No True Gentleman

Books by Liz Carlyle

A Woman of Virtue
Beauty Like the Night
A Woman Scorned
My False Heart
No True Gentleman
Tea for Two: Hunting Season

No True Gentleman

Liz Carlyle

POCKET **STAR** BOOKS

New York   London   Toronto   Sydney   Singapore

An *Original* Publication of POCKET BOOKS

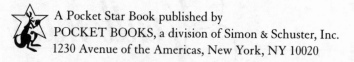 A Pocket Star Book published by
POCKET BOOKS, a division of Simon & Schuster, Inc.
1230 Avenue of the Americas, New York, NY 10020

ISBN: 0-7394-2659-1

Jacket illustration by Alan Ayers

Printed in the U.S.A.

To my dear friends:

Jean Sandilands Steele,
whose expertise in history, politics, culture, cartography,
and life in general
is forever dragging me back from the brink of folly,

and

Denise Cavanaugh, D.Phil.,
a lovely French girl with dancing eyes and a wicked wit,
who can probably translate *Beowulf*
into a half-dozen languages without mussing her hair.

I have been blessed by your friendship.

No
True
Gentleman

Prologue

Give me virtuous actions
and I will not quibble about the motives.

—LORD CHESTERFIELD, 1776,
The Fine Gentleman's Etiquette

April 1826

She was an old woman now. Many believed she had been born so—that she had sprung from the womb that was Tuscany, swathed in bombazine and old black lace, weighed down by her obstinacy and her rosary and her temper, which could, admittedly, be very bad. Sofia Josephina DiBiase Castelli had buried three husbands, her precious daughter, and, sometimes it seemed, even her grandson.

She had seen the world; fallen in love in Paris, married in Florence, and grown old, wise, and weary in London. But once, long ago, she had been as young and as romantic as the starry-eyed lovers who strolled through the square beneath her windows on a Sunday afternoon. And she was not now so old that she could not recognize the gnawing hunger of loneliness when she saw it in others.

No afternoon sunlight permeated the heavy velvet draperies of Signora Castelli's vast dining room. The fire in the hearth fairly roared despite the spring day beyond the stout brick walls of her town house. Regally stiff in her black, high-backed chair, the old woman sat at the table, her hands cold—a circumstance she was resigned to—and her heart churning with thwarted intent. *That* she had never tolerated with any measure of grace. And so, with gnarled fingers, she lifted the covers from the four small, delicately adorned urns before her.

"Earth, water, wind, and fire," the old woman muttered as she took one pinch from the contents of each and tossed it into the ornate brass bowl before her.

In the shadows of the dining room, another woman lingered uncertainly.

"Maria!" Signora Castelli commanded, snapping her fingers. *"I Tarocchi!* Fetch it here!"

The woman in the shadows bobbed. *"Subito,* Signora Castelli." But she opened the small double doors of the sideboard with obvious reluctance. Her hand shook as she withdrew a box carved of ebony wood and banded with tarnished copper.

With an awkward clunk, she set the box down on the table but did not remove her hands. "Signora Castelli," she hesitantly whispered. "You think it wise?"

The old woman's eyes were keen and narrow. "I am old, Maria," she proclaimed in the voice of doom. "My grandson leaves me no choice. He *will* be wed! And his wife will bear me my grandchildren beneath this roof ere I die!" With each syllable, she jabbed a crooked index finger toward the portrait which hung over the hearth.

Maria's skeptical glance spoke volumes. "Your pardon, *signora,* but Maximilian is no longer so young and innocent."

"*Scusa,* Maria, but you have seen how the women look at him."

Maria's gaze dropped to the black box. "*Si,* but Father O'Flynn—"

"—has a new barouche!" the *signora* snapped. "One which my money paid for. He will have no quarrel with this. Besides, Maria, Our Mother speaks in many ways. You do not listen."

Lips pursed, Maria thrust forward the box as if it had just burst into flame.

Lovingly, Signora Castelli took it in hand and withdrew a bundle wrapped in black silk. With a deft snap, she jerked away the fabric to reveal a thick pack of cards which—unlike their owner—had been worn soft around the edges with the passage of time. Holding the pack aloft in one hand, the *signora* lifted one candle from the table with the other and dipped it into the brass bowl, setting the herbs afire. Writhing snakes of white smoke spiraled up. With her right hand, she passed the cards back and forth through the haze.

"Earth, water, wind, fire," she solemnly repeated. "All must be purified."

The smoke receded. Carefully, the old woman cut the cards three times to the right, then dealt them into the formation of a cross with quick, efficient snaps. Her hand darted to the center card, hesitated briefly, then turned it. "Oh, *Dio mio,*" she whispered.

Maria leaned eagerly forward. *"Il Re di Spade,"* she whispered reverently. "The King of Swords. It is Maximilian, no?"

Sourly, the old woman eyed her servant. *"Si,* my cousin. Now you wish to observe?"

Sheepishly, Maria pulled out a chair and sat. Signora Castelli returned her attention to the spread, quickly turning up the next three cards. Maria gave a little shriek and drew back. *"Nerone!"* she hissed. "Oh, my God! Who is to die?"

"No one, you foolish creature," chided the old woman, flicking up three more cards. At the third, she lifted her brows sharply. "Well . . . not yet." Her fingers touched each card in turn. "But there is great evil. A fair-haired man with an impure heart. Deceit. Treachery. But it is elsewhere. Not in this house." The last was said with a touch of hauteur.

Another card was turned. Muttering under her breath, the old woman crossed herself. "Ah, Maria, here is the answer. A woman in grave danger. The Queen of Chalices." With a dry fingertip, she pecked on the card. "A vase full of serpents. A heart filled with avarice. I do not know her, thank God." Under her breath, she made a *tch-tch* sound and studied the adjacent cards. "A pity, a pity!"

"What?"

The old woman shook her head sadly. "She is doomed, Maria, for greed will lead her to a bad end," she said, flipping the Five of Wands with a flourish. "There! You see?"

"But what of Maximilian?" Maria pleaded, leaning insistently forward. "What has this to do with him?"

The old woman lifted her shoulders beneath the stiff black silk of her gown. "The evil is drawing near to my grandson. This woman represents . . . some sort of danger." Slowly, her fingertip traced back across the series of cards. "More than this, I cannot see."

Maria sighed, and Signora Castelli turned over the next card. "Ah-ha!" she shouted, her mood shifting mercurially to one of joy. "Look, Maria! Do you see? *La Regina di Dischi.* She is coming at last! All which we have prayed for is within our grasp. *Si,* I felt it! I felt that it was time!"

"The Queen of Pentacles?" mused Maria. "But you never turn that card . . ."

Signora Castelli cut her off with an impatient hiss. "Because she has never before come!"

Maria lifted her gaze to Signora Castelli. "Who is she?"

The old woman gave a faint, inward smile. "She is *the one,* Maria. The Earth Mother. She is all things—benevolence and sensuality, goodness and truth. You see here—" Signora Castelli paused to tap upon the face of the card. "She holds the mysteries of nature in her hand. But the balance is delicate. There is much cosmic disharmony in her heart. I feel it strongly."

She paused to draw her heavy black brows into a frown. The last cards were turned, a series of pentacles. At once, her head snapped up, her bright, jetty gaze snaring Maria's. *"Che la fortuna ci assista!* Quickly, quickly, where is my rosary?"

Maria leaned forward and pulled it from the pocket of the old woman's gown. "What else did you see, *signora?* What do you mean to do?"

"Now I must pray." The old woman clasped the beads between her palms and lifted her trembling hands toward Maria's face. "She is close. Very close. But the evil is closer still. We must pray that the evil does not touch Maximilian. And we must pray that this woman, *la Regina di Dischi,* will be delivered safely into our hands, so that we can do what must be done."

Chapter One

A true gentleman must take care never
to seem dark and mysterious.

—LORD CHESTERFIELD, 1776,
The Fine Gentleman's Etiquette

Terrible accidents can befall anyone who plunges into the unknown. Catherine knew that all too well. And yet the fog which lay before her, slate gray and cloying, did not give her pause as it should have done. Instead, she pressed heedlessly forward, allowing the damp to envelop her like cold, wet wool. Orion's rapid hoof beats were muted by the soft earth as she mindlessly urged him into the thatch of rhododendron ahead.

Much of her behavior had been just so of late, impelled not by logic but by an inexplicable need to flee something which lay behind, with little thought to what risk might lie ahead. She had let grief and confusion drive her from Gloucestershire. Then into London. But perhaps she should not have permitted it to drive her into this fog alone. Perhaps she should have waited until full daylight, instead of rushing into the distant reaches of Hyde Park before dawn had scarce broken. But as usual, the silence inside the house—inside her heart—had been suffocating.

With an impatient signal, she urged Orion on, vaguely considering how her brother Cam would scold if he learned of her recklessness. Suddenly, a noise sounded in the fog ahead. Sharp yet muffled, like the snapping of a twig beneath a layer of wet leaves. And then she saw him—at the precise instant Orion did. Like a pagan warlock summoning up a dragon's breath, the big man loomed up before them, his long black cloak swirling in the mist, his height eclipsing the path beyond.

With a shrill cry, her horse reared and spun right, pawing wildly at the mist. Floating from the fog, the man snared the gelding's bridle, dragging down his head as if the beast were little more than a willful pony. Orion's eyes flashed with white, his hindquarters wheeled nervously, kicking up divots of turf. But with relentless calm, the tall man held his head. At last, the horse gave a final snort of censure and yielded.

For a long, uncomfortable moment, silence held sway in the gloom.

"Your pardon, ma'am," the man finally said, his voice like gravel. "I fear the dampness muffled your approach."

Catherine stared down at him, then let her gaze slide to his impervious grip on her bridle. "I can hold my mount, sir," she snapped. But, inexplicably, blood was pounding in her ears.

At once, his spine stiffened, and she watched, intrigued, as his long, elegant fingers slid away from the leather. "I thought perhaps you could not," he said coolly, his gaze burning through her. "Apparently, I was mistaken."

"Quite," she managed.

Suspicion was etched on his face, and as he glanced up and down the path, Catherine had an uneasy sense that the man could see things which she could not. "Madam, you ride unaccompanied?" he asked, his tone deceptively casual.

Catherine realized her folly at once. She was completely alone in a pea-soup fog with an intense, intimidating stranger. Straightening herself in the saddle, she looked down her nose and feigned her elder brother's haughty glare. "My business is my own, sir," she retorted. "But if we're to remark upon the obvious, one might mention that you were strolling rather carelessly on the bridle path."

A flash of what might have been acquiescence lit his eyes, and he cast her an odd, sideways look. "Regardless, this is no place for a lady alone."

To her chagrin, Catherine realized he was right. Quickly, she took his measure. Lean and dark, the man was younger than he'd first appeared, though his face was edged with the weariness of age. His eyes were more shrewd than kind. And with his high, hard cheekbones, one would not call him handsome. But he certainly was . . . *arresting*. Oh, yes. Oddly, he spoke with just a hint of an accent. German? Italian? But it mattered little. Despite the heavy, silver-knobbed stick he carried and the grace with which he wore his somber clothing, the man was no English gentleman. He looked far too dangerous for such a civilized term.

The man must have heard her soft intake of breath.

His cold, black gaze returned, capturing hers. "Take yourself home at once, madam," he said tightly. "Hyde Park is not safe at this hour."

Catherine wasn't sure why she lingered. "I must confess, you gave me quite a start," she said, deliberately arching her brows. "Do you always lurk about in the fog like that?"

Orion tossed his head uneasily. With a quiet oath in some foreign tongue, the man seized his bridle once more. "Trust me, madam, my *lurking* should be the least of your concerns," he snapped. "The worst of London's rabble has yet to see their beds."

He was, she saw, entirely serious. Reining her mount back a step, Catherine inclined her head in agreement. "Perhaps you are right, Mr. . . . ?"

His expression inscrutable, the man swept off his top hat and bowed in a gesture which was both graceful and insolent. It was also oddly . . . *un-English*. Then, as suddenly as he had appeared, he walked past her and vanished, his greatcoat swirling into the mist, absorbed by it.

Only then did Catherine notice the huge black beast which followed at his heels. Catherine cut a sidelong glance down, but even on horseback, she had not far to look. *A dog—?* God in heaven. She hoped it was a dog.

A little shaken, Catherine found that her wish to escape the confines of town had suddenly flown with her nerve. And so she did precisely as the stranger had ordered. And an order it had surely been. He had snapped out the command as if he were a man to whom authority came easily.

After winding back along the path for a few minutes, Catherine cut Orion sharply left and uphill, bursting from the trees into the open green space. Here, the muted light of a late April morning had finally leached through the cloud cover, and she could see her way clear for some distance. It was then that she caught sight of him again, standing high on the ridge to the northwest, leaning his weight gracefully onto his walking stick. His stern eyes followed as her horse picked its way along the path up to Oxford Street. Such scrutiny should have made her uncomfortable, but it did not. It felt oddly reassuring. As if he had waited to ensure her safety, or perhaps even hoped to speak with her again.

But she was mistaken. As soon as she emerged, the man stepped onto the footpath and set a determined pace in the opposite direction. At the last possible moment, however, he paused, glancing back at her over his shoulder. In acknowledgment, Catherine inclined her head, lifting one gloved hand in thanks.

The man did not bother to return her gesture.

Scarcely a mile away, daylight had not yet made its way over the high, easterly roofs of Princes Street. In the hearth of Lord Sands's drawing room, a newly lit fire struggled against the damp, the silence broken by nothing but the hiss of coal and the somber rhythm of the longcase clock which stood between the heavily draped windows. In a chair near the hearth, Harry Markham-Sands—or the Earl of Sands, as he was properly known—sprawled gracelessly, looking every inch a country gentleman, complete with the requisite ruddy face, receding hairline, and slight paunch.

The mood inside the room was not a happy one. Lord Sands was a miserable man, and had been so for more years than anyone—especially his sister, Cecilia—cared to count. A less charitable woman would have simply shrugged and said that Harry had brought his misery upon himself. And Cecilia was generally a very charitable sort. Today, however, her feet hurt, her back ached, and her breasts were leaking. Eight years of restraint finally snapped under the weight of it all.

"Well, Harry!" she declared, pacing about the room. "You brought this misery on yourself!"

Harry simply tugged a silver flask from his dressing gown. "Daresay I deserved that," said her brother equably. But he tipped the brandy toward his coffee cup with a trembling hand.

Like a falcon on a field mouse, Cecilia leaned over his chair, snatching away the flask. "And blister it, Harry, this doesn't help one whit. You'll not drown this latest scandal in French oblivion."

Harry's face grew even redder. "It ain't a scandal, Cely." The word *yet* hung unspoken.

"Your wife is nothing but a scandal, Harry!" Cecilia insisted. "And when you threatened to hurl her out of your theater box last night, you added fuel to a bonfire!"

Tentatively, Harry brushed his knuckles over the raw scratches down his face. "I didn't really mean I'd do it."

Cecilia gave no quarter. "How much had you had to drink, Harry?" she pressed, waving the flask between two fingers. "And did Julia claw your hide off then and there? Or did she wait until you could thrash it out in the middle of the lobby?"

Harry threw his arms over his chest and slumped lower in his chair. "No one overheard, Cely," he mumbled. "Well, only those in the adjoining boxes."

Abjectly, Cecilia sank down into a giltwood armchair opposite her elder brother. "Oh, Harry," she whispered, letting her head fall forward into her empty hand. "This is the *ton,* my dear. It only takes one. Already I have heard—and it's scarcely dawn!"

"I'm an embarrassment to you," he murmured miserably. "To you *and* Delacourt."

At that, Cecilia lifted her head and stared at him. "Oh, Harry! David and I are fine. It's not us for whom I worry," she said plaintively. "It's *you.*"

Morosely, Harry shook his head. "Too late, Cely. I married her, more's the pity. I've been a cuckold for years, and all of London suspects. Only thing to do now, what with Julia getting so blatant about it, is sue for divorce. Been threatening her for months, you know."

Thoughtfully, Cecilia chewed at her thumbnail. "Well, I daresay it might be done, Harry," she finally said. "But it won't be easy. You've little influence in the House, and there are too many so-called gentlemen in Parliament who mightn't want any names bandied about. I think you know what I mean."

"Oh," said Harry softly. "Never thought of that." He ran one hand through his already disordered curls.

Poor Harry. He wasn't the most brilliant jewel in the family crown. Urgently, she scooted forward and set the flask to one side. "Listen, Harry, give up the lease on this house and drag her back to Holly Hill. Or . . . or cut off her allowance! Blister it, she hasn't even given you an heir."

At that, Harry sneered. "No, and she shan't get the opportunity to do so," he vowed. "I can't trust her an inch, and I'll bloody well let the title go to Uncle Reggie ere I'll see another man's brat take it. As to *managing* her, a fellow might as well draw water with a sieve. Julia's pin money very nearly exceeds my income. Her marriage settlements saw to that."

Cecilia muttered a most unladylike oath, then surrendered the flask of brandy to her brother.

With a miserable grin, he took it, tipped a generous measure into his cup, then crooked one brow in invitation. For a moment, Cecilia was tempted. Then she shook her head and lifted the unadulterated coffee to her lips. She sipped but once, however, before slowly setting it back down again. "Listen, Harry—who was she with this time? Lord Bodley? Mr. Vost? Or one of the others?"

Morosely, Harry shook his head. "Didn't get a good look. Unmarked carriage."

"Rot. What luck." In silence, brother and sister finished their coffee, and then Cecilia rose to take her leave. "Well, Harry," she said, holding his gaze earnestly. "David and I will stand by you, no matter what. You know that, do you not?"

Mutely, Harry nodded.

Cecilia lifted her hand to cup his bristled cheek. "In a few days, my husband will return from Derbyshire," she said with a reassuring pat. "I shall ask him what's best done about Julia. I daresay David shall know just how to manage her."

At the mention of his rather ruthless brother-in-law, Harry brightened just a bit. Impulsively, Cecilia stood on her tiptoes and kissed her brother. To her surprise, Harry's hands clasped her shoulders, his fingers digging into her flesh with a desperation his voice had not revealed.

"Everything will be fine, Harry," Cecilia whispered against his ear. "It will. I promise." But as her lips drew away from the warmth of her brother's cheek, a bone-chilling scream tore through the house. Suddenly, Cecilia knew that she was wrong. Very wrong.

Everything would not be fine.

Just a short distance south of Princes Street, a far more pleasant morning interlude was being slowly staged in a tall brick mansion on Berkeley Square. By half past ten, the efficient Isabel, Lady Kirton, had already kissed her lover good-bye, ordered her hearths swept and her drapes drawn, directed that breakfast be laid in the small dining room, and then commanded that her niece be fetched down from Mortimer Street to eat it.

Filled with a sense of well-being, and fortified by a wealth of maternal intent, this most worthy woman now gazed across her dining table at Lady Catherine Wodeway, who was stabbing just a bit too violently at a piece of bacon. Discreetly, Lady Kirton gave her footmen the signal to withdraw.

"I am so pleased," she tentatively began, "that you've surrendered to the pleas of a tiresome old woman and come to town at last, Catherine."

In exasperation, Catherine gave up on the bacon. "Is that why I'm here?" she responded, lifting both her fork and her brows. "To amuse my dotty old auntie?"

Lady Kirton laughed, a light, girlish sound which contrasted with her matronly figure and silvery hair. "I want you here for the season, my dear," she insisted. "What with my daughter gone off to India, I am left all alone."

Catherine tossed her aunt a dubious glance. "You have Colonel Lauderwood."

Lady Kirton dropped her gaze to her teacup. "Oh, Jack enjoys only his charities and his military club. He cares nothing for polite society."

"Oh? And you do?"

"Yes, indeed!" Lady Kirton smiled impishly. "I've done nothing but look forward to the season's balls, soirees, and picnics. It is simply not to be missed!"

Catherine laughed. "What nonsense," she proclaimed, setting down her fork and staring straight into her aunt's wide blue eyes. "You've never cared a jot for society."

After a long moment of silence, Lady Kirton leaned forward. "My dear Catherine," she said quietly. "Will was my sister's son, and I loved him, too. But you cannot remain a widow forever. Nor, I collect, would you wish to?"

Catherine felt a rare blush heat her cheeks. "No," she admitted. "No, I don't. But neither do I wish to be placed upon the marriage mart. Or to go about in society."

Lady Kirton turned up her palms in a gesture of exasperation. "My dear girl, can you think of another way?"

"Isabel, I know scarcely anyone in town," she protested weakly.

Lady Kirton smiled benevolently. "I fancy you're making my point, Cat, not yours."

"Good heavens, Isabel! I'm a country mouse. I never even came out! I married Will when I was just seventeen, and I have always known a quiet life. And I prefer it. But it's just that . . . that I . . . ."

"That you wish for a husband and a family," finished Isabel softly.

"Well, I don't wish to be lonely," Catherine slowly admitted. "But I'm not at all sure I could find it in my heart to remarry."

For a long moment, Isabel toyed with a crust of dry toast. "Then take a lover, as I have done," she finally said, obviously struggling with the words.

"Yes," confessed Catherine. "I'd considered it."

Isabel set her shoulders back a notch and lifted her chin. "Well, as long as one is discreet," she began airily. Then, unexpectedly, she gave her head a sharp, impatient shake. "But oh, my dear! You are so very young! Why ever would you wish to do such a thing?"

Catherine was silent for a very long moment. "Will and I were married for eight years, Isabel," she said, her voice very small. "I think . . . well, I think I must be barren."

For a moment, Isabel studied her, as if judging Catherine's strength. "Yes, I do fear that might be the case, my dear," she gently admitted. "So perhaps a widower? One with children. There are a dozen such fellows in town this year—fine men, some of them. And all of them hoping to escape the fate of marriage to some simpering idiot. They could do no better than you, Cat. You are capable and beautiful, and you have a wonderful wit."

"A wonderful wit! Oh, that quality must be at the top of every gentleman's list of wifely virtues!"

"It is if he wishes to grow old with her in some measure of happiness, yes," answered Isabel sagely. "Now! On to other matters. Your elder brother has written at last. I'd hoped he might be persuaded to come to town and take his seat in the House this year. But I'm afraid Treyhern is not as amenable as you, my dear."

"I told you he would not come," warned Catherine. "Besides, Helene is again *enceinte*. Cam would never stir far from Gloucestershire under such a circumstance."

With a sigh, Isabel shrugged and set down her cup with a clatter. "Then why do you not close up his big house in Mortimer Street, my dear?" she begged. "God only knows where your younger brother Bentley may be bedding down, so you will surely wait for him in vain. Come stay with me. Nothing would give me more pleasure."

Gently, Catherine thrust out one hand. "I would merely be in the way of your romance with Jack," she protested laughingly. "Besides, there is that matter of the lover I mean to take. Perhaps I, too, shall want my privacy?"

"Oh, dear me." Isabel looked fleetingly ill at ease. "Treyhern may have my head for this."

Again, Catherine laughed and picked up a pot of jam. "Oh, my sainted brother shall know nothing of my clandestine lover, Isabel. I can keep a secret, depend upon it."

Bemused, Isabel shook her head. "Sometimes, Cat, I cannot make out which of your brothers you most resemble. I begin to fear it's that scamp Bentley after all."

"Enough about my brothers, Isabel," Cat demurred. "Tell me, how does Jack go on? Will I see him at all this season?"

Isabel looked a little wistful. "Oh, he says he's too old for society," she answered. "But I am counting on you to keep me young, Cat, so hand me that stack of invitations. You've brought them as I asked, thank goodness. And I know you've several, for I've seen to it."

Obediently, Catherine produced them, and soon Isabel had sorted them into three little stacks. "Good, good," she mused, taking up one large ivory card for closer scrutiny. "Lady Merton's musicale tonight . . . then Lord Walrafen's charity ball on Thursday."

"A ball?" asked Catherine archly. "With dancing?"

"It is customary to dance at a ball, yes," said Isabel, fanning the card madly back and forth. "And this one is a must! Indeed, we must go straightaway to have the dark blue taffeta fitted. Walrafen is a particular friend of mine—and an exceedingly eligible bachelor!"

Chapter Two

Let your manner, your air, your
terms and your tone of voice be soft and gentle.

—LORD CHESTERFIELD, 1776,
The Fine Gentleman's Etiquette

At half past ten, Maximilian de Rohan shoved his pen into his inkpot with a vitriolic curse and left it precariously dangling. His office felt stifling. He could not seem to write a legible or logical sentence these days. Nothing he learned made sense. Up was down, west felt like east, and the pieces of his most recent puzzle did not fall together as they ought to have done.

And now, *Dio mio!* That woman had come to Hyde Park again. Just as she had done for the last six mornings. He wished she would stay the hell away. There was work to be done—and it was dangerous. Still, from a distance, he could not help but quietly watch her, unsure of just why the woman had captivated his attention so thoroughly. At first, he had told himself it was simply the boredom of his vigil in the park. Peel's latest crusade had obliged de Rohan to skulk about there every morning for a fortnight. And given such a bloody frustrating task, why not let his eyes feast on something pleasant whilst he waited?

But watching her had proven seductive. She was tall and lithe, perhaps twenty-five years old, and possessed of a fresh, earthy sort of beauty. Graceful and uninhibited, the woman cantered along the empty paths of the park, seeming as one with her big chestnut gelding. Sometimes she dismounted for a stroll, the horse following at her heels like a faithful spaniel. But always she moved like poetry, almost skimming across the grass. And as he watched, he had found himself foolishly wondering what she smelled like.

He drummed one finger lightly upon the edge of his desk and permitted his rare flight of fantasy to continue. She would smell like the outdoors. Like home, perhaps. Yes, pure and sweet, like new-mown fields and sun-warmed earth. Things a man could rarely smell in London, for if they existed at all, the oppressive smoke and soot choked out their scent.

Still, she was an English lady born and bred. The set of her spine, the utter confidence with which she moved, made that much plain. No, they would never be well acquainted, despite her rather clumsy effort at forcing an introduction this morning. So he had snubbed her. Quite deliberately. This despite the fact that for six days, he'd been unable to tear his eyes from her. Each time she rode beyond his sight, he would will her to return. And he would wait with uncharacteristic patience until she did so.

It really was embarrassingly foolish. Once he had watched while, in defiance of all propriety, she had veered off the path and taken the big horse sailing over a series of boxwoods, leaping one after another as if nothing could intimidate her. In Hyde Park, of all places! And as she had hurtled over the last and ridden away, he had been left with the strangest notion that she found the park and its urban polish far too confining for her tastes. He began to imagine that she yearned to burst free of some worldly constraint.

What might it be? The constrictions of her family? She was just a little too old for that. A domineering husband, perhaps? He rather thought not. She did not look like the sort a man might easily dominate. Moreover, no man would permit his wife to go haring off alone through any part of London at such an hour. And today, she had come earlier still, long before the fog which rolled off the water had been burnt away by the morning sun. And so today he had not watched her from a distance as had become his habit. No, today she had taken him unaware as he lay in wait amongst the rhododendron. And left him feeling angry and vulnerable. *Maledizione!* A man in his position could not afford to be taken unaware by anyone. Certainly not by a beautiful, well-bred Englishwoman.

Almost of its own volition, his hand went to his desk drawer and extracted a book which he'd shoved inside months ago. It was a fine old copy, probably rare and valuable now. Balancing its weight in his hand, de Rohan stared down at the title stamped in gold upon the spine. *The Fine Gentleman's Etiquette.* Touching it filled him with a strange sense of mortification and regret. Mortification that he'd kept it. Regret that his life had turned out so differently. The latter emotion enraged him.

But still, he had the bloody book out now, didn't he? Bound in red leather and edged with gilt, the volume had been given to him by a man with an appreciation for the finer things in life, a gift in honor of de Rohan's surprising appointment to the Home Office. Of course, he'd glanced at it out of politeness and tucked it away with an expression of gratitude. But he'd had little use for the tome, which had been written by Lord Chesterfield, a pompous, puffed-up old English lord long since dead—of asphyxiation from too much arse-kissing, de Rohan did not doubt. The book was filled with egregiously snooty advice which was at best fawning and at worst Machiavellian. De Rohan looked again at the inscription:

Dear boy,
Eventually, a diamond in the rough needs polish.
Yr. most Humble servant,
George Jacob Kemble

But how bloody ridiculous that he should own such a thing! De Rohan snorted and threw the book back into the drawer just as a sharp, impatient rap sounded at his office door. At first, he felt relieved to be jerked so ruthlessly back into his ordinary world. But it was a relief short-lived when Mr. Hobhouse's plaguing, meticulous clerk popped in. As usual, Feathershaw held a fistful of files and wore a sharp pencil tucked atop his ear. He looked like a keen, overanxious squirrel.

In resignation, de Rohan waved the clerk toward a chair. At once, Feathershaw pulled out the pencil, settled his spectacles a little higher up his nose, and began his relentless tapping upon the chair arm. "You've reviewed the files I sent on the criminal law consolidation proposals?" he began, in a voice which dared de Rohan to disagree.

De Rohan did not disagree. Instead, he merely stared across his desk, his dark brows lifted in a deliberately arrogant gesture. "Pray go on, Mr. Feathershaw."

For a moment, the clerk seemed determined to hold his own, but he could not quite bear up under the scrutiny. "No, you have not, have you?" he challenged waspishly, breaking off his gaze. "The committee meeting convenes in a quarter-hour, and, as usual, you've not so much as looked at—"

"I'm a policeman, Mr. Feathershaw," de Rohan interjected. "Not a bloody politician. And I took this position merely to help—"

"Correction, de Rohan," interjected the clerk. "You *were* a policeman—"

A sharp knock cut him short. Feathershaw swiveled about to glare at the door. He resumed his impatient pencil tapping when the front-office clerk stepped inside de Rohan's modest room.

"I beg your pardon, Mr. de Rohan," began the young man, his brows in a fretful knot. "But a footman just brought this down from Mayfair. He says it's most urgent." Carefully, he passed the note across the polished surface of the desk. De Rohan studied the small, untidy direction scrawled boldly across the vellum. Quickly, his policeman's eyes took in the details. Expensive paper. Good ink. But no seal. Someone in a rush, then. He flipped it open to find a crest he did not recognize.

Dear Max—
I must see you most urgently. Please come to me at
once in Princes Street at the home of my brother, Lord
Sands. Be assured I would not trouble a dear friend
were our situation not desperate.

> *Yr. servant,*
> *Cecilia, Lady Delacourt*

Urgent! Desperate! Good God, Cecilia made it sound
as if someone had been murdered. With a snort of exasperation, de Rohan tossed the note to one side of his
desk. He'd not heard from Lord and Lady Delacourt in
the months since their departure for Derbyshire. And
peaceful months they had been. But now, Cecilia, at
least, was back. All had gone well with her confinement,
it would seem.

He was relieved, of course. If he were honest, he
would admit that a small part of him was pleased to see
her untidy handwriting scribbled across the strange missive. And was he a *dear friend?* Certainly, de Rohan liked
her a little better than he would wish to—which was to
say, more than was prudent for a man in his position.
And he rather thought she knew it. Or possibly not. Cecilia seemed uniquely oblivious to her own charms.

Still, her charms notwithstanding, de Rohan had neither the time nor the inclination to go charging about in
the East End in search of some angel of the night gone
missing. Or some unhinged whoremonger with more
use for his fists than his cock. But that's precisely what
Cecilia would ask of him. Her husband, Delacourt, was
barely able to manage her, and Cecilia's chaotic, near-

futile charity efforts—saving prostitutes, reforming thieves—were forever churning up all manner of trouble. Still, she would ask. And he would go. And he would do what he could, as he'd done a half-dozen times this past year. Because, for some reason which escaped him, he was unable to refuse her.

Ha! Another lie. He knew the reason perfectly well. It was because she was so charming. God, how he hated that. Not her charm, but his susceptibility to charming women in general. But Cecilia was not, he reluctantly admitted, like most women of her class. She truly cared for others. She had an unselfish heart. She was not afraid of hard work, no matter how hopeless. Perhaps that was why he could never resist her pleas?

"Mr. de Rohan?" The voice of the front-office clerk cut into his consciousness.

De Rohan lifted his gaze to find that the earnest young man was still staring at him. "Yes, Mr. Howard?"

"The footman downstairs?" Howard said uncertainly. "He says he's to await your answer. I believe, sir . . . that is to say . . . I think the carriage is waiting. For you."

At that, Mr. Feathershaw abruptly ceased his tapping. "Hobhouse is also waiting, de Rohan!" he said warningly. "The Criminal Law Consolidation bill! He expects your input. You'll not escape this time."

Good Lord. Another bloody meeting. Cecilia's letter, de Rohan decided abruptly, was a godsend. Before he could reconsider, he jerked to his feet, shoving back his chair and snatching up his portfolio in one motion. "The committee meeting must go forward without me, Mr. Feathershaw. Lord Delacourt has summoned me on a matter of some urgency. You know his temper—not to mention his influence. We dare not keep him waiting."

It was not, de Rohan decided, such a very great lie. With his empty hand, he snared his coat from its hook, took up his ebony walking stick, and strolled through the door, leaving Howard and Feathershaw to stare at him as he disappeared into the shadows.

"Arrogant, jumped-up foreigner," hissed Feathershaw. "He's no sort of gentleman at all!"

"You'll not say that to his face, I daresay," snorted Howard. Then he grinned and leaned a little toward his companion's ear. "Besides, his file downstairs says he was born in Middlesex and baptized at Allhallows by the Tower."

Feathershaw's lips twisted. "Was he indeed?" he asked sarcastically. "Such a fine part of town! Now I'm truly impressed!"

Through the wide bow window of Madame Germaine's exclusive establishment, the clatter of midday traffic turning in and out of Bond Street could easily be heard. But Catherine could no longer see the fine spring day which had arrived too late to do her any good. Now she was stuck in the fitting room—probably until teatime—to be poked and prodded and stuffed into fancy garments whose names she could scarce pronounce, let alone fathom any need for.

And why? Because she had been so foolish as to flee the rustic beauty of Aldhampton! On a day like today, the spring lambs would be frolicking. Her orchard would be raining blossoms in a sweet-scented hailstorm of pink and white. Fields would want plowing, and there would be a thousand things to discuss with her steward. But despite the fond memories, or perhaps because of them, Catherine did not think she could survive another spring at Aldhampton. It was too empty.

Certainly, she could not deny the delight her visit was giving Aunt Isabel. And what better thing might one do with one's life, if one could not find personal happiness in it? She might as well give Isabel her companionship for a few weeks instead. And perhaps—just *perhaps*—she might meet someone interesting. Indeed, perhaps she already had. Oddly, her mind turned back to her strange morning ride in Hyde Park.

A pinprick brought her back to reality. "Oww!"

Madame Germaine's seamstress leapt away from the low dais. *"Mille pardons, madame!"*

Lips pursed, Lady Kirton hastened through the heavy draperies and into the fitting room, a bolt of ivory silk in one hand. "It's hardly your fault, Michelle." Isabel scowled up at Catherine. "Your client fair twitches with impatience."

"I'm trying to be still," Catherine insisted.

Critically, her ladyship swept her gaze down Catherine's length and murmured her approval. "My, that does become your long legs, my dear."

Atop the dais, Catherine laughed. "So that I look like a colt instead of a horse?" she asked as the seamstress cautiously resumed her pinning.

Isabel smiled and settled herself into a nearby chair. "You're beautiful, Cat."

Catherine dropped her eyes to the seamstress's nimble fingers. "I'm neither blond nor dainty. And I'm certainly not fragile."

"No, indeed," agreed Isabel. "You're all woman. And you look sensible and elegant." She waved her gloved hand at the shop girl. "Leave that deep ruching off the neckline, Michelle. She's old enough to show off her assets."

"Ha!" Catherine jiggled herself more firmly into the bodice. "From what I've seen, I'll need every asset I've got. Now, go on, Isabel! Whilst we pin up this hem, I suppose you may as well lecture me about this Lord Walrafen. Has he at least some of his teeth? Any of his real hair?"

Having left Whitehall out of impulse rather than any real concern, de Rohan found his mood swiftly altered when he arrived in Princes Street. A knot of pale-faced servants stood whispering on Lord Sands's doorstep, and across the street sat a vehicle which he recognized with a sinking certainty. It was a mortuary van, the spindly black horse in the traces hanging his head as if he understood too well his task.

At once, de Rohan realized he'd taken Cecilia's summons far too cavalierly. He pushed his way past the small crowd, through the open door, and into chaos. Inside, more servants rushed to and fro, while others milled about the back of the hall, whispering feverishly. Beside the drawing-room door, a buxom, golden-haired servant hunched against the wainscoting, sobbing into a wad of her starched white pinafore.

A stately woman in housekeeper's garb strode past. "Genevieve!" she said, frowning down at her. "Do go upstairs and collect yourself!"

"Oui, madame," whispered the girl, and the other servants sheepishly followed her out.

The man who appeared to be the butler stood quietly talking to two men in uniform, both of whom de Rohan recognized as constables from the Westminster Police Court in Queen Square. Seeing de Rohan, the butler hastened forward. "Oh, you must be the gentleman from the Home Office?" He wrung his hands as if in emphasis. "I daresay you wish to view the corp—er, to go straight up?"

"Go up where?" de Rohan demanded. "What has happened?" But his mind was already conjuring up dreadful possibilities.

The butler opened and closed his mouth soundlessly, as if an explanation escaped him. The man de Rohan recognized as Police Constable Sisk stepped forward, his coworker on his heels. "Bring the van on around, Eversole," Sisk quietly instructed, pulling de Rohan to one side.

De Rohan seized the police constable with a barely suppressed violence. "Where is Lady Delacourt?" he hissed. "Good God, man, what has happened to her?"

With a quizzical smile, Sisk let his eyes slide down de Rohan's dark clothing. "Ooh, very pretty company you do keep these days," he mused. "Not like old times, eh, mate?"

"Rot you, Sisk," growled de Rohan. "Where is she?"

"Don't get your ballocks in a twitch, de Rohan," whispered the constable. "She's shut 'erself up in the drawing room with the brother. Wailing like a banshee, that 'un. Seems 'is wife got 'erself done for last night."

De Rohan stared blankly at Sisk. "Lady Sands? *Dead?*"

"Aye, and a very nasty bit of work it was. Bound ter

be all manner of trouble, too, wot wiv 'er being married to a lord an' all. Glad you're here ter take over."

To take over? Belatedly, de Rohan realized he'd not removed his hat. He jerked it off now and ran his left hand through his hair. Cecilia's sister-in-law was dead?

But if so, it was a parish matter. A matter for the Queen Square magistrates. He'd not been involved in a murder since the tragedy at the Nazareth Society, Cecilia's charity mission. That was when he'd first met Cecilia. And Lord Delacourt and Lady Kirton, too. But since then, his job duties had vastly altered. These days, he was more apt to be seen pushing paper in Whitehall than spying on smugglers in Wapping. He felt confused. He had come as Cecilia's friend. He barely knew the Countess of Sands. But he certainly knew her name and reputation. Julia Markham-Sands was a beauty. A notorious beauty, to be precise. And a god-awful thorn in her husband's side, if rumor could be believed.

"How is Lord Sands taking it?"

The constable gave a grisly smile. "Like a guilty man, de Rohan," he cheerfully responded, patting him on one shoulder in mock sympathy. "And being as you're the Home Office's man, you'd best come up and 'ave a look around afore his lordship thinks ter stop you."

The sarcasm bit at de Rohan. "I was sent for," he snapped. "By the man's sister."

But Sisk was already trundling up the stairs. Still clutching his hat and his portfolio, de Rohan followed the constable's heavy boots up to the second floor. They reached the bedchamber door just as the litter bearing the draped body of Cecilia's sister-in-law was being carried out. Eversole and the ambulance attendant paused, looking at de Rohan in respectful inquiry.

Well. Whether he wished it or not, he had apparently been identified as a source of some authority. He shot a quick glance at Sisk, then flipped back just the corner of the linen. Julia Markham-Sands was no longer a great beauty.

"Strangulation?" asked de Rohan emotionlessly.

Constable Eversole made a grim face and gently drew down the sheet with one finger. De Rohan felt a moment of surprise. It seemed that Lady Sands slept in the nude. Dark bruises mottled her throat, fanning almost obscenely toward her breasts.

Sisk eyed the injuries. "Gagged then strangled, I'd say," he answered. "Quick, clever work it was, too. Poor lady never made a sound."

"Oh?" De Rohan crooked a brow sharply. "Who says so?"

"Her lady's maid. And Lord Sands, o' course." The police constable gave a macabre laugh and motioned the attendants out. "Everyone else slept above or below, and no one 'eard a thing."

De Rohan grunted and crossed the luxurious Persian carpet to pick up a pair of silver spectacles which lay on the night table next to an empty wine bottle. But they were nothing more than dainty lady's reading glasses. He peered through them. Lady Sands had been a tad nearsighted. He looked at the bottle. Champagne—but an expensive yet inferior vintage. He shrugged. The English were such philistines. "Where is the goblet?" he snapped. "How many were there?"

Sisk was sharp. "One, empty. The maid dropped it in shock. But you saw 'er neck. This wasn't poison."

Sisk was right. Pray God he wasn't right about Sands. "Perhaps it was someone outside the household," de Rohan wondered aloud. "But someone she knew."

The police constable shrugged. "Robbery then, more like," he responded. "In fairness to Lord Sands, the window does look to 'ave been forced with some sort 'er pry or chisel."

Mildly bemused, de Rohan put down the spectacles. "I take it no one heard that, either?"

Sisk scratched his chin and jerked his head toward the nearest window. "See your point. The way that latch was forced, daresay t'would make one 'ell of a racket, even if it was meant ter flummox us."

"This room has been thoroughly searched?" snapped de Rohan.

"I gave it a quick once-over."

"The servants' statements have been taken?"

"Eversole'll finish up the few wot's left, soon as the body's gone orf ter the morgue." Sisk shifted his weight uncomfortably. "You taking over or not?"

Without answering, de Rohan moved to the window, gingerly opened it, and leaned out. The room gave onto the rear of the house, and under cover of darkness, an experienced cracksman could have scaled the wall using nothing more than window ledges and drain pipes. But experienced cracksmen were rarely foolish enough to break into occupied rooms. And if caught in the act, they were more apt to flee with what they could get than to hang about and murder someone. Not unless it was unavoidable.

But in this case, it had clearly been avoidable. Lady Sands had neither surprised nor accosted her killer. Instead, she had been slain in her own bed, and by the look of it, she'd not even awakened until it was much too late. Not until the killer had the gag halfway down her throat, at any rate. And somehow, Max rather doubted that she'd drifted off to sleep alone.

De Rohan's eyes skimmed over the opulent but otherwise ordinary bedchamber. Other than the window, nothing looked disturbed. It seemed unfair, somehow. Good God, a woman had been strangled, and the bedcovers were barely tousled! For a long moment, de Rohan paused, his eyes shut tight against the scene. But the sight of Lady Sands's swollen visage was burned into his memory. Could Cecilia's brother be guilty of such a heinous crime? If he were, Sands must be brought to justice by someone, no matter how long his family lineage. And after a year in his strange new post at the Home Office—a post de Rohan held through the patronage of Cecilia's former stepson—he still thought of himself first and foremost as a policeman, a job he both loathed and loved.

Still, the hunt was in his blood. No matter how hopeless or grim the work—and it was usually both—he could not resist the challenge. He could never give up the chase. His last position had been as a chief inspector for the River Police. Before that, he'd spent two years in Queen Square and another two as a captain in the elite Bow Street Runners, the youngest man ever to attain such a post. But in those rough jurisdictions, murder was swift and impersonal, the work of one felon against another. He'd seen it so often he was almost inured to the carnage. But this—the killing of a wealthy woman who slept in what should have been the safe haven of her own home—this was something else altogether. And in Mayfair, no less. Despite Sisk's eager deference, de Rohan had been given no jurisdiction here. He was here as a *dear friend*. Worse, he worked for the Home Office, and they would have questions, too. They would wish this handled with the utmost delicacy.

Unfortunately, delicacy was not his forte.

Bloody, bloody hell.

De Rohan stared into the depths of the room, searching for a way out of his coil. Just then, the first clear shaft of morning sun speared through the window, reflecting brightly on something which lay upon the patterned carpet. Swiftly, de Rohan crossed the room and knelt beside the dressing table. Over his shoulder, he motioned for Sisk. "You'd best have a look at this," he said quietly.

"Gor!" The constable squatted beside him. "Looks ter be a bleedin' fortune!"

It was true. In addition to the huge topaz pendant which had initially caught his eye, the floor along the brocade table covering was scattered with ear bobs and brooches. In the dull light, the brightly patterned carpet had made them difficult to see. With one fingertip, de Rohan lifted the table skirt. In an upturned heap underneath lay an elegantly carved jewel chest spilling brilliant colors across the floor.

"Christ Jesus!" whispered Sisk. "What manner o' thief pikes orf leaving a pile the likes o' that?"

A very good question indeed. With grave reluctance, de Rohan stood up. "Well," he said quietly. "I suppose there's no help for it now. You'd best tell me everything."

Chapter Three

Be easy, even forward,
in making new acquaintances.

—Lord Chesterfield, 1776,
The Fine Gentleman's Etiquette

That night, de Rohan dreamt of home. Home as it had been before. No haze of smoke, no blackened rubble. And no sated, soot-stained soldiers lying languidly amidst the ruins, swilling his father's finest *gewürztraminer* like sotted pigs whilst they laughed and belched and awaited a turn with his mother's kitchen maids. Instead, this dream was sweet. The sun was warm on his shoulders, the earth fragrant beneath his bare feet, and the sunlit slopes surrounding his little world were striped with row upon row of rich, ripe green. Beneath his palms, fat grapes exploded in scent and color as he squeezed and smashed. Sweet juice flew, splattering up his arms, flecking his face and shirt.

"Maximilian! Che cosa fai—?"

He looked up from the shallow wooden tub to see his mother hurtling out of the house in a streak of bleached linen and wild black curls, shrieking in a stream of Italian as she flew through the garden gate.

"Max! Ooh, Max, you imp!" she cried, falling to her knees in the warm grass. She dragged him against her, simultaneously dunking one corner of her smock in the adjacent pail of water. "What a mess you've made!" she chided, sluicing the spatters of fruit down his arms and hands. "These grapes are for the kitchen, wicked boy! Not for Papa's cellars!"

But Max knew she wasn't really angry. So he giggled and turned his face into her bosom, comforted by the feel of her lips atop his head, drawing in her scent of soap, lilies, and fresh-baked bread. But the wiping of his fingers was relentless. Noisier now, the rough, wet linen scrubbed his palm and fingers with an urgency. *Dio mio,* did she mean to scrape his skin off this time?

De Rohan awoke with a start.

Lucifer. Just Lucifer. Not his mother at all.

He drew a deep breath, blindly thrusting out his hand to stroke the dog's head. No hint of light shined through the window of his small bedchamber, yet the big black mastiff and his unremitting bladder were heralding dawn. He forced himself to roll over, only to find that Lucifer was slinking onto the bed now, the mattress creaking ominously beneath his eleven-odd stone.

De Rohan forced away the last vestiges of what had been—for once—a soothing dream, wiped his hand on the counterpane, and ruffled the dog between the ears. "Off the bed, you brute." Eyes downcast, the dog edged closer, until his tongue was hanging over de Rohan's face, his breath warm and moist in the chill morning air. "Ugh," he grunted, sliding naked from the covers. "Time again, old boy?"

Lucifer gave a *woof!* of gratitude and bounded off the

bed, landing on the bare floor with an awesome thump. De Rohan padded through the parlor to pull open the french window which gave onto his landlady's walled garden. His neck chain jingling merrily, Lucifer darted over the threshold to begin his patrol.

De Rohan began to shave and dress in his usual haphazard fashion—plain black worsted trimmed with accoutrements of gray and white, clothing which required little forethought. Then, after building up the fire and settling the kettle on the hob, he lit the lamp at his desk beneath the window. His eyes strayed at once to the red leather book. He'd brought it home, he'd told himself, to avoid the embarrassment of having someone at the office see it. He prayed to God that was the truth. Again, as if his hand were not his own, he picked up the book and flipped through it. It fell open at a particular passage. De Rohan snorted. Kemble's favorite, he did not doubt.

Dress is an article not to be neglected. The difference between a man of sense and a fop, is that a fop values himself upon his dress; and a man of sense laughs at it, but at the same time knows he must never neglect it.

With a hearty Italian curse, de Rohan threw it down again and turned his mind instead to a meticulous review of the statements Sisk had delivered. Mindlessly, he downed two cups of black coffee while hastily scratching out notes until they covered a dozen pages of foolscap. Then, from memory, he roughly sketched out the floor plan of Lord Sands's town house, hovering over it with yet a third cup of coffee.

So engrossed was he in his study, time escaped him.
Suddenly, something—a robin, perhaps—fluttered past
his window, causing Lucifer to bark sharply. De Rohan
lifted his eyes to see that dawn had broken over London,
bringing with it a clear, spring morning. Through the
window, he could see the stirrings of life; the creaking
and clopping of carriages coming up the side lane, the
rumble of coal carts and costermongers as they began
their day's journey toward the Chelsea Road. Nearer to
hand, an enterprising spider had spun a fine white web
in the boxwood just beyond the glass. Glistening with
dew, it caught upon the branch tips like a casually tossed
handkerchief. But in truth, it was no more casually
tossed than was his own web in the park. The web he'd
best attend to before the sun peeped over the roofs of
west London.

Abruptly, he laid down his pen, shoved the handful of
freshly made notes into his portfolio, and looked about
for Lucifer's leash. After calling the dog, he took up his
walking stick and strode out to begin his circuitous journey to Whitehall. But on his doorstep, he very nearly
tripped over Nate Corcoran, an erstwhile street urchin
whom he'd befriended and now marginally employed as
his family's errand boy.

The lad leapt to attention, swiping a quick hand
under his nose and setting his cap on a little straighter.
"Bon gorno, guv," he chirped. "Eight sharp, as you said."

De Rohan spared a smile for the boy. *"Buongiorno,*
Nate," he corrected, brushing a smear of dust from the
lad's coat sleeve. He'd forgotten having sent for the boy.
"Come stai?"

Nate screwed up his face as Lucifer began to wag and

sniff. "Nonna Sofia ain't taught me that 'un yet," he said on a resigned sigh. "I don't reckon I'll ever learn enough ter be a river policeman."

"How are you?" de Rohan translated, fishing in his pocket for a coin. "And you'll make a fine constable if you can keep from getting snabbled by one first. Now, take Lucifer to Wellclose Square and tell my grandmother to let him run in the garden this week, for I've a busy schedule."

"Yes, sir!"

Impulsively, de Rohan knelt on the pavement to ruffle the dog's fur. "Now, no digging, old boy!" he commanded, but Lucifer just gave him his usual cockeyed grin.

De Rohan stood to lay a cautioning hand on the lad's narrow shoulder. "Mind the traffic, Nate. And let no one touch him, lest he snap a finger off. And you're to tell Nonna Sofia *niente ricotta!*" He pressed a crown into the boy's grubby palm. "But don't mention this extra money."

"Ah!" Nate's face broke into a grin. *"Una bustarella?"*

Now, how the devil had the boy learned that word? De Rohan scowled. "No, it is not a bribe. Just keep an eye on what she feeds him, and tell me if there's trouble." He cocked his head down at the dog. "You see how fat he's grown?"

The boy flashed a sideways grin. "No ricotta!" he translated cheerfully. "But I dessay she'll feed him wot she pleases, sir."

"She always does," de Rohan grumbled, passing Lucifer's leash with one hand as he clasped the lad's narrow shoulder with the other. "I'll come for him on Saturday, yes? *Sabato.* You tell Nonna Sofia that. And I shan't see her until then, unless she needs me, all right?"

"Righty-ho, guv!" said the lad, setting off with a cheerful wave. *"Sabato! Niente ricotta!* And arriverder-chy!"

"Arrivederci," corrected de Rohan softly. "You're a good boy, Nate. *Grazie."* But the lad had set a steady pace east and did not hear him. He watched them go, the boy and the dog, and felt a fleeting moment of emptiness. His rooms would be empty tonight, and he did not welcome it. But better the dog should be spoilt than left all but ignored while his master worked late into the night.

De Rohan approached Hyde Park via Constitution Hill, then took the footpath which ran west above the Serpentine. At this hour, the park was all but empty. A few moments of brisk walking took him well beyond the most public areas of the park, toward the paths more often frequented by those who wished to put their horses through their paces and by those who desired privacy. It was the latter who most interested de Rohan, and for the first time in a fortnight, it seemed he might be in luck. As he quietly approached the place where the path ran through a clump of rhododendron—the very one in which he'd seen the woman the previous day—he heard the low murmur of voices. Male voices—one almost imperceptibly edged with Cockney, the other a low, hard growl, followed by a cynical, familiar laugh.

At last! They had been working on this police corruption case for months. With a calm sense of certainty, de Rohan circled around so that he might approach at a point rather less obvious. By God, he'd nearly sell his soul to the devil if he could just get a good look at the both of them. Better still would be an opportunity to watch money change hands. It would be proof of his suspicions. And he would make a most credible witness.

The exhilaration thrummed through his blood. But halfway through the knot of high shrubs, he realized he was not alone. Farther along the path was a bench, tucked neatly into a roughly sculpted niche. On it sat a woman—damn it, *the* woman. She was reading a bloody book! De Rohan felt a moment of alarm. It worsened when the voices suddenly rose. Through a thinning veil of greenery, he saw the woman jerk to her feet. Had she heard him? Or the bribery which was occurring not a stone's throw past her shoulder?

His greater fear was confirmed when he rounded the corner. She was not looking at him. Instead, her head was cocked to one side, and she was staring in the direction of the murmurs. Murmurs which now seemed to be moving nearer . . .

Disconcerted, de Rohan set a foot wrong, and the gravel shifted noisily beneath his shoe.

With a soft, startled cry, the woman dropped her book and spun toward him, her dark red skirts whirling about her ankles. A broad-brimmed hat with a long red plume helped obscure her identity—but not from him.

"Wot the 'ell?" came the Cockney voice from the other side of the bushes.

Her hand flew to her lips, and she opened her mouth as if to speak. But heavy footsteps were striding toward them. So de Rohan did the quickest—and the stupidest—thing he could think of. What he'd burned to do for the last seven days. In one swift motion, he dragged the woman hard against his chest, spun toward the shadows, and covered her mouth with his.

Catherine had meant to scream. She really had. Right up until the instant that the square yard of rock-solid chest thudded against hers, sending her bonnet askew and melting her knees to jelly. But instead, she hesitated. This despite the fact that the dark stranger had jerked her into his arms and was forcing her deeper into the shrubbery. In that moment's hesitation, his mouth came down hard over hers, hot and demanding, urging her lips apart. With one arm banded tight about her waist and his fingers curled into her hair, the man drew her to him in a crush of red merino and cascading brown hair.

"For God's sake, kiss me," he hissed, barely lifting his mouth from hers.

Catherine gave a small, indignant gasp, but her good intentions exploded into flame when he seized the moment, sliding his insistent tongue inside her mouth. Desperate, it seemed. Quite inexplicably, she answered. He kissed her more deeply, with the expertise of a man who knew women well. Though his touch was gentle, he held her with a violent intensity. As if he were truly afraid to let her go. His male heat and extraordinary scent filled her nostrils. Her heart pounded in her ears. The men arguing in the bushes were but a vague memory. Dizzy with confusion, Catherine barely heard their footsteps on the graveled path behind her.

"Christ!" murmured a disgusted male voice. "A friggin' lovers' tryst!"

Catherine should have screamed for help, struggled harder in his arms, exploded with rage. Oh, yes—*should* have. But the man jerked his head up like a startled animal. His dark gaze held hers, commanding her silence. Over his shoulder, he spoke, his words harsh, angry barks. *"Go. Away. Now."*

The warning was meant, Catherine knew, for the men on the path. Clearly, he'd not realized that their footsteps were already retreating. For a long moment, the stranger's hard mouth lingered over hers, his eyes still black but no longer cold. He dipped his head again, an awkward, uncertain motion, and Catherine didn't make a sound. But slowly—quite reluctantly, it seemed—he stopped and stepped away, his gaze falling to a spot somewhere near her boots.

Absent the strength of his arms, Catherine's knees began to buckle. Unsteadily, she thrust out her hand to touch the edge of the bench, and his gaze flicked up in mild alarm. At once, a strong, steadying hand slid beneath her elbow.

"I daresay you'd like to backhand me for that," he said, his voice low and thick, his unusual accent more pronounced.

"Sh-should I?" she managed to ask as he drew her just a little nearer.

"Slap me?" His mouth quirked into an uncertain smile. "Yes, soundly." But he was as shaken as she. Catherine could hear the merest hint of it in his deep, raspy voice. But his eyes were as steady as his grip.

Strangely, she had no wish to strike out at him. Instead, she forced a smile. "Did you enjoy it enough to make it worth a good wallop, then?" she asked, tilting her head to one side to study him. "I've a rather strong right arm, you know."

The man cut a quick glance away. "Oh, I enjoyed it," he admitted, his voice rueful. "Enough to be drawn and quartered, instead of merely knocked senseless."

Catherine started to laugh, but it faltered. Good heavens. This wasn't funny. It was . . . she didn't know what it was. But she knew his hand beneath her elbow was warm and strong.

"Tell me your name," she softly commanded, stepping slightly away from him. "Don't just tip your hat and walk off again."

As his fingers slid away, his expression seemed to harden, and he said nothing.

"You've taken some rather blatant liberties with me," she reminded him, thrusting out her right hand. "So perhaps we should be introduced? I'm Lady Catherine Wodeway."

Reluctantly, he took the proffered hand and, instead of shaking it, bowed elegantly over it. "De Rohan," he responded, his tone quite formal. "Maximilian de Rohan."

Catherine did not immediately draw her hand from his. "You were trying to hide me from those men, were you not?"

Surprise lit his eyes, then vanished so quickly she might have imagined it. He was, she thought, a man who was rarely surprised by anything. "They did sound as if they might be unsavory characters, didn't they?" he lightly agreed, bending down to pick up her book and his walking stick.

Catherine did laugh then. "Oh, come now, Mr. de

Rohan!" she said as he pressed the book back into her hands. "Do I look such a fool as that? Why don't you tell me what you're up to?"

De Rohan felt himself bristle at the woman's persistence. She—*Lady Catherine Wodeway*—had no more business being involved in his affairs than he had in knowing her name. Still, he did know it. He'd learned a vast deal more than that, in fact. But she was right, damn it. He had taken liberties—abominable liberties— with her person. The fact that she had not strenuously objected did not obviate her right to an explanation.

"I am with the police," he finally answered. "And those were the sort of men who often discuss matters which they do not care to have overheard. By anyone."

"Oh." Lady Catherine's color drained. "I begin to comprehend."

For a moment, she stared down at the book she now held. It was, he noticed, a rather tattered copy of *The Female Speaker*. Unable to resist, and very much wishing to change the subject, he reached out and lightly touched it. "You are an admirer of Barbauld?" he asked, intrigued.

She looked up at him uncertainly. "Yes. No. I . . . oh, I don't know! I took it from my brother's library. I thought it might . . . oh, improve my mind—?"

"Why?" De Rohan lifted one brow and took her by the elbow again, as if to lead her from the shrubbery. "Does it need improving?"

Lady Catherine shook off his hand, her lips thinning in mild irritation. "Do not change the subject, sir. Tell me about those men. Do you know their names? You were waiting for them yesterday, were you not? That is why you warned me away. That is why you . . . you pulled me into the shadows and kissed me today, isn't it?"

Uncharacteristically, de Rohan hesitated. The woman was even more beautiful up close than at a distance. Her coloring was far warmer than that of most English-women; her heavy hair and intelligent eyes were a per-fectly matched shade of deep, rich mahogany. High cheekbones set off a jaw which was firm and elegant. A stubborn woman, he thought. But her mouth was wide and good-humored, and far too voluptuous to be consid-ered beautiful. But then, de Rohan had never favored the delicate, bow-shaped look affected by most ladies of fashion.

"Yes," he finally responded. "Yes, that's why."

"The only reason—?"

De Rohan felt a spike of irritation. "The only reason what?"

"Why you kissed me," she persisted, her dark eyes re-lentless.

"I did not wish them to see your face," he gruffly ex-plained. "Nor did I wish to be recognized, for that mat-ter."

Lady Catherine cast him a skeptical glance. "Why do I wonder if you mightn't have managed it some other way?"

At that, he took her a little roughly by the elbow and hauled her away from the bench. He did not like being seen through so easily. "I have already apologized, madam, for my gauche, unconscionable behavior, so—"

"Actually, you haven't," she interjected, jerking to a halt again.

He released her arm, whirling about to stare at her incredulously.

"Apologized," she clarified, standing toe-to-toe to glare up at him. "You never did, you know."

"Then *I apologize!*" de Rohan growled. "Now, where, madam, is your mount?"

"Perhaps I walked?"

"You always ride." He snapped out the words without thinking.

"Do I?"

Lady Catherine ran a surprisingly steady gaze down his length, and de Rohan was shocked to realize that, despite his irritation, he rather liked her. She was a strong, capable sort of woman. And sensible, too, he thought. He had kissed her, and yet, instinctively, she'd known he meant her no harm. A more missish sort would have flown up into the boughs just for the attention.

But now he had revealed a bit of his knowledge about her. What would she say if she knew how often he had waited for her? If she suspected for one moment the fanciful thoughts that went tripping through his head each time he watched her ride through the park? For a long moment, silence held sway in the shadows of the rhododendron.

Suddenly, she spoke, words tumbling from her mouth. "Mr. de Rohan, would you . . . or perhaps I should say that I . . . yes, strange as it sounds, I think that I should like to know you better. Would you care to—to perhaps become better acquainted? W-would you care to dine with me some evening?"

Dine with her?

De Rohan couldn't believe his ears. Couldn't believe

his absurd reaction to her invitation. He would not allow himself to fall into that trap again. Of wanting what he was no longer destined to have. Of desiring, even briefly, someone who thought herself far above him. And whose values and motivations were undoubtedly quite different from his own. "I don't think you understood," he said harshly. "I am with the police."

Apparently, Lady Catherine did not take his point. "But surely that fact does not preclude you from accepting dinner invitations? From women who are grateful for having been rescued from—er—*unsavory* characters?"

De Rohan stared at her open countenance and bottomless brown eyes, hating the surge of renewed hope which coursed through him. Hating her for making him feel a moment of regret, an instant of doubt, about the choices he'd made. Perhaps, he abruptly decided, she was just a little too strong and capable. Most likely, she was just another bored society wife looking for some sycophant to ease her *ennui* between the sheets. There was a quick way to find out. "And is dinner all you require, Lady Catherine?" he asked, his voice seductively soft. "Or is there some other, more intimate sort of companionship you seek?"

"I beg your pardon?" Color flooded her face.

Ruthlessly, he pressed on. "In my experience, when a highborn lady asks a man like me to dine, she usually intends to indulge in something a little more decadent than a good meal and a fine bottle of wine."

The woman hadn't exaggerated about her strong right arm. But despite the warning, he failed to see it coming. The blow caught him square across the face, sending him reeling backward, one hand pressed to his mouth. Gracelessly, he stumbled, flailing backward with his walking stick and catching himself up against the edge of the bench. Good God, she hit like a man! More shoulder than wrist, more wrath than petulance. He looked down to see the smear of blood on the back of his hand, then he looked up to see the blazing visage of Lady Catherine Wodeway staring at him across the narrow clearing.

"Here's some intimate companionship for you, Mr. de Rohan," she snapped, stalking off in a swish of red wool and hot temper. "Take that fancy stick of yours and go bugger yourself with it."

Somehow, Catherine managed to make her way back to her brother's house in Mortimer Street. Too shaken by rage and humiliation to trust her fists with Orion's mouth, she had led him out of the park and all the way through Mayfair. After tossing his reins to the footman who miraculously appeared, she hastened into the house, toward the sanctuary of the morning parlor which overlooked the rear gardens. Staring through the broad, lightly draped window into the muted sunshine beyond, she raised both her hands, pressing the fingertips to her lips as if the act might take back her ugly insult.

Go bugger yourself? What on earth had possessed her to say such a vulgar thing to a stranger? No insult could justify it. Catherine felt her face flame anew with embarrassment. Despite her easy, informal ways, Catherine would have washed out the mouth of any servant she'd overheard using such language. And wherever had she learnt such an expression?

Oh, she knew the answer to that one! *From Bentley.* And the only other time she'd ever used it, she'd used it on him, in the heat of a dreadful argument. Her younger brother had stolen her favorite hunter from the stables, ridden it, and returned it to its stall without so much as a rubdown. Over dinner, the quarrel had exploded. Catherine had been but sixteen at the time, and almost as willful as Bentley. Motherless and neglected, they'd been hellions, the pair of them. Spitting out insults like feral tomcats, both had ignored their elder brother Cam's stern warnings. The argument had escalated. And then . . . she had said *it*.

To her undying humiliation, her last salvo had resulted in her first whipping, when finally, her father—who rarely noticed her, let alone bothered to punish her—had handed his best riding crop to the housekeeper with very clear instructions. "An incorrigible hoyden," her father had grumbled over the din of wailing, thrashing, and blaspheming. Only Mrs. Naffles's inexperience had left Catherine able to sit down. Still, once the whipping was over, it was clear that Randolph Rutledge had lost what little will he'd had to manage his only daughter. And so, within the year, she'd worn down his halfhearted objections and won his permission to marry Will Wodeway. In hindsight, Papa had probably considered himself well rid of her.

And now! Good Lord, what was she to do? She certainly would not apologize! Mr. de Rohan had insulted her abominably. He could rot in hell. Suddenly, the sun, which mere moments earlier had seemed muted, became agonizingly brilliant. Her head began to pound.

Oh, how bloody ridiculous! She had never suffered a moment's illness in her life, not even when Will . . . when Will had died. Suddenly, it felt to Catherine as if he'd gotten her into this mess. Damn it all, how dare he do something so blindly stupid and—and just *die?* They had promised to care for one another always. How dare he leave her alone and lonely like this? Anger and fear rushed anew through her bones.

Oh, God. She was so lost. Catherine let her fist fall, striking the top of the sideboard in front of the window with a thud. The headache was making her sick now. Slowly, she turned and made her way through the house and back upstairs to the darkness of her bedchamber.

Despite his early-morning detour into Hyde Park, de Rohan arrived at his office long before everyone save the lowliest of clerks. But, after settling into his chair, he found himself grappling with a restlessness which left him unable to concentrate. Disdainfully, he shoved away the stack of files which Feathershaw had heaped upon his desk. Still, the walls pressed in upon him far more intently than usual. For a quarter-hour, he struggled in vain against the urge to flee into the chaos of London, where real work—not a pile of bloody paperwork—so desperately wanted doing. And in the end, he dropped the criminal law consolidation proposals into the top drawer of his desk, slammed it shut, and thundered back down the two flights of stairs into a bustling spring day.

But in his heart, de Rohan knew what drove him into

the busy streets of Westminster, and it was something rather less pleasant than boredom or duty. It was guilt. He had hurt someone. Quite deliberately. Oh, de Rohan did not delude himself. He knew that many considered him unfeeling and harsh, and the accusation was not wholly without merit. He told himself his job required a degree of callousness. But this morning, he had been worse than callous. He had been spiteful. That was not his way.

Almost unseeingly, de Rohan pushed his way through the throng of morning traffic. Already, the Haymarket was choked with drays and hackneys disgorging their respective cargoes. The smell of meat pies mingled with the odor of horse dung as clerks and merchants hastened along the pavement, pushing past one another in the morning's rush. Here and there, familiar faces—street sweepers, shopkeepers, and the like—shouted out a brisk good morning. De Rohan touched his hat brim in response and kept moving. Near Regent Circus, he passed by his favorite coffeehouse, but for once, the smell which drifted from it failed to tempt him. On the next corner, he hesitated. Two attractive women stood gesturing before a shop window, calling out orders to a small girl inside the glass who was arranging a display of bonnets.

"No, no, the opera turban on top," wailed the first woman. "And mind the plumes, Mary! Mind the plumes!"

The second woman let her gaze drift from the window. "Morning, Mr. de Rohan," she murmured, setting one hand impudently on her hip. "Where've you been keeping yourself?"

The elder sister turned from the window. "Come along with you, Lucy Leonard!" she snapped. "If Mr. de Rohan wishes to call, he'll come inside, not chatter in the street like a magpie."

De Rohan lifted his hat and managed a smile. "Good morning, Mrs. Elden, Mrs. Leonard. Business is brisk?"

"Oh!" Irene Elden threw up her hands with an expression of misery. "The season is upon us, Mr. de Rohan!" Then, with one last gesture at the girl in the window, she swished her way back into her millinery shop.

Her sister did not seem eager to follow. Lucy thought him a bit of a hero, de Rohan knew. Four months ago, he'd saved the pretty widow from being robbed whilst carrying a week's worth of shop receipts. She'd flirted with him ever since. He'd walked out with her a few evenings, even kissed her twice. She had been eager, too, kissing him back with abandon and allowing his hands to roam where they would. Her message was plain, and it had nothing to do with gratitude.

"Irene and I are to get up a theater party for tomorrow night, Max," she purred. "Oh, do come along for once! We're to see *As You Like It . . .*" She let her words trail away suggestively.

De Rohan stared down at the tongue which darted out to wet her lush, half-parted lips. Oh, he could guess precisely how Lucy liked it. Sometimes, he was even tempted to find out. "I'm sorry, Lucy," he heard himself say. "I've another commitment."

The lush lips formed a perfect pout. "Well, you're a fine, big buck of a man, Max," answered Lucy tartly. "But I don't possess the patience of Job. Mr. Kent asked me twice last week to have supper with him—and very prettily, too—so when next he asks, I'm going, Max. I *am.*"

It wasn't a threat, just a statement. Max forced himself to smile. "Then he is a most fortunate man," he answered. He slapped his hat back on, tweaked Lucy on the chin, and set off before he could reconsider what he was passing up.

He was making a mistake, most likely. He probably should have agreed to Lucy's theater plans. And afterward, he should have taken her home, opened a bottle of champagne, and given her a good, hard fucking. It was probably what he needed, and Lucy had made it plain that it was exactly what she wanted. Like most women of her class, Lucy was earthy and uncomplicated; there was no duplicity in her, no feigned emotions or crocodile tears designed to trick a fellow into believing up was down. He felt his fists begin to clench. Good God, when had he become so cynical? Ah, he knew. But he did not like to remember.

In de Rohan's experience, a young man's first *affaire* was a painful and devastating thing. His had also been enlightening—and for that, he supposed, one ought to be thankful. Unlike Lucy, his first love had been ephemeral and disingenuous, not to mention almost achingly beautiful. But Penelope's had been a beauty which went only skin deep. Still, for as long as he lived, de Rohan would never forget the first time he'd seen her. It had been, after all, a matter of duty. And duty meant everything to him, did it not?

De Rohan snorted in disgust and stepped briskly across the next street just as the bells of St. George's began to peal, reverberating off the buildings which fronted Regent Street. By force of habit, he jerked out his watch. A wedding, no doubt, at this hour. He smiled bitterly and thought again of Penelope, who had been married in that very church so many years and another lifetime ago, in a wedding which had been the talk of society.

But not a year later, de Rohan had been sent to her imposing brick town home on Grosvenor Street by the chief magistrate of Bow Street. Her elderly husband, a powerful cabinet minister, had been wild with outrage. His bride's priceless jewel collection had been looted, and only Bow Street's best would do. The youngest man ever to make captain of the Runners, Max had a reputation for being ruthless, persistent, and scrupulously honest. But beyond even that, he had a reputation for persistence, for his willingness to crawl up or down the ladder of society to find the true villain at the root of every crime. Not just the pickpockets, prostitutes, and black legs, but the East End bawds who sucked them into near slavery and the West End gentlemen who financed their perfidy for profit.

He had believed that his father would have been proud of his work. And Bow Street had believed him perfect for this case. He was a vast deal more polished than most of their men, a fact which typically earned him nothing but good-natured ribbing. De Rohan had been wildly flattered and had dutifully trotted off to Grosvenor Street like some witless knight errant, to inadvertently lay his heart at the feet of a cold, manipulative bitch. The crime had been simple, the solution obvious. And he would have known it at once, had he but looked past Penelope's beauty. If he had set aside his sympathy. *If he had stayed out of her bed.* Oh, she had not been the first fine lady of the *ton* to ask for his services. But unlike the others, she had been neither insulting nor demanding. Oh, no. Penelope's seduction had been far more insidious, and she had sought far more than pleasure.

For weeks, he'd hung on her every sob, soon fancying himself in love with her. Poor Penelope was trapped in a loveless marriage, sacrificed by her family for money. Her husband was old, controlling, and cruel. Max, she had said, was her only solace. And so he had all but cried for her, while subconsciously rejecting every circumstance which pointed toward the ugly truth. Slowly, the case had ground down to an embarrassment for Bow Street. Penelope's husband had grown more vociferous; perhaps he'd even suspected her. Max had been discreetly pulled from the case and another, more senior investigator assigned.

Penelope was more perfidious than anyone could have guessed, and in the end, her crimes had been proven far worse than pawning her own jewels. Max had been struck by disbelief. Once, he'd even returned to Grosvenor Street, where she had laughed and called him an impudent upstart. Eventually, the cabinet minister had been faced with an awkward decision. His pretty Penelope could go to Bridewell, or she could go to the Outer Hebrides, forever to live in one of his lesser properties. His power and his politics gave him that choice; Max had had none. His heart was in tatters, his reputation very nearly so. Oh, the depth of his failing had never been fully revealed, but suspicion had clung to him for months.

When he'd been offered a position with the River Police in Wapping, he'd taken it, grateful to escape without the epithets he deserved. *Fool. Adulterer. Failure.* Again, he'd turned tail and run. But why, now, was he reliving this? Better than a dozen years had passed. He had paid for this sin as he had paid for the other: by proving himself over and over again. But the fear was ever present, the thirst to succeed seemingly unquenchable. It was said of him, he knew, that he was fearless. But it was not true. He was terrified—terrified of failure.

Caught up in the past, de Rohan stepped off the pavement to cross the street but leapt back when a horn exploded in his right ear. He jerked up his head to see the afternoon mail coach go flying through Cavendish Square, so close his cravat stirred in the draft. With a self-deprecating curse, de Rohan glanced about to see that he'd crossed the whole of Mayfair and now stood at the foot of Harley Street. He understood at once why his subconscious had brought him here. Briskly, he paced up the street until he arrived at a familiar house. He lifted his stick and knocked. "Dr. Greaves, please?"

"He's with a patient," explained a harried housemaid, throwing wide the door and gesturing toward a small, comfortable parlor. "Take a seat just there, sir, and he'll be with you soon as may be."

"I thank you." De Rohan stepped inside and slipped the girl a card. "But I'm not a patient. I'm with the Home Office."

The girl's brows lifted in mild surprise, but she took the card, bobbed a quick curtsey, and vanished into the nether regions of the house. De Rohan settled into an overstuffed wing chair near the hearth and studied what was left of the morning's fire.

Soon, the guilt grabbed hold of him again. Not guilt over Lucy or Penelope but, strangely, guilt over the woman he did not know. Still, he did know her name. *Lady Catherine Wodeway.* She'd insisted on telling him. Right before he'd insulted her. For a moment, he found himself wishing he shared Nonna Sofia's faith. His grandmother was an implacable Papist, and a quick confession to a reproachful priest would have done him a world of good just now. Certainly, he would not do the right thing—seek out Lady Catherine Wodeway and offer a profuse apology. No, that he could not bear to do, though he'd little doubt that he could bring her address to hand in a matter of minutes. Half an hour perhaps, if his spies proved hard to find. Far better simply to pray they never met again. Certainly he had no wish to meet her right arm again. Absently, he rubbed the tender spot along his lip. He wondered precisely what her dinner invitation had entailed. Perhaps just . . . *dinner?*

Dio mio, what a dreadful thought! Still, de Rohan had learned the hard way that a man could not be too careful with the jaded ladies of the *ton*. He knew too well that a few of them found his line of work horrifically titillating, his dark appearance and grim demeanor challenging. Worse, policemen were near the bottom rung of England's social ladder. His status made rich women rather too bold—and then they expected him to be *grateful* for their overtures. He was not. He was in-sulted.

Still, even if Lady Catherine had made her expecta-tions explicit and then dropped a bag of gold sovereigns into his palm to seal the bargain, his cruelty would not have been justified. He should have simply thanked her for the compliment and moved on. But, inexplicably, he'd instead let her strike a chord inside some part of him. She had made him feel, ever so fleetingly, a sense of regret.

Ah, God. That would not do.

Suddenly, he looked up to see Dr. Greaves standing on the threshold, a curious smile on his face. "Maximil-ian!" exclaimed the portly physician, coming fully into the room, his hand extended.

Warmly, de Rohan took it. "Good morning, Greaves. I expect you know why I am here."

"Constable Sisk said you might be by." With a little grunt, Greaves settled himself into the opposite chair. "You wish to know if I have completed my examination of the corpse of Lady Sands. I have, and I wish I could tell you she died of natural causes, but, of course, I cannot."

Slowly, de Rohan nodded. "I saw the bruises about the throat. Was that the cause of death?"

Greaves nodded and stretched out his legs toward the dead coals. "Without question. She died slowly, of suffo-cation," he answered, threading his fingers over his ample belly. "And unfortunately—or perhaps I should say *fortunately*—she was rather well primed with alco-hol. I doubt she awoke until he had a good grip round her windpipe."

"There was little sign of a struggle," mused de

Rohan. "But in my experience, it takes a good bit of strength to strangle a person, even one so small as Lady Sands. Would you agree?"

The old army surgeon lifted one thick white brow. "Oh, yes. A vast deal of bruising, the throat neatly crushed. Not likely the work of a small man, unless he was near wild with rage. Certainly not a woman."

A mental image of Lord Sands's large hands drifted through de Rohan's mind. He shook it off and forced a tight smile. "No, women much prefer poison, do they not?"

"They do indeed," agreed the rotund doctor. "And now, Max, I should like to impose upon our long friendship and tell you one last thing in confidence. I fear it isn't pretty."

"Go on."

Greaves looked suddenly pained. "I won't say so at the inquest, mind, for I cannot be certain. But I am persuaded the lady had been recently with child."

De Rohan drew in a sharp breath. *"Had been?* You mean . . . a miscarriage?"

"I doubt it." The old doctor shook his head sadly. "The uterus was enlarged, and there were—well, signs of a healing injury. Do you want to hear a clinical explanation?"

"A healing injury?" echoed de Rohan. "An abortion?"

Greaves nodded. "And quite recently, I'd venture." Then, as if to dispel a ghost, he slapped his thighs almost jovially. "Well, there you have it, sir! All very straightforward. Haven't had a murder like this in Mayfair since old Lord Mercer got himself done for."

"I recall it vaguely."

Greaves winked. "And that, by the by, was a woman. With poison. Dangerous creatures, women. Want watching at every turn. Now, Max! About that nasty split lip you're sporting—may I give you a little tincture to put on it?"

Chapter Four

*Our jarring passions, our variable humours, nay, our very
health and spirits, produce contradictions in our conduct.*

—Lord Chesterfield, 1776,
The Fine Gentleman's Etiquette

In the cool shadows of her bedchamber, Catherine
paced. The pounding in her head had not relented. Luncheon was out of the question. Perhaps she ought to lie
down? Or perhaps she ought to discover the location of
Maximilian de Rohan's police station—watch house, office, or whatever one called it—and march straight there
to tell him just what an arrogant bastard she thought
him.

Sharply, she sighed into the silence of the room. No,
no, that would not do at all! Her wicked tongue was
what had gotten her into this mess. And was it possible
she was being unfair to the man? In her social naïveté,
had she said or done something which had given him
the wrong impression?

Of course, it had been a little forward to ask him to
dine. But in the country, where life was more informal
and society more egalitarian, one often did such things.
Was such an invitation considered unacceptable in

town? Catherine did not know, but he certainly would have. For all his outward reserve and simple clothing, the man—who'd neither looked nor acted like a policeman—had possessed an air of sophistication.

Or perhaps, despite her instincts about him, he simply wasn't a decent man. His eyes were wickedly black, coldly mocking. Still, his initial actions had been kind. He really had believed her to be in some sort of jeopardy, of that she was certain. But why had he kissed her? Surely, just as she had suggested, there had been another way? Her challenging question had made him lash out at her with a raw, visceral anger.

It stung Catherine to think she might have misjudged him. Worse still was the memory of how she'd become totally lost in the feel of his mouth. Lord, she'd never been kissed like that in her life. She had desired her husband, yes. They had been friends from childhood, and their mutual affection had been steady and certain. But never flaming hot. Never wild and irrational. Never *frightening*.

Oh! How could she compare her husband to such a dreadful man? Catherine whirled about, paced to the window, and stared into the street below. What must Mr. de Rohan think of her, to kiss her in such a way? He certainly would not now think her a lady, despite her awkward introduction. But he *had* kissed her first. What was a lady to do? Surely, an introduction was in order when two people had been so intimate as to . . .

Good God! There was no logic in this! Why did she even care? With sharp, angry motions, she jerked shut the heavy draperies, hurled herself onto the bed, and tried to shut out her thoughts. She could hear an occasional carriage rumbling along Mortimer Street. Beyond her door, she could hear Delilah, the housemaid, walking briskly down the passageway. The normalcy of it felt soothing, and eventually, she drew a pillow to her chest and fell asleep, curled into its softness.

At half past one, de Rohan received a curt summons to the Home Secretary's office. Many months ago, de Rohan had been introduced to Mr. Peel by Cecilia's stepson, Lord Walrafen. De Rohan had liked him at once. Peel's grandfather had been in trade, and although the English aristocracy had a strange habit of pinching their noses at earned wealth, somehow Peel's father had overcome the stench and netted himself a baronetcy. Behind the younger Peel's back, many amongst the *ton* still referred to him as a *parvenu*. But they whispered when they said it, for Peel's influence had suffered little from his lack of blue blood. And despite his integrity, one did not cross him without care.

On this particular morning, it was hard to judge Peel's mood. The Home Secretary motioned de Rohan toward a chair. Then, as if he were acutely uncomfortable, Peel rolled his shoulders beneath the fabric of his coat and sat a little straighter behind his desk. "I'm told by the chief magistrate at Queen Square that you're involved in the Sands situation," he began.

De Rohan hesitated. "I was called to the scene by Lady Delacourt," he admitted. "Merely as a friend of the family."

Mr. Peel studied him across the burnished surface of his desk. It was surprisingly neat, given the vast number of tasks which vied for the Home Secretary's attention.

"But you have spoken with Lord Sands," he said quietly. "And you've asked the constables to share with you their findings."

"I have," de Rohan admitted.

"And so, whether you wish it or not, you are involved?" When de Rohan made no answer, Peel continued. "I understand you've also been privy to the postmortem findings."

De Rohan nodded. "An inquest has been set for one week from today. A mere routine. There is no doubt of the coroner's ruling."

"Murder by person or persons unknown?" returned Peel.

"It could get worse." De Rohan looked at him pointedly. "It seems that someone—perhaps Sands himself—strangled her ladyship."

Peel's expression turned inward, to one of weary sadness. "I do understand," he softly admitted. "And it will crush Lord Sands's sister, Lady Delacourt, will it not? And our mutual friend Walrafen, too, by association."

"*If* it is true," de Rohan reluctantly agreed.

"*If—!*" echoed Peel, his voice soft with anguish. "But we can hold no one—not even our friends—above the law, can we?" He pierced de Rohan with his steady gaze. "I may depend upon you, above all people, to understand that, can I not?"

De Rohan's answer was swift. "If you do not know that much, sir, then you've chosen the wrong man to clean up your police corruption."

Mr. Peel smiled faintly. "I do know it. And unless I miss my guess, you'd rather handle this case yourself than entrust it to the blundering of others—and that would include Bow Street. Am I right?"

"Unfortunately," de Rohan agreed with a bitter inward smile.

Peel's expression was rueful. "Well, we cannot quite do that, can we? But I've told the chief magistrate that you will be my eyes and ears in this investigation. And there will be certain things which you will be better able to handle."

"What sort of things?"

Peel shrugged. "Some people will be reluctant to consort with the Westminster constabulary, and the Runners would be worse. It will seem—"

"Beneath their blue-blooded dignity?" de Rohan snapped.

Amusement lit Peel's eyes. "Just speak to those who you know will not wish to associate with the police. Push the case forward. Be discreet yet thorough. Try to spare the family from gossip. Pray God it was the work of some madman, but if not . . ." Peel shook his head. "The constables will keep you informed. Report to me each Monday."

"Yes, sir."

At that, Peel shoved back his chair. "Oh! And one more thing. The bribery scandal—I understand you have made progress?"

"I have," agreed de Rohan, coming to his feet. "As we suspected, Bruter is taking bribes to alter the prison inspection reports. And frankly, sir, it may go deeper. Perhaps as deep as the watchmen and constables."

Peel's face fell. "I wish that surprised me."

De Rohan smiled tightly. "As to Bruter, we'll get him,

sir. I overheard him again this morning at his usual meeting place in Hyde Park. Unfortunately, circumstances prevented me from . . . that is to say, there was a bystander. I was concerned."

Peel waved his hand. "No matter. It is but a matter of time." Introspectively, he paused. "You've done well, de Rohan. But let someone else handle the mundane surveillance. I want your attention on the Sands investigation."

De Rohan stood, his eyes going at once to the wall clock. "Then I shall call upon Lord Sands this afternoon," he answered. "He was quite beyond coherence yesterday."

Peel shot him an oddly assessing look, then relaxed into his chair with a satisfied expression. "Do you know, de Rohan, I often think you are a bloody zealot," he said musingly. "You want justice, particularly for the common man, and you want it more ardently than anyone I've ever known. Why, I do not know. But thank God for it, because you are precisely what I need just now."

Acutely uncomfortable, de Rohan bowed and turned toward the door.

At the last possible second, Peel called him back. "Oh, and de Rohan?"

With a sigh, de Rohan spun about and lifted his brows.

The Home Secretary narrowed his eyes. "That's a nasty little cut on your mouth," he murmured. "I trust there was no sort of altercation in the park this morning?"

Catherine awoke from her nap on a choking sob, disoriented as to where she was. Sitting upright in bed, she shoved the hair from her face and looked about. Through the open dressing-room door, she could see her large traveling trunk, its lid still flung open. The breath flooded from her lungs in relief.

Cam's house. London.

With the back of her hand, Catherine began to wipe her eyes. She looked down to see that her pillow was damp. An oppressive sense of grief weighed her down. Through the curtains, she could see early afternoon sunlight. How long had she slept? The last remnants of a dream were slipping from her grasp, and Catherine felt as if she were losing something sad and precious. What on earth had she been dreaming? Faint memory stirred. Catherine's hand flew to her mouth.

Will. Good God. For the first time in months, she had dreamt of Will. Abruptly, she dragged the soft pillow into her lap and buried her face in it. *Please, God. Not those dreams again!* In the period just after her husband's death, sleep had become nothing but a torment. Night after night, memories of his last morning's kiss had haunted her. And each time, they began in the very same way. As if from a distance—as if she no longer lived her life but merely observed it—she could see herself tucked inside her small parlor at Aldhampton Manor.

She could watch herself peering through the bottle-green draperies and into the foggy morning beyond. And then, with a slow, floating motion, she turned to smile at Will, who sat finishing his coffee. Catherine could hear her own voice cautioning him, cajoling him—but not once begging him—to stay home by the fire with her. Then, through the haze of the dream, she would hear the awful gunshot ring out, though, in reality, she'd not been close enough to hear. But Will's dying words—oh, those she had heard.

"I should have listened, Cat." His words had gurgled like water over broken glass. "Ah, Catherine . . ."

But in this new dream, the one which had left her sobbing in her sleep, Will had not spoken. There had been no sense of hearth and home. No warm breakfast parlor. No steaming coffee. Just the fog; not a cool country haze which swathed you in the scents of damp earth and foliage, but the thick, metallic miasma of London which clung to your skin and stung your nostrils.

And she could hear the shot, see Will collapsing at her feet, his body splayed upon the autumn leaves. But she could not see his face. Even worse, in this new dream, she could see the man who'd shot him. A lean, shadowy figure dressed all in swirling black. He stood beside Will's lifeless form—looking down at the face which she could no longer see—the gun still expertly balanced in his hand.

Maximilian de Rohan?

Dear God, she was all mixed up! She was losing her grip. Catherine jerked upright, pressing her palms against her temples and squeezing shut her eyes. Will had been shot by one of his hunting companions, she reminded herself. A hearty country squire like himself, not some long, lethal figure in black. The weather had been bad. The spaniels had scattered into the brush, the beaters' cry lost in the fog. It had been an accident. *An accident!* She needed to forget about Mr. de Rohan. She would never have to see him again. He was a policeman. Even Catherine understood that policemen did not circulate in London society.

Suddenly, a loud, insistent tattoo thundered upon her bedchamber door. Catherine knew at once that it was not a servant. Smoothly, she pulled herself up into a sitting position and neatened her skirts. "Come in."

To her delight, the door flew open to reveal the broad shoulders of her younger brother. "Bentley!" she cried, bouncing off the edge of the bed.

With a swagger and a smile, Bentley thundered across the floor, opened his arms to catch her, and then whirled her bodily about the room. "Cat, my God! Truly here in town?" he said, finally setting her down again. "Why? When?"

"Bentley! Where have you been?"

"Oh, here and there, m'dear." He urged her a little away from him and looked down. "Aw, dash it, Cat!" he exclaimed, running the ball of his thumb beneath her left eye. "What's all this?"

Sheepishly, Cat lowered her gaze to his disheveled cravat. In truth, Bentley looked disheveled all over, which was nothing unusual. "A touch of the headache," she murmured. "Nothing more."

"The devil!" growled Bentley, stomping toward the bed and drawing her along in his wake. "Headaches don't make a female's eyes look like that. Where's your maid?" When she made no reply, Bentley settled her onto the bed and stood back, dragging one hand through his unruly black hair as he stared at her. "My God, Cat! Oughtn't she be doing something? Burning feathers? Fetching you some of that concoction you ladies sniff for the blue-devils?"

Catherine clasped her hands over her face and burst into weak laughter. "Oh, Bentley!" she choked, falling back into the softness of the bed covers. "Would that such things were so easily fixed! Still, you do cheer me up." She dropped her hands and stared up at him. "Now, answer my question—where have you been for the last fortnight?"

Bentley's dark brows snapped together. "No place my sister need know of," he grumbled.

"And doing things that are none of her business?" she challenged.

"Just so," he answered gruffly.

With a resigned sigh, Catherine settled back into the pillows. Restless as always, Bentley began to roam about the room, pacing back and forth like a caged animal. From time to time, he paused to study a painting or to toy with a bottle of perfume. "Missing old Will again, aren't you?" he finally said, taking up the book she'd been reading in the park and flipping aimlessly through it. "I miss him, too."

"Oh!" His sympathy was her undoing. "I do miss him, b-but—" She choked.

Her brother shot her a panicked look. "Dash it, Cat," he muttered, yanking open her bureau to rifle through her handkerchiefs. Leaving it open, he crossed the room to sit on the bed, thrusting one at her. "Now, what is it?"

Catherine felt her shoulders begin to shake. "Oh, I don't know!" She snatched the handkerchief and buried her face in it. "I miss him, but it's just that . . . just that . . . well, I really can't quite *remember* what he looked like, Bentley! N-not exactly. I mean, *before* he died. And I feel so guilty for forgetting him."

"Aw, Cat," Bentley muttered, gathering her awkwardly into his arms.

Catherine flung one arm about his neck. "Oh, Bentley! I can see him as he was that day when they carried him in," she sobbed into his shoulder. "But that's all!"

Awkwardly, her brother patted her on the back. "Now, Cat!" he soothed. "It's going on two years. Of course you don't remember exactly. Life goes on."

Weakly, Catherine fell fully against him. "Oh, Bentley!" she sighed. "Sometimes I think that's what I'm most afraid of."

Just then, a far more deferential knock sounded, and Delilah entered. Catherine barely noticed when Bentley returned to her bureau drawer and, oddly, began to neaten it. "Lady Kirton's come, ma'am," said Delilah with a curtsey. "She says you're to accompany her to tea?"

Shoving shut the drawer, Bentley whirled about, eyes flaring with mild alarm. "Blister it!" he said, rushing to give his sister a quick peck on the cheek, then heading toward the door. "Best cut out the back. Ain't up to doing the pretty for your Aunt Isabel today."

"Bentley, wait!"

But just as he pushed past the maid, something heavy almost fell from his coat. Deftly, he caught it and shoved it deeper into his pocket. "Bentley, wait!" Catherine repeated, bouncing off the bed. "Where are you going? And what on earth do you have in your coat pocket?"

Bentley paused just beyond the threshold. "Snuff box," he muttered, running a disordering hand through his hair again. "And I'm off to Essex. Got a hankering to tool up to Gus Weyden's for a bit."

Catherine followed him as far as the door. *"Where* in Essex?" she cried after him.

But Bentley's heavy boots were already thundering down the servants' stairs, and he had vanished into the depths of the stairwell.

In the late afternoon, de Rohan left Whitehall and set off in the direction of Mayfair. He was admitted to Lord Sands's town house by the nervous butler. But he'd no sooner given over his hat and stick than he saw Lord Delacourt come out of the library.

"De Rohan!" His lordship looked relieved. "Well met, old fellow! I hope you've come to call on Harry and Cecilia? I confess, I've no notion what one ought to say in such dreadful circumstances."

The butler withdrew. De Rohan hesitated just inside the door, studying Delacourt. "I do need to speak with Lord Sands," he admitted, feeling rather like a traitor. "But I must tell you quite frankly, my lord, that I'm here as an agent of the Home Office."

Delacourt smiled regretfully. "I see," he said very quietly. "Well, what can one expect? It is a nasty situation, is it not? And I'm afraid my wife has not yet grasped just how bad things look for her brother. My God, what could Harry have been thinking when he threatened to pitch Julia over that balcony?"

"I beg your pardon?" De Rohan's voice was sharp.

Delacourt looked vaguely uncomfortable. "Oh, the deuce! I'm awfully ham-fisted, aren't I? But I suppose Cecilia never thought it worth mentioning. Harry got half-sprung at the theater the night before last. Then he and Julia proceeded to have a rather public quarrel." He paused to draw an uncharacteristically unsteady breath. "Look here, de Rohan—I don't suppose you would simply believe me if I swore to you that Harry was incapable of murder?"

Awkwardly, de Rohan hesitated. He had often seen Harry about town and had spoken with him for several minutes yesterday. Nothing he knew of Cecilia's brother made him a likely suspect. It was not that Harry possessed an air of innocence—far from it. He simply did not seem to possess enough forethought to commit such a crime.

Apparently taking de Rohan's hesitation as agreement, Delacourt smiled more warmly and patted him on the shoulder. "You may as well come into the drawing room, de Rohan," he said, urging him across the corridor. "Cecilia's inside consoling Harry. She will be pleased to see you. By the way, my friend, that's the devil of a split lip." He elbowed de Rohan suggestively. "Honorably earned, I hope?"

"Shaving cut," de Rohan muttered.

With his free hand, Delacourt threw open the door. "Cecilia, my dear, look who has come to—" Smoothly, he halted, apparently noticing the two ladies who sat opposite Harry and Cecilia, their backs turned to the door. "Your pardon, my dear," he murmured, stepping backward. "I can see we've interrupted."

But it was too late. Harry had risen from his chair. Cecilia bounded to her feet and rushed toward them. "Oh, Max!" she cried a little plaintively, brushing past her husband to clasp de Rohan's hand. "Thank goodness you've returned."

"My pleasure," he murmured uneasily, bowing deeply over Cecilia's small, cold fingers.

But Cecilia seemed unaware of his unease. Urgently,

she drew Max and her husband into the room. "Do come in and join us for tea. Ellie will fetch more cups. And look! Here is dear Lady Kirton—you will remember her from the Nazareth Society, I daresay? She has come to offer her condolences and brought her niece along." Cecilia motioned toward two ladies, who promptly turned to face them. "Lady Catherine, I collect you've not met my husband, Lord Delacourt? And this is our very good friend, Mr. de Rohan."

At once, a sharp intake of breath tore de Rohan's eyes from Cecilia. Afterward, everything happened in a flash. The young woman seated beside Lady Kirton jerked to her feet. A porcelain cup struck the edge of the tea table in a spray of white chips. Hot liquid splashed across the carpet. At once, Cecilia darted forward, frantically dabbing at the woman's skirts.

The woman.

Oh, *merda!*

Blankly, de Rohan stared at her, somehow managing to suppress a burst of bitter laughter. Cecilia seemed oblivious. "Oh, dear!" she cried. "Oh, Lady Catherine! Have you burnt yourself? Was it the handle? Did it snap?"

A maid thrust forward a tea towel, and Lady Kirton joined in the wiping, sweeping, and clucking. Delacourt stepped aside, making apologetic noises in the back of his throat. Harry just kept drinking—from a brandy glass, not a teacup. De Rohan began praying for an earthquake to split the floor and swallow him. His mind churned with embarrassing possibilities. He felt sick. It was little consolation to see that Lady Catherine looked worse. All color had drained from her face, and her gaze was focused somewhere near her feet. Soon, however, her skirts had been dabbed dry, and she was left with no alternative but to reseat herself.

"I do beg your pardon, Lord Sands," she said, cutting a nervous, reproachful glance toward de Rohan as he sat down. "How very awkward of me."

"Oh, pray do not regard it, Lady Catherine!" fussed Cecilia as she picked one last shard of porcelain out of the carpet. "Those cups are too fragile. Did I not say so when Julia bought them, Harry?"

"Just so," said Harry soothingly, lifting his bleary gaze to stare across the tea table at Lady Catherine. "Besides, ma'am, we've a score of 'em. Blasted things ain't made for a fellow to hold on to properly. Like a good, thick mug, myself."

Just then, the maid set down three more of the accursed cups. "Now," interjected Cecilia brightly, lifting the teapot as if to pour again. "I did introduce everyone, did I not?"

"You did, my dear," Lady Kirton answered, bending gracefully forward to set down her saucer. "But unfortunately, Catherine and I must take our leave."

"Really, ma'am!" murmured Delacourt. "There is no need."

"Ah, David, I think there is." Lady Kirton turned the warmth of her smile on de Rohan and began to tug on her gloves. "It was an honor to see you again, Mr. de Rohan. We've not met since the horrible incident at the Nazareth Society last year. If I did not say so at the time, the entire board of governors was grateful to you. Very grateful."

As de Rohan muttered his thanks, the two ladies stood.

The color had returned to Lady Catherine's face. Indeed, it was now a rather livid shade of pink, and her once-lovely eyes were so narrow, one could not discern their color. But he already knew they were brown. A rich, dark shade of brown, ringed with gold and fringed with incredibly long, dark lashes. And at that very moment, Lady Catherine's hand fluttered up nervously to brush back a wisp of hair, and he noticed something else, too.

Lady Catherine wore a wedding ring.

He watched her draw on her gloves over her long, slender hands, something heavy and tight catching in his throat. Well. How odd. He had not thought—or, some-how, he had simply not considered . . .

But he *had* considered, damn it. He'd believed her married, had he not? It had been, in part, that belief—and not his anger toward himself—which had made him lash out at her. Had it not? Awkwardly, he forced a stiff, formal bow. "Lady Kirton, Lady Catherine," he said coolly. "It was indeed a pleasure."

At last, her gaze snapped to his, and he could see the wrath which burned there. If looks could have killed, Lady Catherine's eyes would have dropped him like a plumb-line, right in the middle of his lordship's Aubusson carpet. As if fearing contamination, she swished her skirts in a wide arc around him, then lifted her chin to shoot him one last go-to-hell look as she headed for the door. De Rohan should have been mortified. But, to his horror, all he could do was stare at her lush, wide mouth and remember how it had felt beneath his.

A quarter-hour later, de Rohan was almost relieved to find himself in Harry's library, a room which looked as little used as his lordship's intellect. Harry carried in two glasses and his decanter from the drawing room.

"Eye water, Mr. de Rohan?" he offered, motioning toward a chair.

De Rohan shook his head. "No, thank you, my lord."

Harry heaved a deep, weary sigh and settled himself behind his desk. "Daresay I ought to give it up myself," he admitted, eyeing the brandy a little sorrowfully. "Yes . . . perhaps. When this is all over."

Cecilia's elder brother was a large, bluff man of perhaps thirty years, portly, with a gently receding hairline. Setting down his goblet, he turned to de Rohan. "Well, have at it, sir. Daresay everyone thinks I'm too witless to know how this looks—Julia getting herself strangled and all—but I ain't. It looks deuced bad for me."

De Rohan lifted his brows in mild surprise. "Did you kill her?"

With a twisted smile, Harry Markham-Sands shook his head. "Julia and I had an ugly argument, de Rohan. Of course, one thing led to another, and I . . . well, I said some things."

"You threatened to kill her—?"

"No." Harry looked bemused. "Specifically, I threatened to hurl her over the edge of our theater box and 'into the hoi polloi of the pit where she belonged.' "

De Rohan found himself suppressing a smile at Harry's unexpected wit. And if half the things he'd heard about Lady Sands were true, her husband's opinion wasn't far wrong. "Perhaps you'd best start at the beginning, my lord?" de Rohan calmly suggested. "Tell me exactly what occurred that night. I shall endeavor to keep your words confidential."

At that, Harry snorted with laughter and tossed off the dregs of his brandy. "Don't trouble yourself," he returned, staring down into the empty glass which he held cradled against his waistcoat. "Everyone knows about Julia. But I'll tell you what I can."

Harry's story was consistent with the statements Sisk had taken from his valet and coachman. His lordship had slept late, spent the better part of the day at his club, then dined at the Adelphi with friends. Afterward, finding himself at loose ends, he had traveled across town to Drury Lane where he kept a box.

He had not expected his wife to attend the theater that night—not until he had seen her alight from an unmarked carriage. From the shadows of the portico, he'd seen Lady Sands turn to speak to someone still inside—here, de Rohan noticed that the tips of Harry's ears turned red—and then he had watched in humiliation as she leaned inside to kiss the man passionately. A shocking breach of etiquette, or so Harry described it. De Rohan thought it rather worse than that. Indeed, he did not greatly approve of the current English fashion which permitted married women to go about in carriages with men who weren't their husbands. And whilst discreet affairs were often tolerated within certain circles of the *ton*—another fashion de Rohan didn't condone—to actually kiss another man in public went quite beyond the pale.

"And then what did you do?" de Rohan asked quietly.

Harry let out another sigh. "I went upstairs to wait for her. She came into our box but a few moments later. She looked damned odd. Distraught, really. Then she saw me. I demanded to know whom she'd been with. Of course, Julia just laughed at me. I threatened her, told her I would no longer be cuckolded in public. She laughed again and said—well, she said words I am ashamed to admit my wife knew. Dash it all, I'd had too much to drink at dinner. Afraid I lost my temper. Must have been shouting. She came at me, slapping and clawing like a lunatic."

"Were there witnesses?" interjected de Rohan.

Harry shrugged and began to toy with a brass paperweight which lay upon his desk. "The lights were dim, but someone sent an usher to ask—well, to ask if we required any assistance. It was clear what he meant. I was horrified. I left at once."

"And what did you do then?"

"Why, I came straight home."

"And what did you do when you arrived?"

"What did I *do?*" Harry looked suddenly surprised and glanced about the room as if searching for an answer. "Well . . . I guess I had a drink in the drawing room and went up to bed."

De Rohan looked up sharply from his notes. He had not missed the hint of uncertainty in Harry's voice. "You *guess?*"

Harry's ears turned red again. "No, I'm certain. I had a drink. Then went up to bed."

Harry Markham-Sands was lying.

The knowledge came to him in a flash of certainty. It happened that way sometimes, and de Rohan had learned to stake his life on his instincts. "And did you go at once to sleep?" he asked quietly.

"Why, to be sure!" Harry sputtered. "What the devil else would a fellow do?"

De Rohan smiled dryly. "Personally, I like to read a bit first," he responded. "Some people say their prayers. Others like to have a glass of hot milk or write a bit in their journal. Can I take it that you did none of those things?"

The color receded in Harry's ears. "Well, I'm not the bookish sort, you know. Went straight to sleep like always, and slept like the dea—" Harry jerked to a halt and blanched.

"Yes, I'm a sound sleeper, too," agreed de Rohan gently. "Now, what happened next? I understand you heard nothing in the night? And Lady Sands's maid—she, too, heard nothing?"

Harry's eyes widened. "How the devil would I know what she heard?"

De Rohan paused. "I was merely attempting to confirm what Constable Sisk reported, my lord," he answered calmly.

"Oh." Harry shifted uncomfortably and set down the paperweight. "Well, that's what she said. I mean, when I asked her. You know . . . whilst we were waiting for the watch to arrive."

De Rohan held up a staying hand. "Chronologically, please, my lord. What happened after you went to sleep?"

Harry's brows drew together in a red-blond squiggle. "Why, I just slept. Next I knew, Overturf—that's our butler—was thumping on the door, saying that m'sister was downstairs in a terrible taking. So I threw on my dressing gown and went down. Figured it had to be something very bad to drag Cely away from the babe at such a god-awful hour."

De Rohan flicked his gaze up. Harry appeared rather pale and shaken. It was time to end their discussion for now. He'd had Cecilia's version of events from this point onward.

"You've told Overturf that the staff is to cooperate with Police Constable Sisk?" de Rohan gently pressed.

Harry nodded. "Cely told 'em. If anyone ain't cooperative, have a word with her. She'll see to it."

De Rohan nodded. Tucking away his pencil, he snapped shut his leather folio. "Thank you, my lord. I regret having to ask such questions in light of your grief."

Harry waved his hand in obviation. "No trouble. Better you than someone else. Hope you catch the blighter that killed her. I didn't—and you'll find nothing to say I did. Still, I don't like suspicion hanging over me. Whatever Julia was, by God, she didn't deserve to die."

As Harry rose to leave, Cecilia stepped inside and kissed him lightly on the cheek. "He's all right, do you think?" she asked, closing the door softly behind her brother.

De Rohan watched Cecilia float across the room. "Well enough," he answered as they seated themselves in the wing chairs by the desk. "He is angry, to be sure. But fully sensible of how things appear."

Cecilia nervously smoothed her hands down her skirts. "You mean he understands people might think him guilty?" She lifted her eyes to de Rohan's. "But he isn't. I swear it. Julia had enemies—scorned lovers, their angry wives. I can make inquiries. I am well known in society."

"Cecilia," said de Rohan gently. "It mightn't be safe.

And you are in mourning. You cannot go haring about asking questions. Indeed, you should take your brother away from town altogether, for his own peace of mind, and let me handle this."

Cecilia began to chew on her thumbnail. For a long moment, she was silent, and de Rohan knew she was thinking. That could cause all manner of trouble. It would be best to divert her. "You have looked through the box of jewelry which we found?"

Her eyes widened. "I never dreamt Julia possessed so many baubles. But there was one thing . . ."

He sensed her mild alarm. "Something is missing?"

"I cannot be sure, but my mother did have one especially fine piece. The Sands Sapphire." Cecilia laughed sardonically. "In the early years when we were all alone and money was tight, Harry and I often considered selling it. But it's been in the family forever. A large single stone in a teardrop pendant." Her hands balled into dainty fists. "Oh, I can't believe that fool Harry gave it to her for the season! It had been safely locked in the vault at Holly Hill for eons, but somehow, he let her wheedle it out of him."

"Could she have returned it?" de Rohan asked. "Or . . . or sold it?"

Cecilia shook her head. "She'd only just got it from him last week. I've told Genevieve, Julia's maid, to search her things again. I mean, why would a thief steal only one jewel out of so many? She had a diamond brooch worth nearly as much, and it was not taken."

Max, too, was curious. "Let me know what you find," he replied. "In the meantime, write down everything you know, and send it round to my office. Begin with your sister-in-law—who she was, how Harry met her. Where she spent her time. And you must tell me who her, ah, *friends* were."

Cecilia scowled. "Oh, her *friends* were almost innumerable. And I can tell you what I know of her, since it is so little. She came to England only a year before her marriage to Harry."

"It was arranged?"

Cecilia shook her head. "No, she was Julia Astwell, granddaughter of the Earl of Hoage. His only daughter had run off with one of their grooms, and the old earl had disowned her. Julia was born into poverty. In Boston, I believe. Her parents died there when she was but fourteen. A few years later, when the earl's health collapsed, he relented and had his solicitors seek out the granddaughter to comfort his last years."

"And in return, he made her his heir?"

Cecilia nodded. "The estate was entailed, but after meeting Julia, Hoage decided all else was to be hers if she could make a good, blue-blooded marriage. While Harry was a bit wild and deeply in debt, our title is an exceedingly old one, and he can be quite charming in his way. Poor Harry fancied himself in love and has lived in hell ever since."

"She was spoiled?"

Cecilia shrugged. "Certainly she wished to be. Now, of course, Harry's man of business oversees the income and outgo of all money. That, too, was in the terms of Hoage's will. But Julia is denied nothing, for Harry hasn't the resolve."

De Rohan nodded. "So you think your brother was just a means to an end."

"And quite an end it has come to, wouldn't you say?" replied Cecilia mordantly.

At last, de Rohan gave in to the impulse to laugh. "They were married how long?"

Cecilia paused to count. "Seven very long years. Indeed, perhaps you ought to investigate me. I often thought of strangling her."

"And have you an alibi, my lady?" teased de Rohan lightly.

Cecilia chuckled. "My dear Max, I fear your sense of humor is showing!" she warned. "And yes, I've an alibi—a cranky infant who keeps me up all hours. Now, what may I tell you about Julia's social life?"

"Did she gamble? Could she have been blackmailed by someone?"

Cecilia considered it. "Gambling never interested Julia. I'll ask Harry's man to let me run through the accounts, but I can't see how she could have paid blackmail without his knowing it. He's very careful."

"Since there were no children, to whom does the money now go?"

Cecilia paused. "Why, I daresay everything goes to Harry. Julia had no one else save her cousin, the new Earl of Hoage, and he is quite rich. Of course, she had a string of lovers. Shall I make out a chronology of those I know?"

De Rohan nodded, and after going to her brother's desk, Cecilia jotted down a column of names. De Rohan sighed inwardly. It was growing increasingly difficult to feel sympathy for Lady Sands. He carefully tucked the list away and stood. Cecilia looked tired.

"I must go," he said quietly. "But Sisk will return in a

day or so to speak again with the servants. Peel has asked me to—"

"To keep an eye on the investigation," interjected Cecilia. "Yes, I know. I asked Giles to arrange it. The great Lord Walrafen has political clout, you know. By the way, you've received a card for his ball?"

"Yes," he reluctantly admitted.

Cecilia nodded. "This time, you must go. Half the people on that list will be there. If I cannot move about in society, Max, you must do it."

For a time, de Rohan made no answer. It was difficult to refuse her. Cecilia and her first husband's heir, Giles, now Lord Walrafen, had remained friends. Through de Rohan's work, he knew them both, and this was not the first time he had been invited to one of their social events. That they meant to be kind he had no doubt. But even with his new position in the Home Office, their stations in life were perceived as too disparate. And in truth, he was not like the English *ton*. He never had been. He had no wish to move about on their fringes, and the fringe was as close as he was apt to get nowadays.

"Promise me, Max," she pleaded.

At last, he nodded. "I will try, my lady—"

"Cecilia," she interjected. "We are friends, remember?"

De Rohan hesitated. "Yes, we are," he finally acknowledged.

Cecilia smiled impishly and laid one hand lightly upon his arm. "Then may I ask you something of a personal nature?" she asked as they strolled toward the door. "Why were you staring so oddly at Lady Catherine

during tea? I mean, do you know her? She seemed . . .
well, that cup fairly leapt from her hands, and I
thought—"

De Rohan came to an abrupt halt. "I do not know
her," he said gruffly. "I was simply distressed on her be-
half."

Cecilia studied him for a moment. "She's quite attractive, is she not? Country-bred and newly come to town.
Oh, the marriage market will be abuzz. Quite the loveli-
est woman this season, I daresay. Unless one prefers a
more simpering sort."

"She has come for the season?" de Rohan heard himself asking. "Is she not married?"

Cecilia's smile warmed. "The widow of Lady Kirton's nephew. She's comfortably off but by no means
wealthy. However, her elder brother is an earl, and
wildly rich. His wife is French. She's his former gov-
erness. Lady Catherine's father was a terrible rake, and
you might recall her younger broth—"

"Do you have a point, Cecilia?" de Rohan interjected.

"Oh, yes!" Cecilia concluded. "My point is to display
my . . . my *detecting abilities*. And I challenge you, Max,
to do as well. On Thursday night. And remember, my
dear, you cannot force the *ton* to tell you much of anything. You must winkle it out, and very cleverly, too!"

Chapter Five

Your evenings should be spent at balls,
at theatre, and in the very best company.

—LORD CHESTERFIELD, 1776,
The Fine Gentleman's Etiquette

The Signora Castelli lived in a soaring brick town house
in what was accounted the finest neighborhood in London's East End. Despite its proximity to slums and dock-
yards, Wellclose Square was an oasis of wealth in a
borough of paucity. Merchants, magnates, and even bar-
risters, whose business regularly took them into the City
and surrounding business districts, were proud to call
the enclave home. The *signora*'s house rose six stories
above the street, casting a wider and more imposing
shadow than any of its neighbors. And it was from this
fine establishment that the *signora* ruled her empire with
an iron fist and a Tuscan temper.

Although she had begun her life in London much as
her grandson had done—as a disheartened war refugee
with a limited command of the language—Sofia Castelli
had not stepped off the boat entirely empty-handed. No,
she had come with her late husband's account books
tucked in her trunk and thirty years of shrewd dealing

tucked in her head. She'd set up her little import house in a cramped and dirty cellar near Wapping Wall, but she hadn't remained in such humble quarters long. Soon it was said the old woman knew more about wine than Dionysus himself, and more about human nature than God. She was respected by—if not popular with—her business associates and was notorious for brooking no opposition from anyone. Well, no one save her grandson, who was both the thorn in her side and the flame in her heart.

On Thursday afternoon, de Rohan arrived in Wellclose Square just as luncheon was being served by his grandmother's footmen. Overhead, Lucifer thundered across the floor and down the landing, bolting into the dining room as if he'd not seen his master in a month. With a laugh, de Rohan went down on one knee to ruffle his fur. "Come sit by me, old boy," he said, giving him a good scratch behind the ears. "We'll see what manner of scraps you can wheedle, eh?"

As if he'd understood de Rohan's every word, the dog gave a joyous yelp and squeezed beneath the table. At once, Maria ordered another place laid and urged de Rohan toward a chair. "Sit, sit, Maximilian!" she said, ladling out soup. "Look! *Ribollita,* your favorite! *Buon appetito!*"

But his grandmother was less sanguine. "To what do we owe this unlooked-for honor, my grandson?" she murmured as he took up his spoon. "Have you at last grown tired of taking your luncheon in filthy public houses?"

"It's the filthy street vendors who supply my usual fare," he corrected with a grin. "So I'm grateful for a good meal. But today I've just come to pick up some clothes."

His grandmother always resented any reminder that he lived elsewhere. "Clothes!" she grumbled, sipping delicately from her wine glass. "What, did you not take three good suits already? Surely, *caro mio,* you need not strip your every possession from this house?"

"I just need my evening clothes, Nonna."

At that, his grandmother's wrinkled face broke into a smile. "Ah, *benissimo!*" she said, settling back into her chair with her glass. "You mean to go about in society at last? It is time, my grandson."

De Rohan shook his head. "I'm to attend a function at Lord Walrafen's," he said as the footmen began laying out salad plates heaped with *panzanella.* "An hour's work, no more. And it *is* work, Nonna, you may be sure."

The old woman jerked upright, shoving away her salad as if she'd lost her appetite. *"Non ci credo!"* she cried, shooting him a disdainful gesture. "Work! Work! Always the work!"

"You may believe it or not as you wish, Nonna," he snapped. "But recall, if you will, that I have a job. A job which, inexplicably, I find gratifying."

But the *signora* would have none of it. *"Basta!"* she cried, waving her hands wildly. "A hopeless task! I cannot listen to this talk! We have work here, too, Maximilian. Or had you not noticed?"

De Rohan eyed her warningly. He knew where this was going. "Don't start with me, Nonna Sofia, please."

But as usual, she would not be silenced. "No, Maximilian, for once you must listen!" she demanded. "Tomorrow I go to St. James's to make a call at Berry Brothers. It is a golden opportunity, my grandson! They seek an exclusive importer of Italian vintages."

De Rohan tried to check his temper. He cherished his grandmother and knew she only wanted what she thought best for him. "I congratulate you, ma'am," he said very civilly. "Berry Brothers is a bastion of wealth and opportunity."

Already, fervor burned in her eyes. "Max, just think of it!" She made an expansive gesture with her hands. "Tuscan chianti. Soave from Veneto. Barolo from the north. Already, we have a stranglehold on the Loire Valley and most of the Germans. If we are shrewd and cautious, we will soon control half the premium vintages imported into this country."

"Indeed? I thought we already did so," answered de Rohan a little dryly. "Certainly, I can be of no help."

Sofia leaned forward, spreading her hands open plaintively. "But I need a man, Maximilian," she answered softly. "These English merchants, they look at me, and bah! What do they see? Just a haggard *vecchia strega* with one foot in the grave. They think to take advantage of me. To pursue aggressive negotiations aimed at driving our prices down."

De Rohan could not suppress a bark of laughter. "Then I wish them luck in their pursuit. God knows they will need it if they mean to come out with their shirts still on their backs."

"Impudent boy!" Sofia hissed. "I wish you to help me! I need you to help me!"

"You wish—yes," answered her grandson softly. "But with all respect, Nonna, you *need* nothing I can give.

Your reputation precedes you. And I have other duties. Why are you not taking Trumbull? He is an excellent business manager, far better than I shall ever be."

Nonna Sofia had been clutching her napkin tightly in her fist. She dropped it now and let her fist come crashing down upon the table, rattling the china. *"Per amor di Dio,* Maximilian! It is time you took the helm of this ship! Have we not had enough idealists in this family? Is there no end to the sacrifices we must make in the name of equality and liberty?"

It felt as if his heart stopped dead in his chest. This time, she'd gone too far. "Just what are you saying?"

Sofia was undeterred. "That you are as stubborn as your father! It will be the end of you, too."

"As it was for him?" De Rohan hissed, going perfectly still. "Is that what you imply? If so, have a care."

The old woman drew back ever so slightly. "I say only this, my grandson," she whispered darkly. "Business and politics make for treacherous bedfellows, a lesson your father learned too late, may God rest his soul." Almost unconsciously, the *signora* crossed herself.

Strangely, the gesture angered de Rohan. "Forgive me, ma'am, but my father was a vintner, not a merchant."

The skin around Nonna Sofia's mouth turned white. "And when he took my daughter to the marriage bed, he became a *merchant.* That was our agreement. My foolish Josephina had to fall in love with him, and so we made a bargain—his vast European vineyards, my Milanese export business—a powerful union. And all of it meant for you, for your future."

"Then someone failed to explain that to the Bonapartists, did they not?" answered de Rohan, stabbing viciously at his salad. "Otherwise, I'm sure they would have agreed not to torch our estate and vineyards."

The fist fell again, but more gently. "Vines can grow again, my grandson," she said sadly. "But it is your heart which I fear is dead. You are nearly thirty-seven years old, and I ask you, where is your passion? Your zest for life? Ah—in your work for humanity, you will say! But you are a fool. You see what happened to your father! They turned on him and caused my daughter to grieve herself into an early grave. Do you think these English won't turn on you someday? You are not one of them, my grandson, no matter the coincidence of your birth."

And then, very wearily, Signora Castelli rose from her chair. "Come, Maria, take me upstairs. I have no appetite. Better I should go to my room and starve myself to death than suffer this bitterness in my breast."

Ruthlessly holding his emotions in check, de Rohan came at once to his feet, tossing his napkin onto the tablecloth. "I am sorry, Nonna, that I so often disappoint you." Impulsively, he seized her hand and carried it to his lips. "My heart is not in the business, it is true. But let us hope that it is not yet dead."

But his grandmother had been again defeated, and, as was her habit in such cases, she simply pretended there had been no battle. "I am tired," she said again. "Let us leave it at that."

He watched her pass over the threshold and into a shaft of sun which streamed in through a window. It reflected the startling amount of silver in his *nonna's* once raven hair. She was no longer just sly and manipulative;

she really was growing old. *Dio mio,* what was he saying? She had been old for two decades. And for much of that time, she had struggled to do the right thing, or at least her perception of it.

Was that, perhaps, precisely what he was doing? Was there an ugly kernel of truth in what she had said? Was his work, in the long run, simply meaningless? He could not think that. He could not begin to believe that his sacrifices had been in vain. He loved his grandmother. He had no wish to cause her pain. But he could not cut off the source of his life's blood. He could not give up the thrill of the hunt—if one could wax so romantically over police work—just to be her errand boy. And that was all he would ever be, for she was still the best in the business, and he had no head—and no heart—for it at all.

Gracefully balanced in a pool of candlelight, Catherine could feel the warmth of Lord Walrafen's hand resting at the turn of her waist. As the soft swell of violins filled the air, her host swept her across the polished oak and into the vaguely familiar steps of a waltz. Laughter, chatter, and the clinking of crystal echoed through the vaulted room, which was crowded but not yet hot. His lordship's ball, it seemed, was a grand success.

Although Lord Walrafen had greeted her cordially upon their introduction earlier in the evening, he now seemed oddly detached. But, as if by instinct, he moved amongst the other couples with an unerring grace. Intent upon her steps, Catherine, too, was quiet.

"You were very kind to reserve the first waltz for me, Lady Catherine," he eventually remarked. "I normally dance it with Cecilia. This is the first ball she has missed in this house in a great many years."

Catherine tried not to stare directly at him, but it was difficult. He was a startlingly handsome man; one of the most powerful members of the House of Lords. And she was a Gloucestershire nobody.

"I was sorry to learn of your stepmother's bereavement," she said quite sincerely.

"Ah, as was I," he remarked. "Though I suppose *stepmother* is an inaccurate term for Cecilia. After all, I am older than she, and she is now remarried."

Catherine looked at him in some surprise. "Family ties can never be truly undone, my lord. Oftentimes, not even if we wish to undo them."

To her surprise, Lord Walrafen tilted back his head, laughed, and swept her into the next turn. "I think you must be very wise, Lady Catherine."

Catherine lowered her gaze to the oval emerald nestled in the flawless folds of his cravat. "And you, sir, are very kind," she remarked, feeling her face grow warm. "I know very well that Aunt Isabel asked you to dance the first waltz with me. She very much wishes me *to take,* you know."

She could feel the heat of his eyes drifting over her face as they floated across the room. "And what of you, Lady Catherine?" he finally murmured, whirling her artfully past a festooned column. "Do you wish *to take?* Or merely to be left in peace?"

He sounded very much as if, given the choice, he would prefer the latter. And yet there was a hint of something more in his question. Mercifully, Catherine was saved from an answer. The last strains of the waltz ended, and, with an enigmatic smile, Walrafen escorted her across the room to Isabel's side.

De Rohan arrived at Lord Walrafen's ball in a hackney, attired in his best evening clothes. By the *ton*'s standards, his dress was not impressive, but nor was it unfashionable. And by those same lofty standards, a hired conveyance was an only marginally acceptable mode of travel. Still, it had seemed vain to bring his carriage the four miles from his grandmother's house, merely to transport him the few blocks which separated his lodgings from Walrafen's house in Hill Street.

As far as his career was concerned, de Rohan had no business possessing either the clothing or the carriage. Yet, whatever he had chosen to make—or in this case, *not* to make—of himself, Nonna Sofia had had no part in it. Still, he was no more a merchant than a vintner. He no longer had it in him—particularly the latter. He had seen too much, had hurt too deeply, and wanted something different.

But having thwarted Sofia's grand plans for his life, he had not the heart to disappoint her in any other way. And since she occasionally required his escort, such luxuries as clothing and carriages became necessities, for de Rohan would be damned before he would let his personal choices cause his grandmother a moment's embarrassment. So de Rohan shrugged his shoulders beneath the tailored fabric of his opera cloak, then went slowly up the stairs like a man going to the scaffold.

She saw him the moment he stepped over the threshold. The surrounding conversation faded to an indistinct murmur as Catherine watched Maximilian de Rohan place his hand solidly into Lord Walrafen's. It was no formal greeting, either. More of a hail-fellow handshake. Good Lord. *They were friends?* Such a thing would never have entered her mind. Indeed, she had no more thought to see him here than to . . . well, than to see him in Harry's drawing room yesterday afternoon.

Tonight he wore a black coat and breeches cut in the severest, most formal style one could imagine. His linen was flawlessly white, unadorned by so much as a pearl. It was the perfect foil for his dark skin and strong nose. He was tall, too, well over six feet. If his legs had looked long beneath trousers and boots, they looked impossibly so in breeches and stockings. Tonight his posture was stiff and formal, as if he were a soldier. Or a policeman.

But he wasn't. He had lied to her. Isabel had blithely confirmed that much. Instead, he was a Westminster magistrate on special assignment to the Home Office, a position which was such a far cry from his professed career that even country-bred Catherine couldn't fathom it.

Oh, he had once been an inspector with the River Police, it was true. According to Isabel, he was something of a crusader, having lived and worked for many years in the docklands and rookeries of the Middlesex parishes, a grim part of London which was far removed from Westminster. And Isabel had whispered the rumor that as a very young man, he'd served as a captain of the infamous Bow Street Runners—that bane of the criminal class and, oftentimes, of the aristocracy.

Of course, police inspectors and Bow Street Runners did not mingle with polite society. It was all but unheard of. And yet Mr. de Rohan recently had been hand-selected by Mr. Peel and Lord Walrafen to work within the Home Office. What a shock it had been to learn that Isabel knew him and, what was more, so highly esteemed him. And so Catherine had been unable to confide in her aunt the ugly thing which Mr. de Rohan had said to her. But she could still put him in his place, could she not? Abruptly, before she could reconsider the idiocy of her actions, Catherine gathered the skirt of her dark blue gown into her fist and began marching across the floor toward him, impelled by another spate of righteous indignation.

But halfway across the dance floor, she was saved from her folly. Walrafen cut a swift glance toward the front entrance as if looking for newly arrived guests and then placed a hand on de Rohan's shoulder. As though they were the best of friends, he drew the magistrate toward the corridor which led to the private rooms of the house.

Suddenly, Catherine felt a light touch beneath her elbow. She turned at once to see that Isabel had followed her. "Catherine, my dear?" she began a little anxiously. "Can we work our way toward the drawing room? Lord Bodley has begged an introduction. Though I cannot like the man, I can think of no way to refuse him."

Lord Walrafen remained sequestered in his private study with de Rohan for only a quarter-hour, which, given his other guests, was probably longer than civility permitted. Still, it was long enough. De Rohan left their meeting with a renewed sense of optimism. He and Sisk had spent the better part of the day speaking with Lady

Sands's neighbors and their servants, in the faint hope that someone had seen or heard an intruder. But they had not. Retracing Lady Sands's movements on the day of her murder had also yielded little. So he had come to this ball tonight with his hopes pinned elsewhere.

Good manners had required that he lay his cards upon the table at once, and so he had shown Walrafen Cecilia's list. His lordship had been gracious and had confirmed that four of the men were present. Indeed, he had gone so far as to offer to make the introductions. Introductions which de Rohan knew were required before members of the *ton* would even trouble themselves to speak with one another, let alone someone who looked suspiciously as if he mightn't be one of them at all. So he spent the next few minutes at Walrafen's side, circulating through the crowd and being introduced to various guests. De Rohan made careful note of those whom he wished to revisit. And if Walrafen was embarrassed to present a former policeman as his guest, one could not discern it from his demeanor.

After making the rounds with his host, de Rohan left him near the card room and went off to question each guest more privately. The first he spotted was Rupert Vost, a languid, golden Adonis of a man who had a dangerous look about his eyes. Cecilia had noted him as one of Lady Sands's on-again, off-again lovers, a man of no known accomplishment and very little means. He was perennially in debt. But, given his looks, would Lady Sands have cared? De Rohan rather thought not.

Vost still stood to one side of the card room, idly observing the play. He caught sight of de Rohan's approach from the opposite side of the room. Then, with an elegant gesture, he lifted his glass of champagne, as if to salute de Rohan's audacity. Reeking of sandalwood cologne and condescension, Vost was beautifully dressed. De Rohan reached him just as a nearby game of whist broke up, the four players shoving back their chairs amidst jovial chatter. "Do you play, Mr. Vost?" asked de Rohan, casually tilting his head toward the table.

With a muted smile, he shook his head. "Not cards, Mr. . . . er—de Rohan, was it? No, the sort of games I prefer wouldn't be appropriate here. Yourself?"

De Rohan shook his head. "I am not a gambling man."

The smile turned cynical. "Oh, we all of us gamble in one form or another, de Rohan," answered Vost, lazily swirling the dregs of his wine in his glass. "Make no mistake about that. Now, did I understand Walrafen to say that you're with the Home Office?"

When de Rohan agreed, Vost nodded. "Ah, yes. I've heard a few rumors about Mr. Peel's newest obsession. I daresay you'd like to ask me about this dreadful mess with Julia. Yet you cannot quite think how."

In spite of himself, de Rohan felt a grim smile tug at his mouth. "There really is no polite way, is there?" he admitted. "But I cannot imagine you would wish her killer to go unpunished."

Vost's brows went up at that. "No, I shouldn't like that at all. Still, one wonders it wasn't old Harry." He tossed off the rest of his champagne. "I might have been tempted, had I been in his shoes."

Vost's casual attitude about infidelity angered de Rohan. "But you weren't, were you?" he quietly challenged. "In fact, you were quite the opposite—"

"Oh, I won't make this difficult for you, de Rohan," Vost softly interjected. "I was her lover. Sometimes. What of it?"

"How long prior to her death had you seen her?"

"Seen her? Or slept with her?" asked Vost. "I'd seen her that night at the theater. It was quite crowded, you know. But I daresay I hadn't bedded her in six months or better. I really cannot recall."

"You cannot recall?"

Vost shrugged. "Julia was, you see, so very available. But she was not—contrary to her own view—anything special."

"You seem almost pleased to say so," de Rohan remarked.

Vost heaved a weary sigh. "Mr. de Rohan, I am not pleased about any of this," he remarked, setting his empty glass down on a passing waiter's tray. "But just now, I cannot afford any untidiness. I'm newly engaged, you see. To a delightful widow from a fine family, who would abhor the very breath of scandal. No, far better I should tell you whatever you wish to know, rather than have you ask about. I daresay you understand?"

"Indeed," answered de Rohan tightly.

Vost smiled again. "So it is like this: I found Julia amusing. She found me charming. Occasionally, we saw one another. I did not care enough to kill her, nor did she care enough to do anything which might make me wish to."

"I am relieved to hear it."

"And as to that night," he dryly continued, "I met my fiancée at the theater, then saw her safely home."

"And did you remain there?"

Vost looked taken aback. "If I had, I certainly would

not impugn her honor by admitting it. But as it happens, I did not. I returned to my rooms at the Albany, probably around three."

"Were you seen, Mr. Vost?"

Vost shrugged. "I daresay the porter saw me enter." With his left hand, he withdrew a thin gold case, extracted a card, and handed it to de Rohan. "By all means, call if you should think of anything else to ask. I shall try to bestir my memory." He made a faint, dismissive gesture with the back of his hand. "Now, good night, Mr. de Rohan. This has all been most fascinating."

A little annoyed by the dismissal, but having little else to ask, de Rohan drifted from the card room into the ballroom. He would save the drawing room for last. There was someone there whom he particularly wished to see.

The responses of the next two men ranged from embarrassment to anger. Lord Trevor Reeves, the estranged son of the very prominent Duke of Wain, seemed almost relieved to speak with de Rohan. Though he was generally considered to be a wastrel—he had an expensive mistress and a string of sadistic creditors—Reeves admitted his relationship with Lady Sands with a touch of red-faced chagrin.

But the connection was an old one, and the young man had an alibi. "Afraid to say I was a bit jug-bitten," Reeves confessed. "Lost a small fortune at the Oriental Club, then seem to have dishonored myself on the carpet. Some chaps I know carried me home to bed. You can ask 'em if you'd like."

De Rohan handed him a card and moved on to Sir Everard Grant.

The wealthy, widowed Sir Everard was an undersecretary in the War Office. With one eye on his debutante daughter who stood across the ballroom, the baronet lifted his nose. "Never laid eyes on the woman," he said coldly. "Or if I did, I don't recall it. She certainly is not the sort I would associate with."

And indeed, he hardly looked the type. Still, de Rohan knew firsthand the power of seductive women. It was likely Sir Everard was lying, but that would not be proven tonight. De Rohan thanked him and left.

The last of the four was a man with powerful political connections. Lord Bodley, in de Rohan's opinion, was the worst sort of man. A rich, aging roué with a penchant for pretty girls, and the younger the better. During de Rohan's early career at Queen Square, Bodley's name had turned up during the investigation of a ring of pedophiles, and de Rohan had never forgotten it. But, as usual, nothing could be proven against the men who supported such a vice. Instead, two bawds from the East End had been sent off to Bridewell for ensnaring little girls, and that was the end of it. With barely suppressed hatred churning in his belly, de Rohan went in search of his quarry. Perhaps once that miserable task was done, he could go home to his own bed and leave these self-absorbed aristocrats to their bad champagne.

He saw at once that Bodley still stood in a distant corner of the drawing room, holding court as he had been half an hour earlier. Slowly, de Rohan made his way through the crowd, but after having pushed his way past the rotund gentleman who partially obscured his view, de Rohan was stunned to realize that the lady to whom Bodley was speaking was none other than Lady Kirton.

A feeling of dreadful unease seized him. But it was too late. Lady Kirton had seen him. "Oh, look!" she cried, sounding just a little relieved. "Here is the very man himself! Mr. de Rohan, have you been introduced to the Marquis of Bodley?"

De Rohan tried to ignore the beautiful woman at Lady Kirton's elbow. Neatly, he bowed. "The pleasure was mine, just this very evening," he murmured.

Bodley nodded civilly. Lady Kirton laid her hand upon de Rohan's arm, as if she wished very much to draw him into the conversation. And, despite his efforts, de Rohan's eyes fixed at once upon Lady Catherine Wodeway, whose face had flooded with color.

"Lord Bodley is a great benefactor of the Nazareth Society, Mr. de Rohan," Lady Kirton continued. "We were just discussing your work last year with our mission."

But Bodley seemed disinclined to chat. "A pleasure, sir," he remarked, thrusting an arm in Catherine's direction. "And now, ma'am, I believe the violins have struck up again. Might I beg the honor?"

Looking suddenly flustered, Lady Kirton somehow managed to drop her reticule onto the floor. "Oh, dear!" she interjected, shooting de Rohan a plaintive look just as Bodley bent down to scoop it up. "I fancy Mr. de Rohan asked Catherine for this dance."

Asked Catherine to dance?

An outright lie. And dancing with the woman was the last thing de Rohan wished to do. But what choice did he have, save calling Lady Kirton a liar? At least she had the good sense to keep her niece from the clutches of a pervert like Bodley. But Lady Catherine was glancing anxiously back and forth between them. De Rohan was certain she meant to refuse. Finally, she gave her dance card a hasty glance. "Perhaps so," she lamely murmured. "I cannot quite make it out."

De Rohan found himself compelled to face the inevitable. He seized Lady Catherine's hand and dragged her toward the ballroom, ruthlessly ignoring the whispers which followed in their wake. As they crossed onto the floor, the swell of the music surrounded them, and it was only then that the tune sank into his head.

A waltz! *Maledizione!* What damnable luck.

Impulsively, he jerked Lady Catherine toward him, catching her in his embrace just as the cellist drew a particularly resonant chord. She gasped into the folds of his cravat. "No doubt I'm about to reap the punishment you think I deserve, Lady Catherine," he murmured as he circled her waist with one arm.

"Oh?" She lifted her gaze to his as they began to move. "Drawn and quartered right here?"

"I should be so lucky," he growled as the crowd surged about them. "I've not danced the waltz in a good while. And now I'm about to publicly humiliate myself by trodding upon every toe you possess."

But Lady Catherine had fully recovered her aplomb. "I hardly think it is my toes which ought to concern me," she remarked as he spun her into a turn. "I did not wish for this, Mr. de Rohan. In fact, what I do wish is that you would waltz me toward those french windows, then do me the honor of vanishing into the darkness and out of my life."

Before de Rohan could answer, another couple whirled perilously near, the gentleman's elbow catching de Rohan's. At once, he felt the toe of Catherine's slipper beneath his heel. She winced, but her steps did not falter.

"Bloody hell," he muttered. He felt heat flood his face.

"Pray do not regard it," she said, her voice coldly civil. "I am unhurt."

De Rohan lifted his gaze, but he could not quite meet her eyes. "And I am sorry," he said quietly. "Perhaps more sorry than you know."

Lady Catherine clearly caught the double entendre. "Are you?"

"Yes." Though his hands touched only her hand and waist, he could feel the strength and energy—the sheer *joie de vivre*—which, despite her anger, coursed through her lithe body. He swept her into another turn and stared down into the bottomless pools of her brown eyes.

He was shocked to see Lady Catherine's expression gentle. "How long has it been?" she asked softly.

Suddenly, his heart lurched. "Since—?"

"Since you've waltzed?"

Relief flooded through him. Silently, he calculated. "Nearly twenty years," he said quietly. "And then only with my mother in the schoolroom."

Catherine considered his words for a moment. Who was this man, Maximilian de Rohan? Certainly, he was not quite what he pretended to be. Catherine might be an uneducated rustic, but even she knew that poor men weren't apt to recognize the literary work of Barbauld. And rarely did they display such innate, Continental courtesy. Certainly, they did not learn to dance in the schoolroom with their mamas.

She looked up into his grim black eyes, then let her gaze drift lower, taking in the lean, hard bones of his face and a mouth which looked forbidding, perhaps even a little cruel. And yet she sensed he was not an unkind man. She opened her mouth to speak, to demand some explanation of such odd contradictions, but could find no words. Could barely find her breath. There was only the searing heat of his hands, the strange, commanding strength of his eyes. And suddenly, something more intense. A stab of longing, keen and quick, more compelling than anything she'd ever felt. Attraction. *Obsessive* attraction. The allure of something beautiful but faintly dangerous, like walking along a cliff ledge while one watched the churning white surf below.

But Catherine had never been a risk taker. What was it about this man that made her pulse ratchet upward and her knees go weak? Thus preoccupied, Catherine failed to keep her beat, entangling her feet with his. On a graceless jerk, her whole body tipped rigidly forward, but, without misstep, Mr. de Rohan caught her, then slowed to a halt. The french windows, flung wide open, were now very near, and, before she could protest, Catherine found herself being swept out of Lord Walrafen's ballroom and onto the terrace beyond.

His touch was tender but implacable. "Mr. de Rohan!" she protested, spinning away from him to glance anxiously about the empty expanse of lawn. "Whatever do you think you're about?"

The moment of gentleness had vanished as abruptly as it had come, but de Rohan had not released her hand. "Preserving our toes," he muttered. Then, without preamble, he drew her to his side and into the shadows. "I fear we are neither of us able to dance with any degree of competence, Lady Catherine. And I, for one, have something to say."

Catherine had never met a man so plainly spoken. "I dance perfectly well, thank you!" she exclaimed, trying to jerk her hand from his. "And I have nothing to say."

De Rohan merely drew her closer, and, strangely, she let him. "Be still, Catherine," he whispered, his voice so near it stirred her hair. "I am no danger to you here."

Was he not? He felt very dangerous indeed. In the cool night air, with his arm about her shoulders, his male heat seemed to drown her. Maximilian de Rohan seemed to exude restrained power and a raw beauty which left her stomach weak and bottomless. Catherine jerked her hand again, and this time, he let her go. "Say what you will and have done with it, Mr. de Rohan," she whispered.

His lips thinned as if he were vexed. But with whom? Himself, Catherine thought.

"I insulted you abominably two days ago," de Rohan began abruptly. "I beg your forgiveness. I am very glad you paid me back in kind at once."

"In *kind?*" she murmured incredulously. "I merely made a suggestion. One which you richly deserved."

Surprisingly, his fingers came up to press shut her lips, his hard black eyes almost twinkling. "And an anatomically difficult one, at that," he said, chuckling softly.

Her face flamed at the recollection of what she'd said. Suddenly, Catherine found the entire situation wildly absurd. Beneath his fingers—and totally against her will—she made a sputtering sound, half laughter, half indignation.

"Oh, no!" he cautioned, his voice a low, seductive rumble. "Don't try to mount your moral high horse now, Lady Catherine. It's far too late. I've already noticed you've got a temper like a wasp and a mouth like a fish-wife."

Catherine felt her blush heighten. He was almost right.

"And that having been said," de Rohan continued, dropping his fingers from her lips, "I should very much like to accept your invitation to dinner. I owe you some sort of explanation. One which I'd prefer to make in a more private setting."

Her face was flushed with lovely color, and her brown eyes flashed with defiance. An utterly irresistible combination. De Rohan spoke rapidly, impetuously, before his brain could catch up with his heart. "Come, Lady Catherine, be impulsive. Run away with me."

"You must be perfectly insane."

"I begin to think it quite likely."

De Rohan watched her intelligent brown eyes flick down his length. To his amazement, Lady Catherine Wodeway drew herself up to her full height, which was indeed impressive. "Mr. de Rohan," she coolly responded. "You have avoided me, kissed me, then insulted me, and now waltzed with me. Why, if I knew you at all—which I don't—then I should probably think you given to very fanciful moods indeed. I can't think why I ought to go anywhere at all in your company."

De Rohan tried to gentle his expression. If he could steal just an hour alone with her, if he could make his apology and obtain her forgiveness—yes, then perhaps he could set aside his strange preoccupation with the woman. "You probably oughtn't go with me," he admitted awkwardly. "Certainly, I would not advise a young woman of good character to leave a ball with a man she hardly knows. After all, I might be dangerous."

An odd, faintly humorous expression flitted over her face. "Oh, I'm quite sure you are, sir," she murmured. "But not, I pray, a danger to me."

De Rohan raised his slashing black brows at that. "And you are astute enough to know the difference?"

"I think so." Lady Catherine stood before him, quietly confident. She was dressed in a gown of cobalt satin slashed with ivory. Low on her shoulders, she wore a shawl of midnight blue velvet, and around her throat three strands of perfectly matched pearls. Her heavy mahogany hair was twisted into an elegant arrangement which accentuated the lovely length of her neck.

Ah, *Dio!* She was elegance personified. Simple beauty. His worst weakness. Inwardly, de Rohan sighed and let his daydream slip away. "So where does that leave us, Lady Catherine?" Strangely, his voice came out as a soft whisper—not his own voice at all. "Admit it, you were almost as miserable inside that ballroom as I was."

In the still, murky night, Lady Catherine paused for a long moment. A dozen emotions seemed to dance across her extraordinary face—anger, curiosity, amusement, and then, to his surprise, understanding. "I shall fetch my cloak," she finally responded, moving as if to reenter the ballroom.

"Will you?" He caught her lightly by the shoulder, and she half turned to face him. "Why?"

Lady Catherine's smile was like a burst of sun, her

wide, full mouth turning up at both corners. "Well, you may be rather mad and moody, Mr. de Rohan," she murmured. "But at least you aren't boring."

He gave her one of his stiff Continental bows. "I daresay a man must take his compliments where he finds them."

The warmth of her smile deepened. "Meet me on the steps in five minutes."

Catherine felt the heat of Mr. de Rohan's stare on her back as she strode away. Good heavens, what had she agreed to? It was a bold thing to leave the safety of a ball in the company of a man whom one hardly knew. A man who felt just a little edgy and dangerous—and who had already demonstrated a shocking disregard for propriety. And yet, was that not a part of his attraction? He made her angry, yes. But any emotion was better than nothing, was it not? She was tired of feeling dead and dull inside. It was time to seize life—both the good and the bad—again. She only wished she knew which Maximilian de Rohan would turn out to be.

Still, for all her brave thoughts, Catherine moved purposefully through the crowd, afraid to slow down. Afraid she might reconsider. But as she approached the corridor which led to the ladies' retiring room, Catherine heard a low, sophisticated voice call out her name. She spun about to see Lord Bodley following her down the dimly lit corridor. The man smiled condescendingly as he drew up beside her.

"My dear girl." His voice was like silk. "I handled that situation very poorly. I do beg your pardon."

Catherine looked at him quizzically. "Indeed, I must beg yours, my lord. Whatever are you talking about?"

His posture stiffened. "Why, that magistrate—that *policeman*—or whatever the fellow is," Bodley continued. "I am sure you did not wish to dance with him. I should have insisted you not. No doubt your aunt is furious with me for not interceding."

Catherine lifted her brows very deliberately. It was not Mr. de Rohan whom Isabel had been concerned about, that much Catherine had concluded. "Pray do not regard it, my lord," she said, turning back toward the retiring room. "Obviously, you did not realize that Mr. de Rohan is Lady Kirton's friend."

But Bodley grasped her lightly by the forearm. Catherine spun about, staring at his hand where it lay upon her arm. "Really, Lady Catherine," he said quietly. "Business associations are not at all the same thing as social connections."

"He is also Lord Walrafen's guest."

"And Walrafen is a liberal-minded fool," snapped Bodley. "I cannot think de Rohan is anyone with whom your family should wish *you* to associate. I have heard a few things about the fellow, you see. You are new to town, my dear. Let me assure you, he is not our kind."

Catherine lifted her gaze to his and pinned him with it. "Be so good as to remove your hand from my arm, my lord," she said very clearly. "I was just on my way out."

With a stiff nod, he stepped back. Catherine spun about and hastened along the passageway. Lord Bodley did not follow.

A few minutes after uttering his inane invitation, de Rohan stood upon Walrafen's top step, his hat and stick in hand, realizing the true folly of his actions. He had come in a hired hackney. A lady like Catherine would assuredly have arrived by private carriage. What the devil had he been thinking? Perhaps, he admitted to himself, he'd wished to test her. To see if the pretty, well-born English widow would indeed appear in public with him.

Apparently, she would. He felt her warm, capable hand rest lightly upon his coat sleeve as he stared down at the row of fine vehicles which lined Hill Street. And yet his pride would not permit him to ask that she call for her own coach.

Lady Catherine saved him from both his pride and his folly. "I came with Aunt Isabel," she said candidly. "So shall we walk? I'm afraid I don't know the proper etiquette for escaping a lavish ball. It's my first, you see."

Quizzically, he looked down at her. "Your first—?"

Lady Catherine grinned. "Lavish ball."

He wasn't sure he believed her, but de Rohan felt his frustration wane. "I came by hackney," he admitted, stepping down to press a vail into the hand of one of Walrafen's footmen. "I'll have another brought round. You cannot walk far in dancing slippers."

For a moment, Lady Catherine looked tempted to argue, then her shoulders fell. "It really would be selfish to ruin these shoes," she agreed. "Isabel spent an hour choosing them."

As de Rohan pondered her words, a hackney coach drew up. "Where shall we go?" she asked as he helped her inside. "I would love a bite of supper, but in this gown . . . ?"

Suddenly, de Rohan realized she was right. He'd hoped to bespeak a private dining room in one of the better hotels, but even there, dressed as she was, she would be uncomfortable. He should have considered that. Lady Catherine's proximity seemed to muddle his logic.

But Catherine was still speaking, much to his salvation. "I'm staying at my brother's house in Mortimer Street," she said a little mordantly. "If we went there so that I might change into something more comfortable, would you again accuse me of being bent on seduction?"

Bent on seduction?

Go home with her?

Two such phrases should never have been permitted to share his thoughts, let alone be spoken aloud. Asking her to dine with him was folly enough. "I shall endeavor to give you the benefit of the doubt," he managed to reply. And with a musing smile, Lady Catherine leaned down to give her address to the footman, who promptly shut the door.

At the sound of the latch snapping shut, de Rohan suffered the unsettling impression of having flung his soul into some sort of an abyss, free-falling in a way he could neither control nor understand. As if to heighten the torment, he let his gaze flow over Catherine. In her elegant fabrics and understated jewels, she looked like a nobleman's wife. She looked like *trouble*. He had convinced himself that he meant only to seek out a private moment in which to make his apology, but was he lying to himself, the most treacherous deceit of all?

"Are you sorry I've taken you away from Walrafen's?" he heard himself ask.

Lamplight flickered over her open countenance as the carriage rumbled through Berkeley Square. "I don't believe I was precisely *taken,*" she answered, turning away to stare through the glass at the lamp-lit street.

Again, her words were gently satirical, as if she knew what he were thinking yet took no offense. Save for Cecilia, de Rohan had rarely met a highborn English lady so seemingly devoid of guile. Was she real? Or, like Penelope and a dozen other women he'd known, was she just a carefully crafted façade? Certainly, it was a beautiful façade, if nothing more. At that thought, de Rohan's gaze caught upon the heavy pearl drop which swung from her left earlobe, and he found himself seized by the oddest impulse. He wanted to suck it, pearl and all, into his mouth. Suddenly, he wanted *her* in his mouth. On him. Beneath him, her long, strong legs entwined about his waist.

Fleetingly, he closed his eyes. Oh, God! *Was there any chance?* Any prayer, however slender, that Lady Catherine Wodeway would do the very thing he had so bluntly—and so wrongly—accused her of? The very idea tore the breath from his chest and left his skin shivering, like a stallion scenting his mate. God almighty! What was wrong with him? He'd be a fool to sleep with her, even if she begged. Max shoved his insane notions back into the black recesses of his mind where they belonged, and opened his eyes. Lady Catherine was smiling at him quite innocently.

"I saw you speaking with Bodley," he said too abruptly. "I hope, ma'am, that you will have a care with such a man."

Lady Catherine looked as if she might burst into laughter. "Why, how blunt you are, Mr. de Rohan," she began in a slightly exasperated tone. "Have you nothing in the way of ordinary conversation?"

De Rohan felt his expression stiffen. "Forgive me. I am not much in society."

"Rather more than you should wish, though, I'll venture," murmured Lady Catherine. "Besides, Bodley is a generous benefactor of Isabel's charity for wayward women. Outwardly, that would seem to speak well of him, would it not?"

De Rohan caught the hint of challenge in her voice. "It is usually easier for a camel to go through the eye of a needle," he retorted, "than for a rich man to enter into the kingdom of God. Their temptations, you see, are so easily affordable."

Lady Catherine looked vaguely amused. "So I've been told," she agreed. "And just what do you think Bodley wishes to do with his donated riches?"

"Perhaps purchase absolution?" he suggested, unable to keep the cynicism from his tone. "His sort always think a little gold can whiten their souls."

Lady Catherine's gaze seemed to turn inward. "Mr. de Rohan, I think you must be an exceedingly hard-hearted man."

For a long, silent moment, he eyed her through the gloom. "I am," he finally answered. "Perhaps we'd both do well to remember it."

"Well, I did not say you were wholly wrong, mind," Catherine continued, undeterred. "Bodley is handsome enough, but he does give one a chill up the spine."

She was, just as he'd guessed, nobody's fool. He relaxed a little against the worn leather seat. "Then it would seem you have good instincts, after all," he said simply. "I hope, ma'am, that you will trust them."

Just then, the coach rocked to a halt. "Apparently, I do," she retorted as the driver leapt down to fling open the door. "After all, I'm just about to admit a very strange man into my home."

Chapter Six

Avoid as much as you can, in mixed companies,
argumentative, polemical conversations.

—LORD CHESTERFIELD, 1776,
The Fine Gentleman's Etiquette

The house on Mortimer Street was quiet. No footman awaited Lady Catherine's arrival, and, as if all was as she had expected, she drew a key from her reticule. Politely, de Rohan took it from her outstretched hand, reached past her to snap open the lock, and followed her in. Inside, the house smelled pleasant but foreign. No aroma of simmering spices and smoldering herbs greeted him as was the norm in his *nonna*'s house. Rather, the fragrance of well-waxed furniture and steeping tea seemed to have permeated the very walls.

He followed the swish of Catherine's blue silk skirts down a passageway lined with a heavy carpet and flickering wall sconces. They turned into a drawing room hung with gold watered silk and furnished in a Chinoiserie style which had been all the rage a decade earlier. Without asking, she poured him a snifter of cognac—his favorite—and pressed it into his hand. Her touch warmed him. Inflamed him. He wanted it to *stop*.

Then, with a serene smile, Catherine let her fingers slide away, leaving him . . . what? Bereft? No, he'd not felt that miserable emotion since the ruins of his father's chateau stopped smoldering. He felt lust, no more than that. Well, perhaps he found her beautiful and amusing. And intriguing. But those emotions were safe enough. Still, as he watched her walk out of the room, her stride long and confident, the sway of her hips sensuous and natural, he felt the unwelcome desire heighten again. And, to his exasperation, he felt the old doubts stir anew.

Her brother is an earl . . . wildly rich.

Cecilia's words echoed in his head. He told himself he did not care. This house was no more ostentatious than Nonna Sofia's, its furnishings comfortable rather than elegant. Still, de Rohan looked about, unaccountably ill at ease. Why? He was not a poor man. He was probably quite a wealthy one. And while the success of Castelli, de Rohan & Co. was no secret, he had always quite deliberately—and perhaps a little ruthlessly—distanced himself from it. In his world, wealth made a man suspect. Besides, he wanted nothing his money might buy, and to recklessly display his wealth might undermine his credibility. It might give the impression that his career was little more than a rich man's lark. He was not on a lark. He was deadly serious.

No, he gave not a tinker's damn for Catherine's brother's position. It was the lady herself, or rather, his reaction to her, which troubled him. But raw lust, surely, he could manage? A strong man did not let his appetites control him. Max had done so only once, and once had been trouble enough.

Somewhat reassured by that, he settled down on a

soft leather sofa and let the alcohol kindle a soothing fire in his belly. Eventually, he relaxed enough to turn his attention to the fine paintings which adorned the walls. One portrait inexplicably held his interest—a striking man wearing a brocade coat and powdered wig, his handsome face already running to fat. By God, he knew that face! Those harsh black brows, those hot, arrogant eyes . . .

But no, it was impossible. De Rohan would have been a boy in Alsace at the time of its painting. Perhaps it was someone he'd met during one of his parents' trips to England? No, the man looked like none of his father's associates. And yet it drew his eyes again and again. He had finished but half his brandy when he suddenly sensed Catherine standing in the doorway, her long, elegant shape limned by the light of a lamp which burned in the corridor beyond. At the sight, his breath caught again, and a sweet, melancholy ache shafted deep into his gut, twisting like a dull dagger.

Gaea, the earth goddess, he'd begun to call her in his head. For when he looked at her, she made him think of home. If he but squeezed shut his eyes for a moment, de Rohan could see the gently rolling hills, verdant with fields and forests and vineyards. The air flowed cool and clean through his lungs once more. The sun felt warm on his back again. That was a part of the seduction.

"You are admiring my brother's art collection?" Catherine still wore her pearls, but she had exchanged her gown for a walking dress of forest green wool.

De Rohan rose at once. "The portrait between the windows caught my eye."

Catherine stepped fully into the room. "My father,"

she admitted, her words tight and cool. "Dead these five years past. A bit of a bad seed, I fear."

Even de Rohan knew better than to pursue such a remark. "Are you hungry?" he asked instead.

Catherine's expression brightened. "There is a quite good chophouse not far from Cavendish Square. Will it do? The evening is clear, so I thought we might walk."

"It's chilly, Lady Catherine," he said gruffly. "And I can well afford to hire a carriage."

"Why, I never thought otherwise, Mr. de Rohan." Her face lit with veiled amusement. "But it's just around the corner."

"As you wish." De Rohan put down his glass.

The restaurant she'd selected was one he knew well but certainly not one he would have expected her to choose. Popular with businessmen and the lesser gentry, it was informal and a little boisterous, but the beef was excellent and the wine tolerable. With his hand cupped lightly beneath her elbow, de Rohan escorted Catherine through the door. Two or three respectable-looking females were scattered about the dimly lit room, but a woman of her class still looked vaguely out of place.

After being seated, they each ordered veal, and de Rohan asked that a bottle of Chambertin be fetched up from the cellar. As they waited for their food, he poured, discreetly observing her across the table. Catherine had grown very quiet. He wondered what that might mean. Did she regret her hasty acceptance of his offer? If she did, he wasn't about to agonize over it. The lady was here of her own volition. He found her amusing and attractive. And he owed her an apology. Beyond that, he did not wish to become obsessed with another person's thoughts and feelings. He was a loner, and he liked it that way.

At last, Lady Catherine relaxed against the back of her chair, stretched almost imperceptibly, and gave a little exhalation of contentment. No, she suffered no regret. "I'm glad we escaped the ball," she confessed. "How fatiguing these social events are!"

"Dancing can be quite strenuous," murmured de Rohan.

Nearby, a group of shopkeepers burst into laughter, covering up Catherine's hoot of amusement. "Oh, what a poor-spirited creature you must think me, Mr. de Rohan!" she chuckled. "I can spend all day in the saddle or the garden without flagging. It is only these town habits which weary me. This incessant fanning, fawning, and smiling! However do you bear it?"

She was poking fun at him. Well, let her have her light banter if it pleased her. "I'm given to understand your estate is in the country?" he murmured politely.

Again, Catherine gave him that pleasant, faintly teasing smile. "It is hardly an estate," she returned. "I have a small manor house and a good home farm surrounded by a smattering of tenant cottages. No one, however, could mistake Aldhampton Manor for a grand property. But we digress, sir. I believe you were about to prostrate yourself with an apology?"

He felt his mouth crook unbidden into a smile. "Lady Catherine, I think you must be an exceedingly hard-hearted woman," he said, turning her own words into his.

He watched her struggle to glower at him, but hers was not a face that shifted easily into a frown. "Sir, your apology?" she demanded.

As she stared at him across the table, the recollection of what he'd said returned, acute and uncomfortable. He did not like to owe anyone anything. But he was no coward. And so he tried to find the right words, words to justify that which could not be justified. "I leapt to an assumption about your character, ma'am," he finally said, setting aside his pride. "It was wrong. No, *I was wrong.*"

Catherine leaned a little forward in her chair, cradling the bowl of the glass against her bodice. "And why did you do that, may I ask?"

De Rohan stared into the depths of the crowded dining room. In one corner, a table full of young swells was growing rowdy, their boasting and toasting ringing through the room. "I don't know."

Still, Catherine held his gaze without wavering. Her silence drew him in a new and unfamiliar way, and he was not at all sure he liked it. "I knew someone once," he finally managed. "Your invitation—so unexpected—it made me think of her. I believe that I wanted you to . . . to *prove* something to me. But I hardly know what." And there he fell short again.

Catherine cast him a quizzical look, then settled back into her chair. "Well, that's a rather lame explanation," she said, eyeing him narrowly across the table. "Why don't I have a go?"

"I beg your pardon?"

Catherine shot him a tight smile. "I've two brothers, you see, so I've some notion of how the male mind works. Shall I tell you what I think?"

De Rohan would have preferred to have his fingernails yanked out by Spanish guerrillas. "By all means," he coolly answered, reaching for the decanter of Chambertin.

As the crowd about them buzzed with chatter, Catherine swirled the ruby liquid which shimmered inside her glass. A passing waiter put down their plates and went on, the wafting aroma all but unnoticed. "I think you were sexually attracted to me, Mr. de Rohan," she finally suggested. "And for some reason, that made you angry."

De Rohan went absolutely still inside. "Lady Catherine," he managed. "Are you always this blunt?"

She nodded. "My undying sin. Now, I also think that you were cross with yourself for permitting your attention to wander from your work." She paused, looked up, then gave a little shake of her head. "No, that's not quite right, is it? But you did . . . well, *desire* me, perhaps? And you did lash out at me. It was very unfair, but I daresay I've done it, too."

Her ability to see through him was annoying, but he could hardly deny the truth. "Whatever the cause, I've offered you a poor excuse for poor behavior," he admitted tightly. "Why are you so willing to forgive a man who does not deserve it?"

"Why do you care?"

De Rohan lifted one brow in a deliberately arrogant gesture. "I rarely do." But again, he hesitated, carefully measuring his words. "However, it seems we have many acquaintances in common. I should not wish there to be any sort of strain between us."

At once, both light and humor fled from Catherine's gaze. "Is that what this is about, Mr. de Rohan?" she asked, her shoulders going remarkably rigid beneath the fine fabric of her gown. *"Your* work? *Your* acquaintances? Preserving *your* reputation?"

Almost imperceptibly, she drew away from him, and a wild, irrational sense of loss slammed into his chest. "Good God, no!" he snapped, his hand darting across the tablecloth to seize hers. "How can you think that?"

"I . . . don't think it," she finally answered, her voice soft, almost resigned. "No, I suppose I don't."

De Rohan stared down at their joined hands, the pale porcelain of her skin contrasting harshly against his long, dark fingers. Hers were slender, the nails short and neat. Her hand felt strong, capable. Suddenly, he realized he was crushing her in his grip. At once, he let go. "I just could not bear there to be animosity between us, Catherine," he murmured, drawing his hand away. "Even though I expect never to see you again, I do not wish us to part badly. I fear I cannot explain it any better than that."

"I see." A look of what might have been disappointment sketched across her face, but at once, her smile reappeared. "Then—*poof!*" she said with a quick snap of her fingers. "All is forgiven." And on that note, Catherine took up her fork and dug into her food.

De Rohan had not expected it to be that simple. "Are you always so easily satisfied?"

Fleetingly, Catherine's expression softened. "Sometimes perhaps too easily." Abruptly, she set down her fork. "Now, tell me about yourself, Mr. de Rohan," she said brightly, as if the odd moment had never passed between them. "For example, just what is it that you do for the . . . the *police*, was it? I am inordinately curious."

He felt his smile stiffen. "So. Not so easily satisfied after all?"

Lady Catherine looked at him very strangely. "If you're asking if I'm willing to be placated by whatever evasive half-truth you might care to tell me, then the answer is no."

Unwilling to hold her gaze, de Rohan relaxed against the back of his chair. Her response was not unreasonable. He *had* been less than honest. "I work for the Home Office," he finally answered.

"Indeed?" she airily responded. "So you aren't really a policeman, are you?"

"I am, in a manner of speaking."

"How exciting," she answered simply. "And what, pray, do you do at the Home Office?"

"We're preparing for the new police reform bill. Peel means to push it through the House next year."

"Hope springs eternal!" remarked Catherine, tilting her head quizzically. "I admire his willingness to try again. Just what does your work involve?"

De Rohan shrugged. "Mostly, I write very dull reports and attend a great many dull meetings," he answered, then added more honestly, "and I—er—I investigate police corruption. Amongst other things."

"Ah!" Catherine nodded knowingly. "The little *tête-à-tête* in Hyde Park! I was wondering when we might return to that."

Ruefully, de Rohan smiled. "You do make a habit of rising remarkably early, Lady Catherine."

She seemed to give a little start at that. "A habit?"

"I would call every morning for a sen'night a habit, yes."

Catherine cut him a very strange look. "You were aware that I rode in the park every day?"

De Rohan hesitated. "It is my duty to know such things."

Veiled amusement flitted across her face. "What a head you have for details," she mused. "But there's one you seem to have omitted. Isabel tells me you are a sort of magistrate. A common enough gentleman's occupation, isn't it? And rather a far cry from being a policeman, if you ask me."

De Rohan deliberately lifted his gaze to hers. "Are you by chance trying to determine if my company is exalted enough for you, Lady Catherine?"

Suddenly, she looked as if she wished to slap his face again. "Why, how unfailingly narrow-minded you are!" she snapped, pressing her palms flat against the table as if she might rise from her chair. "Indeed, it strikes me that you, Mr. de Rohan, are the only person in this relationship who is obsessed with social status. Have I ever said one word about it?"

"We don't have a relationship, Catherine," he said quietly.

Her posture relented, but her glower did not. "No, and I rather doubt we ever shall," she hissed, settling back into her chair. "Really! How do your friends get beyond that hedgehog demeanor of yours? I begin to wonder if you're worth the trouble."

Over the empty bowl of his wine glass, de Rohan stared at Catherine. "I daresay I'm not," he finally answered. "In any case, a man in my position can rarely afford friends."

Just then, two exquisitely dressed men brushed past

their table, almost unnoticed. One of them slowed, and a warm hand came to rest on de Rohan's arm. "Why, Max, you old charmer!" said a rich, melodious voice over his shoulder. "Oh, happy circumstance indeed!"

De Rohan looked up to find himself staring into the warm, wide gaze of George Kemble. Good God, this he did not need!

Kemble smiled, revealing a mouth full of flawlessly white teeth. "Ooh, aren't you nicely turned out!" he murmured, his expressive eyes sliding from de Rohan's formal attire to Catherine. "And what's this, *mon ami?* Some semblance of a social life?"

De Rohan felt his jaw clench involuntarily. "Good evening, Kemble."

The dapper fellow made a willowy bow to Catherine. "Really, old chap! With such exquisite company to drape upon your arm, you should get out more."

Bloody hell. This gossipy tidbit would be too rich for Kem to pass up. Faced with no alternative, de Rohan jerked to his feet. "Lady Catherine," he interjected gruffly. "May I present Mr. George Kemble, a man of business here in town."

The telling phrase *man of business* affected Lady Catherine not one whit. "Charmed, Mr. Kemble," she said, extending her gloveless hand across the table, willingly acknowledging him. "I'm Catherine Wodeway. What sort of business are you in?"

Kemble drew himself up proudly. "Oh, rare antiquities of all sorts!" he answered cheerfully. "Prized porcelain, heirloom jewelry, the occasional *objet d'art*. I have a great fondness for beauty, ma'am. As does my dear friend Max, one can plainly see."

De Rohan waved his empty glass toward the expanses of the room. "Pray do not let us keep you, Kem. I'm sure you've someplace else to be."

Kemble preened ever so slightly. "Indeed, yes. I'm having dinner with a special friend," he confessed. "But enough about Monsieur Giroux! Now, *à propos de rien,* old boy, I hear you've been given a new assignment." His voice dropped to a sly, horrified whisper. "And one can scarce imagine congratulations are in order!"

De Rohan lifted one brow. "It would seem," he said dryly, "that bad news travels along the Strand at an extraordinary speed."

As if it were second nature, Kemble bent down and snapped a little wrinkle from one corner of their tablecloth. "Oh, in my line of work, one hears everything!" he returned, smoothing his fingers over the fabric. "In this case, your trusty bloodhound Sisk was in my shop yesterday investigating the—er—shall we say, the *misappropriation* of a rather rare Byzantine icon. Trying to solve the crime before the Runners are set upon it, I don't doubt."

Mockingly, de Rohan drew back. "Dear me, Kemble!" he softly exclaimed. "You wouldn't be consorting with sneak thieves and pawnbrokers?"

Kemble struck a pensive pose. "Ah, it's a hard life in the Strand, *n'est-ce pas?* One must earn one's crust."

"*C'est dommage,*" returned de Rohan dryly. "For I fancy you'd not fare very well kissing the clink, and that's where you might end up."

Kemble smiled tightly. "I know you've an incredible command of languages, de Rohan," he answered. "But from French to cant in one fell sentence?"

"I suspect you understand me."

"Quite so, old boy." Kemble turned to Catherine with a wicked grin. "Did you know, ma'am, that our mutual friend can say *kiss my arse* in six languages?"

Catherine found herself obliged to smother a giggle. "Keep to the subject of that stolen icon, Kem," growled de Rohan.

"Oh, don't waste that nasty scowl on *moi!*" Kemble paused to give de Rohan a maternal pat on the shoulder. "I'm not normally in the business of receiving stolen goods. Not if I *know,* for pity's sake! Pure as the driven snow, that's me." He winked, tossed the tablecloth one last look of disdain, then bowed. "And now, if you will pardon me, I must go and upbraid the *restaurateur* for permitting this piece of shockingly cheap cotton to masquerade as table linen! What can he be thinking? It quite turns one's appetite."

Kemble turned to go, but at the last possible second, de Rohan stopped him, placing one hand hesitantly upon his arm. "A moment, Kemble," he ventured. "You still know a great many—er—people about town, do you not?"

"Merci du compliment, dear boy!" The former gentleman's gentleman quirked one perfectly shaped eyebrow. "The exchange of knowledge has always been my true stock-in-trade."

A little reluctantly, de Rohan withdrew the paper Cecilia had given him and passed it to Kemble. "I'd like you to take a look at this list," he said very quietly. "You'll find it self-explanatory. But I'm afraid it mayn't be complete. I should very much like to know."

Kemble's eyes caught on Cecilia's hastily scrawled

heading, and his lips pursed with amusement as he ran down the list of names. "Oh, dear Lady Sands!" He chortled. "I quite take your point, old fellow! It seems rather a short list. Shall I make inquiries?"

De Rohan exhaled a breath of relief. For all Kemble's pomposity, he seemed to have one finger perennially upon the pulse of Mayfair—if not the whole of London—and his information was reliable. Gratefully, de Rohan cleared his throat. "I will call upon you tomorrow, if I may?"

At that, Kemble lifted both his brows. "Ooh, well! Call me intrigued!" he answered, tucking the slip of paper back into de Rohan's hand with another little pat. "Be a dear and make it four-ish so we can take tea. And do bring Mr. Sisk. One never knows when one will need to sharpen one's claws on something that's overstuffed and inanimate."

Catherine watched Kemble swish away, her mouth quirked into a smile. "What an exceedingly interesting fellow!"

"I have often remarked it," answered de Rohan wryly.

Her face brightened. "I quite liked him, though. I think you have very nice friends."

De Rohan scowled. "Kemble is not *a friend.*"

Catherine gurgled with laughter. "Then what would you call him, pray?"

De Rohan frowned down at his veal. What the devil would one call Kemble? He was one of those rare fellows who simply defied description. Indeed, de Rohan was willing to bet that there was far more to Kemble than he wished people to see. Being with him was rather like watching a sleight-of-hand artist at a county fair. Your eye caught upon the flamboyant silk scarf being drawn out his sleeve, but all the while, the reality lay hidden elsewhere.

Still, for all his odd mannerisms, Kem was a good man to have at your back. And if he trusted you, he could provide a wealth of information. Since meeting him in the midst of the Nazareth Society scandal, de Rohan had consulted with him more than once, and on all manner of unusual subjects. Kem knew everyone. And everything.

"Very well," de Rohan tightly admitted. "He's a friend."

Apparently satisfied, Catherine relaxed into her chair and began to pick haphazardly at her roasted vegetables. "You're working on Lady Sands's murder, aren't you?" she suggested, cutting him a sly glance. "Dear me, I certainly was right about your not being dull."

De Rohan crooked one brow and stared at her. "I cannot imagine that discussing a murder investigation over dinner is considered good *ton,* Lady Catherine."

But her interest merely warmed. "Oh, I'm not the least bit fainthearted!" she reassured him. "Besides, I'm persuaded that's why you called upon Lord Sands yesterday. To help solve the murder. A terribly gruesome crime, wasn't it? The authorities don't really think Harry guilty, do they?" She leaned companionably nearer, her gaze steady and earnest. "Of course, it does sound as if he had means, motive, and opportunity—but the *will,* Mr. de Rohan? That is where I think you'll find him lacking."

Though he hid it well, he was surprised to see how

closely her logic paralleled his own. And it was at that precise moment that de Rohan realized that Catherine Wodeway was like no other woman he'd ever known. He found her deeply desirable, yes. But it was her good sense, her practicality, indeed, the very earthiness which had first attracted him—yes, those were the things that invited the level of intimacy which made him uncomfortable. Good God, he wasn't about to confide in her, as tempting as it might have been.

And so he drew his face into a stern, darkly forbidding expression and glared at her across the snowy white linen. Smugglers, bawds, pimps, opium traffickers— hundreds of such hardened criminals had withered beneath his glower. "A murder investigation," he responded, "is completely confidential."

But the glower had no effect whatsoever on his dinner companion. "Well, I don't think it," Catherine calmly answered. "He just doesn't seem the type. But— *oh!*—perhaps you believe her death had something to do with police corruption? Perhaps bribery or some sort of coercion is involved? Is that why they've called you in?"

It was hopeless to try to dissuade her. Better to turn the tables. "Lady Catherine," he answered. "Have *you* nothing in the way of ordinary conversation?"

Drawing back just a little, Catherine blinked at him. "I beg your pardon?"

De Rohan narrowed his gaze. "Common dinner repartee?" he suggested. "Are you not stitching some exciting piece of needlepoint? Have you no excellent herbal remedy to recommend for my incessant headaches? An ardent interest in gothic novels you'd like to prattle on about?"

"Well, no . . ." Catherine's high, aristocratic forehead drew into a confused frown. "No, I really don't read a vast deal."

De Rohan felt his jaw tighten. "Then perhaps you might prefer to talk of the latest fashion in ladies' bonnets? Or even to ask me—and I never thought I'd welcome this—why a man of my advanced years isn't married? In short, ma'am, can you not indulge in some sort of idle feminine chatter rather than probe into matters which are inappropriate for a lady's ears?"

At last, she took the hint, but her big brown eyes merely lit with amusement. "Really, Mr. de Rohan!" Catherine leaned forward to prop her chin upon her fists, almost laughing at him. "I should imagine a man of your superior intellect would find needlepoint and novels tedious. Perhaps *that* is what gives you the headache? Too many tedious women in your life?"

"Given time, all women become tedious," he asserted. But oddly, he let himself smile back at her.

A hint of a challenge lit her eye. "I shan't."

De Rohan had no answer for that one. He jerked his gaze from hers, very much fearing she was right. She was a dangerously interesting woman. And dangerously attractive, too.

But Catherine returned to her earlier topic. "Anyway, I daresay one of Julia's lovers did it," she speculated, her brows drawn thoughtfully together. "That's usually how it goes, you know."

"Catherine, I really don't think—"

Suddenly, her eyes widened with excitement. "Oh! I've got it!" she cried. "Perhaps a jealous wife hired someone—you know, a thug?—and had old Julia done in!"

De Rohan stared at her, vaguely intrigued. "Done *in?*"

Catherine nodded solemnly. "Jealousy is an evil thing, Mr. de Rohan," she answered. "Why, in our home village of Cheston-on-the-Water, the baker's wife tried to do in her husband! And all of it over that mousy little Molly Spratt who came in to do the dusting at the rectory."

"Molly Spratt?"

"It was arsenic, you see," she said matter-of-factly. "Right in the bread dough."

"*Arsenic?*"

"Oh, yes." Catherine lifted one perfect eyebrow and nodded. "Poor devil saw her—the stuff is grayish-white, you know—but he thought it some new sort of yeast. It brings on a miserable death; cramping, convulsions, retching."

"Yeast?" he said dryly.

"Arsenic," she corrected without missing a beat. "But old Dr. Clayton—he's our local sawbones—caught it, and just in the nick, too."

"Lady Catherine, really . . ."

Catherine simply shook her head. "Oh, it's jealousy, I'm telling you." At that, she dropped her voice. "I daresay this is a good a time as any to, well, to tell you about my sister-in-law."

Despite his better judgment, de Rohan was intrigued. "By all means."

In the candlelight, Catherine's face seemed to lose a bit of its color. "Cassandra, my elder brother's first wife," she blurted. "We hushed up the worst of it, but let me tell you, I'm lucky to be received in the best drawing rooms. Besides, if I don't tell you, *someone* else shall. Particularly if we go on like this."

De Rohan almost wanted to laugh, but he wasn't sure why. "If we go on like *what?*"

"Why, being friends," she said with a weak smile. "And in Cassandra's case, it was the rector at St. Michael's. Can you believe it?"

"And so your brother did in the rector?" he gently teased.

Catherine's face fell. "You heard?"

Good God, was she serious? Amazed, de Rohan shook his head. "I heard nothing of the sort."

"Well, thank heavens." Catherine shot him a tight smile. "But that was years later—and only after he'd kidnapped my niece, Ariane. You see, the rector had had an *affaire d'amour* with Cassandra. And when she attempted to break it off, he killed her. Well, we think it was an accident. But I daresay we shall never be sure, now that . . . well, now that—"

"—your brother did him in?" suggested de Rohan.

Almost cheerfully, Catherine nodded. "Just so, but only after the kidnapping. And it was my *younger* brother who shot him. It's all very complicated."

"I begin to see." De Rohan grappled for something he understood. "Wine?" Preemptively, he thrust the decanter in her direction.

Her smile brightened. "Oh, thank you," she said as he filled her glass. "A stimulating conversation always leaves one thirsty, doesn't it? Now, where were we?"

De Rohan sighed, set the bottle down, and propped his elbows on the table in resignation. "I collect that one of your brothers had just shot someone," he said, addressing the wrinkled tablecloth. "The—the vicar, was it?"

"The rector, actually," she corrected. "But enough family gossip! What I'm trying to say is this—I'm not a bit squeamish. And I'm quite sure I can be of help to you. I am, you see, so very experienced."

In despair, de Rohan emptied his glass again. "Experienced in what?"

"Oh, in murder!" she calmly responded. "And since Isabel means to lead me about society like a lamb to the slaughter, I may as well make good use of my time."

Total silence fell across the table. De Rohan's blood ran cold. Swiftly, he pinned her gaze with his. "Doing *what,* damn it?"

The shopkeepers at the adjacent table had fallen silent. One of them, fork still in hand, craned urgently forward. Catherine tossed the fellow a reproachful glance, then turned back again. "Really, Mr. de Rohan!" she chided, but her tone was teasing. "Isabel says one cannot get a voucher for Almack's if one uses language like that in public."

"Doing *what?*" he repeated.

Catherine's gaze held firm, but her smile was fading. "Why, simply making inquiries!" she answered, making an airy little gesture with her hand. "Nothing more! Ladies gossip all the time—it's my only feminine skill, truth to tell. I can't stitch or paint especially well. And really, what is the difference between a juicy bit of gossip and a police inquiry? Very little, I'd wager."

De Rohan scrubbed one hand down his face. "Catherine—" he began, speaking very clearly. "Your late husband, did he ever beat you?"

Catherine merely laughed, a light, cheerful sound, and patted his other hand where it lay splayed upon the tablecloth. "Who, Will?" she answered incredulously. "Why, he hadn't a mean bone in him."

Will. Her husband's name had been Will.

De Rohan really had not wanted to know that. It was just one more detail he did not need to know about Catherine Wodeway. Nor did he wish to consider the feeling—he could not quite bring himself to call it regret—that being with her churned up. She was lovely and intriguing, yes. She was also exasperating and quite obviously willful. Why should he feel anything for her, other than lust? He had chosen his path in life and could not now look back. He could not change what he'd so willingly made of himself. His old life was dead. As dead as her husband. And his father.

Suddenly, her smile brightened. "Mr. de Rohan, why do we not return to the privacy of Mortimer Street?" she suggested. "I will pour you a glass of port, and then we may privately discuss the ways in which I might help you."

De Rohan stood firm. "You cannot help me," he answered. "Not in *any* way at all."

He wasn't precisely sure what he'd meant by such a reply, but Catherine simply looked exasperated. "Why, that's silly! You seem perfectly willing to let that Mr. Kemble help."

"Catherine!" de Rohan finally exploded. "He's a man, blister it!"

She flashed him a sly smile. "I'm not perfectly sure everyone would agree with you on that."

De Rohan hurled his napkin down in frustration.

"Well, they would if they'd ever been backed into a dark corner with the bloody fellow," he hissed. "I have been! And at the very least, one can depend upon him to behave rationally."

Catherine made a quieting gesture with her hand. "Oh, do sit down," she softly insisted. "I *liked* him. Immensely. I was just making a point."

"And that would be . . . ?"

"That people are almost never what they seem."

He could see just where this was going. "Oh, no." De Rohan glowered at her, hating her logical mind. "No, no, no!"

Catherine batted her eyes innocently. "No, what?"

"Just *no!* No to everything you've suggested. To everything you've asked. And to everything you are even *considering.*"

"Everything?" she echoed, her voice dropping to a throaty whisper.

De Rohan felt as if someone had just dragged the breath from his chest again. Good God, she really was flirting with him. "Yes," he managed, trying to sound firm. "Yes, absolutely."

"Unequivocally?" Her tone was unmistakably suggestive. "All of it?"

De Rohan steeled his expression. "Did I not just say so?"

Her gaze slid away from his, and her cheeks turned pink. "But how do you know what I was thinking?" she softly asked.

A long moment of silence held sway over the table. The rumble of conversation, the aroma of good food, all of it faded from his consciousness, leaving him awash in some miserable mix of desire and regret. But there were some risks even a bold man dare not run, and Catherine damned sure felt like one of them.

"I believe I do know what you were thinking, Catherine," he finally answered. "And, regrettably, the answer will always be *no.*"

A part of him wanted to jerk back the words as soon as they were spoken. But he did not. Even if she were a different sort of woman altogether—just as his every instinct said—he still could not go through that again. Even with total honesty between them, nothing but pain could come of such a liaison. Whether his office lay in Whitehall or Wapping, in this strange world of the English *ton,* he was considered at best a member of the affluent bourgeoisie and at worst a policeman—a thing he was proud of but would never rise above. It was a choice he'd made willingly, with every awareness of what he was giving up. And now, his duty came first, which was as he wished. He would make neither explanations nor apologies. Not to anyone.

Chapter Seven

*But virtue is, in itself, so beautiful, that it charms us
at first sight, and engages us more and more
upon farther acquaintance.*

—LORD CHESTERFIELD, 1776,
The Fine Gentleman's Etiquette

They finished what was left of their meal in relative silence. Soon, de Rohan found himself settling the bill and escorting Catherine out into the night which seemed somehow colder than before. The wind had kicked up, too, and toward Oxford Street, two street lamps had fallen victim to its caprice. Despite the strain between them, de Rohan instinctively drew Catherine a little nearer but resisted the urge to pull her fully into his warmth.

Suddenly, a huge black coach and four came rattling out of Princes Street and into the main thoroughfare. It clattered past, but almost at once, the coachman drew the vehicle to a halt, rolling up short near the chophouse. A crested door, obscured by the shadows, flew open, and a bonnet topped with bouncing black feathers protruded into the gloom. "Max!" cried a soft, desperate voice. "Is that you? Lud, what luck!"

By now, Lady Delacourt's footman stood by the door,

clearly uncertain whether he should assist m'lady in or out of her equipage. Gravely concerned, de Rohan hastened back along the pavement, Catherine still clinging lightly to his arm.

Urgently, Cecilia waved him nearer. "Oh, Max," she insisted, "do climb up at once. We must talk!"

De Rohan drew Catherine a little nearer. "Good evening, Lady Delacourt," he said quietly. "Is something amiss?"

"Oh!" returned Cecilia sharply. "Is anything *not* amiss?" And then she paused to squint into the gloom. "Dear me, Lady Catherine, I did not recognize you. My pardon!"

Impelled by the desperation in Cecilia's voice, de Rohan assisted Catherine up and followed her in. "Oh, thank you!" Cecilia exclaimed as the footman closed the door. "I'm sorry it's so late, but I've this instant come from Harry's. He's in an awful state! Max, it's the necklace. The Sands Sapphire. It is gone!"

De Rohan exhaled sharply into the darkness. "You are quite certain?"

"We are now." By the light of the carriage lamp, de Rohan watched Cecilia's pale, anxious face. "Genevieve can't find it, and Harry and I have searched from top to bottom. We went through the drawers, the desks, and, out of desperation, I finally sent a footman up to Holly Hill. I was hoping Julia had sent the necklace back to the vault, but she had not. Max, it was a family heirloom!"

De Rohan had a very grim feeling. "So there's little doubt it was taken from her jewel chest on the night she was killed."

Cecilia nodded. "It would seem so," she admitted. "And the only good thing to come out of it is that it proves Harry didn't kill her. I mean, why would he steal his own necklace?"

"Why, indeed?" de Rohan murmured. He had not the heart to tell Cecilia that such subterfuge was commonplace. A few harsh scrapes around the window lock with a rasp, plunk some bit of jewelry down a drainpipe, and *voilà,* a motive for murder. A burglar had been seemingly caught in the act and turned violent. But just as quickly, he reconsidered. Something about that theory did not fit—

"A suspicious person might argue that the disappearance of the necklace was a setup," interjected Catherine, cutting into his thoughts. "But had your brother done such a dreadful thing, he would never have chosen a family heirloom. He would have chosen something valuable, yes, but never something so sentimental."

"That's right," de Rohan suddenly admitted. Good God, her mind was as quick as her tongue.

Catherine slid urgently forward on the seat. "Lady Delacourt, was there just the one necklace stolen? Most ladies possess a great many jewels."

"Why, just so!" answered Cecilia, her expression suddenly hopeful. "A small fortune was left behind. Indeed, the Sands Sapphire was the finest piece, but why would a thief stop at that?"

"It wants answering, does it not?" replied Catherine pensively.

Almost unconsciously, de Rohan lifted his hat and raked one hand through his hair. "I want the rest of those jewels, Cecilia," he quietly added. "Will your brother agree to it?"

Cecilia looked vaguely surprised. "To be sure! Just send someone along to Harry's tomorrow. And another thing. About Harry's finances? So far as I can tell, all is as it should be. They were appallingly lax with their creditors, but that's the extent of it."

Catherine gave a soft laugh. "From what I've seen here in town, Lady Delacourt, if murder were done over unpaid bills, two-thirds of Mayfair would have been struck dead by now. There must be more to it."

"I fear so." Cecilia frowned, and turned her gaze to de Rohan. "Constable Sisk has already been through most of Julia's things, but she'd left her traveling desk at Holly Hill. It contains her old calendars, an address book, a bit of correspondence. Shall I bring it all round to your rooms? I could do it on Saturday."

Saturday. He had been expected to dine with his grandmother. "Yes," he answered, noting the dark circles beneath Cecilia's eyes. Nonna Sofia, it seemed, would have to wait. He would send Nate to Wellclose Square with a message.

Gracefully, Cecilia leaned forward to touch him on the hand. "Thank you," she whispered, her voice finally breaking. "Oh, Max. Thank you."

De Rohan smiled gently. "And now, my dear, you must go straight home. At once."

"Yes, I must! I've a fear my husband is at home with a colicky baby." Cecilia leaned across the carriage to clasp one of Catherine's hands in her own. "And dear Catherine! How glad I am that we have become friends. Will you and Isabel call on me soon? Perhaps tomorrow?"

"Certainly, if that is your wish." Catherine sounded mildly surprised.

Cecilia relaxed back into her seat. "Then I thank you both again. I must apologize for having disturbed your—" She hesitated, coloring ever so slightly as she searched for the right word. "Your evening alone."

De Rohan did not know what to say. Was that what he and Catherine had had? *An evening alone?* The phrase implied a great deal. Resolved not to think of it, he threw open the door, leapt out, then lifted Catherine down. Cecilia's coachman whipped up his cattle and rattled away into the night.

As they walked in silence, Catherine held herself a little away from him, her hand barely grasping his arm. It was as if the brief conversation with Cecilia was forgotten, and the words he'd spoken over dinner had returned to drive an invisible wedge between them. He regretted such words had been necessary. But he had needed to speak them, had had to discourage her, for his sanity's sake.

Along the lane, most of the houses lay in darkness, with many of the street lamps blown out by the wind. At the next corner, yet another sputtered and died. With his vision limited, de Rohan's remaining senses leapt to full alert, a reflex honed by years of prowling pitch-black alleys and fog-shrouded rivers. He became acutely aware of the faint fragrance which rose from Catherine's hair. He could taste the hint of salt and smoke in the damp air. His ears caught the soft strains of a Haydn quartet carrying on the wind from some elegant drawing room near Cavendish Square. All of this he drew in, as intuitively as he breathed. And so it was that de Rohan sensed rather than saw the man who moved through the gloom toward them.

On gut instinct, he jerked Catherine nearer to his side and shot a protective glance over his right shoulder. There was nothing. He tried to shake off the unease which suddenly gripped him. It had been a strange night, that was all. Ever cautious, de Rohan moved to urge Catherine across the street, but a passing dray cut them off, its lone lamp barely piercing the gloom. It was enough, however, to cast shape and shadow to the man up ahead.

The dray rattled past, and darkness swirled in again. Instinctively, de Rohan fisted his hand about his walking stick and rolled onto the balls of his feet. The man neared, his footsteps slowing. "Beg pardon, gov," said his disembodied voice. "Can yer direct me ter 'Enrietta Street?"

De Rohan jerked his head over his shoulder. "Henrietta Street is opposite the square," he snapped impatiently. "Go through, and you cannot miss it."

In the murk, Catherine sensed that the man raised one hand. "Obliged," he said, his voice strangely soft. A little *snick* sounded in the darkness, and she heard de Rohan curse beneath his breath.

The man laughed. "No need ter cut up rusty, sir," he whispered as de Rohan shoved Catherine behind him. "I'll just 'ave the lady's pretty ear bobs and be on me way, awright?"

Catherine's shoulder scrubbed the wall as de Rohan urged her deeper into the darkness. "Stand aside, you fool!" he growled. "I'm an officer of the Crown. The lady is under my protection."

"The baubles or me knife?" growled the man, edging toward them. "What's it ter be?"

Everything happened at once then. The man floated from the gloom, and Catherine felt de Rohan's muscles harden powerfully. She sensed rather than saw his arm whip up and out. The man feinted, then lunged. Swift as lightning, de Rohan's stick came crashing down. It thudded sickeningly against bone. With a cry of agony, the man reeled into the wall, his knife clattering onto the pavement.

In that instant, however, Catherine was seized from behind. A cold hand thrust over her shoulder, clawing roughly at her pearls, yanking them until she choked. Fleetingly, her fingers struggled at her throat. The pearls were cutting into her flesh. De Rohan had spun about, cursing as he shoved her between his body and the wall. His stick came up again, and the second attacker staggered back. The clasp broke. Catherine sucked in her breath on a wheeze.

"Stop, thief!" de Rohan bellowed into the night.

From the direction of Cavendish Square, Catherine heard pounding feet racing toward them. And then the strange man from the chophouse came hurtling out of the darkness. "Max, behind you!" cried Mr. Kemble. Smoothly, de Rohan whirled about. Catherine's pearls clattered and spilt across the cobblestones as Kemble took the thief down into the filth of the street.

In the darkness beside her, Catherine heard de Rohan pounce upon the first man. Fists smacking into soft flesh. Grunts and curses. The sound of someone gagging. And de Rohan spewing a string of vitriolic Italian as he pummeled the thief into submission. Catherine pressed herself flat against the wall, trying to stay out of his way. Across the street, a window flew wide. Yellow lamplight washed the pavement.

"Murder! Murder!" screeched the onlooker.

One hand pressed to her mouth, Catherine stared. De Rohan had shoved the first man up and against the brick wall by means of his walking stick. With a violence she'd not dreamed he possessed, he repeatedly rammed one knee into his ballocks as he forced his stick across the man's windpipe, choking the breath from his body with both fists. Impotently, the man clawed and kicked, his toes no longer touching the pavement. De Rohan did not relent.

Then, from the corner of her eye, Catherine saw Kemble emerge from the shadows. With surprising strength, he dragged the second thief onto the pavement and tossed him in a heap at de Rohan's feet. He slid a wicked-looking piece of metal off his knuckles and into his coat pocket, watching dispassionately as de Rohan strangled their assailant. By now, the man's tongue had protruded from between his bluish lips.

"Really, Max, must you do murder in the middle of Marylebone?" asked Kemble dryly. "He'll lose his bowels, and you know I cannot abide a stench!"

As if pulled back into reality, de Rohan gave a satisfied grunt, jerked back the stick, and let the man slither down the brickwork. Grasping his throat and wheezing for breath, the thief surrendered, bent double, and collapsed across his partner. *"Vaffanculo!"* de Rohan spat down at him, whirling about to seize Catherine.

Roughly, he dragged her into the murky light. "Good God, are you hurt?" he demanded, his hard black eyes running over her. Only his viselike grip on her arm betrayed the depth of his fear for her.

"I'm f-fine," she managed. "Wh-what did you say to him?"

In the gloom, she felt a bit of the tension flow out of him. "Something like 'go bugger yourself,'" he muttered. "I recall you've a passing familiarity with the phrase."

Catherine suppressed a hysterical laugh. But in truth, she'd begun to tremble down to the soles of her slippers. He sensed it and slid a wide, warm hand up her spine, drawing her against him. "My God, Catherine!" he murmured against her hair.

Wordlessly, she pressed one temple into the soft fabric of his cloak and melted into the comforting scent of warm wool and male heat. Kemble prodded at the groaning men with the toe of one boot. "These handsome fellows anyone you know, old chap?"

Max shook his head. "Petty cutpurses," he said grimly. "I should have expected it when the wind whipped up."

One eye on the thieves, Kemble fished about in his pocket, then thrust out his hand with a flourish. "For you, madam." He let Catherine's pearls spill from his fist, cleverly catching the last strand on the tip of his index finger. "Bring them to my shop next week. It will be my pleasure to clean them for you."

With a cry of relief, Catherine plucked them from his finger. His eyes still on the fallen men, Max continued to slide a soothing hand up and down her back. "I owe you, Kem," he said quietly. "Again."

"Yes, a new pair of gloves, to be specific!" agreed

Kemble, peering down at his hands, his nose wrinkled in disdain. "I swear, Max, you are the very devil on a fellow's wardrobe. These bloodstains will never wash!"

"Maurice Giroux may bill me for a score of 'em," said de Rohan wryly. "If it will put an end to your carping."

Without fully releasing Catherine's hand, de Rohan knelt to study their assailants' faces. Kemble joined him. In the darkness, de Rohan's gruff voice rumbled softly, while Kem snapped out pithy retorts. Like some mystical shape-shifter, it seemed Kemble had reverted to his earlier façade, the charming, sharp-tongued fop. Not an hour past, she'd remarked how rarely people turned out to be what they first seemed. That was certainly true of Kemble. But Max de Rohan? Oddly, no. He was precisely what she'd thought him upon their first meeting: swift, ruthless, and—when pressed—quite cruel. And so why were her knees still knocking? She was safe. And his actions had been by no means unjustified.

Just then, a commotion arose behind them. "Ah," said Kemble, rising gracefully to his feet. "That would be Maurice now, bringing the watch. Take Lady Catherine away, Max. I shall see these rogues taken up before the Queen Square magistrates. Your statement can wait until tomorrow."

Catherine thanked him profusely for the return of her necklace. And then, placing a firm hand in the small of her back, de Rohan urged her away from the scene. For many minutes, Catherine walked beside him in silence. Halfway home, she found her tongue. "Max, what will happen to those men? I mean, after your statements are given and they have a trial? What will become of them?"

For a moment, he was silent. "They'll hang, Catherine."

"Oh." Fleetingly, Catherine squeezed shut her eyes. "That seems . . . harsh."

"Tonight, I think it most merciful," he said grimly.

"But whatever their intentions, you did stop them. And we are relatively unhurt."

De Rohan sighed deeply into the darkness, and she could sense the doubt and resignation in him. "Had they attacked someone other than you, I'd probably press for transportation," he quietly admitted. "We'll hang a man for bloody near anything in this country. That is why Peel wants criminal law consolidation."

That was one of his tasks at the Home Office, Catherine recalled. "It would be more fair for these men to be sent away, would it not? So that they might be punished for their crimes but have a second chance to make something of themselves?"

De Rohan was quiet for a time. "If that is what you want, Catherine," he finally answered, "then I shall see to it."

Strangely, and despite her earlier terror, it was precisely what she wanted. "Thank you," she said. "And thank you, too, for saving me. You were very brave."

"Or very stupid," he said, shaking his head. "I should have hailed a hackney."

Together, they stepped off the pavement and crossed the street to the opposite corner. "I really have been too long in the country, have I not?" she said, still holding his arm. "As you once said, it really is not altogether safe in town."

Max could not miss the apology in her tone. He

tucked her hand into his elbow, and laid his own over it. "I blame myself, Catherine," he said quietly. Somewhere in the midst of the excitement, he'd stopped using her title. And for tonight, at least, he did not wish to pick it up again. "It is my duty to keep you safe."

"And so you did," she interjected. "But why should I be your responsibility? I was a fool to go out on foot wearing such jewelry. You cannot be the savior of the world, you know."

He stopped in the middle of the pavement and spun about to face her. It was as if his heart had leapt back into his throat, and for a long moment, he was unable to speak. "It is my duty," he repeated firmly. "When you are with me, Catherine, you *will* be safe. Always."

She nodded, and stiffly, he jerked back into motion. What had he just said? Why had he spoken as if they had a future? They didn't.

Good Lord, there was a disquieting sort of comfort in Catherine's companionship, as contradictory as that sounded. He found her just a little too easy to be with. She was neither haughty nor pretentious. She possessed a forgiving nature. And despite her effortless dinner conversation, she was one of those rare women who seemed equally content with a man's silence, filling it with nothing but the warmth of her smile. Will Wodeway, he was beginning to suspect, had been an exceedingly fortunate fellow.

At once, he shook off the thought and slid his hand beneath Catherine's elbow, carefully escorting her up the unlit steps. A silent night now enveloped the fringes of Marylebone. Up and down the lane, coal fires had been banked for the evening, spiking the air with wisps of sour smoke. In the shadows, Catherine turned to face him, fumbling in the depths of her reticule. She extracted a key and looked up at him. Even in the darkness, Max could feel the heat of her eyes on his face.

"I'm going to be perfectly brash, Mr. de Rohan, and say what I fear you will not," she whispered, her voice sounding anything but bold. "I should like to see you again. Would that be possible?"

Max dragged the sharp air into his lungs and slowly blew it out again. "It really would not be prudent, Lady Cath—"

"I asked if it would be *possible,*" she gently interjected. "As to prudence, I'll gladly argue that one, too. But not on a stone-cold doorstep."

Suddenly, Max realized Catherine's teeth were chattering. Good Lord, was chivalry dead? His, apparently, was comatose. He reached nearer to take the key from her hand, but just as their hands touched, another blast of wind swept down the street, tearing a strand of Catherine's hair from its neat arrangement and whipping it into his face. She was so near, he could hear her breath catch. Could smell the scent of her hair again. Suddenly, his restraint felt . . . not prudent but a little foolish, when mere moments ago, she'd been half strangled to death. Life was so uncertain.

Yes, suddenly, it seemed the wisest thing in the world simply to pull her into his warmth. With a soft gasp of pleasure, Catherine came against him, sliding her hands up the fabric of his lapels and brushing her cheek against his shoulder. Shuddering ever so slightly, Max cast his eyes to the heavens. *"Dio confonda i superbi,"* he muttered, drawing her to his chest.

But what had once seemed like madness now felt perfectly necessary. He opened his hands against the wool of
her wrap and let his palms press beseechingly into her
shoulders. She felt so warm, so wonderfully alive. Her
hand slipped farther up his back, her palm opening,
spreading wide against the wool of his cloak. Somewhere near her feet, he heard metal tinkle against marble, then go bouncing down the steps. *Maledizione!* The
bloody key!

He did not care. He cared only that in this one fleeting moment, Lady Catherine Wodeway felt as if she belonged right against his heart. In the darkness, it seemed
easier to surrender, as if that which he could not see was
somehow not real. But she felt real. So real that he somehow dipped his head and brushed his lips over hers. To
his surprise, Catherine angled her head, rose unsteadily
onto her tiptoes, and kissed him back. Her effort was
artless, almost awkward, and yet the explosion was in-
stantaneous. Raw need driven by fear slammed into him
like nothing Max had ever known, and roughly—too
roughly—he jerked her nearer, deepening the kiss.

Catherine gasped but did not draw away. Instead, her
fingers curled into the fabric of his cloak, dragging her
body against his. The gasp became a soft sound of need.
Again, he raked his mouth over hers, heedlessly chafing
her with the stubble of his beard. Max did not need to
see the elegant line of her jaw or the inviting swell of her
bottom lip to know that he had to taste her more deeply.
His body had thrummed with lust the moment he'd
seized her hand and swept her across Walrafen's ballroom.

As if reading his thoughts, Catherine slanted her

mouth, invitingly parting her lips. Gave herself up to him. Max captured her face between his hands. The rush of sensation when he thrust his tongue into her mouth was wild and fierce. Uncontrollable. He could feel her breasts flatten against his shirtfront, could feel his own heart pounding again. Blood rushed to his groin. His head swam with the scent of her. His breath came fast and shallow.

Dio mio, he thought. Madness. A madness he could not stop. She was *una bella strega.* A beautiful witch. He had to force himself to slow. His hands left her face, caressed her throat, slid lower.

Catherine had convinced herself that she'd wanted just one more taste of Max de Rohan. But his mouth was still redolent of expensive burgundy—rich, velvety, intoxicating—and she knew at once she was addicted. Stroking and exploring, tongues sliding sinuously together, she savored the heat and scent of him. His hands were strong, his mouth skillful. And yet he trembled as he touched her, shivered as he seemingly lost himself in her. His caresses flowed over her, cupping her breasts, curving around her waist, and stroking the swell of her buttocks, as if the shape of a woman were something new and wondrous to him.

She rose higher and gasped. He was fully aroused, his erection hard against her belly. His teeth caught her lip and feverishly bit, and something feral and urgent shot through her. His large hands lifted her, pressed her back against the door. She felt the wood scrub against the back of her cloak. Willingly, wantonly, she arched into his body. Passion burning out of control, his mouth tore from hers to trail down her throat. His breath was searing against her skin, as if her every nerve ending had suddenly come to life.

In a confusing mélange of foreign words, he murmured hotly against her skin, nipping and tasting as his mouth moved. *"Dio, cara,"* he whispered.

She found his mouth again and kissed him deeply. "Max," she whispered urgently. "Oh, Max, please."

His embrace banded about her like steel as a deep groan rose from his chest. *"Tesoro mio,"* he breathed against her collarbone.

"Max, come inside with me. Please."

Her breathless plea began to drag him back from the brink. He had to stop kissing her. Had to. *Had* to. The thought ran wild through his head as he rolled his hips into hers, lifting her feminine mound against his hardness. Then, dimly, he recalled where he was.

Her damned doorstep.

Christ Almighty. He tried to set her away from him, but he'd backed her up against the door. And she was still kissing him. "Catherine," he rasped against her mouth. *"Finiscila!* Stop!"

At last, Catherine let her hands slide down his arms, and Max pulled away. In the darkness, they stared at one another, both still sucking in air in desperate pants. Heat and vitality and pure feminine desire radiated from Catherine. Max felt like a callow boy who'd just tried to tumble his first tavern wench. He felt blood rush to his face, and, as if to hide it, he stepped deliberately down to the street, fumbling in the gloom for her key.

He found it and thrust it up at her. "Catherine," he rasped in the darkness. "Catherine, this isn't . . . this isn't me. This just isn't what or how I am. How I behave."

She reached down to enfold her fingers about his. "It isn't *me,* either," she whispered weakly. "Good God, it isn't what I am. But perhaps—just perhaps—it is *us,* Max? The way we are together?"

But she could sense at once that he did not mean to listen. Pressing the key into her palm, he spun gracefully about and started away. "Go inside now, Catherine," he ordered over his shoulder.

"Max, wait!" she cried, and in a flash, he turned back to her. "Must you go?" But he did not answer.

She tried again. "Max, that thing you said—*Dio confonda* something—what did you mean? And the other words, too. What did they mean?"

In the near-darkness, she watched him standing motionless for a long moment. Heard his long sigh of frustration. "It's an old saying," he finally answered. "Like a curse or a warning. 'May God confound a proud man.' The rest of it was . . . just foolishness. Now get inside, Catherine. It is not safe. Lock the door."

Then, with his long opera cloak swirling about his heels, the man simply melted into the night. "Bloody hell!" hissed Catherine, crossing her arms stubbornly over her chest. That disappearing trick of his was becoming an annoying habit. For a time, she listened as his rapid, purposeful footsteps rang off the towering town houses which lined the street. But quickly—too quickly—the echo faded.

Catherine let her mouth curve into a knowing, feminine smile. The night had grown miserably cold. Taking pity on him, she slid the key noisily into the lock, opened the door, and slammed it shut again without entering. In the darkness, the distant echo of his steps resumed. Catherine's heart sang.

Oh, yes! No matter how ruthless or uncivilized he might be, in this one thing, Maximilian de Rohan *was* a gentleman. And a gentleman would never abandon a lady on her doorstep, no matter how acute his frustration. So Catherine, like the mooncalf she now feared she'd become, stood alone in the cold until the sound of his footsteps had faded completely into the distance.

Chapter Eight

Men are oftener led by their
hearts than by their understandings.

—LORD CHESTERFIELD, 1776,
The Fine Gentleman's Etiquette

The following morning, Max managed to do the un-thinkable. He overslept, awaking from another hazy dream in a foul humor, still infuriated by his behavior of the preceding evening. What in heaven's name had he been thinking? He had kissed Catherine again—right on her damned doorstep, grinding his body into hers as if she were some dockside whore, to be taken in the shadows of a doorway. But what was perhaps even worse, when she'd insisted she was not his responsibility, he'd argued. He'd even implied that they might have a future together. Had he run stark mad?

Of course, he wanted to bed her—wanted it badly. And she was willing. He knew the signs, that softening of the gaze, that lowering of the voice. He'd been invited to sample a woman's favors in just such a way a hundred times. He often accepted, so long as no one was apt to get hurt. So why did it feel as if bedding this particular woman would come with strings attached?

After leaving Catherine alone in the dark, Max had refused himself the small luxury of a cab, resolutely hiking the three miles across town in the cold wind in some futile attempt to exorcise the demons which possessed him. But the brisk walk had done nothing to ease his more tangible discomfort. A throbbing cock-stand had plagued him all night, then saluted him again at dawn, cheerfully tenting two wool blankets and a counterpane as if they were nothing more than satin sheets.

He'd tried valiantly to ignore his dilemma by pounding his pillows and thrashing at his bedcovers. But eventually, he rolled over with a grunt, stared up into the depths of the ceiling, and surrendered to the weakness of his flesh. He stroked himself gently at first, easing his hand back and forth along his shaft with that same sweet rhythm he'd used to plumb the depths of Catherine's mouth. The weight of his cock was hot and heavy in his palm. For once, he willingly let himself remember her— the curve of her face, the swell of her breasts, that lush, wide mouth . . . the heat and heaviness in his groin were maddening. He grew harder. Stroked faster. Burned for the pleasure of release. Good God, he had to do something to ease his frustrations.

But it was no use. He could not quite do it. What had once been a straightforward means of physical release had become suddenly distasteful. He let his hand fall away. While frigging himself senseless might occasionally ease his physical frustrations, it apparently couldn't slake what he was starting to feel for Catherine. And why? Because he was beginning to have a worrisome notion of what *strings attached* might mean. Because with Catherine, he might want . . . *what?* He might want *more*.

He did not dare let himself consider what more might entail. He had a job to do. It was important. No, it was his life. God knew he was no monk, but bedding Catherine could wreck everything. And then where would he be? He was not of her world, and his had no place for her. With a violent curse, he hurled back the sheets, stumbled naked from the bed, and tried to drown himself in a basin of ice-cold water. By God, he would not give in to this. He would not put his job on the line. And he would not make a fool of himself over another woman—even an honest one—whom society believed so far above him.

By sheer force of will, he shoved away all thought of the previous night. Hastily, he bathed and dressed, but, to make matters worse, his landlady's unmistakable knock sounded upon his door before he'd had time to wipe clean his shaving razor. Bloody hell, had he forgotten the rent, too? As he stood before the mirror hastily jamming his shirttails into his breeches, Max caught one last glimpse of his bleary countenance, wondering as he did so just how the English *ton* managed to keep such god-awful hours. But then, they did not have to work for a living, did they?

And nor, precisely, did he. Max reluctantly admitted it just as he shrugged into his waistcoat and headed for the door. Yes, he, too, could fritter away his life with impunity, could no doubt drink and dissipate himself into an early grave long before his family's coffers were bankrupted. For a moment, he stared at his hand, his skin dark against the sheen of the brass doorknob, and quietly admitted that there had been more than a few bleak nights when the notion had tempted him. Life on the river had been brutal and grim, the stews and slums of London worse. And a policeman, no matter how noble his intent, no matter how deep his dedication, could put but a dent in the inhumanity which surrounded him.

The knock came again, more impatient this time, forcing him back to the present. Max abruptly jerked open the door, only to be surprised by Lucifer's happy yelp, which rang sharply through the corridor beyond. "Good morning, Mr. de Rohan," announced Mrs. Frier in a cool, mildly chiding whisper. "It seems you've visitors already."

The good lady was notoriously disapproving of early callers, but it mattered little. The person who stood in the shadows beyond her shoulder was not one easily refused. Impatiently, Signora Castelli stamped her walnut cane against the floor. *"Buongiorno!"* she announced, pushing imperiously past Mrs. Frier just as Lucifer dashed between them and into the parlor. Sofia turned her glower on the dog. "Impatient beast! *Accuccia! Sta' fermo!"*

"Woof!" countered the beast, his claws clacking anxiously as he pranced about Max's feet.

"Bah!" said the old woman, shaking her cane at Lucifer's glossy black head. *"Il mastino,* he does not listen! He is spoiled, that one!"

After giving Lucifer a sympathetic pat, de Rohan bent to kiss his grandmother's parchment cheek. *"Buongiorno,* Nonna," he responded. "What an unexpected pleasure. Ah—and Maria! *Salve."*

His grandmother's companion bobbed a quick curtsey and cut him a quicker grin. *"Come sta,* Maximilian?"

she asked, passing him a covered terra-cotta dish, still warm from the oven. It smelled heavenly.

Max spared her a rare smile, along with a little wink. "I'm well, Maria, thank you." He waved them hospitably toward the chairs in his small parlor. "Sit, sit, *per favore.*"

In a cloud of rustling silk and old black lace, the two women swept through the room, Sofia gesturing dismissively to Mrs. Frier as she went. The latter shut the door with an insulted thump, while the *signora* paused just long enough to glance heavenward, as if she expected the ceiling to fall. Then she slid out of her flowing black cloak and settled herself gracefully upon the armchair nearest the hearth.

Setting the dish aside, Max extended a hand to take her wrap. Sofia waved him off with an impatient gesture. "We have but a moment before my appointment in St. James, Maximilian," she began, her eyes roaming about the meager chamber. "But please, God, let me understand this. Why does my grandson keep himself in such straits when a fine suite of rooms sits empty in Wellclose Square?"

Max yanked Lucifer's blanket off the wooden settle and sat down, hoping that the ladies would not notice the resulting cloud of dog hair. "As I've said, I work long hours, Nonna," he answered. "I would not have you and Maria inconvenienced by them."

With a dubious expression, Sofia let her gaze roam over his face. "From the look of it, my grandson, it would appear these long hours are inconveniencing *you.*"

Max knew he looked even more haggard than usual.

"I was up quite late," he admitted, bending down to stroke the big Neapolitan mastiff, who had settled with a grunt on the floor. "At Walrafen's. The, er, assignment."

A ghost of a smile flicked across his grandmother's face as she craned her head to stare at his bedchamber door. "Ah, *veramente?*" Her voice was soft and suspicious. "Then it is merely business which keeps you abed until midday?"

It was not yet half past ten, hardly midday. But at his grandmother's words, the memory of Catherine last night suddenly broadsided Max again. It had not been business at all, had it?

He must have hesitated just a moment too long. An odd expression passed over his grandmother's face. "It was not just work, was it?" Her long, arthritic fingers clawed almost spasmodically at the arms of her chair. "You were with a woman. I know it. I have *seen.*"

"No," Max lied, his gaze focused blindly on the huge ruby ring which winked upon her left hand.

"No—?"

Max forced his eyes to hers. "Nonna, have we not been over this time and again? Police inspectors—wise ones—don't have wives. And they don't have children."

"You are not a policeman!" she countered. "You are a *magistrate* who—"

"Who investigates police corruption," interjected Max.

Sofia's lips thinned. "What you ought to be is a wine merchant," she retorted. "Then you could have it all."

Then you could have it all. For once, Max paused to consider. Could he? And would he be happy? Suddenly, the thought of being chained to a desk from daylight until dark did not sound quite as wretched. But it would still feel meaningless. It would still feel as if he had turned his back on his father. Max dropped his gaze and shook his head.

His grandmother settled back into her chair, looking suddenly tired. "Perhaps, Maximilian, you have met no one yet who is worth sacrificing your freedom." She paused for just a heartbeat. "But you *will.*"

Maria leaned forward, her excitement barely contained. "This time, Maximilian, she is sure," she said, almost rising from her chair. "This time, *la signora* has seen her—*la Regina di Dischi!*"

The old woman snapped her fingers. "Sit and be still, Maria! *Per amor di Dio,* you're worse than that dog."

But Max was still hanging on Maria's last words. "The Queen of Pentacles," he said slowly, turning to face his grandmother in amazement. "Please tell me, Nonna, that you do not toy with *I Tarocchi* again?"

The old woman's face tightened. "You are a dreamer, Maximilian!" she declared, slashing at the air with her hand. "You live in the past and refuse to see what the future must be." Abruptly, she stood. *"Vieni,* Maria. We must go."

Gently shaking his head, Max rose and bent to kiss her worn cheek. "Do not believe all that you see in your tarot, Nonna," he said gently. "And do not fret for me. I may be a dreamer, but I am happy with my life."

His grandmother acted as if he had not spoken and reached for her cloak. *"A proposito,* Maximilian," she said coolly as he swirled it about her stooped, narrow shoulders. "You wish that *il mastino* should return with me?"

Max had turned away to assist Maria into her wrap. "It would be best for Lucifer," he answered reluctantly. "But if he annoys you, I will keep him. Nate may come here and walk him."

Half listening, Lucifer uncurled himself and stood. Flopping his head over the arm of the chair which Sofia had just vacated, he cast his big, limpid eyes up at her and sighed through his jowls. He was thinking, no doubt, of her table scraps. The ones which she pretended not to feed him.

Already drawing on her gloves with neat, hard jerks, Sofia cut a sharp glance down at the big mastiff. Fleetingly, her expression softened. "Oh, *va bene!*" she growled at him. "But there will be no more digging in my garden! And no more sleeping in my bed!"

With grief and anger warring in his heart, Max knelt to say good-bye to Lucifer, then watched them go. Sofia leaned lightly on Maria's arm as they led Lucifer down the steps and into the sunshine. She looked older and even more frail today, if such a thing were possible. He wished he could please her. He truly did. His heart heavy, he turned and went back inside the house.

Sofia heard the door close softly behind them. She looked beaten, she knew. But, by God, she wasn't. Gathering her temper, she paused by her carriage. "Maria," she hissed, leaning toward her companion's ear. "Fetch me that boy. Nate."

"*Si,* Signora Castelli," Maria responded evenly. "You will wish him to bathe the dog?"

Sofia turned her piercing gaze on the younger woman. "*No!*" she whispered, her voice lethally soft. "I wish to bribe him again. Maximilian is lying to me. He has been with her, this woman! I know it! Perhaps Nate can learn something."

"Si," answered Maria glumly, and started into the carriage. But Sofia's clawlike hand shot out to stop her.

"And Maria!" the old woman whispered, drawing her backward with surprising strength. "This afternoon, when you go to confession, you must pray, *per favore."*

"Oh, *va bene,"* agreed Maria wearily. "For what now?"

Signora Castelli looked at her with a sour expression. "That she is Italian!" the old woman hissed. "And, God willing, a good Catholic!"

At that, Maria finally burst into hysterical laughter. "Mother Mary!" she cried, holding up her hands to heaven. "This is England! Better we should seek a needle in a haystack. Let us begin by simply praying she'll put up with him, eh?"

Spring had returned to England again. Somehow, without Catherine ever having truly noticed, the brave daffodils of April were giving way to the brighter blooms of May, and the branches which had clattered barrenly in the wind mere weeks ago were unfurling with green. The morning's mist was a full two hours gone, and Catherine could already sense the smell of earth warming beneath the sun, since she'd begun her morning ride through Hyde Park far later than was her habit.

Although the *ton*'s more devout revelers were yet abed, a few of Mayfair's hardier residents had begun to trickle across Park Lane to take their morning constitutional. It was a pity, really. She had particularly wished to be alone with her thoughts today. Impatiently, Catherine nudged Orion through the upper gate and into a faster pace, but was compelled to rein him back at once. Several yards in the distance, a tall, well-dressed gentleman in a gray top hat paused along the path, judiciously eyeing Orion's flashing hooves. In his right hand, he clutched the leash of a grizzled pug, and for all his intrusion into her solitude, the man looked friendly. And very, very familiar. As Catherine approached, she nodded down at him.

Thus acknowledged, the gentleman lifted his hat. "Good morning, Lady Catherine!" he said. "What a dashing sight you cut!"

"Good morning," she returned, smiling brightly as she touched her crop to her hat brim. But out of sheer embarrassment, Catherine did not pause. She had met him at her first London dinner party and had spoken briefly with him at Walrafen's. Yet she could not now remember his name!

The fault was hers, she admitted, her gaze sweeping over the park's green expanse. She had come to town to meet people, to search for something which might drag her from her mire of lethargy and despair. And she had liked the fellow when she'd met him. He'd reminded her of Will: large and a little pompous but also warm and amusing. A very eligible widower, Isabel had whispered. An important undersecretary, Sir Everard . . . something. Catherine shook her head. The details had slipped away, and she knew why.

Maximilian de Rohan. The man had cast a spell on her.

And a strange sort of spell it was, too. Catherine hardly knew whether she was captivated or infuriated. Both, it seemed. Impatiently, she pushed Orion forward, allowing the spring breeze to blow back the tendrils of hair which teased her forehead. But her thoughts of Max were not so easily tamed. An extraordinary new awareness pulsed through Catherine's veins this morning, and it had nothing at all to do with the fact that the man was dark and dangerous looking.

He was desirable, yes. But there was more to it than that. Catherine couldn't quite put words to it yet, but in his long, harsh face, she saw a kinship. Perhaps it was some mutual understanding of loss. Or perhaps disillusionment? Still, his were emotions she couldn't fully comprehend. Good God, she barely understood her own. She knew one thing, though. While she would always remember her husband with an abiding fondness, at long last, her grief was truly fading. Suddenly, life seemed rich with intrigue. At least she could thank Max de Rohan for that.

Against her better judgment, Catherine let the memories of the previous night come flooding back. How dreadfully she had prattled on during dinner, pushing past the edges of his self-imposed privacy, even deliberately goading him at times. And all of it done in some vain hope of either cajoling him or shocking him out of that perpetual state of antagonism in which he seemed to exist.

He had seen through her, to be sure. She suspected he was the sort of man who could see through everyone, who could cut to the truth of anything—laughter, lies, and even, yes, lust—with the same swift blade of intuition which he'd so deftly wielded on her. Over dinner, Catherine had implied nothing by so much as a suggestive tilt of her eyebrow, yet he had known her innermost thoughts. Did women want him so frequently, then? Had he seen the signs so often that he had come to recognize them effortlessly? Or was it simply her?

Her elder brother Cam had once warned her that she wore her emotions on her face. Then it had mattered very little, for she'd never had anything to hide. And she wasn't perfectly sure she wished to hide anything now. It had always been her way to be frank, perhaps inappropriately so. But Catherine was not at all sure she wished to change. She was rather like her elder brother, single-minded and set in her ways.

So perhaps Max de Rohan would simply have to put up with her. Inwardly, Catherine smiled. Yes, perhaps it would be just a little bit intriguing to watch him writhe with discomfort under her onslaught. And perhaps—just perhaps—she could break through that self-imposed wall again. She was, after all, a Rutledge. And as her cantankerous old Aunt Belmont was ever fond of saying, Rutledges were the most accursedly stubborn people ever to draw breath.

The thought was so liberating, Catherine literally tipped back her head and laughed. The very sound of it shocked her. But mere weeks ago, it had felt as if life couldn't be much bleaker. Certainly, it had held no challenge. But now, something was different. Perhaps frighteningly different. Surprisingly, Catherine didn't care, for she now knew one thing which gave her hope: Max de Rohan was no more immune to her than she was to him. Spirits rising, she wheeled Orion about and headed home.

De Rohan stood rigidly at his single, soot-covered office window, watching the late-morning traffic surge toward Whitehall. Absently, one hand kept pushing through his heavy hair, which was already too long and now thoroughly disordered. "A bloody awful day," he muttered. He'd been shocked to see Sofia at his door so early in the morning. For once, it had been an escape to come to work. But now, trapped in a musty office with nothing save last night's memories, restlessness began to eat at Max.

The walls pressed in. The air felt stale. To hell with Peel and Walrafen and all their high-minded Tory notions about reform bills and committee meetings and parliamentary debates. He needed to do real work, help real people. God, how he wanted to return to his old job, where he need never rub elbows with the upper crust. Where his efforts had made a more tangible difference. Or perhaps he just craved the clamor of the river, needed to feel the surge of the tide beneath his launch.

At least he could *see* the Thames from his office, he bitterly mused, though the scene little resembled the one he'd long observed from his old office at Wapping New Stairs. Westminster lay too far upriver from the Pool of London for serious traffic. No hulking merchantmen, no low-riding lighters could venture here. Almost unseeingly, Max watched a light skiff go slicing toward Westminster Bridge, sailing high, fast, and proud. Inexplicably, it made him think of Catherine. And once again, he found he could not escape the feeling that he was on the verge of entering the wrong place, the wrong world. And this time, it had nothing to do with the location of his office.

Suddenly, a faint sound caught his ear, and, like the policeman he really was, Max spun about with blinding speed. Mr. Howard, the front-office clerk, jerked back from his threshold in alarm. "A visitor, Mr. de Rohan . . . er, sir."

A mere slip of a woman seemed to float in the shadows behind Howard. With a jerk of his head, de Rohan sent the clerk back down the stairs. Her lips thin and tight, the woman stepped into his office, clutching a brown velvet reticule as if her very life were contained in its depths. With a policeman's eye, Max took her measure. Just past thirty, neither pretty nor plain. Her clothing reeked of Bond Street, but her gestures displayed a painful lack of confidence. Still, she stiffened her spine with a resolution which surprised him. "Mr. de Rohan?" Her tone was haughty, but her voice wavered.

"I am de Rohan." He gestured toward the chair opposite the desk. "And you are . . . ?"

The woman did not deign to sit. "Mrs. Lane," she said, lifting her chin another notch. "The Honorable Mrs. Amelia Lane, daughter of Lord Welbridge."

She placed far too strong an emphasis on the words *honorable* and *lord* to suit Max. Ruthlessly, he folded his hands behind his back and forced his face into a mask of perfect politeness. "And what may I do for you, Mrs. Lane?"

"What may you *do* for me?" As if kindled by his civility, her antagonism burst into flame. "You may stop harassing my affianced husband!" she exploded, her fingers digging still deeper into the brown velvet of her reticule. "That is what you may do!"

De Rohan lifted one brow. "I beg your pardon?"

"Mr. Rupert Vost!" she answered with a little stamp of her foot. "We are to marry in a few weeks. He will be my husband. And if you insist on insulting him or—or questioning him, why, I will . . . I will tell my papa! And he will put a stop to it, you may be sure!"

Unfazed by her threat, de Rohan studied her. Nothing about the woman made her seem like Vost's type. It was money, then, at a guess. "Ma'am, I'm afraid you misunderstand—"

"No!" she cried sharply. "It is you, sir, who does not understand. I know what you are—what you are doing. You are little better than a policeman. And you're involved in a murder of a woman no one cares about. Rupert was *not* seeing her. Not any longer. He was at my home in Arlington Street that night. *All* night! If that admission damages my reputation, so be it. But you will stay away from him. He loves me."

Her words were tinged with fervency, as if she sought to convince herself as well as de Rohan. "I'm sorry for your distress, ma'am," he said, bowing toward her with extreme civility. "I regret you felt it necessary to come here today. Does your carriage wait, or shall I have Mr. Howard fetch you a hackney coach?"

She stepped back a pace, clearly nonplussed. "Well, I—I . . . does that mean you shall do as I ask?"

De Rohan smiled tightly. "I serve at the pleasure of Mr. Peel, ma'am," he said very carefully. "I fear I'm not at liberty to discuss a criminal investigation with anyone else."

Mrs. Lane's brows pulled into a pucker. "But—but . . ."

She was still opening and closing her mouth soundlessly when Max seized the moment and rang for Howard, who bounded up the stairs with alacrity. "Mrs. Lane was just on her way out," he explained. "Be so good as to help her with her carriage."

Upon Catherine's return from the park, she led Orion around to the mews and gave him over to the blushing, bobbing stable boy who seemed chagrined that she'd had to seek him out. Catherine merely smiled and trudged back along Mortimer Street. The sense of elation she'd felt in the park had faded ever so slightly. Max was a complicated man. Theirs would be a complicated relationship. And were they even going to have a relationship?

Quickly, Catherine washed, changed, then drifted into the dining room in a fog. She could not help but recall how naturally Lady Delacourt had leaned on Max for support or how brave he'd been with the street thieves. He certainly was chivalrous, in the most old-fashioned sense of the word. Musingly, she poured a cup of coffee at the sideboard and settled into her chair. Other than her brother Cam, had she ever known a man strong enough to lean on? Certainly not her father. The late Randolph Bentham Rutledge had been a gazetted drunkard and womanizer who had impoverished his children without compunction. Now all Catherine could hope was that his namesake, her younger brother Bentley, wasn't headed in the same direction. So far, it was a near run thing.

Of course, she'd had Will, and she had loved him. But for some reason—call it the clarity of hindsight—she was beginning to face a few truths she had long preferred to ignore. Her husband had been strong and comforting, but he'd possessed little appreciation of life's realities. Hounds and hunting he'd understood. But it was she who'd been left to make their most grave decisions.

She remembered one particularly bad year—a cold spring followed by a dry summer and a drenching autumn—when what little they'd managed to grow had rotted in the ground before harvest. Will had just drained their cash to purchase new bloodstock and build a fine stable. Suddenly, routine farm tasks such as roofing and draining and fencing—the things *she* had to worry about—were financially beyond them. When their bailiff had thrown up his hands and whispered the word *mortgage,* Will had turned to her with a helpless shrug. It hadn't been the first time.

Suddenly, a noise disrupted her thoughts. Catherine was almost relieved when the housekeeper entered, her shoes clicking quickly across the marble floor, then muffling on the thick carpet beneath the dining table. Mrs. Trinkle looked like a woman on a mission. "Begging your pardon, my lady, but may I speak frankly?"

Catherine smiled. "I wish you would!"

"Perhaps it's not my place, ma'am," she began, her tone peevish. "But I need to ask—have you any idea how long you mean to stay in town?"

"How long?" asked Catherine, stalling. The truth

was, just as she'd given no forethought to coming to London, she'd given none to returning home. Lately, she seemed incapable of logical action of any sort. Her behavior last night was, perhaps, an example.

Just then, Delilah staggered in, bearing a tray impossibly laden with food. Mrs. Trinkle turned and began methodically to set the dishes out. "What I mean to say, m'lady, is that perhaps it might be prudent to take on a cook and hire a proper staff?" she continued as she worked. "Why, you've not so much as a lady's maid. To be sure, Delilah and I don't mind doing what we can, but . . ."

Catherine let her eyes drift over the sideboard. A half-dozen chafing dishes stared back. Guilt struck her hard. She'd never thought to discuss her plans—or lack thereof—with Mrs. Trinkle. And because he'd spent years in grinding poverty, her now-wealthy brother was probably the only nobleman in England too frugal to keep his town house fully staffed.

Catherine smiled ruefully. "I should have mentioned it sooner, Mrs. Trinkle, but there's no need for grand meals. Tomorrow, a little porridge will do nicely."

"*Porridge—?*" Mrs. Trinkle looked aghast.

"Porridge," confirmed Catherine. "As to staff, I shall post a letter to my brother today."

"Oh, dear!" Mrs. Trinkle's eyes popped wide as saucers. "The post!" She thrust forward the salver, which held a large, overstuffed letter.

At once, Catherine recognized the childlike scrawl splashed across the vellum and promptly slit it open with her knife. A stiff, folded watercolor slid out and fell open on the table. Catherine laughed, then turned her eyes to the letter. As usual, it was more postscript than forethought.

> *Dear Aunt Cat,*
> *When are you coming home? Lud, can it be soon? It's dull as ditch-water here at Chalcote. Papa is busy with the plowing, whilst Mama is always vomiting. Milford says that's a vulgar term, but I don't know another. I'll bet Uncle Bentley does. He always knows the best words. Anyway, Papa says that you've run away to London to kick up your heels, but I heard Mama say that you are just trying to outrun your ghosts. So I am sending you this knight in shining armor to protect you. I'm sorry the red and yellow ran together on the coat-of-arms. Gervais drooled on it.*
>
> Your devoted niece,
Lady Ariane Rutledge

> *P.S. Uncle B. has gone missing again. If you see him, tell him Janie at the Rose & Crown says she hopes he will pay her another call soon, as she has a special treat for him. She winked when she said it, and Milford called her a saucy piece. He wouldn't tell me a piece of what. Oh, and P.P.S.—I will be twelve in three weeks!!!!!*

In the distance, a door opened, then thunked shut again. Catherine was making a mental note to upbraid the indiscreet Janie at her first opportunity when Mrs. Trinkle returned. "It's Lady Kirton, ma'am," she announced on a sharp exhalation. "I've put her in the drawing room."

Isabel? Memory stirred. Oh, drat! She'd given her promise to go shopping today. No doubt she was to be quizzed unmercifully about her evening with Max de Rohan. If she cried off now, it would only get worse. Resigned, Catherine patted her hair into some semblance of order and rose. Within a quarter-hour, her ever-efficient aunt was tucking Catherine neatly into her carriage.

"Piccadilly, Jonas," Isabel ordered as her footman closed the door.

Chapter Nine

*A rake is a composition of the most ignoble and shameful
vices; they conspire to disgrace his character while wine and
pox contend which shall soonest destroy his constitution.*

—Lord Chesterfield, 1776,
The Fine Gentleman's Etiquette

Burlington Arcade was a narrow enclave of small, chic
shops which catered to West End wealth. Jewelers,
glovers, shoemakers, and furriers lined the pristine corridor, all of them offering the most luxurious goods
money could buy. London's lesser citizenry were dis-
couraged—occasionally even bodily removed—by a
staff of stern, uniformed beadles whose job it was to ensure that the gentry and nobility were able to squander
their money in rarefied perfection.

It was not, however, the sort of place Isabel normally
preferred to shop, so it took only a few moments before
Catherine realized why they were there. The quiet corridor provided them with a measure of privacy. Indeed,
they had strolled no farther than the third shop window
when Isabel paused as if to consider a set of garishly
carved candlesticks.

"Oh, Cat, I meant to ask," she began, peering noncha-
lantly through the glass. "Whatever took you in such

haste from Walrafen's last night? I found your message rather vague."

Catherine cut her aunt a sidelong glance. "Did you?" she asked dryly. "I thought it quite clear myself. Mr. de Rohan asked me to a late supper."

Isabel pursed her lips for a moment. "How interesting."

Inwardly, Catherine sighed. Though gentle, her aunt's interrogations were nonetheless formidable. And in truth, Catherine was burning to talk of Max with someone. "Oh, it was an interesting evening," she admitted as they resumed their stroll. "Were you aware, Isabel, that Mr. Peel has asked him to supervise the Sands investigation?"

Isabel's face lit with curiosity. "How do you know?"

Catherine relayed the details of their conversations with Mr. Kemble and Cecilia. When she was finished, Isabel paused to look up at her with wide blue eyes. "Oh, my!" she said a little breathlessly. "What an exciting dinner companion Mr. de Rohan must have been."

"Yes," answered Catherine hesitantly. "But I must say, he occasionally shows a dreadful stubborn streak. In fact, he practically tried to bully me."

Isabel steered her deftly into a haberdashery and paused beside a stack of cashmere mufflers. "Really, Cat!" she chuckled, picking through the stack. "Rutledges aren't *bullied* by anyone. Whatever did you do to plague the poor man?"

"I didn't *do* anything!" Catherine hid her blushes by examining a charcoal scarf, gently rubbing the cashmere between her fingers and considering how magnificent it would look on . . . well, on someone with a dark complexion. "I merely offered to help him just a little." Impulsively, she thrust the scarf at the clerk who stood impassively waiting.

Lips tight, Isabel watched suspiciously as the clerk wrapped Catherine's purchase. "You tried to involve yourself in the investigation, did you not?"

"Not at all." Catherine picked through her reticule, finding nothing but a tattered ten-pound note. "I simply suggested I could ask a few questions whilst I'm out in society," she explained, passing the money to the clerk. "What possible harm could there be in that? But he tried to act quite indifferently toward me."

"Men generally do not argue with women they feel indifferent toward."

Catherine's head jerked up at that. "No, I suppose not," she said softly.

For a long moment, Isabel stared at her niece, as if seeing her for the first time. "It chills my blood to say this, my dear," she finally whispered. "But if you really want Max de Rohan, you'll have to be very discreet."

"Want him?" echoed Catherine as she took the wrapped package from the clerk's hands. "Why on earth would you think that?"

Slowly, Isabel resumed her stroll through the arcade. "Are you thirsty, my dear?" she asked, slipping her arm through Catherine's. "Would you fancy a spot of tea?"

"Isabel," she persisted. "Why on earth would you think that?"

But Isabel merely smiled her quiet, Madonna-like smile. "Perhaps because it is almost noon?"

Catherine drew Isabel to a halt in front of a jeweler's. "We were speaking of Max de Rohan," she hissed as a gaggle of giggling debutantes brushed past. "Pray do not change the subject now that you've tormented me with it."

A handsome man paused to peer through the window opposite the door. Isabel did not notice him. "You seem terribly eager to discuss a man you don't want, Cat," she teased. "Admit it, you're intrigued by de Rohan. Who isn't? And from his expression when he saw you about to dance with Bodley last night, one can only surmise that he is equally fascinated—whether he wishes it or not."

For a long, pensive moment, Catherine dropped her gaze to the package she held in her hand. "He is a good man, Isabel, is he not?"

"Oh, the very best, says Delacourt, who accounts him a great friend," Isabel agreed. "And Walrafen is his political patron. Still, my dear, one must remember that his background is not—"

"Oh, devil take his background!" interjected Catherine. "Really, Isabel! You sound as class-conscious as he. And besides, it isn't as if . . . as if—"

"As if you mean to marry him?" supplied Isabel softly.

Suddenly, the man at the jeweler's window turned toward them and started. Then his expression brightened at once. "My dear Lady Kirton!" he exclaimed, closing the distance between them, then sweeping into a deep bow. "I didn't see you there. And is this your niece? I've not yet met her."

A bit hesitantly, Isabel made the introductions.

"Mr. Vost," said Catherine politely. "A pleasure, I'm sure."

Rupert Vost flashed her a startlingly handsome smile.

"The pleasure is mine, Lady Catherine," he said, gently holding her gaze. "I confess, I vied desperately for an introduction at Walrafen's. Saw you across a crowded room, and all that—"

Sharply, Isabel cleared her throat. "How is your fiancée, Mr. Vost? I must say, your betrothal quite took us all by surprise."

"Amelia is well, I thank you." Vost's smile deepened ruefully. "And yes, I'm well aware I'm not considered fit to lick her boots, ma'am. She does me a great honor. I should do anything to please her, and that is the very reason I wished an introduction to Lady Catherine."

"To me?" interjected Catherine.

Vost turned his electric smile on her. "The matched pearls you wore that night, my lady," he clarified. "Utterly exquisite! Though, to be sure, they barely did your fine complexion justice. Still, I am looking for just such a thing for Amelia. A wedding gift, you see." He waved rather uncertainly toward the jeweler's window. "I confess, I feel a bit of a clodpole, knowing so little about what is fashionable."

"Indeed?" said Isabel archly. "I should have wagered you've bought many a pretty trinket in your day, sirrah."

With laughter shimmering in his eyes, Vost seized her hand and pressed his lips with mock fervency to her glove. "Oh, how you wound me, ma'am!" he said, rising with a wink. "And quite rightly, too. But you see, buying a gift for one's future wife is quite a different matter from buying a trinket for one's—"

"Yes, yes, we understand!" interjected Isabel, no longer able to suppress a smile. "Now, off with you, you rogue."

Vost pulled a pathetic face. "You won't help me shop, Lady Kirton?" he asked in a hurt voice. "And what of you, Lady Catherine? Yes, I see a bit of sympathy in your eyes! Perhaps I may call upon you later for advice?"

Isabel seized Catherine's arm. "You may call upon your fiancée, scamp, and she will advise you," she retorted, waving as they strolled away.

Catherine looked over her shoulder to see Vost wink yet again. "Help me!" he cried, silently mouthing the words, but Isabel gave a hard jerk on her arm, and Catherine turned away.

"Good Lord!" she exclaimed. "Who *was* that man?"

Isabel propelled her deeper into the arcade. "An unrepentant rake," she snorted. "Don't fall for his charm, Cat, no matter what he says. That one must marry for money, which is just what he's doing. No one could fall for that desperate, sour-faced Amelia Lane."

"Isabel, you act as though I'm the veriest babe," grumbled Catherine. "Was I not raised by the worst rake in Christendom? Besides, Vost must wait his turn. Weren't you about to ring a peal over my head regarding Mr. de Rohan?"

"Why, yes, thank you! I was!"

Catherine's glower did not forestall her next words. "Just beware, my dear," Isabel gently resumed. "Even a discreet *affaire* with de Rohan could end any chance of your marrying into a title."

Catherine very nearly dropped her package. "A *title*?" she answered incredulously. "Good God, what need have I of a title? I begin to doubt I even want another husband."

"Very well." Isabel nodded succinctly. "If your heart is set, just have a care how you go about it. De Rohan doesn't strike me as the sort who gives his heart. And if you would but give me a chance, I might finish my comment on his background by saying that I mean only to point out how little we know of him. He isn't English. Not precisely. And he was raised abroad, so he might be a Papist. Or celibate. Or, God forbid, married. Had you considered any of this?"

Catherine heard only one word. *"Married?"* Her eyes widened in horror. "But he isn't! He told me so."

"Did he?" Isabel flashed her sly, inward smile again. "Still, the man is a mystery, dear. And his former career notwithstanding, he seems terribly sophisticated—"

"Ah—! And I've still got straw sticking to my shoes, is that it?" asked Catherine, chagrined. "Perhaps I do feel a little out of my depth with him, but oh, Isabel! I don't know what I want, but I certainly do find him interesting." Wordlessly, she pressed the carefully wrapped scarf to her chest.

Isabel slowed to a halt near a wrought-iron bench at the rear of the arcade. "Oh, lud!" she sighed, urging Catherine down beside her. "I see he's to be the one, then. And I'll confess to a little envy. But beware your heart with that man, my dear."

Catherine paused to consider her aunt's gentle admonition. Was Maximilian de Rohan the sort of man who broke women's hearts? Probably. Yet Catherine was no longer sure she cared. Still, how could she explain such recklessness to Isabel? How did one describe that awful emptiness which brought with it an almost desperate need to *feel* something—anything—again? And why did this man, with his grim, too-serious face and dark, avenging angel's eyes, make her feel life and lust and passion so intensely? Still, no one—not even a dark-eyed angel—could keep the ghosts at bay indefinitely. Catherine had already learned that they could be neither outrun nor ignored. They had to be *overcome*. "Perhaps I buried my heart with Will," answered Catherine quietly.

"Did you?" Isabel shot her an odd look.

Doubt was plain in her tone. And for the first time, Catherine realized that she was utterly certain she had not. Despite her sense of loss, her heart was whole, willing to be freely given, and the knowledge shook her. But, instead of admitting it, she settled onto the bench, straightening her spine and pushing back her shoulders. "I'll be fine, Isabel," she said calmly. "My heart can handle Max de Rohan."

"Very well," said Isabel briskly. "But a certain amount of discretion is required by society in an *affaire d'amour*. One mustn't be blatant or go about looking besotted. And, to be sure, one must be careful of one's servants."

"Dear me!" replied Catherine dryly. "There are ever so many rules of etiquette here in town."

"Indeed." Isabel's eyes twinkled. "And remember that I spoke of taking matters into your own hands?"

Feeling heat flood her face, Catherine cut her eyes away. "Yes, but how? He's very stubborn and prideful."

"Well," said Isabel briskly. "A Rutledge would know, I daresay."

"*Isabel—!*"

Her aunt patted her lightly on the knee. "Oh, just come along, Cat," she said, pulling her companion to her feet. "All will be well. But first, we must call upon Cecilia. She will know whatever there is to know about de Rohan. And did you say she means to call upon him Saturday?"

Catherine nodded and jerked into motion. "Yes, to give him a box of Julia's things."

"Ah, well!" said Isabel over her shoulder. "That will do nicely!"

"Will it? For what?"

But Isabel's round, tidy figure was already winding swiftly through the crowd ahead. Catherine picked up her pace and followed the bobbing swath of blue and yellow feathers atop her aunt's bonnet, wondering as she did so just what she had gotten herself into.

The Strand was a wide, shop-lined street which led from the posh, polished West End into the slightly disreputable Fleet Street and thence into the darker environs of the east. The church of St. Mary-le-Strand sat smack in the middle of—rather fittingly—the upper end, whilst at the bottom lay the dubious gateway of Charing Cross. Thus positioned by fate, the thoroughfare was usually filled to overflowing by all manner of London's citizens, and nowhere was this confluence more keenly felt than at the intersection where St. Martin's Lane disgorged its flow of traffic from Covent Garden and Mayfair.

Dilettantes and dandies, stonemasons and statesmen, demireps and duchesses—all of them regularly turned the corner of St. Martin's into the Strand. A shrewd fellow would have thought it the perfect location for a unique sort of business. And so it was but a few yards beyond that de Rohan halted, looking down at the small brass plaque on the door which bore a familiar but peculiar inscription:

Mr. George Jacob Kemble
Purveyor of Elegant Oddities and Fine Folderol

With his usual skeptical grunt, de Rohan lifted the latch and entered, Sisk hard on his heels. Eversole, the junior constable, paused to stand guard outside.

The bell jingled merrily as Sisk shut the door. Behind one of the glass counter cases, a willowy, well-dressed young man lifted his eyes just long enough to give them a bored, brooding look. Then he returned to his task of polishing an ornate silver lamp—a curiosity which looked as though it might have leapt still smoking from Queen Scheherazade's own hands.

As always, de Rohan's gaze was drawn through the room. Perhaps it had been an injustice to liken Kemble to a cheap carnival magician when, in truth, he seemed to have purchased the entire carnival and stuffed it into his shop. Yet there was nothing cheap about any of it. Countertops were littered with bric-a-brac of opal, jade, and Venetian glass. Flemish tapestries and Turkey carpets warmed the walls. An Indian punkah hung from the ceiling, and, beneath it, a bizarre collection of jewel-crusted kaleidoscopes covered a small marble table. Moroccan silver, Chinese porcelain, and antique jewelry lined the showcases, all of it flawlessly arranged.

De Rohan paused to study a glistening suit of medieval armor just as Kemble emerged from the bowels of the shop, swishing around a glass display case. "Isn't he just lovely?" Kem simpered, sliding one hand caressingly down the silvery arm. "Danish, fourteenth century. And notice the impressive codpiece. We like to call him *Thor.*"

De Rohan couldn't contain his laughter. "And what the devil do you mean to do with him?"

Kemble smiled sardonically. "Oh, just sell him to a rich cit," he said with a little toss of his hand. "They're always keen to create the illusion of ancestry." Suddenly, his gaze lit on the jewel chest Sisk carried snugly under his arm, and his expression shifted from cynicism to anticipation. "Oh, my God!" he said breathlessly. "You've brought them already?"

"Aye, well, we can't very well leave 'em lying about Queen Square, can we?" muttered Sisk.

De Rohan had sent word of their secret mission, and clearly, Kemble was excited. "I'm ready," he whispered. "Come into my office."

Ignoring Sisk, Kemble motioned them toward a door which clearly gave onto the rear of the shop. De Rohan pushed through the heavy curtains and into a well-lit room. High, spotlessly clean windows opened onto the alley, their drapes drawn wide to the afternoon light. On a worktable beneath the windows sat two lamps, and, beside them, an assortment of silvery tools lay in a neat row atop a long, padded cushion.

After hitching himself onto a tall stool, Kem turned up the wicks of both lamps, then motioned for Sisk to set down the chest. The constable did so, and, without further comment, Kem unrolled a length of padded velvet and unceremoniously dumped the box. Julia Markham-

Sands's priceless collection of jewelry spilled out in a glimmering, slithering rainbow of hues.

"Ooh, lovely!" Kem began to poke through the pile with quick, clever fingers.

De Rohan watched, amazed, as he sorted the jewels into three heaps, flinging pendants and hatpins with equal abandon, pausing now and again to mutter to himself. Occasionally, he took up one of his little tools to scratch, or to measure, or even to tap upon the stones or their mountings. Once or twice, he lifted the globe of his lamp; then, using a pair of heavy tweezers, he would pass a brooch or an ear bob back and forth through the flame.

Finally, he selected a jeweler's loupe from the padded cushion, set it carefully to his eye, and began to peer at the pieces in the nearest heap, one after the other. When he had finished, he spun about on the stool and looked up at de Rohan with a smug smile.

"Well—?" growled de Rohan.

Kem's smile widened. "Pinchbeck, old boy!" he gleefully announced. "Every bloody one of them."

Sisk exploded first. *"Pinchbeck!"* he shouted. "Why, those 'er the Countess of Sands's jewels, man! They can't be fake!"

Kem shrugged sympathetically. "They're as near as makes no difference, constable," he clucked. "The whole collection isn't worth the price of this topaz in my cravat."

De Rohan merely stared. It wasn't as if Kemble's announcement was wholly unexpected. He'd known something was wrong. Very wrong. And this sort of thing happened all the time. Still, he could not help but seize the largest brooch—a large, oval ruby edged with pearls—and rub his finger over it. "Imitations, then?"

Kemble sniffed disdainfully. "Not even good ones."

"What the deuce?" Sisk turned to stare at de Rohan.

Kemble leaned forward with one of his sharp little tools and tapped upon a tiny scrape he'd made in the metal backing of the ruby brooch. "See here—that's soft brass underneath. Good pinchbeck should be an alloy of copper and zinc. And the stone!" He cast his gaze heavenward. "Pure paste!"

Sisk scrubbed at his jaw with a large, callused hand. "Don't like this above half."

"Well, there are bits and pieces which are real," Kemble admitted, poking scornfully at an opal hatpin and a slender bracelet made of pearls linked with jade. "But just those bits which weren't worth copying."

"But Lord Sands told me that most of this jewelry was heirloom," interjected de Rohan. "And the remainder he'd given her as gifts."

Kem pursed his lips for a moment. "Then she had it copied to throw Lord Sands off," he insisted, shaking his head. "It is not uncommon. A lady of the *ton* finds she cannot pay her debts and resorts to pawning or selling her jewels."

"Oh, de Rohan's seen that trick before," muttered Sisk a little snidely. "Still, I can't credit these ain't real."

Kemble's eyes flashed with anger. "Well, by all means, constable, haul this pile of rubbish down to one of your fancy St. James jewelers if you question my veracity," he snapped. "But I'm an expert."

"Yeah?" demanded Sisk. "Says 'oo?"

In retaliation, Kemble cut a scathing look at the constable's wardrobe. "Mr. Sisk," he said haughtily, his gaze settling on his waistcoat. "Did anyone bother to tell you that mustard is out?"

Sisk drew back a pace. "But I can't eat me bacon without it," he answered, rubbing his fingers over the rumpled fabric. "And it's just a dollop or two, so what's the 'arm?"

Kemble shot him a tight smile. "The color, you imbecile!" he exclaimed. "Yellows and browns are *passé* this year. That atrocious police uniform would better suit you."

Sisk shook a beefy fist in Kem's face. "I ain't on duty, so just sod off, Mr. Priss!"

"Stop squabbling, both of you!" ordered de Rohan gruffly. "And there'll be no jewelers. Someone made every piece of this rubbish, and until I know who, we say nothing."

Kemble dropped his argument at once, his gaze turning suddenly inward. "Now that I think on it, jewelers do have their own special techniques," he said, lifting one slender finger. "A method of soldering or mounting that is not quite like anyone else's. Sometimes even a tiny hallmark."

"What are you suggesting?"

Kemble smiled tightly. "Why not let me keep one of the antique pieces—say, that large Tudor collar—and I'll pretend I'm too witless to know it's fake." Here, he shot Sisk another dirty look. "Then I'll trot it about to some of the local boys for appraisal. Someone will recognize the work, and no one will dare to ask too many questions, since—"

"They'll fear it's been pawned or stolen," finished

de Rohan wearily. "Thanks, Kem. Just be careful. Sisk, I guess we'd best take this pile of paste back to Lord Sands and give him the bad news. Whilst we're there, perhaps we should ask after the servants again."

"Aye, p'raps," grumbled the constable, still eyeing Kem nastily. "But put that fancy French piece on the top o' yer list."

Already refilling the jewel chest, de Rohan stopped and spun about. "Who, the lady's maid?"

Sisk sneered. "Genevieve, she calls herself. A knowing little trick, that one."

"Now, there's a phrase which jogs one's memory!" interjected Kemble, crossing the room to a massive desk filled with pigeonholes. Thrusting his fingers inside one, he extracted a sheaf of foolscap and passed it to de Rohan. "Was there ever a more knowing trick than dear old Julia? You'll want to add these well-serviced gentlemen to her list of lovers."

Quickly, de Rohan scanned the paper with Sisk and Kemble staring over his shoulder. "Anyone look familiar?" Kem asked almost gleefully.

There were only three names. A wealthy American banker, a minor French count, and . . . Good God! *Bentham Rutledge?* The name was all too familiar to de Rohan. Rutledge was a rake and a gamester of the worst sort, and this was not the first time his name had turned up in a criminal investigation.

De Rohan must have sucked in his breath sharply. "Turns up like a bad penny, doesn't he?" remarked Kemble, tapping a well-manicured fingertip on Rutledge's name.

"Lady Sands was sleeping with *him?*" De Rohan

could not hide his shock. "Why, he hardly seems polished enough—not to mention rich enough."

Kem hesitated ever so slightly. "Well, just a quick tumble or two, so far as I can discover," he confessed. "But remember, some women find rough edges appealing. After all, even *you* managed to get a dinner date this week."

Spewing with sudden laughter, Sisk bent nearly double. De Rohan felt his face flame. "Keep your bloody opinions to yourself, Kemble."

Kemble just smiled and pinched de Rohan on the arm. "Oh, don't get your drawers in a knot!" he responded. "Unlike Rutledge, you're fine enough in your ways, dear boy. It's just your personality that's rough-edged. And where did you find that farm-fresh lovely, anyway? My God, I'd kill for skin like that!"

"None of your business, Kem." Swiftly, de Rohan urged Sisk back through the velvet curtains and into the shop.

Kemble followed them through the shop and jerked open the door. "Well, there's a bit of intrigue! I know *everyone* in town—and I'd never seen *her* in my life." Kemble handed the jewel chest over to Sisk with a calculated flourish, then gave it a little pat. "Now, off you go, boys! Time to break the bad news to old Harry."

Chapter Ten

Take care that conversation
does not lead you into any impropriety.

—LORD CHESTERFIELD, 1776,
The Fine Gentleman's Etiquette

After a rather dismal half-hour spent explaining to Lord Sands the unfortunate truth about his family jewels, de Rohan sent Sisk back to Queen Square with the jewel chest, which, technically speaking, had just become police evidence. It was agreed that he and Sisk would resume work later in the day. Hastily, de Rohan wolfed down a pork pie he'd snagged from a vendor in Green Park, then made his way toward the Chelsea Road. He arrived to discover that Mrs. Frier had let Nate into his flat, and set the boy to work. With a forced smile, de Rohan ruffled Nate's hair and exchanged a few pleasantries.

When de Rohan had first gone in search of a suite of rooms near Whitehall, Mrs. Frier had looked upon Lucifer rather suspiciously, and after a scant two weeks in residence, the mastiff had fallen into outright disfavor. First, there'd been a "digestive indiscretion" deposited in the good lady's rose garden. Then she'd caught sight of the "nose smears" on the windows. De Rohan had simply found himself a couple of buckets, and Nate, the erstwhile pickpocket, had found himself gainfully employed. Between the myriad errands the lad now performed within de Rohan's two households, Nate could now feed his mother and six siblings.

De Rohan let his gaze drift over the boy's tattered clothes. *Dannazione!* How, in a land of rampant plenty, could children be left to starve? Had the Revolution taught the English nothing? But he knew too well how little one man could do, and so he turned his mind to the wrong he had some hope of avenging, settling at his desk to jot down all that he'd learned from Kemble. He'd barely set pen to paper, however, when Nate's chirpy voice cut into his thoughts.

"Yer looks fair fagged t'day, gov," said the boy as he scrubbed the parlor window.

De Rohan looked up from his notes. "A bit, yes."

Nate lifted one pale brow, all innocence and solicitude. "Late night, was it?"

"Umm," agreed de Rohan vaguely.

Suddenly, he caught Nate glancing toward the small table where de Rohan washed and dried his meager dishes. "Must a' had a bit o' company last night, eh?" the boy persisted, his wet rag squealing across the glass. "See you got a couple o' them fancy wine goblets laid out to dry."

"Do I indeed?" An ugly suspicion began to dawn.

"I'm thinkin' it must a' been that Lucy Leonard," continued the boy conversationally, his arm working in broad, sweeping circles. "A right proper armful, she is. Clean, too, and got all 'er teeth."

With a muttered oath, de Rohan stretched out one hand, snapping his fingers impatiently. "Get down, Nate," he growled. "Give it here."

"Wha—?" demanded the urchin, holding up his hands. "I ain't pinched nuffink."

With utter confidence, de Rohan snapped his fingers again. "Nonna Sofia's money," he warned. *"La bustarella! Subito!* And don't bite the hand that feeds you."

For a moment, Nate looked as if he wasn't at all sure which hand that might be. Nonna Sofia, de Rohan guessed, had been sharing her leftovers with more than just Lucifer. Finally, with a huff of resignation, Nate tossed down his rag and crammed his hand into his pocket, but his surrender was forestalled by Mrs. Frier's knock. De Rohan opened the door to find his landlady, her nose tilted haughtily upward. Constable Sisk stood at her elbow, looking grubbier than before, if such a thing were possible.

"I brought the files," the policeman grumbled.

Soon, de Rohan had set the kettle on and cleared the glassware from the small table. Together, he and Sisk hefted it nearer the windows. Sheepishly, Nate took up his wash bucket and slunk out into the garden to wipe the outside glass, and for the next hour de Rohan poured over Sisk's records. Methodically, he compared his notes and sketches to Sisk's, finding no discrepancies. Then he settled down to skim over the interviews again. There was nothing new or meaningful that he could see.

De Rohan gave a weary sigh and tossed down his pencil. "Blister it!" he whispered, frustrated. "Nothing!"

Sisk settled back in his chair, hooking his thumbs in the bearer of his trousers. "P'raps we'd best go over the suspects again. You went to that Lord Walrafen's to-do on Friday night, didn't you?"

De Rohan ran his finger up their list of names, stopping at the top three. "I spoke briefly to these gentlemen," he explained, shaking his head. "But I daresay we've little prospect amongst them. Reeves in particular. He claims to have been drunk at the Oriental Club."

"So the porter says," Sisk grumbled. "Cast up his accounts on the card-room carpet."

With a grunt of disgust, de Rohan marked off the name. "I heard."

"And cross off Sir Everard Grant whilst you're about it," continued Sisk. "He spent the whole week at a fancy house party in Maidstone. Lots o' witnesses there."

De Rohan shoved himself away from the table with another oath. "Then why in God's name did he deny even knowing Lady Sands?"

"Did 'e?" Sisk seemed unsurprised.

"Yes," hissed de Rohan. "And now, you're telling me he had an alibi and never mentioned it?"

For a long moment, the constable was oddly silent. "The fancy don't care to bow to the police, de Rohan," he finally answered. "You knows that as well as anyone. And you still got the hard, cold eyes of a Runner."

When de Rohan opened his mouth to protest, Sisk lifted one hand to forestall him. "Oh, aye, you might be a fine Westminster beak now. But as far as the nobs 're concerned, most of 'em still think you stink of Bow Street."

"Thank you, Sisk, for your social commentary," grumbled de Rohan, pressing the heels of his hand into his eyes.

Sisk shrugged ambivalently. "No insult meant. You were a bloody fine constable and a better Runner, for all that you'd no business being either. And w' them languages you speak—why, it's no wonder the River Police come beggin' for you. Even after that all trouble wi—"

De Rohan cut him off with an icy glare.

"Aye, well, never mind that. I'm just telling how things are. You're not like them. Hell, you're not like *me*. So there it is, y'see?"

He did see. Sisk, devil take him, was right, and de Rohan had always known it. But only now had he begun to give a damn. To consider what he'd given up. Good God. He did not wish to think of that just now. "Back to Lady Sands," he muttered, shoving away a stack of files. "Who's next on our list?"

"Bodley." The constable spat out the name like sour milk. "Says he was home alone, no witnesses. Frankly, I'd wager he was down at Covent Garden trying to diddle the little orange girls."

De Rohan heaved a weary sigh. "Jesus, Sisk, you're disgusting."

Sisk yawned, then gave a little stretch. "Ah, well, it's a disgusting world, de Rohan," he said, scratching himself inappropriately. "Now, what of our pretty Mr. Vost? Anything there?"

De Rohan shook his head a little morosely. "I'm persuaded he's done for, too. A wealthy widow showed up in my office yesterday to explain that Vost had been warming her bed that night. *All* night. She was very clear on that point."

"Hmph," said the constable. "What did Vost say?"

It was de Rohan's turn to shrug. "Initially, he was

vague. Protecting her reputation, of course. He may be a Queer Street rogue, but there must be a bit of the gentleman in him."

Even Sisk looked disappointed now. "Aw, frig it," he said, drawing a thick line over Rupert Vost's name. "That leaves us w' Kemble's three. They've already sent Eversole and one o' the magistrates to Calais to try 'n run that Frenchie count to ground."

De Rohan was impressed. "So swiftly?"

Sisk smiled, showing all eight of his yellow teeth. "Yeah, but I s'pect it'll come to naught, for he's known in town, and got no motive as I can see. And then we're down to . . ." He paused to squint mightily at his notebook. "Aye, just that scoundrel Rutledge, and Fordham, the banker from Philadelphia. Can't find neither of 'em yet, but if Sands didn't do the deed, then I'll put two quid on Rutledge. Pure trouble, that 'un."

"What do you mean?"

Sisk snapped shut his notebook. "Bad blood, I hear, on his sire's side, though the old man's long dead. But add that to the latest rumor which says he owes Tommy O'Halleran's gaming hell two thousand pounds, and I'm thinking it was theft, plain and proper."

Two thousand pounds? De Rohan heaved a sigh. "You'd best go look about Hampstead," he muttered. "Rutledge sometimes holes up there."

But he still couldn't imagine the killer was Sands. Nor had he wished it to be Rutledge. The young man had gotten himself horribly entangled in the Nazareth Society murders, but based on what little de Rohan had seen, he hadn't the look of a thief. Still, Rutledge was a wastrel who kept very low company.

Worse, de Rohan was uncomfortably close to with-holding evidence, for he'd said nothing to Sisk of Dr. Greaves's suspicions about an abortion. But the truth wouldn't bode well for Sands. If Sands had guessed Julia was pregnant . . . well, no nobleman wanted another man's child as his heir. But then there was Rutledge, an-other grim prospect. He'd lost a child once, de Rohan re-called. Initially, and irrationally, Rutledge had blamed the child's mother. He'd been insane with anger and des-peration. If he lost another babe by the hand of its mother . . . *Dio,* the thought was appalling. He looked pointedly at the constable. "Do you still think it was Sands?"

Sisk was just beginning to shake his head when Mrs. Frier knocked again, much more impatiently. With a deep sense of misgiving, de Rohan opened the door. This time, the good woman's nose wasn't just turned up; a steady rain could have drowned her. Max looked past her shoulder and started praying for a monsoon.

"A lady has called," she coldly announced. "On *police* business!" The last was pronounced with the same chilly edge she had hitherto reserved for Lucifer's rose garden *faux pas.*

In the shadows of the corridor, a tall woman threw back the hood of her red carriage cloak. "Good after-noon, Mr. de Rohan," said Lady Catherine, her voice un-usually soft and throaty. "I've come to deliver the materials her ladyship promised last night." She held up a remarkably large rosewood lap desk and gave it a little twitch.

He stared at Catherine's burden, and memory stirred. Lady Sands's personal effects! Cecilia had said she'd bring them. So why was Catherine here? "Where is Lady Delacourt?" he demanded.

Catherine feigned innocence. "I believe the babe still had a touch of colic, and his lordship was called to a special session in the House."

"Then how kind of you to help out, ma'am," he said, reaching out his hand to take the lap desk by its handle.

But Catherine did not surrender so easily. "There are also some things Cecilia bade me discuss with you, Mr. de Rohan," she interjected. "In private."

Mrs. Frier began to tap her toe disapprovingly.

Max was astonished. *Catherine meant to come in?* Mrs. Frier would ruin her good name. Certainly, he could not introduce her to a boor like Sisk. And it was beyond foolishness to let Nate get a glimpse of her. Still, he was almost as glad to see her as he was angry with her for being so foolish as to come. But why should he turn her away? He was tasked with stopping crime and corruption, not feminine folly. If Catherine had no better sense than to call upon a man in his private lodgings, on her head be it.

She was looking at him impatiently. "I suppose you mean to come in?" he responded.

With a faintly apologetic nod, Catherine swished her skirts around Mrs. Frier, who thumped shut the door at once. Sisk, of course, was already on his feet, grinning like a river rat as he ineffectually smoothed the wrinkles from his yellow waistcoat. In the garden beyond, Nate had plastered half his face to the window glass in a wet, pink smear of flesh so that he might better peer inside. It only wanted a barking seal, a trick pony, and a burst of applause to complete the horrible sensation that de Rohan was standing naked in the center of Astley's Amphitheater.

Catherine seized control, thrusting out her empty hand at the grinning policeman. "Catherine Wodeway," she murmured, eschewing her title. "I'm just running an errand for a friend."

The policeman's smile grew to his ears. "Charmed, mum," he answered, eyeing her assessingly. "I'm P. C. Sisk, Westminster Police Court, and I'm just running—"

"Along," interjected Max, violently sweeping up the files and thrusting them at Sisk. "As in leaving. Now. He's expected back at Queen Square."

"True! Very true!" agreed Sisk, waving back at Catherine as Max propelled him inexorably toward the door. "A pleasure, Mrs. Wodeway! A pleasure!" Shooting Max one last speculative grin, Sisk winked and slipped away, his arms wrapped awkwardly about the bundle of papers.

Max turned to Catherine, the skin drawn tight around his mouth. "Sit down," he barked, striding across the room to deal with Nate.

Catherine tried not to laugh at Max's obvious irritation. Clearly, he did not normally entertain ladies in his lodgings. On that rather intriguing thought, she watched as he stalked across the room to yank open the french door. "Nathaniel Corcoran!" he roared at the boy in the window. "Come down this instant!"

At once, the lad scrambled down from his perch, dropping his wet rag into the bucket at Max's feet and slopping soapy water over his boots. Max did not seem to care. Instead, he jerked a surprisingly thick roll of banknotes from his coat pocket and ripped one off.

"*La bustarella,* blister it!" he growled, thrusting it at the wide-eyed boy. "And if so much as a whisper of this passes from your lips to you-know-who's ear, I'll be serving your gizzard as Lucifer's luncheon."

The lad rocked back on his heels and studied Max through slitted eyes. "I get to keep the *signora*'s money, too?" he challenged, stuffing the note into his trousers.

"You'll put it in Father O'Flynn's alms-box!" grumbled Max. "Now, out over the garden wall! And don't let Mrs. Frier see you leave." But just as the boy went slithering over the stone enclosure, Max's parlor door cracked again, and Sisk poked his head back in. Max whipped around to glare at him.

"The lady's maid!" Sisk demanded, thrusting out his hand and snapping his fingers impatiently.

"*What—?*" roared Max.

"Genevieve Durrett. You left 'er statement out." Impatiently, Sisk motioned toward the desk. "Give it 'ere. I'm ter question the chit again tomorrow."

With short, impatient motions, Max rifled through a pile of papers on his table and extracted something. Soon the flurry of activity was over. Nate was gone, Sisk had finally vanished, and Max had bolted all the doors behind them. A grim silence fell across the room.

"Perhaps," Catherine mordantly suggested, "you might wish to draw the draperies as well?"

Max rounded on her at that. "Lady Catherine," he harshly began. "What on earth do you think you're doing here?"

Catherine tried to look confident. "Nothing as exciting as you seem to think, I'm afraid," she answered, sliding out of her carriage cloak. "Dare I hope you're at least a little disappointed?"

She passed her cloak to Max, and in a true testament

to his loss of composure, he did not notice. Instead, he merely stared. "This is a bachelor's household," he reminded her. "And you are a lady. An *unmarried* lady. For the nonce, my landlady will assume the boy is here, but you need to go."

His voice was harsh, but his eyes, she saw, were already softening at the corners. Relieved, Catherine simply tossed her cloak over a blanket-covered settle. "It's all right, Max, really," she said, discreetly waving away the ensuing cloud of dust and dog hair. "I've two of Delacourt's brawniest footmen outside. I'm sure they'll leap to my aid should you decide to make some inappropriate advance upon my delicate, ladylike personage."

Max's black brows snapped together over his hawkish nose. "That isn't funny, Lady Catherine."

"Just Catherine, please." She blinked her eyes innocently. "And is there any chance, do you think?"

"Any chance?"

She stepped closer, held his gaze. "That you might make an inappropriate advance?"

Max cut her a dark, sidelong glance and stepped away, dragging one hand roughly through his hair, which was black as night and far too long. He no longer looked irritated. He looked wary. "Don't flirt with me, Catherine," he said quietly.

He turned his back on her, leaving Catherine to chew nervously at her lip. Perhaps a more neutral topic was in order. "You'll find that box most interesting," she remarked as he picked up Lady Sands's traveling desk. "Cecilia and I picked through it over tea. It seems Julia kept most of her letters and calendars."

With a thud, Max laid the wooden box on his table,

set his hands wide to either side of it, and stared down at it for a long moment. Drawing in a deep breath, Catherine looked about at her surroundings. The room in which she stood was a small parlor cum dining room, and to call it spartan would have been a kindness. The furniture was almost shabby, the planked oak floors devoid of carpets. But a low fire burned in the hearth, and the room smelled pleasantly of warm wool and strong coffee.

As to Max himself, gone was the suit of evening clothes which had made him look . . . well, not like a staid English gentleman but something rather more intriguing. Today, he wore what she now recognized as his work clothes: ordinary charcoal trousers and plain white linen with a severe black stock, and all of it topped off with a dark superfine coat which definitely hadn't seen the inside of a Savile Row tailor's shop. Yes, today, he could have been anyone, could have melted effectively into any middle-class crowd of clerks or solicitors. Except for those obsidian, all-seeing eyes. And that slight stoop in his broad shoulders, as if he'd spent too many years attempting to blend in with men of shorter stature and lesser character.

Suddenly, Catherine wanted to go to him, had to resist the urge to wrap her arms about his narrow waist and press her cheek to that broad, muscular back. Instead, she joined him at the table, bending forward to insert the key into the lock. "Here," she said a little breathlessly, snapping it open and throwing back the lid. "Let me show you what's inside."

At once, his hand came out to stay hers, his long, elegant fingers catching her own, wrapping around them, holding them perfectly still. In the electric silence, she could feel the pulse in his thumb beating against her palm, steady and strong. Then, slowly, his head swiveled around, his dark, piercing eyes commanding hers, forcing her to look into them. Suddenly, Catherine was deeply grateful she was not a criminal under his scrutiny.

"Why the devil did you come here?" he demanded harshly.

She faltered. "I—I just need to see you," she admitted. "Is there anything so terrible in that?"

De Rohan forced himself to exhale. Carefully, he watched Catherine's eyes for any evidence of duplicity, the slightest hint of hesitation. But there was no mistaking the anguish in her voice, the vulnerability in her words.

I need. Not *I want.* Not *you must.*

But those were the demands he'd half expected to hear, weren't they? A little roughly, he took her chin in his hand and drew her face back to his. Deep brown pools of innocence looked back, causing his breath to catch. *Dio mio,* he thought, forcing himself to breathe. Surely, no woman could feign such wide, honest eyes? Such a tender, trembling mouth? Or was he just blinding himself to the truth again?

In the fading afternoon light, he laughed, the sound soft and bitter in his ears. He had been taken in before by wide eyes and trembling lips. But this time, he was rapidly ceasing to care. She wanted him. There was no other reason for her to have come here. Suddenly, the thought of having Catherine in his bed seemed a worthy risk. What did it matter if, in the end, he was merely servicing her? Being used by her? But would Catherine treat anyone so shabbily? He was beginning to think not. Hope not.

He wanted Catherine. So badly. And in the end, lust edged out cold logic. Still holding her chin, de Rohan simply bent his head and kissed her. She came against him on a whispery sigh, the tension melting from her body.

"Max." Sweetly, almost uncertainly, she kissed him back with lips like silk, wrapping herself around him and rising onto her toes. Catherine was not a small woman, and yet she felt so delicate in his embrace. He was too tall. Too rough and too impatient. He stooped lower, and she opened her mouth beneath his, inviting, coaxing, slowly firing his blood like a fine Bordeaux. He hesitated, his lips lingering on hers. In response, she slid one warm hand around his waist, beneath his waistcoat, and reality spun away.

"God, Catherine." His plea was but a whisper as his mouth slid down her face, down her throat. She answered him, but he could not absorb the words. He drew her warm, sweet scent into his lungs like a drowning man.

"Max," she pleaded. "Look at me. Kiss me."

Instead, he let his hands run up the taut muscles of her back and dropped his forehead to her shoulder. "We should stop, Catherine," he rasped against the warm, white curve of her neck. "I would not hurt you for all the world."

Her lips brushed gently along the curve of his ear. "It might be worth it."

He lifted his head, his eyes drawn to her face. The late-day sun streamed across the garden wall through the newly polished windows, outlining her hair with a halo of red-gold light. She looked like an earthbound angel with her winsome mouth and fine, full breasts.

"The afternoon light is so beautiful," she said softly, as if reading his mind. "I would like to . . . to stay with you for a while."

De Rohan knew what she meant, and he hadn't the strength to send her away. "Do you want me to make love to you, Catherine?" he rasped. "Is that what you want?"

She licked her lips, a quick, nervous motion, then nodded.

"God, Catherine!" he muttered. "What a mistake that would be." But he kissed her again, this time sliding his hands around to cup her face. In response, Catherine gave a soft moan of pleasure. Max drove his fingers into the hair at her temples. A hairpin went skittering across the floor, unnoticed. He could feel the rapid pulse beating faster and faster beneath her skin. Could feel his own, throbbing in his groin. She delved into his mouth with her tongue, and he shuddered as if he'd been struck by lightning. She was soft, womanly soft, against his male hardness. And suddenly, mistakes didn't matter.

He drew her higher, closer, sliding his tongue inside her mouth. With a little moan of delight, she sucked in his tongue, curling her own about his and sliding sinuously back and forth. The kiss rolled through him, rocked him deep in his belly. Sent more blood rushing hotly into his loins. She moaned again, instinctively pressing her breasts and belly against him. He could have her. So easily. And he wished to God he knew why she wanted him. Remembering his torturous dawn fantasies, Max fought the urge to beg her to touch him. Instead, he tightened his hands on her waist and lifted her hard against the heat of his erection, easing himself up and down, deliberately tormenting her. He wanted her to *know*. Wanted to feel her reaction.

It took only an instant. Catherine let her breath out raggedly. "Oh, Max," she rasped, her head falling back, her breasts nearly exposed. "Max, please!"

He cut her off with a groan, covering her mouth with his and praying he didn't disgrace himself before he got his clothes off. But Catherine's hands went urgently to his waist, and she tore her lips from his. "Oh, please, Max," she panted, beginning to rip his shirttails free. "Make that big mistake with me. Take me to bed."

Max let his mouth slide down her throat, nipping gently at the tender flesh. "Ah, Catherine," he rasped, losing himself in the flood of sensation. *"Sei molto bella. So very beautiful. I will make it perfect. Perfect for you."*

Her hands tore free his shirt, found the bare skin of his back. His flesh rippled in delight, and, unable to resist, Max quite literally swept her off her feet. He carried her down the narrow passageway and kicked open his bedroom door before he could come to his senses. The room was almost monastic, his bed a jumbled mass of last night's knotted sheets, but she didn't seem to notice. He laid Catherine on the mattress, hurled his coat and waistcoat onto the floor, then followed her down, kicking off his shoes as he went.

They touched one another with a heated desperation. Her fingers went to the buttons of his trousers. She kissed him again, her tongue as hot and demanding as her hands. His rough hands shoved at her skirts, caught in the fine lawn of her shift, tore at the silk of her drawers. Dimly, he heard fabric rip. He was behaving desperately, brutishly, he knew. And yet he could not seem to stop himself. His fingers cupped her flesh, caressed the heat and dampness, slid inside. She reached out to touch him. Greedily, Max seized her hand and carried it to his erection, throbbing for release.

Catherine swallowed hard, and then it happened. She went rigid beneath him. "Max, wait," she blurted. "Just . . . wait. Please."

Dio mio, he knew that tone. At once, he stopped, ruthlessly tearing his weight away from her body. But Catherine drew him back, pulling him ever more tightly into her embrace. "No." She shook her head, scrubbing her hair against his pillow. "Not *stop.* Just—"

"What?" he demanded, breathing hard against the bare skin of her throat. "Good God, what do you want of me, Catherine?"

He heard her exhale, low and soft. "I just want you to understand, Max," she said in a small voice. "I don't usually do this. I'm not . . . experienced."

He lifted his head to see that she was blushing up to the roots of her hair. Sweet heaven, what was she trying to say? Lust had clouded his thoughts. Perhaps sensing his confusion, she widened her eyes and cupped his face between her warm hands. "I mean, I was married, Max. Of course, I've done it. But just not . . . like this. So casually. I thought that might matter."

So casually. The words—her meaning—seeped slowly into his brain. And she was right. It bloody well did matter. It mattered more than he wished. Ruthlessly banking his desire, Max levered himself up on one elbow and let his gaze roam over her face, struggling unflinchingly to see this strange, new creature for what she was. But the only thing that came clear to him was what she was *not*. Certainly, she was not what he was used to. She was not just another casual lover. And she was not just another whore with a title dangling from her name.

Was that what he had thought? Despite all evidence to the contrary, had he still imagined her to be like so many other women he'd known? Like Lucy? Or worse, *like Penelope?* Was that why he was willing to bed her so swiftly? And so roughly? With no soft words of wooing, or even seduction, between them? Yet Catherine had been willing. Still was, it seemed. She stared up at him in all innocence, her hair in utter disarray, the neckline of her carriage dress pulled wantonly down, exposing two inches of womanly cleavage to his eyes.

He knew what he ought to do. He ought to stop. But he was no gentleman. Whether she meant to or not, Catherine had come here asking for it. Max meant to oblige. "I will make sure, *cara mia,*" he whispered, easing one finger between the warmth of her breasts, "that you never regret this." And with that, he allowed himself the luxury of tugging firmly but gently downward on her bodice. Catherine moaned and arched toward him as the lace ruching dragged across her nipples, baring the hard, perfect tips.

For a moment, she watched him as he stroked and teased. Then she whispered his name, and her eyes dropped shut, fanning fine black lashes over her cheeks. He shaped the weight of her breasts in his hands. "Oh, Catherine," he heard himself whisper. "Never have I seen anything so beautiful."

Her breasts were high and heavy, the taut aureolas dusky pink against her pale flesh. A slice of evening sun cut through his draperies, warming her jaw, her shoulder, and slanting lower. She was all feminine curves and soft, creamy flesh, and de Rohan was suddenly, unutterably certain he'd waited the whole of his life for her. Instead of rucking up her skirts and rutting with her as he had burned to do mere moments ago, he suddenly wanted to make love. To feast languidly, reverently. He bent his head, felt his breath against her breast, heard her soft gasp of anticipation.

Catherine cried out when Max drew her breast into his mouth. Instinctively, irrepressibly, her body surged to his as he sucked and laved, first tender, then hungry. Drowning in sensation, she felt the heat of him surround her. Max's scent clung to the bedcovers, teasing at her senses, enticing her. She imagined him naked, his long legs tangled in the sheets. The vision was wildly arousing.

As he turned his attention to her other breast, Catherine cried out and reached for him. She wanted him inside her now. Did not want—did not *need*—to wait. The wantonness of her hunger shocked her. Dear heaven, she'd never even made love in the daylight before! A little desperately, she reached up and urged him fully on top of her. Beneath him, she felt small and vulnerable. But safe. So safe. Beautiful and seductive. She let Max urge her legs apart with one knee and felt his hard, heavy thigh settle into the vee of her legs. He kissed her again, open-mouthed and lingeringly, pushing his tongue deep into her mouth, probing her. She heard him groan, felt another shudder rock his body, and a heavy, languorous warmth began to pool in her belly. She could feel his erection, unmistakably hard against her leg, and the thought of it made her ache with a need she'd never known.

Her drawers went slithering to the floor somewhere amidst the heated caresses and melting kisses. Max pushed up her skirts until his hand could shape the roundness of her belly. He made another sound, a growl or a moan, then slid his long, warm fingers lower, until his palm cupped her thatch of hair. His middle finger began to rub and tease, sliding deeper with each tormenting stroke. Softly, she cried out.

"Here, *cara?*" he crooned, his eyes never leaving his hand as he watched himself work her so intimately. "Do you ache for me here? Say it, *cara mia,* and I promise I will leave you gasping."

His words were so wicked, his thick, rasping voice so seductive. "Yes, there," she whispered.

Catherine moaned with pleasure when his finger eased inside, his thumb sliding up to tantalize her quivering bud. It felt as if her very core were on fire for him. "Ah, *bella,*" he murmured, his touch holding her prisoner. "So eager. So needy." Another finger slid inside, spreading her. The thumb again, more torturous, more demanding now.

On another helpless cry, Catherine answered him, arching her pelvis higher, riding down on his hand, whimpering for release. She shuddered again and felt her breath begin to quicken. "Max, oh God. I can't . . . I want . . . now, Max. *Please.*" Of its own volition, her hand went to his trousers, her fingers clawing at the impossibly large ridge which strained against the fabric.

Roughly, Max laughed and seized her hand, pulling it to his mouth. "Patience, love," he murmured. To her shock, his tongue came out to tease at the palm of her hand, and, inexplicably, Catherine arched off the bed again. Lazily, he drew her middle finger into his mouth, his wicked black eyes holding hers as he sucked at it, drawing more and more of the aching warmth into her loins with every pull. For long, languorous moments, his eyes never left hers. One hand still teased at her swollen flesh, while the other held her hand captive to his mouth.

And then, suddenly, Max sat back on his haunches and slid his palms between her legs, pushing them wide apart. With his knees, he pushed them wider still. "Aah, Catherine, *sei molto bella,*" he rasped again. "So beautiful." Watching her body from beneath hooded eyes, he slid his warm, long-fingered hands up the soft skin of her inner thighs—all the way up—then opened her flesh with his thumbs.

Despite her raging desire, Catherine thought she would die of embarrassment at such intimacy. When he bent his head and kissed her there, she was sure of it. A flush of heated color ran from her toes to her ears, and then his mouth found her most delicate flesh, and Catherine's hips came off the bed on a jolt of pure lightning.

At once, his head jerked up, even as his hands forced her hips hard against the mattress. For one long moment, he held her prisoner with his sinful black gaze. A question passed. An answer came from her, unbidden. Her aching need was too great. She was his, to do with as he pleased. With his eloquent, lazy half-smile, Max dropped his eyes and lowered his head again. At his touch, a sound, part whimper, part plea, caught in her throat. His fingers found her, one, then two, spreading her wide for his mouth's sensual assault. Catherine had never known such sweet torment could exist. He teased and touched her. Over and over, he slid his tongue through her flesh, barely grazing her clitoris and leaving her quivering. She felt her fingers slide through his hair, then dig into the fabric of his shirt, into his broad shoulders.

"Please, oh, please . . ." she begged blindly, arching against him without shame. The provocative, gliding pressure of his tongue slid deeper. Catherine's head went back, her throat convulsing as she clawed at him. She felt her body seize and shudder. Twice. Again. And then Catherine cried out as the uncontrollable pleasure rolled over and over her, carrying her away on a raft of sensation.

The last trembling slowly faded, leaving her dazed and gasping. She came back to full awareness to see that Max knelt between her legs, his expression raw and intense. She lay spread before him, her embarrassment eroded on waves of passion. "Now, *cara mia,*" he whispered thickly, his expression suddenly wild and unguarded. "I must have you." Their fingers went at once to his trousers—hers to caress him through the taut fabric, his to rip clumsily at the last buttons. His erection sprang free from the crumpled clothing, a shaft of satiny, throbbing iron. At once, Catherine captured it, wrapped one hand around him. "Oh!" she whispered, taking in the size and strength of him. Above her, Max shuddered with pleasure. Emboldened, she eased a hand down his heated length, her eyes widening as one perfect pearl of moisture seeped from the swollen tip.

Max squeezed shut his eyes and prayed for control. *Oh, God, he was close.* So close. Watching her orgasm had nearly sent Max over the edge. And now her caress was a sweet, sweet agony. He groaned, and Catherine guided his cock nearer, lifting her hips to take him. "Come inside me, Max," she whispered. "Don't stop."

He couldn't have. No, not even if she begged. But she wouldn't. He could see the depth of her emotion in her somnolent brown eyes—that feminine longing to pleasure him—and it touched something deep and fragile inside him. Willingly, Catherine opened herself to him, and his entire body shook with the restraint as hers enveloped his, drawing his male hardness slowly and inexorably into her feminine softness. For a moment, she stilled herself, one leg wrapped around his body, as if she were adjusting to a new and unfamiliar sensation.

Almost, he thought, ruthlessly holding himself in check. *Almost all the way.*

But almost was not enough. And he had never been a patient man. He could not wait. He withdrew, raised himself high above her, reentering on one deep thrust. "Aah!" he shouted as his head went back. It was a roar of triumph, a sound of pure male need. He drew out, thrust hard again and again, squeezing shut his eyes.

Sweetly, she clung to him. "Max," she whispered. And then his lips found hers, opening over them greedily. Curling her other leg below his hip, Catherine dragged herself higher, urged every inch of her body against him, driving him insane. Driving him to thrust

himself madly inside her until, at last, he tore
from hers and looked down into her eyes.

"Catherine, *per favore!*" he said pleadingly.
Slow down."

She shook her head, dragging her hair across the
low. "Not slow, Max," she whispered. "Not now. Pleas

He sank his teeth into his lip, shut his eyes, and gently
rocked his hips back and forth. Oh, sweet heaven, she
was still tight! Impossibly tight. He was on the jagged
edge of explosion. It had been too long. He wanted her
too desperately. Max thrust deep again and felt his testi-
cles draw taut. Oh, too close. He tried to grapple for control, tried to think of something else. The minx pressed
her lips to his ear, her sharp teeth scoring his earlobe.
"Don't, Max," she coaxed. "Don't be gentle now."

It had been too long. Her mouth and her body and
her words were too tempting. He'd meant to go slowly.
Pleasure her again. But she rocked her hips tantalizingly
upward, and he began to thrust again. Hard, and harder
still. Max lost himself in the sensation. He tried to heed
the first shudder, swore he would pull out. But the rush
of pleasure was unbearable. Too late. Or almost so. He
slid deep inside one last, perfect time. Felt his body
racked to the bone with an intense trembling. And then,
with a harsh cry of release, he exploded, shattering into
sweet, perfect ecstasy.

Max tore himself from Catherine just as his seed spilt
from his body in a rush, draining away with it his frustration and anger and loneliness. He fell half across
Catherine, gasping for breath, trembling with pleasure
and awe. Together, they rolled to one side, the breath
still heaving in and out of his chest.

After a long, blissful moment had passed, Max lifted a corner of the sheet and wiped away the damning evidence with a hand that still shook. Catherine nestled her head against his shoulder and pressed her lips to the turn of his jaw. "Oh, you did not need to do that, Max," she gently chided. "You really did not."

Max pressed his lips to her temple and felt the taste of her on his mouth. "It's safer, Catherine," he murmured. "You know that." But he had the unsettling sensation that what he'd done might have been just a split second shy of *safe*. Catherine did not seem at all concerned. Instead, she gave a feline stretch, wiggled her toes, and fell fully against him.

Briefly, they drowsed, nestled in one another's arms until dusk began to settle over the room. Max gazed up at the ceiling with its familiar cracks and rough white plasterwork, watching as it quickly shifted from dusky peach to fiery gold, and realized that what he was experiencing was probably the most exquisitely peaceful moment of his life. But peace and sweetness were things life had always meted out to him in incremental doses. It would not do to grow accustomed to either when they could not possibly last.

Not two minutes later, fate, ever a cruel mistress, obliged his expectations. The knock on the door came, soft but insistent, echoing hollowly in the empty parlor. Violently, Max cursed. Catherine's eyes flew open, and she struggled awkwardly onto her elbows.

Lifting his weight onto his arms, Max dropped his forehead to touch hers. *"Maledizione!"* he managed to choke. "Do I live in a bloody coaching inn?"

Catherine let out her breath in a dejected sigh. "You'd

best answer it," she whispered, stroking one hand through the heavy hair which fell forward to frame his face. He started to shake his head, but she insisted. "Oh, Max, I'll still be here. What if it's something important? What if it's your work?"

His work. At least she'd called it important. But more important than his work was the fact that Catherine could ill afford for anyone to suspect she was alone with him. "Yes," he finally rasped. "Yes, all right."

He was never quite sure how he found the strength, but somehow Max rolled to the edge of the mattress and stood, stabbing his shirttails in as he headed for the door. One of Catherine's red kid slippers had tumbled from her foot onto the floor, and he nearly tripped. Suddenly, he was seized with the impulse to snatch it, to hide it away. But he was not, and never would be, any woman's Prince Charming. Max snatched up his waistcoat instead and kept on moving.

Catherine sat up and swiftly began to adjust her clothing. The knock came again, and with one last backward glance, Max strode through the corridor and toward the parlor. He opened the door to a blast of Italian, torrid and scathing. Maria rushed into the room, hands gesturing, eyes flashing. "Maximilian, *che cosa fa?*" she demanded. "What are you thinking? *Dio mio,* it is half-past five. *La signora,* she expected you! Hours ago! She is old, Max! She is not well!"

As Maria's tongue-lashing burst into bilingual fireworks, Max pressed the heel of his palm to his forehead. Saturday! *Merda!* He always spent Saturday with his grandmother. Had he forgotten to send his regrets? She'd probably been flogging the kitchen staff for hours.

Such days together were the highlight of her week, though she would sooner have died than admit it.

"Ah, Maria!" Max tried to look contrite. *"Scusa per il ritardo."*

"Late? *Late?* No, you simply forgot——" Suddenly, Maria stopped, her hands held expressively heavenward. She was staring past him and into the depths of the parlor.

Max experienced a sudden sinking feeling. Oh, God. Surely Catherine would not be so foolish as to——

"What is that?" Maria suddenly demanded.

Slowly, Max turned around, relieved to see nothing. "What?" he asked innocently.

Maria strode toward the settle. *"This,* Maximilian!" she answered, shaking a fistful of red wool at him. "This!"

Catherine's carriage cloak! The deuce! Max squeezed shut his eyes.

But Maria was still speaking, her words suddenly soft, her tone as sly as his grandmother's. "Ah-ha!" she exclaimed. "She is here, is she not? *La Regina di Dischi.* That woman your grandmother saw—she is here?"

Suddenly, a faint rustling sound arose from the shadows of the passageway. "Am I causing a problem, Max?" said a soft, uncertain voice. "Because, truly, I was just on my way out."

Max swallowed hard as Catherine moved uncertainly into the light, looking hurt and confused. And her embarrassment was his fault. "Maria, be quiet!" he sharply demanded. "This is my home. She is my guest. You will mind your tongue."

But Catherine was still warily watching Maria. "Your pardon, ma'am," she said, reaching out to take her cloak.

"I did not realize that Mr. de Rohan was expected elsewhere. I simply dropped by to deliver something."

Max spared no thought for the meddling Maria. "Catherine," he said softly, turning to face her. "Trust me, this has nothing to do with you. Mrs. Vittorio will apologize at once."

As quickly as they had come, Maria's thunderclouds vanished, and her soft, round face broke into sunshine. "Oh, no, no, *bella!*" she soothed, refusing to relinquish the cloak. "No, no! You must pardon me. I meant you no insult. It is just that Maximilian's grandmother, she is old. Since Max took these rooms, she is all alone in a big, empty house. She wishes only to see him, her beloved grandson, for dinner. That is all."

At once, Catherine's eyes softened with sympathy. "All alone?" she echoed, her gaze shifting from Maria to Max and back again. "Like a shut-in?"

Maria nodded enthusiastically. *"Precisamente!* A shut-in. Very sad, very sad."

A little brusquely, Max lifted the red cloak from Maria's hand. "She is nothing of the sort, Maria, and well you know it," he grumbled. "Lady Catherine, this is Maria Vittorio, my grandmother's companion and cousin. Maria, Lady Catherine Wodeway."

Maria's eyes grew round. "Ah, *eccellente!*" Energetically, she seized Catherine's hand and began simultaneously to pump and to pat it. "Come, *bella,* you must go with us to dinner. Visitors are the highlight of the *signora*'s week. Shed joy on an old woman's life, yes?"

Catherine still looked dreadfully confused, glancing back and forth between them. "I . . . well, I'm really not dressed for dinner—"

Maria smiled broadly. "Oh, but you are *un tocco di grazia, cara mia!* Pretty, like a fashion plate!"

With a perplexed smile, Catherine stared down at her clothing. "Well, of course I should be hap—"

"I am sure, Maria," interjected Max, "that Lady Catherine does not have time for us. *Any* of us."

Catherine's confusion shifted to hurt as she stepped back. "Well, no. Not if you think—"

Maria beamed again and brushed past Max. "Ah, *bella,* don't be foolish," she said, seizing Catherine's shoulders as if she might give her a little shake. "He is a man! He does not think at all! Now, tell me, have you other plans?"

Chapter Eleven

*Have attention even in the company of fools,
for even they may drop something worth your knowing.*

—LORD CHESTERFIELD, 1776,
The Fine Gentleman's Etiquette

Mrs. Vittorio, it seemed, was a determined woman. Mere moments later, Catherine watched almost dazedly as Max dismissed Delacourt's carriage, then assisted her into another almost as fine, but his words were brusque, his actions abrupt. The equipage, she guessed, belonged to the great *signora,* Max's grandmother, who Catherine already suspected was not the shut-in Mrs. Vittorio wished her to believe. In fact, as she gazed at the woman's flashing eyes and flying hands, Catherine began to suffer the unsettling sensation of being drawn inexorably toward a tightly woven spider's web. Why, then, was she going? Why had she not simply made some excuse? She could so easily have done so.

But, as usual, Catherine's curiosity had gotten the best of her—a fact she would probably regret. Soon, the three of them were rumbling through Westminster at a brisk pace. Maria Vittorio continued to chatter, but when Max responded, his words were clipped and cool.

He was angry. And apprehensive, too, she thought. He had not wished her to come. And yet he had said not a word to forestall her.

For her part, Catherine was not at all sure what had just happened. One moment, she'd been basking in the afterglow of a swift but extraordinary lovemaking, and the next, she was busy pretending she was just a visitor who had slipped down the corridor to tidy her hair. She had overheard Maria refer to *that woman*. Whom had she meant? Was there someone else in Max's life? Catherine felt a shaft of pure jealousy. But one could hardly expect such a fine example of manhood to sleep in an empty bed. Not unless he chose to.

She cut a careful glance at the lady who sat next to her. A curious creature, Maria was a plump, middle-aged woman with a genial face and wide, expressive eyes. His cousin, Max had said. And Italian, to be sure. Which would help explain his dark complexion and fluent languages. And what of this mysterious grandmother? A woman of means, judging from the carriage. Catherine wondered, too, about Max de Rohan. Somehow, she had imagined him alone in the world. That was certainly the impression he gave, and quite deliberately, too, she thought.

Doubts and questions rushed in again. What manner of man was he? Not an impoverished policeman, certainly. Probably not even a middle-class bureaucrat. Indeed, did she know him at all, this man to whom she'd just given her body? In many ways, the answer was a resounding *no*. She should have had regrets, yet, oddly, she did not. And what of Max? She flicked a quick, assessing look up at him, but his expression was again unreadable. The carriage picked up speed along Whitehall and eventually made a swift turn into the Strand.

Maria stopped chattering just long enough to regain her balance, and Catherine seized the moment. "Your accent is quite lovely," she politely interjected. "You are Italian, are you not?"

The woman looked at her in some surprise. *"Si,* you did not know this?" she asked. "Our family is from— *come si dice Toscana,* Maximilian?"

"Tuscany," he answered softly.

"Ah, *si.*" Mrs. Vittorio nodded. "But *la signora*—Maximilian's grandmother—she lived for many years in Milan. Then came the war." Equivocally, the woman shrugged. "Lombardy was bad, Italy little better. We had to leave."

Despite her worry over Max, Catherine found herself fascinated. "And so you came to London? Why?"

Mrs. Vittorio opened her hands wide. "For the business, *naturalmente!*" She cut a curious glance across the carriage at Max, then returned her gaze to Catherine. *"La signora,* my cousin, she always said that the English, they would triumph in the end. She sees things. *Knows* things."

"How extraordinary!" Catherine murmured, not at all sure what Mrs. Vittorio meant. She turned to Max. "And how old were you, Mr. de Rohan? Did you find it exciting to come to a foreign land?"

But Max had no opportunity to answer. "No, no," interjected Mrs. Vittorio, waving her hands. "Maximilian was but a boy, still living at his father's chateau on the Rhine. But did he tell you he was actually born here? While his parents were traveling on business?" She flashed an impish smile. "We often tease him that he is really one of you, an Englishman."

Swiftly, Max interrupted, leaning forward, his big body swallowing up every inch of space within the carriage. "Maria," he said darkly. "I'm quite sure Lady Catherine finds our family history singularly uninteresting."

The hands spread wide again, lifting expressively upward. "But Maximilian, did she not just ask?"

He was silent for moment. "Ah, so she did."

Max settled back onto his seat and turned his gaze on Catherine, as if measuring his words. "Most Englishmen would consider me something of a mongrel, Lady Catherine," he finally said. "I'm descended from a mélange of Catalonian vintners, Spanish peasants, and Italian merchants. Perhaps even some less desirable things. But my father was born in Alsace. A small place. I expect you do not know it."

Mutely, Catherine shook her head, and after a long pause, he continued. "It is a place of hills and vineyards wedged between the Rhine and the Vosges mountains."

Catherine's memory stirred. "It is a part of France, is it not?"

His lips turned up into a bitter smile. "It depends on whom one asks," he said softly. "Certainly, Napoleon considered it so."

"Ah!" said Catherine. She was beginning to understand his bitterness. "And when did you come to this country? How old were you?"

Max held her gaze for a long moment, his eyes suddenly flat and black in the shadows of the carriage. "Long after the Revolution," he finally answered. "And

I was nearly a man grown." His tone did not invite questions.

"Molto bene!" said Maria brightly. "No more of this sad talking! Tell me, my lady, do you like the food of Tuscany?"

Catherine lifted her shoulders and smiled. "I confess I do not know," she admitted. "I'm afraid I'm not well traveled."

"Ah, and the world is a very big place, is it not?" she said gently. "But Max has seen much of it. He can tell you all that you wish to know. But me, ah! Now, I can tell you about food!"

And she proceeded to do precisely that. As the *signora's* carriage spun along Fleet Street, Maria Vittorio described the many culinary delights which would be served at dinner—strange, foreign-sounding foods which were totally unknown to Catherine's plain beef-and-mutton palate but which sounded delicious and exciting all the same. And the journey was not a short one, for they were going, Maria explained, beyond the financial heart of the City, beyond the Tower, and deep into the East End, a place Catherine had only heard of.

Throughout Maria's pleasant chatter, Max sat stoically opposite them. His eyes never left Catherine's face, it seemed. And when from time to time she shifted her gaze to the window, she would feel the heat of his stare intensify, burning through her. She wished suddenly that they had not answered the door after all. She had needed more time in Max's bed. They had made love, yes. But they had had no opportunity to forge that sweet bond of intimacy which lovers share afterward as they drowse in one another's arms. No opportunity to shut away the uncertainty and whisper, however tenuously, of the future.

Was there a future? Was that what she wanted? Catherine felt as if something crucial had been left undone. Questions had been left unanswered. And now, Catherine could feel the distance and the doubts returning. She could *see* it in Max's shuttered gaze. With a sense of grief and loss, Catherine turned her attention to the passing scenery. And what she saw disturbed her.

Interspersed with elegant homes, fine churches, and private gardens were expanses of abject squalor the likes of which Catherine had never dreamt could exist in London, a place which seemingly promised wealth and opportunity beyond imagining. There were pockets of poverty near Mayfair, yes. But nothing like this. And yet, even here, enclaves of wealthy businessmen and prosperous merchants coexisted with the destitution, drawn east by their need to be near the City and the docks.

Why, she wondered, had Max lived here? Why had he given so much of his life to these people? Isabel had called him a crusader. A reformer. Catherine could well believe it. Past the Tower, they turned away from the river and into a particularly disheartening neighborhood. Gutters overflowed with black, fetid water. Bleak-faced children ran barefoot in the streets. Thin, ill-dressed women trudged along the pavement past shabby storefronts and public houses, questioning every man they met. Their shoulders were slumped, their eyes were expressionless, and even in her naïveté, Catherine knew what they were. Saddened, she squeezed shut her eyes, but Max apparently mistook the gesture.

"Tell me, my lady," he said, his voice tinged with sorrow and sarcasm. "Just what do you think of our East End scenery? Is this fair prospect all that you had imagined?"

Making no answer, Catherine turned her gaze to the window again. She could almost guess what he was thinking. A part of him wanted to believe that these scenes repulsed her, that her opinion of him was somehow caught up in where he had once lived. Perhaps in his strange, proud way, Max expected her to cast disdain upon the people whom he had served so diligently. Well, he would wait in vain.

At last, they turned north into a narrow but well-kept lane which opened up into a great square filled with towering town houses which looked very like their West End counterparts. The *signora's* coachman drew up before a particularly imposing, double-fronted house, and a servant came down to take the horses. Soon, she stood in the shadows of a large, dimly lit entrance hall, Max at her elbow. As Maria chattered instructions, a tall, elderly servant came forward for their wraps. Catherine took a moment to look about the house. Cavernous rooms opened to either side of the hall. Not the reception rooms Catherine would have expected but, rather, offices whose floors were covered by work tables, bookcases, and stacked-drawers.

Suddenly, a slight, bespectacled man appeared at Max's elbow, a leather-bound ledger tucked beneath one arm, a pencil over one ear. "Ah, Mr. de Rohan!" He was dressed much as Max was, but his tone was one of both deference and frustration. "How glad I am to see you!"

"Working late again, Trumbull?" murmured Max.

The man smiled faintly. "Mr. de Rohan, a word about the warehouse we need at St. Katharine's? I've found something, but your grandmother thinks the price too dear."

Max looked at him pointedly. "You'll have to haggle it out with her, Trumbull."

The man's smile faded. "But every inch of real estate is being snapped up, and the new docks not even finished!"

Max turned to lift Catherine's cloak from her shoulders. "The *signora* is well aware of the construction schedule," he answered firmly but gently. "Go home, Trumbull. Your family is more important than a new warehouse."

Cutting an uncertain glance at Catherine, the man bowed subserviently and withdrew. Without explanation, Max turned to offer her his elbow. With Maria Vittorio in the lead, they made their way deep into the house and up a twisting flight of stairs. With every step, Catherine struggled to suppress the butterflies in her stomach. The house was large and dark, the furniture in each room massive and polished to a near-ebony sheen. Opulent draperies and hangings covered the walls and windows, while the air was redolent with strange, spicy fragrances. It seemed a house of wealth, elegance, and mysterious restraint. Catherine felt at once lost and intrigued.

Suddenly, a noise like thunder rolled over their heads and down the steps. Alarmed, Catherine jerked her head up. In the gloom, a massive black shape came hurtling around the newel post toward them. At once, Max let go of her arm and knelt on the landing. "Lucifer!" he shouted, his voice suddenly happy. *"Vieni qui!"*

"Bad doggy!" chided Mrs. Vittorio just as the huge black beast leapt onto Max, very nearly sending him tumbling back down the stairs. "Bad, bad! We have a guest." But Lucifer, his powerful hindquarters wiggling and his massive dewlaps flopping, had eyes only for his master. And Max was caught up in the moment, his hands and his gaze running over the dog, as if to reassure himself that all was well.

This, then, was the horrific beast Catherine had seen trailing after Max in the fog of Hyde Park. Catherine did not think him quite so horrific now, but he was still a beast, outweighing her by a stone or better. Murmuring soft words in a language Catherine could not understand, Max gave the dog's fur one last ruffle, then pushed him down. Immediately, the dog rolled onto his back in the middle of the landing, his tongue lolling out to one side like a small puppy.

"What a lovely creature!" said Catherine, kneeling on the steps to study him more closely. "But what on earth is he? Some sort of mastiff? I've never seen a black one."

"This one is from Campania," answered Max, his voice suddenly rich with affection. "More gentle than the French or English mastiffs and easily trained for police work."

Max scratched him once more behind the ears, then snapped his fingers. "Lucifer, *senti!*" Abruptly, the dog leapt to attention, all playfulness vanishing. They proceeded up yet another flight of stairs, Lucifer close on Max's heels. To the left of the second-floor landing, oak double doors had been flung wide to reveal a vast, opulently furnished sitting room. Like the rest of the house, it was dimly lit and faintly overheated.

And then, Catherine saw the *signora*. She sat stiffly in a high-backed chair near the hearth, dressed in formal black silk from head to toe and looking as if she'd leapt straight from one of the Grimms' fairy tales—one of the decidedly less benevolent ones. Her face was long, her nose sharp as a meat cleaver, and a swath of black lace framed her shoulders and her hair. This picture of regal disdain was completed by an enormous shield which hung high above her head on the massive chimney piece. Enameled in azure and sable, it was emblazoned with arms, a black lion rampant beneath a coronet of pearls. The sight was so unexpected, Catherine almost slowed to a halt.

Maria, too, slowed to a more deferential pace, but Lucifer plunged boldly across the room to flop down with a groan at the old woman's feet. "Ah, *signora,*" said Maria. "You have awakened from your nap!"

The old woman cut her off with a short, chopping motion of her hand. "*Si,* but only to discover that I was abandoned—not just by my grandson but by my cousin as well."

Max came swiftly forward and bent to kiss her hand. "Mind your temper, if you please, Nonna." His voice was gentle but intractable. "I was detained. And as you see, Maria's errand was a worthy one, for she has brought you a guest."

With no sign of surprise or insult, the old woman let her gaze run down Catherine's length. "Ah, and who is this?" She crooked one finger commandingly. "Come closer, *bella,* so that I might see you."

Swiftly, Maria swept forward. "This is Lady Catherine Wodeway, a friend who had called upon Maximilian," she announced with a hint of triumph. "My lady, this is Maximilian's grandmother, *la* Signora Castelli."

Catherine approached and took the old lady's dry, bony hand. She felt almost as if she were expected to make a sweeping curtsey, kiss her hand, then back slowly away. "It is a pleasure, *signora,*" she managed. "I hope I do not intrude. Mrs. Vittorio insisted."

Signora Castelli nodded. "Maria often does," she admitted. "And you, *cara?* You are a friend of my grandson's, *si?* But you have not, I collect, known him very long."

Catherine shot Max an anxious look. "No, not long."

"Come, Nonna," interjected Max, as if to forestall an interrogation. "We have kept you waiting past your dinnertime. Shall we go into the dining room?"

Together, they went back down the stairs, with Signora Castelli leaning heavily on her grandson's arm. He touched her gently, giving the elderly woman his strength without any attempt to steer or control her, and Catherine could sense that there was much love between them. Inside, the dining room was furnished in keeping with the rest of the house: dark furniture, burgundy velvet draperies, and a blazing fire. They moved around the table at the *signora*'s direction, and, at once, Catherine's breath caught, her gaze captured by the stunning portrait which hung over the mantel, dominating the room.

Clearly, it was not the work of some itinerant portrait artist but that of a master. The colors were dark and opulent, the scene one of utter domestic harmony. A strikingly handsome young man sat in a thronelike chair, dressed in Continental elegance, with lace spilling from his throat and cuffs. A book lay open over one knee, and his jaw was propped languidly on his fist which sported a huge cabochon emerald the color of his eyes; eyes which burned with a strange zeal above a stubbornly squared chin. Long raven hair was drawn back off his face to reveal a high forehead and slashing black brows.

A beautiful young woman sat beside him, a soft half-smile curving her lips, a toddler held affectionately in her lap. At their feet lounged a black and gold shepherd dog, and, oddly enough, in the background hung the same arms which Catherine had seen in the *signora*'s sitting room. But for the green eyes and somewhat paler skin, the man could have easily been mistaken for Maximilian de Rohan. Quickly, Catherine glanced down at the small brass plate, but it appeared to be in French. The date and part of the inscription, however, she caught. *Louis-Armand de Rohan, le Vicomte de Vendenheim-Sélestat, 1792.*

What on earth? Clearly, this nobleman was Max's ancestor, but Catherine could make no sense of it. As she recalled herself to the present, Lucifer wedged himself under the table, flopping down between the *signora* and her grandson. Catherine slid into her seat, only to find the heat of the *signora*'s assessing stare. Max was busy helping Maria with her chair and did not notice. Catherine lifted her chin and returned the *signora*'s gaze with a confident smile. It would not do, she sensed, to permit herself to be cowed by this woman. In response, Mrs. Castelli's expression shifted to one of mild bemusement, and she turned away to confer with the butler about a tureen of soup which was being carried in by a footman.

Catherine let her gaze run over the table, which was

exquisitely laid, the food exotic, spicy, and delicious. At first, the conversation was pleasantly neutral, but soon, despite Max's diligent parrying, the talk had turned to Catherine. Before the covers were removed for the fourth course, Signora Castelli had already managed to learn that her guest was a childless widow from Gloucestershire, newly come to town to attend her late husband's aunt. While the *signora* nodded approvingly, Catherine tried to study Max, who was polite but distant with everyone. She felt a vague sense of remorse for having come. Why could she not learn to constrain her curiosity? She should have refused Mrs. Vittorio's invitation. Max was a private man, and perhaps with good reason.

Clearly, his grandmother was interfering and difficult. And yet Max stood firm in the face of it, managing the old woman with a gentle resolve. He was, she realized, a far more compassionate man than she'd first thought him. Suddenly, Catherine wanted desperately to speak to him, to say something which might ease the tension between them, but there was little opportunity. Already, the *signora* was gently prodding her with questions about religion and children; specifically, what did she think of the former, and why had she none of the latter? Catherine felt her face flush with heat. Deftly, Max again turned the conversation, this time to the weather, but such a diversion would not last long. His gaze caught hers, swift and brilliant, his unease now tinged with a rueful sympathy.

Throughout the meal, the butler and a footman flanked the hearth, running and fetching during the eight courses, each of which was accompanied by a different decanter of wine. From time to time, the *signora* would pause to confer with Maria and her grandson upon the merits of a particular vintage, using terms Catherine did not understand. Three times, the *signora* ordered the butler to jot down their comments in a large, leather-bound book atop the sideboard.

"Your knowledge of wine is most impressive, Signora Castelli," Catherine remarked as they finished the last course.

The *signora* crooked one eyebrow very regally. "Is it not my business to be knowledgeable?" she answered, sounding mildly surprised. "We are vintners and merchants of fine wines. Did you not know this?" But she looked at Max, not Catherine.

Max laid down his fork. "My family has been in the wine business for over a century, Lady Catherine," he quietly explained. "My grandmother is justifiably proud of her empire."

At that, the *signora*'s black eyes flashed. "Of *our* empire!" she sharply corrected. "The one which you neglect in pursuit of foolishness. What do you think, my lady, of a man who abandons his heritage for such a hopeless task?"

Understanding struck Catherine with swift certainty. Gently, she cleared her throat and laid aside her fork. "I think I understand your disappointment, ma'am," she answered. "But your grandson's work is vital to all of us. I cannot think *hopeless* is the right word."

"And our business, it is not vital?" asked the *signora* bitterly, her eyes still on her grandson. "I think—"

"*Basta,* Nonna!" interjected Max. "We will argue in private." His eyes were fierce and hard.

Fleetingly, the *signora* hesitated, then sheathed her

claws. *"Molto bene,"* she said in a conciliatory tone, motioning that the last course be removed. "You will permit us, my grandson, to join you for your *porto?*"

Tightly, Max nodded. His grandmother smiled. "Then, for the ladies, a fine sherry," she remarked, snapping her fingers at the butler. "A bottle of the *colheita, per favore.* And a decanter of *amontillado."* Then she turned her piercing black eyes on Catherine. "And now, *bella,* a bit of entertainment, if you will?"

Catherine felt a moment of uncertainty. Pray God she was not being asked to sing or play the pianoforte. But Max was watching Maria, who had risen from her chair and crossed to the sideboard. "Oh, no, Nonna!" he growled. "Don't even consider it!"

With awkward, nervous motions, Maria was extracting a small wooden box from the door of the sideboard. The *signora* sat quietly, looking the very picture of innocence. "What is the harm in a little amusement?" she said, opening her hands as she shrugged. "Lady Catherine will not be opposed. English ladies, they like this very much."

"What?" asked Catherine. "What is it that English ladies like?"

The old woman beamed at her. *"I Tarocchi,"* she whispered conspiratorially. "I will see your future. In the cards."

Deeply, Max groaned. Catherine looked back and forth between them. "You mean to tell my fortune? Like a gypsy?"

With an expression of disgust, the *signora* shook her head. "No, no, foolish girl! Gypsies can tell only when your pockets are plump and your head is empty."

"It is all foolishness," said Max, his voice like gravel. "No matter who does the telling."

But Catherine was intrigued. "Then if it's foolishness," she answered, "you'll not object to my indulging?"

Max scowled across the table at her. "By all means," he grumbled. "If you wish to be embarrassed, indulge."

Maria had returned to the table with the small wooden box and several brass dishes filled with herbs. Soon, the *signora* was going through some sort of ritual, setting the herbs afire and muttering to herself as she passed a tattered pack of cards back and forth through the smoke.

As if he were accustomed to such scenes, the butler began serving their wine just as the *signora* placed the cards in front of Catherine. "Touch them," she commanded in a deep, throaty voice. "Yes, caress them, *cara*. It is good to impart something of yourself into the cards. *Buono!* Now, you must separate them into three small stacks. No, no! *A sinistra!* Move them to your left. Use only the left hand."

A little breathlessly, Catherine did as she was commanded. The *signora* restacked the cards in the opposite direction, then, with her long, gnarled fingers, lightly shuffled them about. "Now, tell me, *cara mia,* what is it that you wish to know, eh?"

Catherine shot a surreptitious glance at Max, who was sipping broodingly at his port. He refused to look at her. "I should wish to know my future," she said simply, allowing a hint of a challenge to light her eyes. "Is that not the purpose?"

The old woman shook her head. "Sometimes, *bella,* it

is wiser to tell the past first." And, with that, she began to lay out the cards, facedown in a huge circle. Once done, she crossed the circle with another seven cards, placing the last in the very center. Almost nervously, her hand hovered over the center card, then flipped it face up.

At the opposite end of the table, Maria gave a sharp cry, clasped her hands together, and looked heavenward. Max shot her a sour look and polished off his port. "What is that card?" asked Catherine. "What is the meaning of it?"

The old woman smiled as if pleased. *"La Regina di Dischi,"* she said quietly. "The Queen of Pentacles, an exceedingly positive card. She represents generosity, economy, and wisdom, all that is good and productive. And above all, she brings great fertility."

"Fertility?" Catherine blurted.

The *signora* narrowed her eyes shrewdly. *"Great* fertility," she corrected, her words tinged with warning.

Max made a sound of disgust, but the old woman lifted a staying hand. "No more, *per favore,* until I have finished." At that, she began to turn the circle, running clockwise. From time to time, she paused to study, her fingers sometimes tracing backward, as if she were perplexed. Eventually, she flipped the last card in the circle, then sat back in her chair, looking far more exhausted than one would have expected.

Lifting the decanter of port to refill his wine glass, Max shot Catherine a dark look. "I told you this was foolishness."

"Basta!" cried his grandmother, pressing her fingertips into her temples and staring down at the cards. "I

must think. This is . . . *affascinante."* Suddenly, her head snapped up, and she stared at Catherine piercingly. *"Dio mio,* but you have many men in your life," she said softly as one finger traced around the circle of cards, stopping at the left. "But this one, *bella,* oh, he was wicked."

"Was?" Catherine asked. Max had jerked upright in his chair now, his eyes burning through her—with jealousy, she thought.

The old woman nodded solemnly. "A bad, handsome man. But no more. Death has suppressed what life could not."

Catherine glanced from the *signora* to Max. "No." She gave her head a little shake. "That does not sound like my late husband."

Signora Castelli nodded. "Oh, no, *carissima,* for he is here." She drew her finger to the top of the circle and pecked on the topmost card with her fingertip. "A large, fair-haired man with a good heart. You knew him many years, *si?* But this card—*mazze*—the Ten of Wands. *Tch, tch!* He let you carry too many burdens alone. He will have little influence in your future."

Fleetingly, Catherine felt unnerved. She was not at all sure she liked this parlor game. And Max seemed angered by it. But it was too late. The *signora* was tracing back to the left. "But this wicked man, *bella,* he did you much harm," she said, returning to the first card. "See this—the Four of Pentacles? He took what was yours—money or something of value?—and he left you sad. No, no! You need say nothing!"

Catherine balled her napkin tightly into her fists. "It no longer matters," she admitted quietly. "I think he must be my father."

Max set his glass down with a harsh clatter. "*It* isn't *anybody,* Catherine," he insisted. "It's just a bloody card. Part of an old woman's parlor game, nothing more."

"*Pensaci su,* my grandson," said the *signora* a little bitterly. "I am never wrong."

"I just do not wish her overset," he insisted. "And this family is enough to scare the hell out of anyone." The last was said grimly, under his breath.

Despite her unease, Catherine leaned urgently forward, unable to resist the temptation. "Tell me, *signora.* Tell me the rest of it."

The gnarled finger returned to the bottom of the circle. "Another man, very handsome, very stern. A lover, perhaps?" She cut a quick glance up at Max, then shook her head. "No, someone else. You have suffered much together. You look to him for strength."

Catherine gasped. "My elder brother, perhaps?"

"*Si, è probabile.*" The old woman nodded. "But do you see this card above? *Sabino,* the card of hidden things. It signals the approach of deceit. You are doing something a little wicked. Something you will seek to hide from him, this man whom you respect."

A little shiver ran down Catherine's spine as she remembered her words, so casually spoken to Isabel. *Oh, my sainted brother shall know nothing of my clandestine lover,* she had laughed. *I can keep a secret.* She swallowed hard, unable to hold the old woman's gaze. "Will I be successful in my duplicity?" she asked, feigning a light, droll tone.

Signora Castelli smiled faintly. "*Si,* perhaps." She moved on. "But this, ah! This is the card I find most fascinating—*il Cavaliere di Dischi*—the Knight of Pentacles. But it is . . . how do you say, *sottosopra?*"

"Upside-down," supplied Max crossly.

"*Sì!* Upside-down. That is significant. He is a handsome young man, very dark, very brooding." Again, she looked at her grandson, bit her lip, and shook her head. "No, this one has left you only recently, I think? He is adventurous, profligate. Still, I see only grief and guilt in his heart." She studied the next card and made a strange little noise in the back of her throat. "Ah, this young man will return to you soon and throw much into disarray. He is in trouble, very bad trouble. And you will argue, *carissima*. Vehemently. You must have a care—for yourself and for him."

Catherine shook her head. "I can't think whom you mean," she said softly. "I have a younger brother, yes, but we haven't quarreled since we were children."

The *signora* shrugged equivocally. "Ah, well, only you can say. Let us move into the future." Her hand moved into the center of the circle, touching in turn the six cards which framed the Queen of Pentacles. "Ah, yet another man, *bella*. See this—*il Re di Spade?*"

"That means a sword, doesn't it?" Catherine whispered.

With a soft oath beneath his breath, Max shoved his chair away from the table, his every muscle taut. He wanted to jerk to his feet and hurl his wine glass into the hearth. By God, he now knew what Sofia was about. His grandmother meant to deliberately torment him, and Max was not sure how much of this his frayed emotions could take.

But Catherine seemed caught up in his grandmother's spell. Nonna Sofia was still speaking. "Oh, *sì,* this is the King of Swords, a card I have often seen," the *signora* said, cutting a swift glance at her grandson. "And he, too, is very stern. But you see this?" She touched the next card, a wounded warrior in violet armor. *"Catulo.* It tells us the King of Swords has had victory in his goals, but at a great price to himself. His self-control is great, too great. He is solitary. He suffers much. He will be a part of your future, *bella,* whether he wills it or no. And now there has come a trouble which is not of his making." She paused and drew a sharp breath. "A great evil."

At the foot of the table, Maria gave a tiny shriek. Catherine must have sensed Max's heightening unease, for she cut him a swift glance beneath lowered lashes. "Trouble?" she echoed hollowly. "What sort of trouble?"

"This woman—" Sofia paused to tap upon another inverted card, a beautiful woman seated before a vase filled with serpents. "Danger surrounds her. Already, it is too late. She has passed from this world, *bella,* and into the next. And these cards—you see them here?—ah, it was a crime of both passion and greed. A dark-haired lady, very lovely, but not loved. Did you know her?"

"I—I'm not sure . . ."

Catherine looked terribly shaken. Max was beginning to feel as if his head might explode. What the devil was Sofia about? By God, this time she'd gone too far with her tricks. And yet, tonight, she was playing her charade for all it was worth. Her hands were shaking, her eyes were wide, and her face was as pale as death. His breath seized as he watched her lightly touch the adjoining cards. *"Eccola,* here is death," she whispered more certainly. "And with it, the possibility of destruction. Listen to me, *cara mia!* You must be very careful."

Max slapped his open hand hard onto the table. "Stop it, Nonna, before you terrify her," he demanded. "This is ridiculous! Come, Catherine, I am leaving."

But Catherine shook her head, as if unable to tear her eyes from the cards.

His grandmother, too, seemed mesmerized. "Remember!" Sofia hoarsely whispered. *"Il Re di Spade* is a seeker of vengeance. Yet he will bring strength to your life. But first, *bella,* I fear you must pay a price."

Max watched as Catherine leaned forward, barely breathing. He felt out of control. He did not believe in the tarot. Somehow, Sofia had stacked the deck. *It had to be.* The cards never fell this way. He'd been forced to watch often enough. Well, by God, he was done with watching. Max shoved himself roughly back from the table. "Are you coming, Catherine?"

As if mesmerized, Catherine reached out and touched the King of Swords. "What sort of price must I pay, *signora?"*

Signora Castelli shook her head. "Ah, it is not clear," she admitted sadly. "Perhaps too great a price. Already, you have argued with him. Oh, *cara mia,* but he is a stubborn one! You wish to bend him to your will, and he argues. He resists. But this time, he just might lose." She examined two more cards and sighed. "He needs you, *di sicuro,* and yet he pushes away the knowledge. Be patient. In his own time, *bella,* he will learn."

Max's heart was pounding in his ears now. Something inside him snapped. How dare Nonna Sofia manipulate him this way? God damn it, she could *not* will his future with a pack of bloody cards! He would not stand for it. Suddenly, as if his hand were not his own, he shoved away his empty glass and stood. *"Maledizione!"* he said harshly. "Nonna, *che assurditá é questa?* I have no time for this foolishness! I have work to do."

But Sofia ignored him. Instead, Maria rose uncertainly from her chair. "Wait, Maximilian, you have seen the cards!" she cried, tossing her hand toward the tarot spread, but Max was already half out the door. "Max, *per favore!* You cannot leave!"

Suddenly, Max whirled on her. *"Cannot?"* he roared. "This is partly your doing, Maria! You dragged Catherine here! You got the damned tarot out! Now you can just deal with it!" He spun on one heel, pausing only to snap his fingers at the dog. "Lucifer, *vieni qui!*" he commanded. "At least you have some sense."

The dog bolted for the corridor without a second glance, and Max slammed the dining-room door behind them, his hands shaking, his forehead beaded with sweat.

Chapter Twelve

On a bleak Friday evening in late May, Max found himself alone in his rooms with nothing save a dying fire and a snoring hound for companionship. In the Chelsea Road, the doddering old charley had crawled from the warmth of his watch-box to call midnight, and despite the season, southwest London lay swathed in a still, frigid silence. Inside, the parlor had grown cold, but Max could not muster enough concern to get up and stir the fire. As if bent on self-flagellation, he turned his book a little toward the light.

"If you have not a graceful address, engaging manners, a prepossessing air, and a good degree of elegance, you will be nothing. I recommend to you an innocent piece of art: flattering people behind their backs, in the presence of those who will not fail to repeat the praise. . . ."

With a disgusted curse, Max pitched Lord Chesterfield's self-serving tome over his shoulder, where it landed on the floor with an awful thud, then skittered into the wall. What egregious, scheming tripe! Was that the way of the English gentleman? If so, Max was glad to be *nothing* in their eyes. He'd been perfectly happy for years being *nothing,* had he not? He had no notion why he'd brought the bloody book home from the office to begin with. In the last few days, he'd spent several evenings thus; bored, cold, and oddly unmotivated. But this time, for some reason, he had engaged the services of a bottle of blue ruin to ease the monotony. At least it was better than Kem's damned etiquette lessons. Blister it, what use had a policeman for fine ways and pretty words?

Lucifer, devil take him, dozed on the hearth rug, rumbling like a brewer's dray. Max envied him the luxury. He couldn't sleep—hadn't slept, really, in some days. It was just the work, he told himself, as he stretched out his booted legs and stared into his empty glass. It had nothing to do with the lovely, long-legged lady who had so briefly shared his bed, and had seemingly carried off a sliver of his soul. How could it, when he'd scarcely seen her these last few weeks?

After stalking out of Sofia's house in a blind rage, Max had sworn off women. It had seemed easier than asking himself why his grandmother's prognostications had so disturbed him. And so Max had spent the next day with Sisk, dredging the nearby rookeries of St. Giles for jewel thieves and willing his mind away from Catherine. Neither was successful. And on Monday, he had returned to work to find Whitehall in an uproar. Hobhouse had called an emergency meeting to thrash out two particularly controversial criminal law proposals, Feathershaw was harping like a fishwife over a few overdue reports, and the bribery investigation had exploded into a roaring scandal.

At Lambeth Street station, a magistrate—a bloody *magistrate!*—had been discovered on the dodge. Two constables at Queen Square followed soon after. Not Sisk, thank God. That would have been more than even Max could have stomached, for, despite the fellow's rough ways, Max liked him. *Trusted* him. A rarity, that. But, just as Peel had hoped, the stones were being turned with regularity now, and more dark and slimy truths were bound to slither from beneath.

Disgusted, Max jerked the stopper from his bottle and tried to remind himself that these were the very problems he'd sworn to resolve. His work kept him sane, and he could not bear to give up. No, not for anyone or anything. And this time, it was work which might—just *might*— improve the lot of London's poor and oppressed on a larger scale. He told himself he was glad and that the heightening responsibility would give him less time to dwell on other things. Such as Catherine.

Dannazione! The woman now tormented not just his dreams but most of his waking moments as well. He sloshed out another measure of cheap gin and studied it. Why her? Why now? And why the devil had he bought this bottle of rat poison? Tonight there were no answers. He knew only that he should never have gotten involved with *her*—a woman with the power to ruin life as he knew it. And to kiss a woman with such intimacy—to

lay her down on his bed and spend himself inside her—
oh, yes, that was *involved*. So involved he ached with the
loss of what had felt, ever so fleetingly, like hope.

Yet, since that fateful evening, Catherine had not
sought him out. He had spent the first few days both ex-
pecting and dreading that she would. And then suffered
a week of agonizing disappointment when she did not.
He told himself that it was for the best. That it was what
he deserved, too, for his boorish behavior. Spring had almost turned to summer, and still there had been nothing. Max sipped generously from his glass and told
himself he was grateful.

But London suddenly seemed a small town. It had
eventually been his misfortune to run into her at a
crowded rout in Berkeley Square, where Lord Bodley
was expected to make an appearance. To his shock,
Catherine was on the arm of Sir Everard Grant, laughing
as if they were old friends. She did not look as if she had
suffered overmuch from Max's disappearance from her
life. And then, unexpectedly, across the crowded drawing room, his eyes had caught hers. Despite his suddenly
pounding pulse, he had somehow managed to bow in acknowledgment. She had returned the gesture with a polite smile, then cut her gaze away, her lashes demurely
lowered. As if they were the merest acquaintances.

He had left at once, Bodley—and his duty—forgotten. And he had tried to forget about Catherine, too.
But, as fate would have it, the following week, he'd seen
her window shopping in Bond Street with Colonel
Lauderwood, whom he knew vaguely as Lady Kirton's
lover. This time, Catherine spoke. Indeed, there had
been no gracious way to avoid it. She had inquired after

his health and that of his cousin and grandmother, but coolly, almost too politely. In response, Max had doffed his hat and paused just long enough to be civil. She had not encouraged him to linger.

And then today! God help him, what had he been thinking? He had been returning from Kem's shop shortly after five when he'd caught sight of her. She was strolling arm in arm along Pall Mall with her aunt, their heads bent in quiet conversation, their fashionable bonnet brims obscuring his approach. At the lending library near St. James's, Lady Kirton had paused to fumble beneath her shawl for her watch chain and then had drawn Catherine inside. Neither of them had seen him. He was free to go on about his business, which was precisely what a wise man would have done.

But he had not been wise. Seized by some inexplicable mix of angst and frustration, he'd followed them inside. Lady Kirton had gone at once to the counter, while Catherine had drifted along the rows of shelves, her expression one of disinterest. And so he had silently stalked her into the depths of the empty library, telling himself that he meant merely to watch her. To reassure himself that she was well. To see if she looked happy. For a long moment, he'd stood quietly in the shadows as she aimlessly tugged one book after another from the shelves. But after glancing at them, she would simply shove them back again with sharp impatient motions, as if nothing could possibly please her.

Well, he was not especially pleased, either. And at that moment, it somehow felt as if she were to blame for his misery. She wasn't, and he'd known it then as he knew it now. But he had cleared his throat, with no notion of what he'd meant to say or do. Her eyes had flicked up from the pages of her latest selection, and their gazes had caught and held for an instant.

But her surprise had swiftly faded. "Why, good afternoon, Maximilian," she'd said coolly. "This is becoming most disconcerting, is it not?"

Lazily, he had stirred himself from the shadows, uncrossing his arms and strolling toward her with far more nonchalance than he'd felt. "Hello, Catherine," he'd said quietly. "What is it you find so disconcerting?"

Her eyes had gone narrow and hard, but she had refused to step back. "It is simply that for the first few decades of my life, I've gone blithely about my business knowing nothing of your existence," she'd answered, snapping shut her book. "And yet nowadays, we seem to be forever tripping over one another."

He should have remembered his vow to keep his distance, but the bitter edge in her voice had goaded him. He had placed one palm flat against the shelf above her head and leaned into her, deliberately using his body to intimidate her. "What I find disconcerting, madam, is that for the last three weeks, you've scarce given me the time of day." His voice had been a hard, dark whisper. "Why is that, I wonder?"

"Why is that?" Eyes suddenly ablaze with amber fire, Catherine had shoved her book hard into his chest, forcing him to grab it. "Perhaps it's because I think myself so far above you?" she'd bitterly suggested. "Or perhaps I just wanted a good hard bounce on some man's mattress, and yours was convenient? Or maybe I was just trying to complicate your life and ruin your career? Choose the one which suits your mercurial mood, Max."

"Stop it, Catherine."

But she'd shaken her head with a violence. "No, it's true. I could not possibly have any sincere interest in your police work. Or your family. Certainly, I could not possibly care for you as a man. I've simply been amusing myself with you. Had you forgotten?"

He had never believed those things! Well, not many of them. But the sting of truth made Max want to shake her, to hurt her. And that thought had both revolted and enraged him. "Stop it, Catherine!" he'd hissed. "I don't know what you are suggesting."

"I'm suggesting you just keep believing your own carefully crafted poppycock, Max," she'd snapped, half turning as if to leave him. "That way, you'll never have to deal with any uncomfortable notions like intimacy. You'll never have to worry about your work conflicting with your personal life. You'll need never apologize for your unutterable discourtesy in practically abandoning me on your grandmother's doorstep. And you'll never, ever need to wonder if I ever really gave a damn for you."

She had started away from him then, her spine rigid as a rifle barrel. He had tossed the book aside and reached out, grabbing her by the shoulder. She whirled on him then, her face a mask of fury. "You arrogant ass!" she hissed. "Don't you lay a hand on me!"

He was on her in an instant, not even realizing it until his mouth came down on hers, crushing it beneath his own. He had trapped her between his body and the shelf, forcing her hard against a wall of books and forcing her mouth with his tongue. It was assault, plain and simple. He'd arrested men for less. And yet he had kept kissing and kissing her, his mouth rough and desperate.

Fleetingly, she fought him, the heels of her hands shoving against his shoulders, her face twisting frantically beneath his. They stood chest to chest, thigh to thigh, so close he could hear his own heart pounding. Somewhere near his elbow, a book fell to the floor, echoing like a slap in the cavernous chamber. And then the fight had gone out of Catherine. Her body melted into his, and a noise which sounded perilously like a sob caught in her throat.

Anger he understood. But grief was beyond bearing. Max had shoved the weight of his body roughly away from her and stepped back, awaiting the scream or the slap which he richly deserved. But Catherine had had a more potent weapon. She had simply stood, arms at her sides, palms flat against the wall of books, her bottomless brown eyes wide, wary, and glistening with tears. Unable to tear his gaze from hers, he had lifted the back of his hand to his mouth as if he could take back what he'd just done. But he could not. He was ashamed. And yet he ached for her so badly he thought he would die.

Then, abruptly, she pushed herself away from the books with both hands. A shaft of dying sunlight sliced between them, filling the air with dancing dust motes. "I *won't* do it, Max," she had whispered, as if speaking as much to herself as to him. "I will *not* chase after you. I will not make this easy for you. Is that what you'd expected? And did you hope it? Or dread it?"

Finally, Max dropped his eyes and shook his head. "I don't know."

"Nor do I," she sadly replied. And then she turned and walked slowly back along the narrow row of shelving, her hems sweeping smoothly over the fallen book, her spine once again rigidly set. He had watched her go with some inexplicable mix of relief and agony churning in his breast.

Suddenly, a nervous-looking clerk had materialized, cutting into the shaft of light at the end of the row. "Madam?" he said as Max melted back into the gloom. "We are closing. I'm afraid it is time to go."

"Yes," answered Catherine in a distant voice. "Yes, it is."

A knot caught in Max's throat at the memory. How the devil had it come to this? He did not want to see her, did not wish to have an *affaire* with her. And yet her very withdrawal seemed to be ripping away half his heart. The truth was, during the visit to his grandmother's, Catherine had been nothing but warm. It was he who had behaved abominably. Driven by an anger he'd not fully understood, he had simply walked out, abandoning her to the mercy of two meddling old women. Thank God Catherine was no fainthearted fool. But perhaps he was? Max was afraid to consider it. And, in disgust, he simply yanked the stopper from the bottle again and hurled it decisively into the fire. It was time, he abruptly decided, to do something which he'd not done in almost twenty years. It was time to get piss-pot drunk. Lord Chesterfield and his fine, elegant airs could just go hang.

In Mortimer Street, the day dawned, overcast and cool. Catherine had found the past few days a misery, and for a variety of reasons. But Isabel, perhaps sensing what was wrong, had forced her to carry on. Since that dreadful evening at Signora Castelli's, Catherine had attended an assortment of balls, musicales, and dinner parties. To make matters worse, Mr. Vost kept asking her to go driving with him, and Sir Everard Grant still seemed determined to court her. She'd danced with them both last night, and this morning, Sir Everard had sent her flowers, as if he thought her some silly debutante.

She had also done her domestic duty, shuffling through piles of paper sent by the employment agency. Mrs. Trinkle had beamed in satisfaction, but Catherine had felt a little guilty hiring servants when she was no longer certain her heart could bear to be in town. But she couldn't quite bring herself to leave, either, and so, by ten o'clock on Saturday, she was industriously interviewing butlers when an all-too-familiar coach and four came rattling up the street.

Through the library window, Catherine watched as a footman dressed in the gray and black Castelli livery leapt down and hastened up the stairs. At once, her heart began to race. She entirely forgot the question which had been on the tip of her tongue. But Mrs. Trinkle saved her. The housekeeper entered, bearing a note of heavy vellum, her lips tightly pursed. With a quick word of apology to the man who sat across the desk from her, Catherine slit the seal with her pen knife.

"I believe," said the housekeeper, in a put-upon voice, "that the carriage has been told to await your answer."

But, to Catherine's astonishment, the carriage awaited more than just an answer, and clearly, the housekeeper suspected it. For a long moment, Catherine considered her predicament, skimming the note twice more. But at last, as always, curiosity grabbed a choke hold on her good intentions. Ruefully, Catherine turned her attention to her guest. "I do beg your pardon, er, Mr.—?"

The housekeeper gave a gloomy sigh.

Decorously, the man cleared his throat. "Umphelby, my lady."

Umphelby. Well. That sounded like a butler's name, did it not? Pompous, with lots of vowels and syllables. It was the best criterion she had, for Catherine had never hired anyone more sophisticated than a threshing hand. Mrs. Trinkle sighed again. The poor woman wanted a staff hired, and she wanted it done yesterday.

Catherine swept to her feet, the *signora*'s note still in her hand. "Very well, Umphelby," she said, thrusting the other hand out to shake his. "When can you start?"

The man jerked awkwardly from his chair. "Why— er—a sen'night hence, madam."

Catherine smiled at Mrs. Trinkle. "Advance Mr. Umphelby a quarter's salary, and give him the grand tour," she cheerfully suggested, knotting her frothy blue shawl about her shoulders and striding toward the door. "Good day to you both. I'm afraid an emergency calls me elsewhere."

Leaving them murmuring in her wake, Catherine moved swiftly through the house, gathering up her cloak and reticule. Her wits seemed scattered, too. She had no notion what Signora Castelli might mean by such a summons. Her note said only that she hoped Catherine would join her at breakfast. The fact that ladies did not "join" anyone but family for breakfast at such an hour seemed to have escaped the *signora*. Or perhaps she did not care. Certainly, Catherine didn't. She was perishing of curiosity.

As the carriage spun east, Catherine recalled her last visit to Wellclose Square. She was, without a doubt, a

fool to return. She had sworn she would never think of
Max de Rohan again. Good Lord, he had stormed out of
the dining room, abandoning her without explanation
or apology. As if his grandmother's macabre card reading hadn't been enough to terrify her, he'd left her
stunned, struggling to collect her thoughts, when but a
few hours earlier, they'd been making heedless, passionate love. Of course, in all fairness to Max, Catherine was
mindful that neither the dinner nor the lovemaking had
been his idea. There had been no promise, no commitment, between them. And yet his withdrawal from her
life had been crushing.

If ever she had doubted that Will was in her past, she
had her answer now, did she not? She was obsessed with
the mysterious Maximilian de Rohan. He awoke all of
her senses, stirred all of her emotions, and in a way she'd
never dreamed possible. And as she struggled to understand herself, Catherine had been forced to reexamine
all that she'd learned of him. Slowly, it had all begun to
fall into some semblance of order. The opulence in
which his family lived, his frustration and anger, the
portrait hanging in the dining room—all of these odd,
disjointed images had converged, and Catherine had
begun to understand what a fool she had been. She had
always known Max was no ordinary man. That was the
very quality which had first attracted her to him. Still,
she'd kept playing with fire, pursuing a man who apparently did not wish to be pursued.

Well, by God, she was tired of chasing after his regard. And if she were honest with herself, perhaps she
was just a little scared. His kiss yesterday had been
something of a warning, she thought. Catherine had be-

lieved she wanted only a light flirtation, perhaps a handsome man to warm her bed and ease her heart. But Max de Rohan was not the sort of man one pursued casually. He was too serious, too passionate. She had seen him three times since that strange, awful night, and until yesterday, she'd been quite successful in keeping her emotional distance from him. Yesterday, however, she had pushed him to the edge, and she was not sorry.

Damn him. Damn him and his regret *and* his bloody pride! If he wanted her, let him say so. She had grown too old for silly games.

So why was she now in this carriage, jumping at the beck and call of his imperious, eccentric grandmother? Catherine sighed into the shadows of the carriage. She really had no wish to consider that question too closely. Suddenly, it seemed more prudent to fold her hands into her lap and focus on the scenery whirling past her window.

Upon her arrival, Catherine was shown at once up the dark, twisting staircase to Signora Castelli's private parlor. Max's grandmother sat in the shadowy depths of the room, looking much as she had weeks earlier: stiff, regal, and draped in flowing black lace. In the hearth, a roaring blaze had been newly stoked, and to her left, a small satinwood table had been laid with linen and silver. Tentatively, Catherine crossed the length of the room.

"Ah, *bella!*" the *signora* greeted her. "How good of you to honor an old woman's request." She did not rise but, instead, motioned Catherine toward the chair opposite her.

"It is my pleasure," answered Catherine, settling into

the proffered chair. "But I confess, ma'am, I cannot think why—"

"*Sì!*" interjected the old woman, her voice impatient but cheerful. "You cannot think why I, an old Italian woman, presume to call one of your station here? But let us both be honest, *cara mia*. You know. Oh, yes, I think you do."

Catherine lifted her chin. If it was frankness the old woman wanted, why not oblige? "I daresay I can guess," she agreed. "You are curious about the nature of my relationship with your grandson. And I suspect that he will tell you nothing. But pray do not concern yourself, ma'am. Mr. de Rohan and I are merely friends—and even that might be an overstatement."

At that, the old woman threw back her head and cackled. "Oh, *bella*, I might be old, but I am not a fool. What Maxmilian feels for you is not friendship."

Soundlessly, Catherine opened her mouth and then closed it again. The *signora* stopped chuckling just long enough to order the footman to draw up the table and serve. Then, impatiently, she motioned him out. The servant bowed and drew the double doors soundlessly shut.

For a long moment, the old woman studied Catherine, then shook her head. "Too late, my lady," she said matter-of-factly. "Wipe the regret from your face. I have again consulted the cards, and we must press on."

Catherine was confused. "Where, pray, are we pressing?"

But the old woman continued on as if she'd not spoken. "Now, I don't suppose—" She lifted her fork and stared across the snowy linen into Catherine's eyes. "No, you would not convert, would you?"

Catherine stared back, stunned. "I do beg your pardon," she somehow managed. "Convert? As in my *religion?*"

"No?" The old woman shrugged, lifting her hands in a now familiar gesture. "Ah, *molto bene!*" she said lightly. "I ask too much. But, as you English say, nothing ventured, eh?" Then she motioned toward the gold-rimmed plate laden with food. "Eat, *cara,* eat! You will need your strength."

That Catherine was beginning to believe. But she could not manage a bite. The frail *signora* suffered no such inappetence, digging into her food with surprising relish. "Now," she said, after swallowing a mouthful of eggs. "We need a plan. Max must be dealt with, and he is—how do you say it—*ostinato?*"

"Stubborn," guessed Catherine. "And where, ma'am, do you think he gets that?"

The old woman cackled again and stabbed her fork at Catherine. *"Bene, bella!* We will deal well with one another, you and I. Now, the plan."

Catherine looked at her in exasperation. "But what, pray, are we planning, ma'am? I confess, you've quite lost me."

Signora Castelli stared at her as if she were a foolish child. *"Il fidanzamento, bella!* The betrothal!" She crooked one chastising eyebrow, and shook her finger at Catherine's belly. "I *see.* I *know.* And Maximilian—*Dio mio!* That one has no time to waste, either."

"Oh, my God." Catherine fought for breath, gaping at the *signora,* realization swiftly dawning. "Oh, my

God." And then, thinking something more restorative was in order, she seized her coffee cup and swilled it. Another mistake. Her eyes flew open wide, and it took all the ladylike grace she possessed to refrain from spewing the bitter brew across the tablecloth.

The *signora* winced sympathetically. "Ooh, *caffè espresso,*" she said apologetically. *"Scusa!* I should have mentioned. Now, the banns. *Non c'è problema!* My Josephina's husband was a Protestant, may God forgive me." She paused to cross herself.

Abruptly, Catherine jerked from her chair, sending her blue wool shawl slithering to the floor, unnoticed in the heat and confusion. The woman was stark raving mad! "Er—I'm sorry," she blurted, backing slowly toward the door. "I have to go now. A-an engagement. The, er—the altar guild."

Signora Castelli curled her lip in frank disdain. "What, *bella?*" she challenged as Catherine turned away. "My Josephina's boy, he is not good enough for you now? You are too fine an English lady?"

That got Catherine's attention. She'd had just about enough of these high-handed Italians. She stopped dead in her tracks and whirled about to face the *signora.* "Why, how dare you!" she exclaimed. "That isn't it, and you know it! I'm just not—"

"Bah!" The old woman cut her off, slapping down her hands and leaning forward as if she might leap across the table. "Perhaps you are just a coward! Not fit to bear my grandchildren!"

A shaft of raw anger impelled Catherine forward. She pointed one trembling finger straight at the old woman's face. "Let us be perfectly clear on this point,

Signora Castelli!" she gritted. "I won't be bearing any-one's children—"

"No—?" she interjected, one brow flying up.

"—and certainly not those of a man who possesses the temperament of a snarling dog!"

"Ahh!" said the *signora* slowly. The disdain fell away at once, to be replaced by an expression of infinite weari-ness, and the old woman fell back into her chair. "I see how it is, *bella mia*. Maximilian is full of rage and confu-sion. And he has made you angry. Insulted you, perhaps."

Catherine took another step toward the table. "Re-peatedly."

With a sigh, the old woman gestured toward Cather-ine's vacant chair. "Oh, sit, *bella,* for God's sake, sit. I'm too old to chase you."

Her surrender struck an unexpected chord with Catherine. "Are you quite sure?" she grumbled, sliding slowly back into her chair.

The old woman looked briefly penitent. *"Per amor di Dio,* I haven't even enough teeth to bite. Now, *bella,* you must tell me what has transpired between you and Max-imilian since we met."

Catherine lifted her brows. "Why, nothing at all!" she murmured, still on guard. "I've scarce laid eyes on the man in weeks."

The old lady looked only a little surprised. *"Vera-mente?"* she asked. "But, *bella,* I do not understand. In his twenty years beneath my roof, Maximilian has never brought home a woman. Well, a few prostitutes. But only for a hot meal or a bath."

"Ha!" barked Catherine. "You make him sound like an altar boy."

Faintly, the old woman smiled. "Oh, no, *cara mia*. Far from it. But he is often foolish, and driven more by his heart than his head."

"You think that a bad thing?"

The *signora's* eyes narrowed. *"Si,* usually. Max's father was the very same, and he paid a terrible price for it."

At that, Catherine jerked fully to attention. "The man in the portrait in your dining room?" she interjected. "Is that really his father? The Vicomte de Vendenheim?"

"De Vendenheim-Sélestat," she confirmed in a flawless French accent, casting her gaze heavenward. "Armand de Rohan. My Josephina's husband. Please, God, what was I thinking? To marry her to such a one!"

So, he was a legitimate child, Catherine thought. She'd suspected—well, something else, perhaps. Intently, she leaned forward. "She did not wish to wed him?"

The *signora* looked at her in amazement. "Of course she did! It was a love match! That was the very problem."

"I'm afraid I do not perfectly understand."

"He was a starry-eyed democrat—and in a land wedged between the strife of France and the imperiousness of Germany! Better to have been wedged into a powder keg, given his sort of politics. *Liberté! Fraternité! Egalité!"* Again, her pronunciation was perfect. And bitter.

Catherine's eyes widened with horror. "Good Lord, he was a revolutionary?"

The old woman squeezed shut her eyes and slowly shook her head. "Not quite, thank God," she whispered. "At first, Armand merely supported the disbanding of feudalism on his estates and vineyards. He tried to lead by example, establishing tenancies and schools. He brought teachers and physicians to his people. He paid fair wages."

"But those sound like good things," protested Catherine.

"And they were expensive things!" the old lady snapped, her eyes flying open. Then her face assumed a more conciliatory expression. "To my shock, however, they were not wholly unprofitable. But then came the Revolution in full force. For many years, Armand kept his distance, but eventually, he was called to Paris. Bonaparte wished to ensure the support of the noble families along the Rhine, and Armand believed very deeply in the rights of the people."

"What happened?"

"Initially, all went well. But, as you know, the Corsican pig grew greedy, and Europe was to be his trough. The work of the guillotine had been hard for Armand to stomach, the armies marching through the countryside harder still. Soon the extravagances of the new regime were quite obviously as bad as those of the old. The peasants' lives were little improved. Armand, ever honest, demanded improvements. Vehemently. Many in Alsace did. But none with so much to lose. None with so grand an estate or so beautiful a wife and so promising a son."

"Dear God," Catherine whispered. "And what of you, ma'am? Where were you?"

The merest hint of tears appeared in Signora Castelli's eyes. "In Milan," she softly answered. "Until the fall of Marengo. After that, I could see what was destined. Already, my husband was in his grave, and half our business was lost to the war. I saved what I could and fled to England. But Armand, he would not leave his vineyards. And Josephina, she would not leave him. Not until it was too late."

"Why? What happened?"

"They turned most swiftly on their own, the damned French dogs! A traitor to the cause, they called him, and they made of him an example. As the Grand Armee marched toward Ulm, a party of cavalry were diverted to torch his farms and vineyards. And when that was done, they barricaded his chateau and burnt that, too. Thank God he had forced Josephina out of the house."

"He . . . he died?"

The old woman barely nodded. "And a part of her with him," she said quietly. "But Armand, he had ordered Maximilian to take Josephina away, to hide in the village. If the worst should happen, they were to come to me in England, which they did. And I think he has lived with the guilt ever since."

"The guilt? I do not understand."

"The guilt of a survivor, *bella,*" she whispered. "Myself, I have buried three husbands and a child. Trust me when I say that to live when others do not can be the worst pain of all. He was sixteen, older than some French soldiers. And yet he was not allowed to defend the land he cherished. He was sent away to a foreign country and told to hide behind the skirts of his *maman.* That, I daresay, is how he sees it."

"But that is ridiculous!"

The old woman gave one of her noncommittal shrugs. "Oh, *cara mia,* a man's pride is a confusing thing.

He wanted to die for the cause. He is his father's son—the same political beliefs, the same fervid emotions, and, I fear, the same bad end."

Catherine could certainly attest to the first two, but she was not at all sure she believed the last. For a long moment, she was silent. "And has he never returned home? He has no wish to see his lands?"

The *signora* shook her head sadly. "There is nothing left, save what Josephina frantically piled into a hay wagon." She pointed to the majestic shield which hung above the fireplace. "The arms of the house of Vendenheim-Sélestat. The portrait of his father. A few family heirlooms. But these are worldly possessions, creature comforts. Maximilian is scarcely aware of their existence. You have seen how he lives, how he thinks. He loved the land, *si,* but that was taken, and the house burnt, and he chooses not to fight for what remains."

Catherine's brows rose. "But—but the Peace of Amiens, did it not make things right?"

The old woman laughed bitterly. "Nothing, *bella,* is ever made right after war. Do not believe what you read in your English newspapers. Armand was viewed as a supporter of the *sans-culottes* by most of the English and as a traitor by half the French. It is sad, really, when all he wished to do was feed his starving peasants."

Catherine stared down into her plate of uneaten breakfast and felt a deep sense of guilt. Even on the brink of insolvency, her family had always had food. "Tell me, *signora,* what will become of Max?"

Signora Castelli spread her hands open wide. "This, *bella,* is what I ask you," she plaintively answered. "If it matters to you, then I will tell you that for all his simple ways, my grandson is no longer a starving refugee. I have rebuilt my business into an empire, and half of it is his. All of it, when I die. And from his paternal grandmother, he has many vineyards in Catalonia. A small estate, too."

Catherine drew her brows into a knot. "That's lovely, but . . ."

The old woman smiled, and here, the mischievous glint returned to her eyes. "And, of course, if you would agree to marry him, and *if* you could persuade him to acknowledge his title, why, then you could be a viscountess! Such things are important to an English lady, *si?*"

"No." Catherine said the word firmly. "Not to me. But with all respect, Signora Castelli, I have no wish to marry your grandson. I just don't . . . want him."

The *signora's* smile deepened. "Oh, *bella,* lie to me if you must. But never lie to yourself. You want him. And what woman would not, eh? He is a big man, a strong man. And, *Dio mio,* is he not handsome?"

"No. Not . . . not in the conventional sense." Her face flushed with heat, and Catherine cut her gaze away.

The old woman cackled with glee. "Not in the *English* way, no. He is not blue-eyed or fine-boned. He has much Spanish and Tuscan blood. Temper, too." Then, pensively, she took up her coffee and sipped at it. "I suspect it is his work which troubles you. He was once a policeman, in a culture which thinks a gentleman should not sully his hands with work. Perhaps you could persuade him to stop, *bella?*"

Catherine shook her head. "Only a selfish woman would try to change a good man into something frivolous," she answered. "But I do not plan to remarry. It has nothing to do with Max. Please, ma'am, let us speak of it no more."

The old woman opened her mouth as if to argue and then closed it again. For a moment, she silently contemplated the still-roaring fire. "Ah, such a pity!" she said very quietly, setting down her empty cup. "Certainly, I have been unable to divert him from the battle which his father died fighting. I pray it will not be the end of him, too."

Catherine leaned intently forward. "But mightn't it be that he does not wish to feel his father died in vain? The tide is finally turning here in England. Everyone speaks of reform. If he gives up now on what he thinks right, isn't that perilously close to saying that his family's sacrifice was for naught?"

At that, the old woman took up her napkin and began to dab gently at the corners of her eyes. "Oh, *cara mia,*" she snuffled. "How wise you are! And so beautiful! I knew that when Maximilian chose, he would choose well. I am so sad to know that it has come to this. What will happen, I wonder, to my poor boy? No one can understand the grief I feel—like a cancer, eating at my heart!"

Catherine rose and circled around the table to place one hand on the *signora*'s shoulder. "Oh, there, there, Signora Castelli," she said, patting her lightly. "You pay me a great compliment. And your concern for your grandson is admirable. But you've misunderstood. Max hasn't *chosen* me. We are acquaintances, nothing more."

Face still smothered in her napkin, the old woman nodded, waving Catherine toward the door with her other hand. "*Si,* I am but a foolish old woman," she whispered. "But bless you, *bella,* for coming. You must leave me now, so that I might grieve in peace for the empty life of my beloved grandson. You are a good girl. I regret having troubled you. Go now, go on with your life. And be so obliging as to ring for Maria on your way out."

A little sadly, Catherine picked up her reticule and drew on her gloves. The old woman was quite obviously manipulative, perhaps even a little mad, but Catherine still felt a strange sort of affinity for her. Once, as she walked toward the door, she glanced back over her shoulder, but Signora Castelli was still sobbing quietly into her napkin. She felt a moment of regret and very nearly turned back. But the *signora* had asked for privacy.

At the door, Catherine paused just long enough to tug the bell pull. And then she went down the long flight of twisting stairs, out the front door, and into the bright light of day, leaving the warmth and the darkness and the redolent spices of the Castelli household behind. As she climbed into the carriage, however, she could not resist one last glance up at the heavily draped windows which overlooked the square. To her surprise, one of the velvet panels dropped shut, obscuring the small face which had been pressed to the glass. How very sad! The *signora* had been watching her departure. With a strange sense of loss, Catherine motioned for the footman to close the carriage door.

Above, in the *signora's* private parlor, the coal still crackled and hissed. The worthy lady herself sat as stiffly as ever in her high-backed chair, her linen napkin already restored to the table, as dry and pristine as the day her laundry maid had pressed it.

"What do you see, boy?" she demanded of the lad who stood perched upon her best velvet footstool.

"Gawd love 'er, she's pale as milk, mum," answered Nate, peering through the glass and down into the square. "Sickly-looking, too, like she's 'eaded ter the scragglin'-post."

The old woman smiled in satisfaction. "She is getting into the carriage?"

Just then, hooves began to ring smartly off the cobbles below. "Orf she goes, mum. Just as yer said." Cheerfully, the boy shut the drapery and hopped down off his perch.

"Eccellente!" Impatiently, she motioned for Maria to be seated. "A fine-looking woman, is she not, my cousin?"

Maria nodded enthusiastically and leaned forward to pour herself a cup of the rich, black coffee. *"Si,* and from the country, too," she casually replied. "Good skin. Strong bones."

"Hmph!" snorted the *signora*. "A good breeder, you mean to say."

"Oh, *si,* that, too," she agreed, sipping delicately from her cup. "Did you persuade her, do you think?"

The old woman snorted again. "Ha! Tough as old shoe leather, that one," she grudgingly admitted.

"Oh?" asked Maria archly, taking up the butter knife. "Never say that you have met your match?"

The *signora* smiled wickedly. "Don't be fool enough to doubt me, Maria," she answered. "I played that girl like a violin." Suddenly, she snapped her fingers for the boy. "Nate, *vieni qui!* You have eaten?"

The boy dragged his cuff under his nose and shook his head. "Not ter speak of, mum."

The *signora* gestured emphatically toward the door. "Go belowstairs and ask Cook for eggs and sausages. Tell her it is my explicit command. And then take yourself off to this place—" Eyebrows raised, she shot an inquiring glance at her cousin.

"Mortimer Street," supplied Maria, taking a generous bite from a buttered roll.

"Va bene," replied Signora Castelli. "Mortimer Street. Take yourself there and hide. When you are not required by my grandson to walk the dog, you will watch the Lady Catherine's house. I wish to know every person who goes in or out her door."

"Front er servants' entrance?" he eagerly clarified.

"Bravissimo, Nate," she answered. "You think ahead. The front. And if Maximilian comes, note how long he stays, then follow him. See where he goes. Report here at cock-crow every day. Breakfast and two shillings will await you."

"Gor, mum!" The boy looked as if he would have done murder for such a sum, but she shooed him toward the door with the back of her hand. Already patting his belly, Nate hurried out and down the stairs.

Chapter Thirteen

*The adoption of vice has ruined
ten times more people than natural inclinations.*
—LORD CHESTERFIELD, 1776,
The Fine Gentleman's Etiquette

As any practiced rakehell can tell you, there really is no agreeable way to bestir oneself following an evening of drunken revelry. A pounding head is the price of pleasure, to be endured with as much grace as a chap can muster. Max de Rohan, however, possessed nothing remotely approaching grace, and, as best he could remember, had enjoyed neither pleasure nor revelry the previous evening. So it seemed rather unfair that he should be plagued by the symptoms of a morning after. But life was rarely fair, and a dull blade began to hack at his brain shortly after dawn.

At first, Max tried to lie perfectly still, stoically awaiting the death which felt inevitable. When Old Scratch didn't turn up, Max considered suicide but drowsed off trying to remember where he'd hidden his pistol. Finally, after hours had seemingly passed, he roused to the odd but unmistakable sound of snarling, snapping teeth. They were not, so far as he could tell, his own. Shaking off a horrific dream—something about having his head chewed off by wolves—he heard another low, malevolent growl rumble somewhere near his skull, vibrating the floor.

Definitely not a wolf. Through the pain, Max cracked one eye. *Maledizione!* A suspicious shadow cowered in the open french window. Max could hear rain splattering on the garden path beyond. He tried to shout, and it came out as a croak. Lucifer snarled again, lower and more malevolent.

This time, the shadow whimpered and drew back into the rain. "N-n-nice p-poochie, poochie!"

Max squinted into the gloom as the fellow again poked one well-shod foot over the threshold. Loyally guarding Max's near-lifeless body, Lucifer curled his massive lips back, revealing a perfect set of three-inch incisors and a reeking case of dog-breath. *"Grrr!"*

The man shrieked and jerked back. "Christ, Sisk, you call those *teeth?*"

A sardonic chuckle sounded from behind him. "All the better ter eat yer wiv, Kemble!"

"Sisk, you're a bloody pervert." Kemble poked another toe inside. "We must get past that dog! Throw him a bit of raw meat—something you never use, like your brain or your prick."

"Sod off, Kem, yer little shite," grumbled Sisk. "I ain't the one wot wanted ter stand out 'ere in the rain an' pick the bloody door lock!"

"Unghh," Max finally managed. His brain, mouth, and eyes were getting slowly reacquainted. With another agonizing groan, he realized he was looking up and a bit sideways at his visitors. Bloody hell! How the devil had he managed to pass out by the hearth?

Kemble eased the door open another inch. Lucifer lunged with a bloodcurdling snarl.

Unsteadily, Max forced his head up, but the hearth rug stuck to his cheek. "Lucifer, *vieni qui!*" he managed to rasp. *"Dio mio, basta!"*

The snarl receded only slightly, but the dog retreated. Sisk thrust his head over Kem's to survey the room. "Aw, frig it!" he exclaimed, gesturing at Max. "Kem, 'e ain't dead, just shot in the neck, so ter speak."

Gingerly, Max struggled onto all fours. He felt as if he had been shot somewhere, that was bloody certain. Finally, he staggered to his feet, then thought better of it when the room dipped beneath his feet. He threw out a steadying hand, seized the mantel, and stared up at the two dripping men who now stood just inside his parlor.

Sisk roared with laughter. "By God, this I never thought to see," he wheezed, heaving himself out of his overcoat. "The great de Rohan, half-sotted! And wot the devil are yer all tangled up in?"

Max stared down at the roiling floor. Lucifer's wool blanket bagged around his knees and ankles, while his coat lay upon the settle, covered in dog hair. *Merda!* The last thing he remembered was being miserably cold. Cold, and too drunk to stoke the fire. A little desperately, he scrubbed one hand up his face and through his hair.

Kemble had come gingerly nearer. "Have you got that beast under control?" he demanded loudly, walking a wide swath around Lucifer. "Because Maurice just finished these new gabardine trousers. I won't have them—"

Abruptly, Max threw out a staying hand. "Kemble!"

he bit out, his voice like gravel. "Quiet. Good God, I beg you! How did you get in?"

"Over the garden wall," confessed Kem, tossing his coat at Sisk. "That battleaxe Mrs. Frier hates early callers, and I wasn't in the mood to be left standing in the rain just for spite. And really, old boy, that scowl of hers! It quite shrivels a fellow. But we had to see you at once."

Max shifted his gaze back and forth between them. "And so you simply picked the lock on my back door, Kem?" he asked coolly. "Frankly, I find that oversteps the bounds of friendship."

Kemble drew himself up a full three inches. "Well, what I *feared* I'd be overstepping was your cold corpse, de Rohan," he snipped, tossing his hand haughtily toward the hearth. "We could see you sprawled on the floor. What, pray, were we to think?"

"Aye, an' we knocked, too," chimed Sisk. "But yer didn't so much as twitch."

Kem turned up his nose. "And so pardon the hell out of us, old boy. Next time, we'll just let you lie there and be eaten by wolves."

Max clapped the hand back over his eyes. "Wolves...?"

Sisk snickered. "Yer was mumblin' something about wolves when we first come in."

With a deep sense of mortification, Max let go of the mantelpiece. "Well, you're in now," he said, making his way gingerly to the small table. "I thank you for your concern, misplaced though it was. Sit down. Why have you come?"

But as soon as the men moved toward Max, Lucifer was back on his feet, teeth bared, growling menacingly.

A little roughly, Max jerked a chair from the table. *"Accuccia!"* he barked at the dog. *"Sta' fermo!"*

Lucifer promptly flopped down on his blanket with a disgruntled whimper.

"How many languages does that hellish beast understand, anyway?" asked Kem, crossing the room to Max's cupboard and throwing open the doors.

"Several Italian dialects, Alsatian, German, a little French," muttered Max. "And get out of my goddamned cupboard."

"Goodness! He's linguistically well rounded," answered Kem, extracting a bag of coffee beans.

"Aye, an' 'e can understand the words *flea-bitten mongrel* in Turkish, too," Sisk cheerfully added.

"Oui?" Kem gave the bag a delicate sniff, then dumped it into the grinder. "And how would *you* know?"

Sisk gave one of his wicked chuckles. "I watched 'em rip the left ear orf the smuggler wot said it."

"Ooh, nasty!" Kem gave a shudder and began grinding vigorously. "Have you any sugar, Max?"

"Bottom door, left," Max mumbled, turning his gaze on Sisk. "Now, what is this about? Have you found me that bloody Frenchman?"

Sisk smiled. "Eversole caught up with him in Calais. Chap said 'e'd gorn orf ter 'is mother's funeral in Paris a month ago. We'll check, o' course, but a fellow ain't apt ter lie about such a thing, and 'e was on 'is way *back*."

Softly, Max swore. "Mark him off for the nonce. What else have you got?"

With a harsh clatter, Kemble set the pot on the hob. "A jeweler!" he sang, whirling about to face them, his hands pressed together like a choirboy. "Miller and Soames in Charles Street. They recognized the Tudor collar." He sauntered back to the table and, almost as an afterthought, wrinkled his nose at Max.

"What—?" Max demanded.

"You smell like an unwashed dog who's been steeped in cheap gin." Kemble lifted his nose a notch. "Besides, one cannot think straight in soiled linen. Go make your toilette whilst the coffee brews, then we'll talk." He beamed around the table, but his expression was implacable beneath the smile.

With another grumble, Max jerked from his chair. A half-hour later, he was washed, dressed, and halfway through a mug of strong, steaming coffee. Kemble had been right, of course. Max felt almost human, and nearly sober. Kemble fussed over him for a moment, retying his neckcloth and poking at his shirt points, but Max waved him off impatiently. "Stop fussing over me, damn you, and start talking!"

And at last, he did. Kemble's story was a simple one. A few well-placed inquiries had eventually led him to a discreet shop in Charles Street. "The word around the St. Giles fences was that old Mr. Soames had a good hand for imitation," explained Kemble. "So I took the necklace round. He was suspicious, to be sure, but I greased him pretty liberally, and soon he started trying to impress me." He paused to bat his eyes innocently.

"Get on w' it, Kem," groused Sisk.

Kemble's smile deepened. "So then I went round to Queen Square to fetch dear old Sisk and the rest of the jewels. And, of course, in the face of Sisk's irresistible charm, the old boy spilt."

"Spilt?" Max turned to look at Sisk. "Just what did he say?"

"Plenty," grunted Sisk. "Soon as I explained ter him as how the jewelry was all caught up in 'er ladyship's death. I explained a couple o' technical terms, like *fraud* and *murder,* and wiv no trouble atall, 'e picked out two more pieces from the chest which 'e claimed was 'is work."

Sisk laid three pieces on the table: the collar, a ruby brooch, and a heavy bracelet. Max studied them. "Just these?"

Succinctly, Sisk nodded. "Aye, and 'e was telling the truth. Terrified, he was. Said a lady w' a black veil visited several times two years ago," he said, handing Max a list of dates. "Between February and April, it were. Each time, she brought 'im a piece ter copy, paid cash, and took both pieces away after."

Max leaned intently forward. "Was it Lady Sands? Did she go alone?"

Sisk quirked his mouth into a strange smile. " 'E suspicioned it was 'er but wasn't sure. The first time, she came wiv a tall, well-dressed gent 'oo waited outside. Soames didn't get a look at 'is face. After that, she came wiv a lady's maid. Again, the girl waited outside, but Soames said she was short, buxom, and golden-haired."

Max let his fist fall onto the table. "Genevieve Durrett!"

Kemble nodded. "That's just what Sisk said!"

"Got ter be 'er," said Sisk emphatically. "I always 'ad a bad feeling about that bit o' muslin."

Max jerked to his feet. "Have you a carriage waiting?"

Sisk urged him back down again. "I've been up ter

Princes Street already, de Rohan," he said. "Genevieve's gone orf ter Cirencester ter see about a position. She's to return late Sunday, but I've set a man on her trail, just ter make sure."

"You sent Eversole?"

Sisk shook his head. "No, Eversole asked ter go back over all the files again."

"A bloody waste of time," muttered Max.

"P'raps, but not all of us 'er livin' in luxury over at Whitehall, de Rohan," answered the constable with a grunt.

The pounding in Max's head intensified. "Just what the devil is that supposed to mean?"

"Mayhap a fancy magistrate can afford to let a case drag on, de Rohan," said Sisk derisively. "But us fellows in Queen Square bloody well can't. We're just a bunch o' witless charlies, er so everyone believes—an' noffink atall compared ter the Home Office or Bow Street. But mark me, sooner or later, Peel's new police will be voted in. And one way er another, I mean ter move up."

"Well, just fuck all this, then!" Max exploded, shoving away his empty cup. "I didn't realize this was a career move for you! Why not just throw up a scaffold in Princes Street and hang Genevieve Durrett first thing Monday? That should serve everyone well!"

"Go fuck yerself, de Rohan, yer bloody upstart," returned Sisk, springing to his feet and leaning across the table. "P'raps I'm not so fine in me ways as you, but I'm as honest a man as they come."

"Now, now, boys!" tutted Kemble, leaning gracefully forward to refill their coffee cups. "Such vulgarity! Apologize at once."

Both men turned and glared at him, but Kemble stared back, prim and implacable.

Sisk capitulated first. "Aw, de Rohan, 'e's got the right of it," he admitted, falling back into his chair. "I'm out o' line, and yer head's just sore. All I'm saying is this—'ow long d'yer think it'll be before Peel jerks this case and gives it over ter the Runners? That'll do neither of us a bit o' good, eh?"

Max pressed his fingertips hard against his aching temples. He'd sooner dance naked down Piccadilly than be outdone by Bow Street. And twice last week, he'd been summoned to Peel's inner sanctum. The pressure on the Home Office was intensifying. Yes, the *beau monde* wanted someone to hang—preferably not one of their own—so that they might sleep more easily in their big feather beds. Genevieve Durrett would be ideal; nothing so convenient as a servant, especially a foreigner. Of course, the American or the Frenchman would do in a pinch. And then there was Rutledge. He moved on the merest fringe of society. There was a rich, reclusive brother somewhere, yes, but it was said they were somewhat estranged. Perhaps the brother would think himself well rid of a bad bargain.

Max finally looked up at Sisk. "You're right," he said quietly. "I'll keep a civil tongue, or try to. Now, what news of the others?"

Sisk grunted. "Bodley's servants won't talk. That American banker says he was in Edinburgh on business—some of that newfangled folderol about building railroads, if you can imagine! And o' course Rutledge can't be found."

"Have you sent a man to Hampstead?"

Sisk nodded. "Aye, we found his cottage," he admitted. "But his elderly servant said 'e'd not been 'ome in three weeks or better, and she knew naught of 'is whereabouts. Very tight-lipped she was, and refused ter answer any other questions. Bloody suspicious, if you ask me. Why else would a fellow pike off right after a murder was done?"

Max sighed in quiet resignation. "Something about this bothers me."

Kemble leaned intently into the conversation. "Set Rutledge aside for now," he said, waving his hand over the jewelry. "Here's what troubles me—if all this is fake, how do we know that the Sands Sapphire was real?"

Max recalled what Cecilia had said. "It was real," he said swiftly. "Sands kept it in the vault and had just taken it out."

Kemble nodded as if he'd just proven a point. "And do you not find it remarkable that our killer managed to choose the one *real* piece of jewelry from a pile of pinchbeck?"

Max swore. "You're right, Kem. He must have known the rest was fake. All that jewelry left behind . . . that fact has troubled me from the very first."

"And since we know Julia didn't gamble," murmured Kemble, tapping one finger thoughtfully on the tabletop, "then it would seem she was liquidating the one asset which couldn't be watched by Lord Sands's man of business. It fairly reeks of blackmail."

Sisk snorted. "Aye, and bein' blackmailed for wot? Everyone knew 'er 'usband was a cuckold."

"Over something uglier than infidelity, to be sure," Max coldly replied, pushing away from the table. *Such as an abortion*. But he still did not mention Greaves's suspicions. "Sisk, let's meet at Coble's Coffeehouse at nine Monday. We'll go have a chat with Miss Durrett. But perhaps they won't wish us to hang her. Not yet, at any rate."

"It's only Saturday," said Kem, fretfully shoving away his coffee. "Are we to have no excitement at all for the next two days?"

"Oh, I have a feeling it's time for me to pay another call on Harry Markham-Sands," grumbled Max. "But I doubt it will be exciting. You might take a few baubles from that jewel chest, Kem, and display them in your window. Who knows what will turn up?"

Sisk shoved the three fake pieces at Max. "And you may as well take these."

Max nodded. "Yes, as soon as I finish with Sands, I'll send notes around to the gentlemen on our list of suspects—*all* of them. I'll ask them to come have a look at these three pieces. Perhaps one of them will recognize something or betray his nervousness."

"Good luck," muttered Sisk.

Suddenly, a loud knock sounded. Max opened the door to find his grandmother's footman waiting in the shadows behind Mrs. Frier. "A message from Mrs. Vittorio, sir," he said, reaching past the landlady to hand him a sealed note. De Rohan sighed again and shoved it into his coat pocket.

Max spent the next hour dashing off letters to most of the suspects save Rutledge and Sir Everard Grant, who still denied knowing Julia. It was a risk, perhaps, to alert them to his knowledge of the jewelry, but perhaps it would push the killer into revealing himself. That done, he hailed a hackney in the rain and proceeded to Harry's house. Max arrived at what society considered an ungodly hour, but the butler didn't quibble, showing him at once into the drawing room. Soon a florid-faced Harry appeared in his dressing gown, a footman trailing behind with another pot of coffee.

Cecilia's brother appeared unkempt and unwell, his visage now bloated, his hair too long. And yet the earl seemed not at all surprised to see Max. Muttering a greeting, he cast a rather detached glance at Lucifer, as if a ten-stone mastiff stretched out on his Turkey carpet was a common occurrence, then threw himself into an armchair and offered Max coffee. His cup chattered on its saucer as Harry passed it. All of this Max noted with growing concern, and he reached gratefully for his cup.

Max took a deep swill and thanked God. Like most experienced rounders, Harry had his coffee brewed strong enough to peel paint. Oh, Max's head still ached, and his eyes still felt as if they'd been gored out with a hot poker, but he would live.

At last, as if fortified against an unpleasantness, the earl looked up to meet Max's gaze. Max drew a deep breath. "Lord Sands," he gravely began. "I daresay you've guessed that I've come to speak with you about Genevieve Durrett."

At once, every shade of color drained from Harry's face. Somehow, his empty coffee cup seemed to explode in his grip. "Oh, God!" he cried, leaping to his feet and dashing what was left of the cup onto the floor as if it were afire. "Oh, God help me! I just knew it!"

Briefly pondering his deleterious influence on

Harry's coffee cups, Max jerked to his feet, but Harry was already flying across the room, crushing shards of china beneath his slippers. He reached the window, lifting his fist to hammer upon the frame until the glass rattled. "I knew you would find out!" he cried, his voice anguished. "By God, I'm glad it's out! Glad, I say!"

Max reached the window, seizing the earl's fist before he could do himself some harm. Only then did he realize Harry was already bleeding. "What has she said?" the earl demanded, turning from the window, heedless of his injury. "What had she accused me of?"

Jerking a handkerchief from his pocket, Max took the earl's hand, gingerly plucking a shard of porcelain from his palm. Unflinchingly, Harry stood, still muttering and cursing. "Bitch!" he swore hotly as Max drew out another sliver. "Bloody bitch! I daresay she put Genevieve up to it. I should have suspected it that very night. Damn me for a fool."

Perhaps it was his weakened mental state, but Max was thoroughly in the dark. He was not, however, fool enough to say so. "And what makes you think she put her up to it, my lord?" he murmured as he balled up the linen and gently folded Harry's hand around it. "I daresay you'd best tell me everything now."

His eyes darting and feverish, Harry nodded. "I think she just wanted to catch me," he whispered, picking frantically at a protruding corner of the linen square. "She wanted to laugh at me. To suggest that I was no better than she was. Because I'd seen her in the carriage that night, d'you see?"

Max urged Harry back toward his chair, but his lordship would have none of it. "You are speaking of Lady

Sands?" he asked, hazarding a guess as Harry began pacing the room again. "You think she wanted to catch you?" What in God's name was the man babbling about?

Harry whirled on him, his eyes narrowing. "Oh, yes," he hissed. "I've had lots of time to think about it, de Rohan. Do you know what it is like to live in a house in mourning? Dashed dull, that's what. And Genevieve has done nothing but run the other direction every time she sees me. I think she'd sooner die than warm my bed now."

Warm his bed? Suddenly, the truth—at least a part of it—came horribly clear to Max. "And Genevieve Durrett was in your bed on the night your wife died, wasn't she?"

At last, Harry stopped pacing and sank into his chair. "Oh, devil take me if this doesn't look worse and worse," he sobbed, clasping his bloated face between his hands. "But I only bedded the girl, de Rohan. Whatever else I may have done that night, I didn't throttle my wife. Perhaps she'd sent her, hoping to catch us. I don't *know*. But she didn't. And I didn't kill her."

Max was inclined to believe him, though he'd long suspected Harry was hiding something. "This relationship with your wife's maid," he quietly asked. "Was it of long standing?"

"God, no," he said witheringly. "If that's what she says, it's a damned lie. Daresay I must have made a particularly pitiful sight that night. The chit practically threw herself at me. And in my state of mind—embarrassed by Julia and all that rot—well, a fellow wouldn't be apt to say no, would he?"

Some men, de Rohan considered, would have said precisely that. And from what he had seen of the world, women never slept with men out of pity. "Lord Sands, I am sorry to ask this," he gently pried. "But when you say Miss Durrett threw herself at you, what, exactly, do you mean?"

Without looking up, Harry shrugged. "Genevieve knocked on my door that night after Julia came in," he explained, mumbling into the carpet. "Struck me as dashed queer, for she asked me something silly—what, I can't recall—then she toyed with her hair a bit and made as if she meant to neaten the folds of my neck cloth. I tried to back away. Told her that I would just ring for my man."

"And then what?" Max encouraged.

Harry swallowed hard. "And then she looked me straight in the eyes, winked, and offered to do the job for me. 'The entire job, *monsieur,*' says she, in that pretty little accent of hers." At that, he finally looked up, abjectly holding Max's gaze. "It was sheer torture, de Rohan," he said quietly. "I don't keep a mistress, and I didn't dare sleep with my own wife for fear she'd get with child, and I wouldn't know it if was mine."

Max could scarcely bear to ask his next question. "Did she, Lord Sands?" he asked softly. "Did Julia ever become pregnant?"

A little sadly, Harry shook his head. "No. I've thought and thought about it, and unless—no, no, she was just barren. A great many females are, they say." His tone was one of anguished confusion. Few people, and certainly not Harry, were clever enough to feign such depth of emotion. The earl had not known about his wife, and whatever her sins, Julia was now answerable only to God.

"Lord Sands, I'm very sorry."

Still clutching the handkerchief, Harry shrugged almost hopelessly. "I was bedding my wife's maid on the night she was murdered," he said quietly. "I know how that looks."

Slowly, Max stood. He knew how it looked, too. A sense of grim despair seemed suddenly to envelop him, and he felt possessed by an almost overwhelming urge to flee the room, this house, his life. He was tired, so bloody tired, of all the ugliness and filth his job entailed. He was no longer sure just why he had cared so much about this crime, or any other, come to that.

He had the means to turn his back on it all, and for the first time in his life, he wished to do precisely that. Something in him, some delicate, tenuous emotion, seemed finally to have snapped, and he wanted nothing so much as to go home. No, it was worse than that. He wanted to go home *to someone*. Someone honest and pure. Someone who could make him feel clean and new and hopeful again.

"Dio mio," he whispered beneath his breath. He could not afford to swill another bottle of blue ruin to put that thought from his mind. He had to get a grip on himself. He had to go. He was needed in Wellclose Square, for Maria's note had said that Nonna Sofia had taken a chill. Pray God that, too, would not take a turn for the worse.

His thoughts in turmoil, Max bent down to touch Harry reassuringly on the shoulder. "I will return on Monday morning to speak with Miss Durrett," he said quietly. "However, I want you and your sister to get out of London. Go to Holly Hill or to Delacourt's estate in Derbyshire. Promise me."

Harry nodded weakly. "I shall try."

Max breathed a sigh of relief. "Good. In the meantime, try not to worry. I will do all that I can." Then he gentled his tone. "Now, let us ring for someone to bind up that hand. I think it must be seen to."

Mutely, Harry nodded again.

Upon leaving Harry, Max dashed through the sheeting rain and leapt back into his waiting hackney. He went at once to his grandmother's house, which seemed darker and gloomier than usual. It was, he hoped, just the weather. He let himself in with his own key and hastened past the front offices, lest he be delayed by another of Trumbull's impassioned pleas. Today he was just a little afraid the old boy might tempt him to do something rash, like hang up his hat on the office coat rack.

He arrived upstairs to discover that his grandmother was not quite the bedfast invalid Maria's impassioned missive had suggested. But she did lie limply upon an upholstered divan which had been moved into her sitting room. From the outset, Max had suspected Sofia might have been feigning illness to serve her own purpose—and he shuddered to think what that might be—but, to his shock, she really did not look well. He was more than a little surprised at the alarm which leapt in his chest at the sight of her, so appallingly frail and ashen, her hands folded, corpselike, beneath her bosom.

At once, he went down onto one knee, gently taking

one of her slender hands into his own. "Nonna," he whispered urgently. "Nonna, *come ti senti?*"

Slowly, her parchment-thin eyelids fluttered open, and she looked up at him uncertainly. "Oh, Max!" she rasped weakly. "Oh, Max, *tesoro mio,* I am weak. Weak, and so very cold. Ah, my heart, I think it is frozen."

"Shh, Nonna, you must rest. I will fetch the doctor." Max leaned across the divan to tuck the wool coverlet higher, but, with an agonizingly slow gesture, she lifted her other hand and pointed a quivering finger toward the hearth.

"*Per favore, caro mio,* first give me my shawl. I am freezing to death."

With a sudden sense of dread, Max rose to do as she'd bid, his hand lingering uncertainly over the length of pale blue wool. It looked like nothing he'd ever seen his grandmother wear. But it did look vaguely, uncomfortably familiar. And, by God, it smelled familiar, too.

But, without lifting her head, his grandmother nodded weakly. "*Si, caro mio,* the one on the chair." He returned to the divan and bent to one knee to tuck it gently around her. But she, too, now looked deeply confused, glancing up at him with eyes which were wide and questioning as she pushed the shawl away. "No, Maximilian," she murmured, gently fingering the unusual fabric. "This one, it is not mine. Now, where, I wonder, did it come from?"

Where did it come from?

Suddenly, Max felt as if he were being tormented past all bearing. She knew the answer to her question. And he knew, too. Still on one knee by the divan, Max was unable to stop the odd, choking sound which caught in his chest. Unable to keep himself from burying his nose in the froth of blue cashmere, unable to stop himself from dragging in the scent of woman and lilacs which yet lingered in its softness. The very essence of goodness and virtue, it seemed.

And suddenly, the trip to Harry's, the filth and brutality of his work, the unending emptiness of his life, all of it struck him yet again. He bowed his head as the crushing sense of despair rolled over him once more, and with it came an almost unbearable sense of loss and loneliness.

"Maximilian," said Sofia quietly, lifting one hand to stroke his shoulder lightly. "Ah, Maximilian."

Chapter Fourteen

Some time in the middle of another wretched night's sleep, Catherine awoke to the sound of rain hammering at her windows, the rhythm ratcheting upward until the glass seemed to rattle. In frustration, she rolled over and attempted to punch her pillow into submission. It would not work, she knew. She'd been dozing in fits and starts for weeks now, and her restlessness had nothing to do with her pillow. On an exasperated sigh, she slid upright in bed, lit her lamp, then took up Cam's copy of *The Female Speaker*. If a dry old literary anthology couldn't put her to sleep, nothing could.

Just then, the low rumble of thunder shuddered the sky. Catherine flung back the bedcovers and slid on her slippers and wrapper. She hated storms, hated even worse the fog which would doubtless follow. It always made her remember Will. But, oh! She would not think of that. If she could not read, she would look about for her needlework. But the thunder came again, closer and more ominous, and something—she knew not what— drew her to the window, undoubtedly the most danger- ous place to be.

And on this night, it was to prove especially dangerous. She leaned into the glass and pulled away the drapery, jerking back with a gasp. In a puddle of water and lamplight, a solitary man stood on the street corner, his shoulders slumped, his hat brim crushed limply into one fist. At that very instant, as if his black eyes were drawn by that same inexplicable force which had pulled her to the window, Max lifted his gaze to hers, staring up into the glass. And yet he could not possibly have known which room was hers. Could not possibly see her through the gloom and rain. But she sensed it all the same, his silent plea, as surely as if he'd spoken it aloud.

Oh, God. Squeezing her eyes shut, Catherine let the drapery fall. What did he mean by coming here? By looking at her so . . . so agonizingly? She would do noth- ing. Nothing! And yet she had wanted him to set aside his pride and come to her, had she not? Suddenly seized by an irrational impulse, she turned and flew through the room, grabbing her cloak as she went. Downstairs, she paused just long enough to toss it about her shoul- ders and yank an umbrella from the rack. As if pos- sessed by madness, she threw open the door and dashed down the steps into the drenching rain.

The street was devoid of traffic, the dampness cold on her face. She reached him in a matter of seconds, the puddles seeping through her slippers. "Max!" she cried, lifting the umbrella to thrust it over his head. "What on earth? Do you mean to make yourself ill?"

For a moment, he made no answer. In the cold night

air, the breadth of the umbrella sheltered them, dulling the rain to a roar, creating a strange sense of intimacy. Drops peppered and bounced all about them, the downpour edging toward hail. Max's gaze fixed on hers, his hard black eyes suddenly soft and shattered. As if something inside him had finally given way.

"Catherine, I wanted—" he began uncertainly. "The dog wanted . . . wanted walking."

Catherine looked about, mystified. "Max," she said gently, "you're three miles from home. You haven't any dog."

"Forgot him," he admitted, staring at his boots. "At my grandmother's. My stick, my umbrella . . . I—I forgot them, too. I just needed . . . I don't know."

He really was quite beside himself. Shaking her head, Catherine seized him by the arm. "Oh, I do not believe this!" she said, propelling him into the street. "What a fool I must look, standing in the street in my nightclothes! And you, too, Max. We are idiots, both of us."

Fleetingly, she felt him stiffen. "Where are we going?"

"Inside," she insisted, pushing open the door. "For brandy. And don't cut up stiff with me, Max, else we'll both die of a chill."

To her surprise, he stepped willingly inside and slid out of his sopping greatcoat, passing it into her impatient hands without argument. But his top hat looked a hopeless case. It was soggy and sadly misshapen. She took it from him, meaning to toss it onto the hall table, but something slithered out and fell onto the rug. Catherine looked down to see her favorite blue shawl lying in a pool at her feet.

"I set off with it in my hands," he said as she bent to scoop it up. "It was getting damp, and I—well, it wouldn't fit in any of my pockets."

He was a fool, but she had not the heart to scold him. "I see," she said gently, wondering why he hadn't simply wrapped it around his neck under his coat. "So you stuffed it inside your hat to keep it dry? How very kind, Max. But this scarf won't warm my heart if you die of a chill, will it?"

He stared at her unblinkingly and gave her no answer.

Catherine draped both her cloak and shawl over the newel post and made her way toward the drawing room. Inside, she kicked off her slippers, lit the lamp, and poked up the fire. All the while, Max stood, simply watching her. She rose from the hearth and let her gaze drift over him, drinking in his long, rangy length, his gently stooped shoulders, and when her eyes caught his, something wild and tentative fluttered inside her breast, like a fledgling trying its wings. Sweet heaven, what a striking man he was! And yet he looked miserable—his expression weary, his long, raven hair plastered wetly against his skin, emphasizing the lean, hard bones of his face.

She poured two tumblers of cognac, wondering just how far he'd walked in the rain and the dark. Surely not all the way from Wellclose Square? But the damp had certainly soaked through to his coat. "Oh, Max," she said softly, moving to brush her hand down the sodden sleeve.

Max seemed to draw away from her touch, and in response, she simply shook her head. "Just give me your coat," she insisted, trying to hide her sudden surge of tenderness. "And the waistcoat, too. Yes, yes, have them off, then put your boots by the fire."

But as she took both garments and spread them over chairs near the hearth, Max reached out, suddenly catching her wrist, jerking her none too gently against him. "Why are you doing this?" he rasped.

Catherine lightly lifted her brows. "To keep you from taking ill."

His face seemed suddenly to soften. "That's not what I meant," he said quietly. "Why are you making me . . . driving me . . . oh, Lord, Catherine. I don't know. I shouldn't be here. It is late. Your servants. Good God, your *reputation.*"

"Never mind the servants, Max." Her voice was calm. "They work for my brother. I am an independent widow, and my business is my own."

He released her wrist and began to move restively through the room, like some sort of caged animal. Which, in some ways, he was. Catherine had known Max de Rohan long enough now to understand that his life was on the street and that, so often, walls merely imprisoned him.

"Max," she gently probed. "Why are you here?"

He stood by the pianoforte now, staring blindly down at the keyboard. He reached out to touch one of the ivory keys. It echoed through the room, high and achingly clear, a melancholy note for a melancholy evening. "I don't know," he softly answered. "I just had to come. I miss you."

And suddenly, she understood that strange, tenuous feeling which fluttered so delicately in her breast. She had a name for it, and the name brought her no pleasure. She was in love with him, in love with him in a way in which she had never loved anyone, not even her husband. And damn Sofia Castelli for putting such thoughts into her head. For no matter his grandmother's words, she was not at all sure Max would ever permit himself to love her back.

Catherine moved to join him, and this time, he did not pull away. "I think you do know why you're here, Max," she insisted, staring up at him. "I think we both know."

He laughed, his voice a little bitter in the lamplight. "I begin to think, Catherine, that I know nothing at all. I have never been so confused, so torn, in all my life."

Lightly, she slid her hand beneath his elbow, turning him from the pianoforte to face her. "I think," she said very quietly, "that we should just accept this *thing* that we have between us, Max. Call it what you will—attraction or obsession, I don't care—but it exists. And perhaps you should stop fighting it."

He lifted his hand, lightly brushing the backs of his fingers up her cheekbone. "Catherine," he said, his voice laced with anguish. "I don't have a place for you in my life. Not in the kind of life I lead. You deserve . . . something better. And I can't change who I am. What I need to do."

"Have I asked for a place in your life, Max?" she asked, curving her hand about his and turning to press her lips into his palm. "Have I asked that you give up what you believe in? And if I did, well, what sort of woman would that make me?"

His empty hand slid up her arm and into her hair,

which hung loose to her waist. "What are you saying, Catherine?" he rasped.

She held his gaze unflinchingly. "Simply that I respect you," she whispered, letting his hand fall away. "And that I want you, Max, in the here and now. I've not had much luck in believing in forever."

With an agonizing slowness, he brought both hands up to cup her face, dipped his head, hovered. His eyes held hers, warm as brandy, dark as sin. Catherine shivered and came against him. This time, there was no fever in his touch. But there was a slow, simmering heat, and something which felt like a promise. Max let his lips play over her face, brushing one corner of her eye, her brow, lingering along her cheek, and, finally, settling over her mouth.

She kissed him back, opening beneath him, twining her arms about his neck. "Max," she whispered against his skin. "You are cold. I am lonely. Please, come upstairs with me."

As if she'd set flame to tinder, his kiss turned primal and ravenous. Ah, sweet heaven, this was what she wanted. She should send him away. Shouldn't let him hurt her again. But, unwittingly, she moaned and dug her fingers into his flesh.

In response, Max deepened the kiss, his tongue coaxing, his teeth drawing at her flesh. Catherine had never been touched with such skill or such certainty in her life. As he molded the long, hard length of his body to hers and bent her back into the strength of his arms, Catherine's heart slammed in her chest. The room and the rain faded from her consciousness. Her greedy fingers fisted in the fabric of his shirt, tugged the damp linen from his trousers, then slid beneath. She needed to feel the heat of his skin, yearned to feel smooth flesh and hard muscle beneath her hands. Needed to be bedded, to be one with this man. *This* man, and no other, heaven help her. She tore her mouth from his and whispered one word. "Please."

"Please what?" he rasped, his breath dragging in and out of his chest. "Say it, Catherine. And be sure. This time, there might be no going back. I need you too much."

"Please make love to me, Max," she begged. "I'm so tired of wanting you. Make love to me. Just once more. And maybe it *will* be enough. Maybe we *will* forget one another."

His hands were already fumbling with the close of her wrapper. "It won't be like that, Catherine," he warned, his lips pressed feverishly to her throat. "It won't be like that for me."

Catherine heard the surrender in his voice, heard the aching need in his words. They made their way through the house and up the stairs to her bedchamber. She pushed open the door and pulled him inside. As if they moved to music, they circled one another, caressing, kissing, shucking off clothes. The room spun about them, awash in muted light. His hands went at once to her nightgown, pushing it off her shoulders to bare her breasts. Her head swam, dizzy at the touch and heat of him. They bumped into the bedpost, clawing and kissing, Catherine tugging at the fall of his trousers.

He urged her back against the bedpost, and his lips caught hers again, bruising and desperate, driving her head against the carved wood. His eyes were like black smoke. The kind of eyes, Catherine thought, that could make a woman do something incredibly foolish. Was this foolish? She did not care. His touch was too hot, too insistent now. She needed him too desperately. Catherine shoved the shirt up his back, and Max ripped it over his head with one hand. "Independent widow or no, Catherine," he said, his hands sliding around her waist. "Your brother may well kill me for this."

"He'll never know," she swore. "I promise, Max. Just touch me. Yes, oh. Like that."

Her nightgown slithered down her hips and onto the floor. On a slow groan, Max shucked off his trousers and bent his head to her throat, devouring her, sliding lower. His mouth closed over her breast, drawing her nipple into the warmth of his mouth. He loved her for long moments, sucking gently at first, and then more erotically, nipping at her with sharp white teeth. Catherine whimpered her need, and he dropped to one knee, an almost reverent posture. With his big hands splayed out across her belly, he pushed her back until the carvings on the bedpost dug into her flesh, warm and hard, blurring the edge between pleasure and pain. Max urged her legs gently apart and delved between her thighs with his tongue, forcing Catherine to bite back an agonizing cry.

Oh, sweet heaven! She had always realized that he could do this to her—drive her wild with aching need—though she'd scarcely known what it would feel like. Yet she had wanted it, wanted him to push her beyond the edge of reason, beyond all she'd ever known. Max's tongue slid around, flicking out to tease her into a hard, tight bud of need, tasting and tormenting, until her knees began to buckle and her heart began to throb—not in her chest but between her legs.

"Oh, God," she breathed. "Oh, Max. In bed. I want you. Inside me. *Please* . . ."

Her hands slid down and through his hair, pulling him closer, pushing him away. He rose up, feathering kisses up her belly and breasts as he went. Somehow, she shoved away the tangled bedcovers and drew him onto the mattress. Her need for him was primitive, animalistic, like nothing she could comprehend. She wanted his strength and his heat, on her, crushing her, driving hard inside her.

He exuded masculine grace and raw energy, all of it held in check by sheer force of will. With his manhood erect, jutting powerfully from a tangle of black curls, Max looked at ease in his nakedness. With good reason, too. She'd never seen anything quite so breathtaking. Max was lean and sinewy, his rich olive skin dusted with hair, his chest a wall of solid, sculpted muscle, his thighs broad and hard. Good Lord, Will . . . well, Will had looked nothing like this. She caught her lip in her teeth, tried to shut away the thought. It was wrong, she knew, to make comparisons, but she knew so little of men. Max's hands grasped her shoulders, and he pushed her down and down, dragging his body over hers, wedging one big thigh between her legs to shove them roughly apart.

He gazed straight into her eyes, the silken weight of his erection brushing her thigh, and for a woman once married, Catherine felt shockingly inexperienced. Slowly, she slid her hand down and wrapped her fingers around the hot, throbbing length of him. Max sucked in his breath and squeezed shut his eyes, the tendons of his throat drawing taut. "Ah, Catherine!"

"I . . . should not?" she whispered.

"Should," he hissed, gathering her against him, burying his face into her shoulder. "Touch me, love. Touch me until I die of the pleasure."

Catherine stroked him again, reveling in the silky heat. "I want this inside me," she whispered against his heart. "Show me, Max. Show me what to do. It's been a miserable few weeks. I've probably forgotten how."

He laughed, a choking sob, his breath hot and moist against her throat. "Witch!" he panted. "You've forgotten *nothing."* He lifted his face and came onto his knees, straddling her, his cock reaching halfway up her belly. Sliding his fingers into her hair, he bent down, stilling her for another kiss which was savage and starved. Then, almost worshipfully, he placed one hand over her womb while the other spread her, probed her, drawing forth her desire, hot and slick.

Suddenly, a shudder seemed to rack his body. "Catherine," he choked, still staring down at her wet, swollen flesh. "Catherine, even if we're careful, have you considered that . . . that you could get with child? Might even carry my child now?"

Teetering on that fine edge of madness, Catherine thought that he meant to deny her. "I'm not," she cried a little desperately. "Oh, I wish I were, Max! But I can't."

His fingers still working her, his cock still hard and hot, Max threw back his head, the muscles of his throat working feverishly as he considered. "Catherine, you can't be sure," he rasped, staring up into the ceiling. "And so you must promise me something."

"Yes," she panted, drawing her hand down his length again. "Yes. Anything. Anything."

His head came down, his black eyes capturing hers, commanding her to his will. "Promise yourself to me, Catherine," he said quietly. "God forbid we make a child, but if we do, no matter your feelings, promise me we'll be wed. Swear it!"

"I—I do," she said certainly. "I swear it." But his hand was already on his shaft, and he was spreading her wide to take him. Catherine drew up her knees, set her feet on either side of his hips, and let her head fall back into the pillow, aching for what was to come.

Max let himself slide into her slowly. She was tight. Oh, mercy. So tight. She gasped at the size of him, and he hesitated. She enveloped him with warm, womanly flesh, coaxing, urging, and Max let his body surrender to the rhythm. Oh, God, what a sweet, sweet thing this was, like being welcomed home after a long and harrowing journey. Like feeling, ever so fleetingly, as if he belonged somewhere. And to someone.

Catherine sighed, lifting her legs to better cradle him. He bent his head and kissed her long and deep, and felt her ache answer his as she rose to meet him thrust for thrust. She seemed so delicate and beautiful beneath him, her shoulders pressed into the softness of the bed, her curtain of dark hair spread sideways across the pillow. In the silence, he drove into her, over and over, until sweat sheened his body and dampness slicked her thighs. But, God help him, he already wanted more. Much more. Not just release but a life. With her, this beautiful, brown-eyed earth goddess. On a whispery sigh, Catherine curled her legs about his waist and kissed him again, open-mouthed and eager, inviting him to claim her. He drove deeper, harder, and felt release slide blissfully near.

Then he dragged in his breath and prayed for restraint. He was no green boy. By God, he would not rut like one. He would take Catherine slowly, to better pleasure the both of them. He had to, for what if she'd spoken the truth? *Just once more,* she had begged. Now, with his cock throbbing hot and deep inside her, Catherine's words suddenly chilled his heart. He smoothed his hands around her waist, down her hips. "Move with me, Catherine," he whispered, lifting her as he rolled smoothly beneath her. "Come, love, on top of me."

Long, mahogany hair swaying over her breasts, Catherine came up, straddling him with her ivory thighs. "Oh!" she softly cried, pressing her fingertips into his chest to steady herself.

Max cupped his hands beneath the lush curve of her derriere, lifting her. "Oh!" she said again, more certainly. And then she came up onto her knees, easing up his shaft with an instinctive grace. The flickering glow of the lamp limned her, warming her skin to a pale peach. Again and again, she lifted herself, her mouth open in a silent cry, seeking her pleasure against his hardness. He let one hand drift up to push the hair back over her shoulder, baring her breasts to his hungry gaze. But when his knuckles brushed over her nipple, Catherine gasped, her eyes flaring open, burning bright with desire.

He lifted his hips, thrusting hard beneath her. His body surged, too soon, too fast. His mind raced, willing control. He battled for strength even as she sought pleasure from his body. Her breathing shifted into soft, thready pants. Crooning his name mindlessly, she began to caress herself, sliding her hands over her belly, cupping her own breasts, writhing as she drove her fingers into her hair, and Max was sure he would die of just watching her. His earth goddess. Good God, how he wanted her. Wanted her, *wanted her,* could keep no other thought in his head as he rhythmically thrust himself up and into her.

And then, Catherine moaned into the night, a sound of pure pleasure, her spine drawn back like a taut bowstring. He was undone by the sight. Unbidden, a feral growl sounded in the back of Max's throat, and he jerked up, twisting the rope of mahogany hair about his hand and dragging back her head to bare the tender stalk of her neck. He bit her hard, as a stallion would a mare, stilling her for his cock, pumping his hips furiously upward, driving himself deeper and deeper as Catherine rode him, whimpering.

In the night, flesh pounded against flesh, damp and sliding. Hunger and need sizzled like a lightning strike, came together in a firestorm of sensation. Fleetingly, his awareness faded, and he knew only his own desire, nothing of hers. And then she sobbed, and sobbed again, her tight passageway caressing him, milking him past the point of sanity. This time, there was no question; he had to come inside her. And then, Max felt himself explode, her every stroke lashing him with pleasure, like the crack of a hot, sweet whip.

Bone and muscle shuddered beneath the strain, until Catherine fell forward, her body collapsing across his own. For a long moment, they trembled in one another's arms until, almost prophetically, the lamp sputtered and went out. In the distance, thunder rolled across the night sky once more. Catherine did not stir.

"Oh, Max," she murmured drowsily against his throat. "Oh, my love. We're in serious trouble now. Once was *definitely* not enough."

With his body still inside hers, Max listened as the rhythm of her breathing shifted into a sound, innocent sleep. But slumber did not come to him so easily. *Serious trouble?* Ha. That was a lame phrase to describe the sort of trouble he was in. His body slaked but his mind in turmoil, Max wrapped his arms around Catherine and drew her closer, knowing with a dreadful certainty that his life had just changed forever.

Chapter Fifteen

Never maintain an argument with heat and clamour.
An injury is sooner forgotten than an insult.

—LORD CHESTERFIELD, 1776,
The Fine Gentleman's Etiquette

Catherine awoke long moments later, lifting her head to stare at Max through somnolent eyes, her breath softly stirring the hair on his chest. Max smiled and rolled with her onto his side, unable to tear his gaze from her. She gave him a slow, drowsy smile which curved her mouth and melted her eyes, and Max found himself hoping that his seed had taken root in her womb. And on that thought, his heart seemed to seize in his chest.

What sort of madness was this? This wasn't something he should wish for, for God's sake! He came fully awake, an old admonishment—some long-ago school-boy lesson—leaping unbidden to his mind. *He that hath wife and children hath given hostage to fortune.* True and clever phrasing, but whose? Virgil? No, Bacon.

In his mind, he could hear the mind-numbing clack of Herr Jaeger's chalk. His old tutor had been ever fond of philosophical debate, particularly this one, the notion that marriage was an impediment to those who took up society's most critical causes. But in his father's case, it had proven far worse than an impediment. It had been a tragedy. And Max had seen firsthand the truth of Herr Jaeger's beloved theory. A man who committed himself to a greater—and more dangerous—good could never afford the luxury of a wife and family. It was both foolish and perilous to think otherwise.

He was drawn gently back into the present by the warmth of Catherine's touch, which filled him with a pure, aching sweetness. She slid her hand along his jaw, pushed the hair back off his face, and softly laughed. "Oh, Max, your hair looks a fright," she murmured, her eyes drifting over him. "Did you walk all the way from Wellclose Square in the rain?"

Max frowned. "Yes."

"Ah," Catherine said quietly. "I thought so." Then she kissed him lightly on the chin, tucking her head against his shoulder. "Your grandmother is well, I hope?"

"My grandmother is insane," he muttered, brushing his lips over her hair. "But she's well enough, I'd say. Wouldn't you?"

Catherine didn't answer that one. Instead, she yawned and stretched again, beautiful in her languor. "Do you know, Max," she said musingly, "your appalling behavior aside, I have missed you dreadfully." Her words were spoken without any hint of malice. It was a kindness he scarce deserved.

"I'm not a very pleasant sort of fellow, am I?" he muttered, threading his fingers through her hair. "Really, Catherine, I can't think what you see in me."

With a wry half-smile, she looked up at him. "Oh, I suppose there's always decency and honor?" she suggested. "Then there's your willingness to work hard. And the fact that you care more for others than yourself. All very dull things to be sure, Max, but redeeming qualities nonetheless."

"Spare me my blushes, Catherine," he said dryly.

"Oh, don't blush yet, Max!" she warned. "I've not enumerated your bad habits."

"By all means, do so. I cannot bear suspense."

"Yes, of course," she said cheerfully. "You're stubborn, dogmatic, and appallingly arrogant. You always know what's best for everyone, are far too quick to say so, and your wardrobe sometimes looks like an afterthought."

"Is that all?"

"It will do for the nonce." She let her head fall back, pressing her ear to his chest, and lightened her tone. "Now, tell me what you've been up to. Talk to me, Max. I like to hear that soothing rumble in your chest."

Max felt acutely embarrassed. "I've nothing interesting to say."

"Ah, that sounded wonderful," she sighed. "Come, now, talk! What news of Julia's murder? Have you notched some suspect in your sights yet?"

His work again? It seemed she was always interested in his work, and, fleetingly, he wondered why. But she was Catherine. He could trust her. "Too bloody many suspects," he finally grumbled, reaching out to fondle a strand of her hair.

As if she wished to see his face, Catherine rolled gracefully onto her belly and propped herself up on her elbows. Despite the dim light, the angle provided a breathtaking view of her buttocks. "But what of your friends, Mr. Sisk and Mr. Kemble?"

"Sorry, what?" Max returned his gaze to her face.

Catherine crossed her legs at the ankles and stared intently back at him. "Constable Sisk and Mr. Kemble," she repeated. "Can they not help you narrow down this onerous list?"

Max opened his mouth to refuse her, to tell her he had no wish to discuss his work, but, to his consternation, that would have been a lie. He wanted very much just to rest here, stretched lazily atop her bed, sliding his fingers through her hair and pouring out his frustrations. And, really, as long as he didn't breach anyone's confidentiality, why couldn't he? To some extent, Cecilia had already involved Catherine.

"We've had some success," he finally admitted. "We've discovered there might be an element of jewel fraud involved. And we've eliminated most of the suspects. I'm persuaded we're narrowing in on one or two."

"Professional criminals?" she pressed. "Or one of her lovers?"

Max made a sound of disgust. "Lovers," he grunted. "Lord Bodley, for one, though I daresay I oughtn't mention names. Just continue to keep your distance from that one, Catherine. And there's another fellow, a young rogue with a rather desperate need for money."

Catherine crooked one brow. "You sound displeased."

Max frowned again and stared into the depths of the darkened room. "Oh, I rather liked the scoundrel," he reluctantly admitted. "Though I'm damned if I know why. Sisk, however, is certain of his guilt, and the fellow did leave town rather suddenly. Ah, but better him than Harry, I suppose."

"Max, that sounds rather harsh."

"Police work is a harsh business, Catherine," he answered, letting his fingers toy with a strand of her hair. "It is ugly and, frequently, no matter how hard we work, unfair. But we won't hang an innocent man."

Catherine dropped her gaze. "I never thought you would, Max," she murmured. "Tell me, is Harry no longer a suspect?"

Max shrugged and folded his arms behind his head, feeling rather pleased with himself as Catherine's eyes drifted appreciatively over his bare chest. "Not in my mind," he confessed. "But Harry isn't helping himself much."

"Oh?" ventured Catherine. "Bedding the lady's maid, was he?"

Max felt his mouth drop open. "How the devil did you know?"

Catherine's mouth curved enigmatically. "Oh, Cecilia feared as much," she confessed. "She's half afraid poor Harry will hang himself. Ladies do love to gossip, you know."

Max tried to look stern. "So you have said," he grumbled. "But you'd best have a care, Catherine."

Mischievously, she dipped her head and bit him, right in the tender flesh below his ribs. "Ouch, vixen!" he yelped, jerking away. "Don't bite!"

"Then don't scowl," she murmured, eyeing him across his chest as she soothed his skin with her lips and tongue. "And if you do, then take your punishment like a man."

Weary of the torment and driven just a little mad from staring at the luscious swell of her arse, Max grabbed Catherine's shoulders and flipped her neatly onto her back. She hadn't time to draw breath before he'd dragged his weight on top. "I'll show you punishment, you sharp-tongued wench," he growled, shoving her thighs apart and pressing her arms over her head. "I didn't come to your bed for a bloody lecture."

Eyes wide, Catherine swallowed, the motion of her throat entrancing. "For what, then?" Her voice was thick, husky. "Show me."

"For this," he answered, rising up to sink his shaft deep inside her. "To be pleasured. To ride you hard, Catherine. You begged me to come to your bed, and you may beg me to leave ere I'm done with you."

Catherine tipped back her head, opened her mouth. "Oh, is that . . . is that a threat?"

He barely heard her question, suddenly lost in sensation. "Ah, Catherine, I want to make you scream," he choked, the pleasure sucking him into her again. "I want to make you plead. I want, I think, to punish you for what you've done."

"What?" she panted, lifting her hips to meet his. "What, Max? What have I done?"

But Max did not answer, could not answer, for Catherine had wrapped her legs around his waist and had begun to rise to meet him with a sweet, urgent rhythm. She knew him now, understood his body, matched him stroke for stroke, sigh for sigh. In the near-dark, their eyes caught and held. Forcing her hands hard into the pillow above her head, Max held her down, held himself back, and drew out the pleasure like a fine silk thread. He wanted to thrust himself inside her forever. He wanted to stay forever in her bed, working her body, feeling it shiver beneath him. He was happy, he realized. Blindly happy. Her pleasure drove him, inspired him. Slowly, Catherine's eyes glazed over.

Soon her gasps ratcheted up, and her body began to beg for release even as he held himself in check. "Ah, ah, Max." Catherine fought, struggling to rise up from the bed. "Please—oh—oh, please, higher, now . . ."

But Max just smiled, pressed her firmly into the mattress, and settled in for a long, tormenting ride.

In the course of his long and strange career, Max had slept in some very odd places. Police work was half patience and half persistence, which meant a man often found himself cooling his heels long into the night. Miserably damp cellars, hard tavern settles, and once—while shadowing a corrupt customs officer—stuffed under a barrel in the hold of an East Indiaman. Yes, Max had slept everywhere. But he couldn't recall ever having slept into the wee hours of the morning with his arms about a woman. That had been a luxury he'd been careful never to allow himself. As a distant clock struck four, Max came slowly awake to find Catherine's body molded inside the curve of his own, and he realized just what a luxury it was. Sleeping with Catherine could prove addictive. And he almost didn't care.

A hostage to fortune. The phrase echoed again, but after a bit of sleep, it no longer seemed quite so ominous. He banded his arms more tightly about her, buried his head against the turn of her neck, and drew in the warm, comforting scent of her. Soap and lilacs. Heat and musk. *Woman.* He wanted to stay like this forever, to capture just this one moment for all eternity. Briefly, he let himself consider again. But, of course, he couldn't . . . and Catherine wouldn't . . .

No, it just wouldn't be wise.

But what if there *was* a child? Oh, *Dio.* Then everything changed. Then he would hold her, quite ruthlessly, to her promise. And he would have his own sacrifices to make, of course. Peel would have to find someone else to skulk about London, ferreting out bribery and corruption, because Max would no longer be able to risk taking a knife in the back. And he would have to buy a house far from Wellclose Square, for, no matter his high-minded politics, a wise man did not risk raising a child in east London.

And what, then, would he do with his life? Return to Alsace and attempt to reclaim his home? No, he had not the heart for that fight. Of course, he could quietly tend his vineyards in Catalonia. But Catherine was a bred-in-the-bone Englishwoman, and it was a peculiarity of the English that they could rarely be happy elsewhere. Max supposed he could always accede to his grandmother's wishes and help run the family empire, though they would doubtless agree on little. But empire or no, that would sit ill with Catherine's blue-blooded brother. No English earl would willingly see his sister wed into a long line of Italian merchants, not unless he were desperate for money, and Max had a deep suspicion that his family's wealth would hold little appeal to Catherine.

What a relief it was to realize there was no trickery in her. How, he wondered, could he ever have compared her to Penelope? She was just as beautiful, yes, but artlessly so. And she had that same milky-rose English complexion which, God help him, he found so wildly irresistible. But whereas Penelope had been slight and frail and almost desperately needy—or such was the impression she'd sought to give—there was little about Catherine which was frail, and she seemed to need no one but herself.

Cupped warmly into his body now, she still slept, her exhalations soft and soothing. A rare sense of peace settled over him, and, with a smile, Max rolled onto his back, dragged one arm across his eyes, and felt himself begin to descend again into blissful sleep.

Suddenly, a faint sound jolted him fully awake and set his heart to pounding. Soft footfalls, coming up the steps. Nearing the door. Max sucked in his breath and held it, horrified. Good God, surely not a servant? No, not at this hour. Instinct seized him. Max rolled silently off the bed and onto his feet, jerked on his drawers, and fell to a crouch in the shadows. The footsteps stopped. His every muscle alert, Max peered into darkness as the door swung open on silent hinges. An enormous, sinister figure crossed the threshold, closed the door, and approached the hearth. Christ Jesus, he was broad.

But when he reached the fireplace, the intruder set something down, cursing softly under his breath. The dying coals limned his booted legs, and Max watched as his arms stretched up, high over his head. And then, carefully, the man seized hold of the landscape which hung over the mantel, gingerly lifting it.

A thief? Good God!

But there was no other explanation. How the devil had he slipped in? He bloody well wouldn't be walking out. But Catherine's safety was paramount. He'd have to take the bold scoundrel where he stood, still off-balance, clutching his plunder. Max charged, seizing the intruder low around the knees, pitching him back, almost onto the floor.

The man grunted, his breath escaping on a sick wheeze. He cursed when his head cracked against the mantel. Max's elbow caught something hard. Wood splintered, and canvas ripped. Grunting and flailing, they went down in a tangle of legs and elbows, overturning a chair. Catherine's scream pierced the night, the mattress squeaking beneath her weight. Somewhere, glass shattered. A lamp, he thought. The thief fought back, kicking and cursing, scrabbling for purchase on the carpet. Taking aim in the darkness, Max miraculously planted a fist in his face. "Stand and hold, you son of a bitch," he growled. "You're under arrest by the King's authority."

Just then, Catherine's lamp flared to life. Another cry rang out, this one furious. "Good God!" she screeched. "Ooh, Bentley! I'm going to skin you alive this time!"

The man who lay bleeding on the floor weakly lifted his head and stared past Max, blinking uncertainly at Catherine. "Blister it, Cat!" he muttered, spittling blood. "D'you know you're naked?"

Max exploded with rage. "What the hell?" he shouted, heaving the man to his feet. "What business is it of yours? Just who the devil do you think you are?"

The young man pressed a sleeve to his gushing nose, eyeing him up and down. "And who 'er you, my fine fellow, to be naked in m'sister's bedchamber?"

"*Your* sister—?"

But Catherine had slithered off the bed, wrapping a sheet about her as she came. "Just none of your business who he is, Bentley!" she cried. "Have you no manners? Why can't you knock?"

"Your *sister*—?" Max muttered again, unheeded.

"Ha!" shouted Bentley. "It bloody well is my business! I mean to see this bold chap at dawn over a brace of pistols!"

Something clicked in Max's brain. *"Rutledge—?"*

"You damned fool!" Catherine hissed at the intruder. "Sober up! It *is* dawn. Or all but! And this man is a magistrate!"

Max was suddenly eager to violate the law. "Sir, name your sec—"

The Honorable Mr. Bentham Rutledge cut him off with a violent curse. "A *magistrate?*" For the first time, the young man looked squarely at Max. "Well, damn my eyes!" he whispered almost cheerfully. *"De Rohan?"* And then his gaze took in Max's near-nakedness, and his expression shifted back to fury. Lunging, he seized Max about the throat, catching him unaware, shaking him until his teeth clacked. "You friggin' bastard! I'll kill you for this! That's my sister!"

Just then, a knock sounded on Catherine's door. Max and Bentley froze in a parody of violence. "My lady?" whispered a high, frightened voice. "Is aught amiss, ma'am? We—we heard a terrible racket belowstairs."

Catherine hiked her bedsheet a little higher. "W-we're quite fine, Mrs. Trinkle," she managed to answer. "It's just—er, Bentley. And me. We're just having a bit of a—er—a philosophical difference."

A pregnant silence followed. "Oh."

"Go back to bed, Mrs. Trinkle," Catherine soothed. "Really, feel free."

But the mysterious Mrs. Trinkle's confidence seemed to have been bolstered. "And did I hear something break in there, ma'am?" she asked warningly. "I mean, his lordship, he's terrible particular about his things, you know. And if anything broke . . ."

Catherine smiled weakly. "I'll deal with Cam, Mrs. Trinkle. Please, you may go back to bed."

But the strident, disembodied voice persisted. "And ma'am—?"

Catherine hissed between her teeth. "Yes—?"

"There are a great many damp things strewn about the drawing room," she said, censure plain in her voice now. "Men's coats, ma'am. Stockings and boots, too. Would you happen to know—"

"Mine!" shouted Bentley, scowling darkly at Max. "They're mine, Mrs. Trinkle. I'll see to them at once."

"Very well, Mr. Rutledge," she said disapprovingly. "And about those brandy glasses—"

"Mrs. Trinkle!" screeched Catherine. "Please! Go. Back. To. Bed."

"Well!" harrumphed the voice beyond the door. "Well, I never! Such goings-on!"

Rutledge waited until the footfalls retreated down the steps, then launched himself at Max with a renewed vigor, catching him hard in the ribs. Max faked to the left, then took Rutledge low in the gut with a punch that sent him reeling. Just then, Catherine thrust herself between them, still clutching at her sheet. "Stop!" she growled, throwing out her arm. "Stop, the both of you! This instant!"

Remembering her strong right hook, Max let his fists drop. Even he hadn't the ballocks to take on *two* enraged Rutledges. With a sneer, Catherine's brother stepped away and shook himself off, jerking his head derisively at Max. "I don't know how the devil he wheedled his way between your sheets, Cat," he said in a cold, quiet voice. "But that man is no true gentleman."

"Mind your tongue, Bentley!"

"No! I won't," the young man hotly insisted. "He's nothing but an upstart and has treated you—*my sister*—like a common slut. I won't have it, I tell you."

Catherine's eyes narrowed to angry slits. "As usual, Bentley, you are completely clueless—"

But Max cut her off, shouldering her aside. "I may be no gentleman, sir," he snarled, standing toe to toe with Bentley. "But insult your sister once more at your peril."

Her face a mask of anger, Catherine whirled about, abandoning them. "Oh, have at one another, then!" she snapped, stepping behind a screen and tossing the sheet over it with a furious gesture. "Rouse the whole house! Clearly, my reputation is less important to either of you than satisfying your masculine pride."

With one eye on Rutledge, Max retreated. She was right. This was neither the time nor the place. He moved about the room, snapping up his clothing and jerking it on in silence. As he draped his cravat carelessly about his neck, Rutledge began to wipe the blood from his face with a handkerchief, watching Max like a bad-tempered cur. At last, Catherine swished from behind the screen, her glossy hair still loose but dressed in a green muslin gown. Rutledge, however, couldn't keep his mouth shut. "It just looks deuced bad, Cat, you tossing up your skirts for some police inspector," he muttered into his handkerchief. "And devil take you, de Rohan, if you ain't broken my nose."

Stabbing his shirttails into his trousers, Max returned to the hearth. "Then perhaps you'd like to tell us why you slunk into your sister's room to steal a painting, sir," he demanded, stabbing one finger in Rutledge's face. "Have you some pressing need for cash?"

"That, sir, is a bloody insult." Rutledge laughed derisively. "I never stole so much as a ha'penny in my life. Brought m'sister a surprise, is all. Wanted her to see it when she awakened."

"Well, I've definitely been surprised," Catherine muttered, but Rutledge had turned away to heft up a huge package propped beside the fireplace. "What on earth is that?"

Suddenly, Max understood why the man had looked so large when he'd entered the room. Still reeling with shock and anger, he now added mortification to the pile. Rutledge hadn't meant to steal anything—he'd brought his sister some sort of gift! And if Max had just kept quiet, the fellow would undoubtedly have left it and promptly disappeared. To hide his embarrassment, Max knelt down to examine the ruined landscape which Rutledge had removed from the chimney piece. The frame was broken, the canvas torn, perhaps beyond repair. "I'll send Mr. Kemble round to see what can be done about this," he muttered, almost to himself.

He looked up to see that neither had paid him any heed. Instead, Catherine was watching fixedly as her brother stripped the last of the wrappings from the package. A sheaf of brown paper fell away to reveal an ornate gold-leaf frame which held yet another paint-ing—this one so new it still reeked of pigment and tur-pentine. Rutledge shot Max a snide, triumphant look and set the portrait atop the mantel. Max stood, his eyes drifting over it. He knew art, and this piece was exquis-itely done. In the background stood a pretty little manor house of butter-brown stone—Cotswold stone, the En-glish called it. From the foreground, a hearty, blond-haired squire stared down at them, his eyes merry, his cheeks pink. A pack of dappled spaniels milled at his feet, and in the crook of his arm, he balanced a finely in-laid fowling gun. Of course, there was no mistaking his identity.

Max felt sick, but Rutledge fairly beamed at his sister. "I guess you'll forgive me for filching your miniature now," he said proudly.

All the blood had seemed to drain from Catherine's face as her eyes moved again to the portrait. "My . . . miniature?"

Bentley looked taken aback. "That little picture of Will when he was a lad? I pinched it from your kerchief drawer weeks ago—you know, when you were cry—er, well, dash it, Cat, didn't you even miss it?"

"No." Catherine looked confused. "Why would you take it?"

But Rutledge's face had fallen. "You said you couldn't remember old Will—what he looked like just before—well, you know. And I thought you'd like a big portrait, to remember him as he was."

"Yes, of course," she whispered, her voice hollow. "How kind."

Feeling dreadfully out of place, Max drew away,

deeply confused. What was going on here? Rutledge . . . and Catherine? Of course, he'd never really believed Rutledge guilty. No, not precisely. But this was an unnerving bit of happenstance. Max had learned long ago to trust no one. But, fleetingly, he'd trusted Catherine. And she had asked him a great many questions, offered over and over again to involve herself in the case. Surely she had not . . . no. No, it wasn't possible. It was a cruel coincidence.

But Max had never believed in coincidence. How, then, could it be that this woman he had—well, grown *fond* of—was a sister to such an arrant scoundrel? An awful sense of dread was stealing over him, crushing the air from his lungs, leaving him with a gut-wrenching panic. He had to get away. Had to think this through. Before he said or did something he would forever regret. He couldn't stay here. And he couldn't live without her. What a damnable coil.

But Rutledge was still crowing over the bloody portrait of his dead brother-in-law. "And so I took the miniature up to old Weyden's," he was explaining. "See, his Cousin Evie's got a deft hand with a paintbrush—famous, even, I collect. And Weyden dug up his old sketches from our hunting party a few years back—you remember, he'd done the house, the dogs, even one or two of Will? And she just studied them all and made this."

"How kind," Catherine repeated.

"Don't you care for it, then, Cat?" Rutledge looked at her strangely. "I mean, it was the devil to tote back from Essex."

Clutching her hands like an anxious schoolgirl, his

sister looked back and forth between them, seemingly unable to answer. Max returned to the pool of lamplight. "Catherine, I am quite obviously *de trop* here," he said quietly. "I must go." He sketched a stiff bow to her brother. "Mr. Rutledge, kindly wait upon me tomorrow at my offices in Whitehall."

Rutledge glanced at him as if he were a street sweeper. "Oh, never mind, de Rohan," he said dismissively. "I've nothing more to say to you."

His arrogance inflamed Max. "Ah, but I have a great deal to say to you, sir," he returned. "And a great deal more to ask. In particular, I should like to chat about that rather egregious debt you've incurred at Mr. O'Halleran's gaming salon."

"Who, old Tommy?" Rutledge looked at him in haughty disdain. " 'Twas but two thousand pounds, a mere trifle, and made good this very night. And what business is it of yours, anyway?"

Max smiled tightly. "I should like to know," he said quietly, "just how you managed to pay it."

Catherine's eyes widened. "Really, Max." Her voice was gently chiding. "I can't think why you need concern yourself with my brother's debts. They're usually dreadful, to be sure, but he always makes them good, and—" She broke off uncertainly and placed a trembling hand on Max's arm, turning him to face her. "Max, my dear, what's this about? Surely Bentley is not the one who—I mean, you cannot think he . . . ?"

Max felt a sudden, aching tenderness and tried to will it away. "This is between your brother and me, Catherine," he said gently. "It has nothing to do with you."

Her grip on his arm tightened. "Perhaps, Max, you

do not understand." Realization was chilling her gaze. "What concerns one Rutledge concerns us all. Be careful. Very careful. Despite what others may think, we are an inordinately close family."

Her distant tone cut him to the quick. "So one might begin to suspect," he said softly.

Suddenly, the air about them thrummed with a new tension. "This is about Lady Sands, isn't it?" Catherine's voice was cold now.

At once, Rutledge's dispassion drained away. He stepped closer, his gaze shifting between them, his words arch. "What about Lady Sands, Cat?"

Catherine turned to look at him. "Bentley, did you know her? Is it true? Were you . . . intimate?"

Rutledge lost a bit of his color. "I'd say that's my business," he said quietly. "Will someone tell me what the deuce is going on?"

The muscle in Catherine's jaw twitched. "Well, unless I miss my guess," she answered as she crossed her arms over her chest, "my lover suspects my brother of murder. Do I have the right of it, Max?"

Max hesitated. "This is just an investigation, Catherine," he equivocated. "I have to do my job."

Catherine shook her head. "No, Max. Oh, no. It is not *just* an investigation now."

Rutledge looked truly stricken. "What in God's name are you two talking about?" he rasped, seizing his sister by the shoulder. "Julia . . . she isn't . . . *dead?*"

Slowly, Catherine turned to face him. "Oh, Bentley. Did you not know?"

Mutely, Rutledge shook his head. "I've been—why, I've been in the country for weeks and haven't so much as glanced at a newspaper." His handsome face crumpled a bit. "Why would anyone hurt Julia?"

"Perhaps for money," said Max very quietly. "The famous Sands Sapphire was stolen."

At once, Rutledge's expression shifted to a mask of rage. "And you think I would kill her? *Steal* from her? Good God, man, Julia was harmless! Vain and foolish but harmless! You, sir, are beneath contempt. You come in here, seduce my sister—a *lady*—then dare to insult me beneath my brother's roof?" His tone dropped to a quiet, certain fury. "Get out. Get out, by God, or I shan't be accountable for the consequences."

Catherine held her brother's gaze, refusing to look at Max. "Excuse us, Bentley," she said, pushing him toward the door. "Please go and fetch his things. And then Max will go. I promise."

Rutledge hesitated, then seized the doorknob with a violence. "Then, by all means, let me speed his leave-taking," he answered, slamming shut the door as he went.

Her hands fisting in her skirts, Catherine turned to face Max. "He is not guilty, Max," she whispered. His gaze snapped to hers. "He is not!" she repeated. "Maybe he—he slept with her? I don't know, but, Max, how can you look at me so? How can you think, after all that has passed between us . . . ."

"Think what, Catherine?" he demanded, his fingers jerking a tight knot in his cravat.

Catherine had never seen eyes so black and cold. "Max, do you think I don't know? That I cannot see what you're half afraid of?" She swept her arm toward the bed. "Do you think this has been some sort of elaborate ruse?"

"I have said no such thing."

"I'm not sure you need to." Catherine closed the distance between them and set her hand firmly upon his arm. He froze at her touch and turned away. "Oh, no, Maximilian!" she whispered, tightening her grip. "You'll not use this as an excuse to shut me out. To punish yourself. Question my brother if you must—it matters little, for you'll soon see he's innocent—but don't give up on us. Not now. Not when we have so much at stake."

At that, he seized her hard by the shoulders. "What, Catherine?" he rasped, shaking her a little roughly, drawing her almost against his chest. "What is it that we have at stake? Just your brother's neck? Or something more? You tell me!"

"Oh, Max!" she said softly, feeling her eyes well with dampness, feeling his fingers dig into her flesh. "How can you even ask? What do you want me to say? That I love you? That I wish you to the devil just now? Good God, I'm half afraid that both might be true!"

His face taut with an emotion she couldn't fathom, Max jerked her against his hardness, lowering his mouth to hers. His kiss was swift, unyielding. Catherine gasped, drawing in his scent of spent anger and male sweat. She could feel his heart pounding against hers, feel the rush of emotion through his bones. Hungrily, his lips moved on hers, his mouth at once passionate and curious. And, briefly, she was lost in the storm. She needed him. Needed him to stay, to sort all this out and say it was all a mistake.

A noise in the passageway brought reality crashing down. They sprang apart, but not before the door flew open to admit Bentley. He dropped Max's damp boots

and clothing unceremoniously onto the carpet, survey-
ing the two of them with open disgust. "Will deserved
better than this, Cat," he said quietly. "He was my best
friend, and he was a good husband, too. You dishonor
him. Deeply. And there's no hiding it now. Trinkle's got
all the servants up and at their morning chores."

Max made no answer. Catherine drew away to the
edge of her bed, wrapping her arms about her body as
Max finished dressing in silence. She spun around at
once, however, when she heard her window scraping
open.

Max had shoved up the sash and thrown one leg over
the sill before she found her tongue. "Max!" she cried,
rushing to the window. "Good God, we're three stories
up!"

Max's gaze clouded over, impenetrable in the lamplight. "Better your servants should know nothing of
your *deep dishonor,* ma'am," he answered, and promptly
dropped away.

With a muted cry, Catherine braced herself on her
palms and leaned fully out into the gloom, Bentley cran-
ing out behind her. "Max!" she cried again. "Be careful!"

"Well, bugger me!" murmured Bentley appreciatively. "He's a bloody idiot."

But Max was halfway down the brickwork, deftly
shifting his balance from drainpipe to windowsill and
back again, as swift and as silent as any housebreaker.
Catherine's heart caught in her chest as he neared the
bottom, his weight swaying perilously over the vast
black pit of the kitchen stairwell as he hung from a ledge
by his fingertips. She needn't have worried. Kicking
smoothly away from the house with both feet, Max

twisted about and cleared the wrought-iron balustrade by a good six inches. He landed neatly on the glistening pavement, quiet as a cat, then disappeared into the murk.

Catherine fell to her knees in a crush of green muslin, both hands still clutching the windowsill so hard they had gone numb. "Oh, Bentley!" she sobbed as his arms came around her shoulders. "Oh, Bentley."

Chapter Sixteen

*And when you have found out the prevailing passion
of anyone, remember never to trust him where that
passion is concerned.*
—Lord Chesterfield, 1776,
The Fine Gentleman's Etiquette

Hatless, his clothing still damp, Max made his way
through the wet, poorly lit lane which cut through
toward Regent Street. He felt as if he couldn't move fast
enough, couldn't get far enough from Catherine's
stricken face, her brother's unmitigated arrogance. *Or
that goddamned portrait of her dead husband.* Panic still
clawed at him. Confusion still drove him, all of it over-
riding his street-sharp wits. What had Catherine
known? *Anything?* Where had Rutledge been? *In Essex,*
his instincts screamed. But, damn it, were his instincts
right?

The damp clung to him like a shroud. *A hackney.* He
should have waited near Oxford Street for a hackney. It
was late, the morning fog already rolling in off the river.
Dangerous, he knew. But a blind sense of urgency
pushed him. Something about Rutledge nagged at him,
had done so for days. And he, who forgot nothing, could
not remember. What? *What was it?* On his left, some-

thing small slid from the shadows, low and fast. Max started, spun about. A street urchin? A stray dog? Gone now. Heedlessly, he strode on, skirting the edge of Mayfair which was dark and devoid of traffic.

He crossed over Piccadilly into St. James's. Here it was marginally safer, the bucks and blades of society still dashing in and out of their clubs, milling about the streets, and calling for their carriages. Near the palace, he passed a pair of staggering young officers, blue-coated Horse Guards, singing boisterously as they returned to barracks a little worse for the wear. Closer to the park, an overly perfumed gentleman in a black opera cloak pushed past Max, flicking him a curious glance. But his hat was drawn low, his collar folded up. Max ignored him, and the man moved on, his heavy walking stick clacking furiously on the pavement.

Not when we have so much at stake. Catherine's words echoed in his mind. What had she meant? What had she known? *Nothing.* And it did not matter. He'd had no business in her bed, anyway. But he could not live without her. It mightn't matter what her brother had done. Or what she had known.

Oh, God! Max did not slow down, resisting the urge to burst into a run as he approached the park's fringe. Here, the fog rolled in unimpeded, keeping him to the graveled path rimming the edge. *Careful, careful.* A man could never be too careful. He knew that. He had been a fool to come out so late at night with no dog. Not even so much as his stick or his knife for protection. A fool to go to Catherine's, too. Footsteps crunched in the darkness behind him. Max halted, slid behind a tree. No one. No one at all. He'd simply lost his wits. He moved on, making his way from the park toward Cockpit Steps, a shortcut he often used. But only in daylight, a cautioning voice whispered in his head. *Never in the dark.*

It was his last clear thought.

Max's feet hit the first step just as the cudgel struck the base of his skull with an awful sound. His knees buckled, and his head cracked against stone. His hands came up, found nothing, then clawed at the stairs. Consciousness danced from his grasp. Something caught him hard in the ribs. Then his head, again and again. *Jesus Christ!* The pain was hot and bright, the steps wet on his cheek. Blood? Whose? *Rutledge . . . Rutledge had been bleeding.* No, no, that made no sense.

Another blow. A grunt. *Careful, careful.* Something in his ribcage popped. *A man could never be too careful.* The thought tried to suck him down. Max fought his way up from the blackness, instinctively raising his arm to ward off the next attack. But from deep in the darkness, a quavering voice sang out.

"Stop, thief!" It was a weedy, distantly familiar sound. "Help! Rape! Arson! Bloody murder!" And then the grating sound of a watchman's rattle.

Moments passed, Max in a heap at the foot of the stairs. Then a long, dark silence, stretching to infinity. Small, frozen fingers probed his skull, rolled him over. Cold. God Almighty, something was cold against his spine.

"De Rohan?" The small voice came at him as if through a long, dark tunnel. "Yer ain't dead, are you? Oh, wake up, sir! Lud, wake up afore 'e comes back!"

"Nate—?" Max managed to mutter. "You, boy?"

"It's me, awright, sir," he whispered. "But we've gots ter get yer orf these stairs, and sharp-like."

"You brought . . . a watchman?"

The boy paused for a heartbeat. "Not exactly," he confessed. "Just filched me a rattle orf the Pall Mall watch-box."

Somehow, Max dragged himself to a seated position. Something warm was streaming down his neck. Tremulously, he touched it. *Blood.* Unmistakably his. "Wh-what—" he began unsteadily. "What are you doing here?"

"Noffink," he said defensively.

Max cursed. "The truth, boy!"

Feet scuffled nervously on the step. Max forced one eye open. "Awright," admitted the boy reluctantly. "I was pokin' me forks in a few pockets down in Pall Mall when I seen this big gentry-cove turn about ter follow yer orf into the park."

The boy was lying, but Max let it pass. "A gentry-cove?"

"A swell," clarified Nate. "In a long black cloak. "And 'e 'it yer wiv 'is stick, I'm thinking."

Max gripped the wall and staggered to his feet. "You didn't see?"

The boy shook his head. "No, but I 'eard. I was close on 'is 'eels."

Somehow, Max managed a strangled laugh. "Oh, yes! Arson, rape, and—er—bloody murder, was it? Most effective." He clapped a steadying hand on the boy's shoulder. "*Grazie,* Nate. You're a clever lad, thank God. Now, can you help me get home?"

* * *

Catherine managed to wait until midday before making up her mind. But in the end, she decided to run Max to ground. Again. Had she no pride? No, apparently not. Or perhaps she had too much? Certainly, she was angry, inordinately so. Angry with her brother, who had acted like an ass and been soundly lectured for it over breakfast. And angry with Max, the ass with whom she was not yet done.

She was also just a little desperate. Catherine had come to London seeking something which had been missing from her life. And she had found it. Now, after a night in Max's arms, Catherine feared for her sanity. Indeed, she very much feared she had inherited her father's sexual appetites and, perhaps, his judgment.

No! She would not think that. It was not true. Max de Rohan was a good man, and what she felt for him went far beyond sexual desire. Perhaps that was what frightened her, what made her willing to throw her pride to the wind. Max was . . . oh! There were no words for what he made her feel. And it made Catherine realize that some things were worth more than pride, that some emotions burned hotter than anger.

She had to go to him. Had to reason with him, set things right between them, sooner rather than later. And she had to defend Bentley, of course. Though, as usual, her brother was his own worst enemy. What in heaven's name had he been thinking? Sleeping with Julia Markham-Sands! She had been an amoral cat—not to mention a vast deal older than he. And Bentley was, plainly put, a rakehell of the first water. He ran with bad men and wicked women and he was forever turning up where he had no business. *Like last night.*

Oh, perhaps Max deserved a tiny bit of sympathy. And so Catherine dashed toward Regent Street and hailed a hackney, giving the address of Max's rooms near the Chelsea Road and praying that he would be there on a Sunday afternoon. He had to accept her help now. This murder had suddenly become very, very personal.

The carriage drew up along the pavement, and Catherine looked out apprehensively at the large, rather ordinary house. A small boy sat on the doorstep whittling on a slat of wood with a rusty pen knife. The big black beast lay at his feet. Catherine paid the driver and stepped down. At once, the beast rose to his feet, his every muscle suddenly taut, his eyes keen. The lad, too, was watching her with a wary expression. He looked plumper and cleaner than she recalled, but she recognized him. "Nate?"

At the sound of her voice, the dog relaxed, stretched, and came padding down the walkway, his tail wagging. The boy, however, was not so easily won. "Afternoon, mum," he said without rising. "Did de Rohan send for you?"

Nate looked as if he'd been sitting thus for hours, like some sort of diminutive sentry. Catherine felt just a little uncomfortable, as if she'd just been asked for a secret password or the answer to a trick question. "I'd like to see him if he isn't busy," she equivocated.

The boy snorted. "Aye, well, the surgeon's finally gone," he answered. "But yer'll 'ave ter get past the gargoyle. Except for the old *signora*'s footman wot brought the dog, she's sent 'em all orf wiv their tails between their legs."

"The *surgeon?*" Alarmed, Catherine dropped to a

crouch, staring at the boy. "What happened?" As if disturbed by her tone, Lucifer began to nuzzle reassuringly about her face. Gently, she stroked a hand over his head and pushed him back to look at the boy. "Nate?" she demanded.

The lad's eyes flicked over her, careful, assessing. "Couldn't say, mum," he finally responded. "But 'e'll be awright."

Catherine stood up, clutching her reticule against her ribs. "I must go in at once," she insisted anxiously. "The landlady, she—well, she cannot very well keep me out. Can she?"

"Oh, she might do," he said, looking up at her with an amused twinkle. "But I reckon yer could go over the back wall, if you've a mind. That way, no one knows 'ow long yer stays, neither."

Uncertainly, Catherine licked her lips. "Go through the garden, do you mean? Right to the back door?" It was a bold move, but it could avoid all manner of potential unpleasantness. Particularly when she was not at all sure Max would wish to see her.

As if she'd agreed to the scheme, the boy stood and shook the wood shavings from his trousers. He muttered something in Italian to the dog, who lay back down to guard the steps. Then, mutely, Catherine followed him around the house and down the alley. Halfway along the wall was a low spot, obviously well used. With an oddly dapper gesture, the boy squatted down and tapped on his shoulder. "Put yer foot right 'ere, mum," he invited. "Then hop up and heft yer bum inter that swag."

Refusing to consider the oddity of the situation,

Catherine did as instructed, then swung her skirts up and over. For a moment, she teetered, hesitating. The garden looked deceptively deep, and it had been a long time since she'd pulled such a prank. But her hesitation was short-lived, for, to her shock, the boy's hands came up, settled firmly on her rear, and gave a hearty push.

With a little yelp, Catherine half slid, half leapt. Arms flailing and skirts billowing, she landed square in a clump of burgeoning peonies. It was a strangely exhilarating experience. Staggering gracelessly to her feet, Catherine righted her bonnet with one hand, shot a peevish glance back at the wall, then made her way to the french window which gave onto Max's parlor. Again, she briefly hesitated, then bit her lip and rapped sharply upon a windowpane.

"Damn you, don't break the glass!" shouted a rusty, disgruntled voice from deep within.

Taking that as permission to enter, Catherine pushed open the door and stuck in her head. The parlor was empty. Catherine bolted the door, dropped her cloak and reticule onto the settle, and walked straight down the corridor and into his narrow bedchamber. At once, terror leapt in her chest.

"My God, Max!" she whispered, rushing across the room. "What happened to you?"

Propped on a half-dozen pillows, Max opened one eye. "You!" he barked. "My God! What are you doing here?" But there was little anger in his tone. Awkwardly, he struggled to sit up. Near his elbow, a pair of well-worn notebooks lay upon the coverlet, and in his efforts, they slid off and onto the floor.

Catherine tried to urge him back down again. "Be

still," she insisted, scooping up the notebooks. "You're hurt, you fool."

Max grunted, dragging himself onto his forearms. "I suppose that's what attracts me to you, Catherine," he said dryly. "Your endearing terms of affection." But he fell back into the pillows, his eyes searching her face, his expression almost gentle. "Your brother did not by chance follow me and exact his revenge last night, did he?"

Catherine stiffened her spine and stood up. "He certainly did not," she hotly insisted. "Bentley did not leave my side until . . . well, for quite a while." *Until I stopped crying,* she silently added.

Max lifted his hand from the coverlet, offering it to her as if in peace. "I rather thought it wasn't him," he admitted, drawing her fingers into his. "I almost wish it had been. It's a bit disconcerting not to know one's enemies."

His tone was so self-deprecating that Catherine relented. "You've been struck some rather nasty blows," she said, leaning across to gently push the hair back off his forehead. "Worse, even, than *I* thought you deserved. Are you concussed, do you think?"

Max gave a bark of laughter. "It depends on how many beautiful women are leaning over me."

"Umm, I thought so." She flicked a fretful gaze back and forth between his pupils. He would live, she decided, but he had been lucky. Another inch to the left, and his eye would have . . . Catherine shut away the thought. "You've no idea who did this?"

An odd half smile curved his mouth. "Oh, I have a list," he said softly. "The Sands suspects."

Catherine lifted her brows. "Made someone nervous, have you?"

Max gave a sound of disgust. "What I've made is an incredibly stupid blunder," he grumbled. "And yes it's made someone very nervous. I sent letters round to almost everyone, mentioning the forged jewelry, hoping to flush the killer out of the bush. Most effective, was it not?"

She smiled and tucked his sheets a little higher. "You're very bold," she murmured. "Now, sir, may we declare a truce? I've come to offer you my services, and you certainly look as though you need them."

He flicked her a wary glance. "What sort of truce? Dash it, Catherine, you oughtn't be here at all."

She pursed her lips for a moment. "My brother did not plot an attack against you last night," she quietly began. "Frankly, he doesn't think that far ahead. Nor did he murder anyone. And this beating proves it, I should think."

Max glowered at the coverlet, clearly weighing his words. "Officially, Catherine, he's a suspect," he quietly insisted. "Because it is remotely possible that the man who attacked me last night had another reason for doing so. I doubt it, but in my line of work, a man makes enemies."

"I am not one of them, Max."

He shook his head, squeezing shut his eyes. "I've never wished to think your brother guilty, Catherine," he rasped. "But don't you see that such a wish is the very thing which can make a man careless? It means one must try twice as hard to be impartial—"

"But Max," she interjected. "Have I hidden anything

from you? Ever evaded your questions? No, because you've asked me nothing. Instead, you've seized every opportunity to thrust distance between us. And you have shared nothing of yourself, either, Max. *Nothing.* I have had to learn the truth about the man I . . . *I care for* from his grandmother!"

Suddenly, Max's eyes sparked with icy black fire. "Oh! I can only imagine the romanticized rubbish she's fed you!" he growled. "But I am not the person Nonna Sofia has led you to believe, Catherine. If I ever was, I'm not now. Pay no heed to the tittle-tattle of a meddling old woman."

Despite his sharp words, though, she could see the reluctant acknowledgment in his eyes. Catherine drew a deep, steadying breath. "You are you, Max," she said simply. "Inside, you are the man I care for. The façade you show the world is no business of mine. Be whomever you please for them, but never try to fool me."

Finally, his expression softened, as if he were considering something.

"Pax, Maximilian," she encouraged, offering him her hand.

He took it and, to her shock, lightly pressed his lips to it. "Sit down, then," he answered, drawing her closer. "I need your help with those." He jerked his head toward the notebooks.

Lightly lifting her brows, Catherine settled herself on the edge of the bed, flipped opened the first, then hesitated. "But these look like old case notes, Max. And half of it's in Italian."

"Yes, Nate dug them out for me. But he can't read,

and my eyes won't focus," he grumbled. "Can you make out the one labeled Mary O'Gavin? It's near the front."

It took her a moment. "Ah," she said finally. "Here it is. Oh, dear! A—a murder?"

He nodded sharply. "An old one," he said curtly. "Just skim until you see a note about a ship. In the top margin of a left-hand page. English, I think. *The Queen of . . .* something. And a docking date. Find me that date."

"Ah, the *Queen of Kashmir!*" she said softly. "December third—"

"The year?" he demanded impatiently.

"—eighteen twenty-four," she snapped.

Max collapsed back into his pillows, the tension suddenly draining from his body. "I thought so," he murmured, almost to himself. He reached out to take the book away. "I'm sorry, Catherine. My head aches like the devil, but it's a poor excuse for my temper."

Catherine hovered over him. "I see that you are relieved," she quietly responded. "That date—may I ask what it means?"

She watched Max's face grow warm. "It's the date your brother returned from India," he quietly admitted. "Almost a full year *after* Lady Sands began selling off her jewelry."

Catherine's brows drew into a puzzled frown. "But I do not understand."

"Whoever stole the Sands Sapphire knew it was the only authentic jewel remaining in her collection," Max confessed. "It was not a random theft. And so it could not have been your brother."

Catherine gaped at him. Half of her burned to know why he'd been tracking Bentley's return from India, but the other half was afraid to know. Max let his gaze drop to the coverlet. "Something about your brother had been nagging at me for weeks," he quietly admitted. "It seems to have taken a blow to the head to make me recall it."

She managed a wry smile. "I shall remember that next time you're being stubborn."

Max exhaled, a sound of deep relief, and returned his gaze to hers. "It would seem I owe him—and you—an apology."

A little nervously, Catherine began to neaten the pleats of her skirts. "Accepted," she said swiftly. "And so I have my truce. But I am still offering my services."

"A truce, then," he said gruffly, flicking an inscrutable glance up at her. "But no services, Catherine. I'm just not up to it."

Catherine's eyes flew open wide. "Wretch!" she screeched, bouncing off the bed as if it had burst into flame. "Arrogant dog! You inveigle your way into my bed, then have the audacity to assume—"

"*Inveigle?*" Max interjected, rising up from the pillows again. "I seem to recall having been invited."

"—and then, after all this, you can so easily assume I still want you?"

With surprising strength for a man so badly beaten, Max lashed out, capturing her wrist, dragging her halfway across him until they were nearly nose to nose. His voice was harsh, but his eyes were laughing, his expression deeply relieved. "Oh, you want me," he growled. "You want me, Catherine, or you wouldn't be here. A woman doesn't play hard to get by crawling over a man's fence—"

"Why, how dare you!" she interjected, trying to jerk from his grasp.

Max looked at her chidingly. "Catherine, you've grass stains on your delightful derriere."

"What a detective you are!" She felt her face flush with heat. "And it was peonies, not grass. But all I've offered you, sir, is my help. I wish to sort through Julia's letters and journals. I thought you could scarce refuse after . . . well, after you'd accused my own brother."

Max let his eyes drift over her face, down her throat, lower. "I've been through it all," he murmured, his voice more like gravel than usual. "There's nothing there."

Concussed or not, Catherine could see desire beginning to simmer in his gaze. "Then you won't mind my hanging about to look at them," she whispered. "I could just sit quietly on the other side of your bed. After all, you aren't using it."

His eyes grew hungry, his grip more certain. "Am I not?" he answered. "What a fool I am."

It sounded like another invitation. Impulsively, Catherine kicked off her slippers, hiked up her skirts, and, careful of his ribs, crawled fully onto the mattress to straddle him. She stared down into his face, and her breath caught hard in her throat when she felt the length of his arousal, already growing hard beneath the sheet. "I thought you were incapacitated," she said softly.

Max released her wrist and set his big hands on her thighs, sliding his hands slowly up the silk of her stockings, inching up her skirts as he went. "And I thought," he whispered, his voice rich as sin, "you didn't want me."

Catherine struggled to remember her purpose. "But I have to see Julia's letters," she insisted. "Max, may I?"

But his eyes were already growing warm, opaque. "Take them," he rasped, letting his thumbs massage the tender, naked skin above her garters. "But later, Catherine. Later."

It sounded like a promise to her. And Catherine almost didn't care. A deep sense of relief had swept over her. Oh, God. She had not known how desperately she needed him. How terrified she'd been of losing him. Perhaps he did not quite trust her—or, more precisely, was afraid to trust anyone. But, instinctively, she understood him.

For her part, she had come here half indignant. And then the sight of him, nearly lifeless on this bed they had so briefly shared, his beautiful olive skin drawn, almost pale—oh, how that had terrified her. She loved him. So much. And his reaction last night, the explosion of passion and anguish, the tortured expression on his face—oh, it told her that what Max felt for her ran deeper than simple masculine lust.

In a strange, unsettling way, Catherine felt as if she'd finally seized hold of life, and she wasn't about to let go. For a long, sweet moment, she stared down at him. His sheet had shifted when he'd grabbed her wrist, exposing a sculpted wall of chest muscle. He was magnificent, yes, but that wasn't why she wanted him. And suddenly, Catherine knew that this wasn't going to be just an *affaire* for the season. Not if she could help it. But could she? She let her gaze drift over his face, which was mottled with bruises and heavily shadowed with a day's growth of black bristle. He looked rough, thoroughly disreputable, and just a little frightening—but enticing, nonetheless.

"Max," she asked tentatively, "are you quite naked beneath the sheet?"

"Yes." His voice was dusky, rich with desire.

Wordlessly, she unwrapped the lace fichu around her shoulders and let it slither onto the floor. He made a soft choking sound in the back of his throat, and his hands came up to shape her face, her neck, then skim lightly over her shoulders. Strong, cool fingers seized the fabric of her bodice. "You really shouldn't have come here," he said, his words a silken whisper. "Should never have crawled into my bed again. I'm not even sure I can give you the welcome you deserve, but my God, Catherine, I have to see you."

Catherine stared down into his glittering black gaze and nodded, not entirely certain just what she was agreeing to. "Yes."

Roughly, he jerked the bodice down, and Catherine heard a stitch rip. The full swell of her bosom was laid nearly bare. "Beautiful," he said, slowly drawing the fabric down so that it dragged a little roughly over her hardening nipples. He watched her breasts, his eyes hungry.

Catherine felt wanton, decadent. And when his hand shoved up the froth of her petticoats, slid higher, seeking the slit in her drawers, she felt something inside her give way. "Ah, *Max . . .*"

Max felt the trembling need shudder through them both the moment he touched her. Forcing himself to be gentle, he held himself in check, easing one finger back and forth through the nest of curls. Deeply, Catherine blushed. The warm circle of gold around her irises seemed to glow with a new radiance as her eyes began to heat, then melt. She made a small sound—eager, uncertain—and pressed against his hand. Max caressed her more intimately, heard her breath ratchet sharply upward, and found himself wondering what kind of lover her husband had been. A poor one, judging from the innocence of her reactions. Most Englishmen, so far as he could determine, either did not know how or did not bother to properly pleasure a woman in bed.

And perhaps he shouldn't be pleasuring this one. Sweet heaven, he *knew* he should not. But Max couldn't stop. She rocked against his erection wantonly, acting on pure, feminine instinct, and his physical pain was forgotten. He slid one finger deeper, seeking and finding the tender bud of her desire. She gasped at the intimacy and tried to wiggle away.

"No!" he growled, clutching at her thigh, forcing her down. "No, *tesoro mio,* don't be afraid to let me watch."

He touched her again, and she shivered, arching backward, riding down on his hand. Hunger surged through him on a deep, rumbling growl. He wanted her. *Burned* for her. He stroked her deeply, tenderly. Again and again. Wet, silky warmth rewarded his touch, invited him. He watched himself caress her, work her, until he could hear her little gasps of pleasure. Until her wetness covered his fingers and slicked his palm. After long moments, he heard her moan deeply and flicked his gaze up, judging the moment.

Her tongue darted out to touch one corner of her mouth, and her eyes glazed over with desire. "Come for me, *carissima*," he crooned. *"Sei molto bella.* So beautiful in your passion. Let me help you. Find the edge."

"I can't—not—not *like this,*" she rasped, staring down at him as if he were something just a little foreign and frightening. And perhaps he was both. But she wanted him. He stroked her more certainly, and Catherine whimpered, her eyes wide and dark.

With his other hand, he caressed her breast, rolling the nipple between his fingers until she cried out. "Catherine, *cara,* don't be frightened," he soothed, still stroking her clitoris with the ball of his thumb. "Come for me, *bella.* I want to watch you. I want to see you."

She writhed beneath his touch. Tendrils of hair had begun to tumble from her neat arrangement, and, with her skirts hiked up, her generous, perfect breasts jutting over the top of her stays, she somehow looked the very picture of both innocence and decadence.

"Ah, ah!" she said breathlessly.

"Yes, like that," Max coaxed. "Like that, *amore mio.* Does my touch pleasure you? Yes, yes, let me see how much."

God, how he loved to watch her. And so he kept touching her, crooning to her in a stream of half-Italian, uncertain himself of the words, lost in the rich brown pools of her eyes. And then, suddenly, her eyelids dropped shut, and Catherine's head tipped back, her mouth parting in a sweet, silent cry. Her release shuddered through her as her thighs clasped his. She rode down on his hand once more, and Max plunged two fingers deep inside her, reveling in the feel of her tight, dripping sheath as it clutched at him.

"Aha, ah!" she cried, falling half forward, her hands set on either side of his neck. "Oh. Oh, Max."

Max felt a moment of triumph, and fast on its heels came a surge of raging desire. He drew in Catherine's scent, the warmth of her hair, her skin, the delicate musk of her arousal, and lust exploded, licking at him with small, hot flames. "Ah, *cara mia,*" he breathed. "If it kills me, I must have you."

Bracing her weight on her hands, Catherine pushed up, her expression both sated and chiding. "Max, you cannot move," she murmured, sliding back onto her knees as her smile shifted to something slightly wicked. "In fact, you are more or less my prisoner, are you not?"

And then, with a tantalizing lethargy, her fingers slid down his torso and slipped beneath the sheet which was now snarled about his waist. Quite deliberately, she drew it down, inch by inch, allowing cool air to breeze across the hair which dusted Max's stomach. He'd grown agonizingly hot watching Catherine shudder against his hand, and when she dragged the linen over his sensitive, swollen head, he gasped with pleasure. Another swift tug, and the length of his cock rose up from the tangled sheets, hard and insistent.

She made a little sound in the back of her throat, and swiftly, his hand shot out to snare her wrist. "On top of me," he begged, wrenching her toward him. "Now, *bella,* if you have an ounce of mercy!"

To Max's shock, she jerked away. "But what if I'm still just a little annoyed with you, Max?" she whispered, sliding her hands slowly up his taut thighs, then smoothing them over his stomach until his flesh shivered.

"Why, I am not at all sure I ought to show you any mercy."

With a soft oath, Max let his head fall back into the pillows. He jerked it up again when her fingers slid lower, one into the thatch of black hair which surrounded his jutting cock, the other between his legs. "Christ, Catherine! What do you mean to do to me?"

"Torture you?" she whispered, curling her right hand around the base of his shaft. "Will it work?"

Will it work? A foolish question when a shudder ran through his body at her every touch. But Catherine, it seemed, was not done with him. Her palm felt cool as she cupped the weight of his sac in her left hand. And then, very tentatively, she slid the other hand up his shaft, and down again.

Max sucked in air through his teeth. "Ah, *cara,* have mercy!"

Catherine loosened her grip. "You do not like—"

His hand lashed out again, holding hers tight to the base of his cock. "Yes!" he hissed, squeezing shut his eyes. "Yes. Oh, God, don't stop, please."

For a moment, he held her in his grip, the corded tendons of his wrist and arm taut and trembling. And then Catherine's hand began to ease up and down with a perfect rhythm. Max exhaled sharply and let his fingers slide slowly away. Her heated gaze burned him. Her every stroke was pleasure of the purest sort, like nothing he'd felt before, and Max, lost in the rhythm of her touch, let his eyes drop shut. Suddenly, something soft and seductively feather-light brushed his sensitive head.

"Aah!" Max jerked, his eyes flying wide open to see the tip of her pink tongue flick out to touch him.

"Max, lie still!" Catherine knelt over him, her lush, full mouth curled into a wicked smile. "Let me pleasure you as you have pleasured me. Would you enjoy it? Will you teach me?"

Max felt his eyes roll back in his head. Not twelve hours earlier, he'd feared he might die. Now he was sure of it. "Anything, love," he managed to croak. "Just touch—God, yes, that—in any way you please."

Steadying her balance, Catherine leaned forward, tentatively stroking him with her tongue as her hand held him fast. Max sucked in his breath again as she licked his length from the tip to the base. "Shall I take you into my mouth?" Her tone was soft and uncertain.

Was she serious? Max had to force himself not to beg. "If you wish, love," he said softly. *"Only* if you wish."

"Oh, I do wish," she whispered.

Watching her lips hover over the crimson head of his cock, Max thought of his erotic, frustrating dreams, none of which could compare to the reality of Catherine. And then, with her hand tight at his base, her lips touched him again, opened, and slowly devoured him, inch by heated inch. Max drove his fingers into her hair as a groan of pure pleasure tore through him. His thighs and legs trembled. Primitive lust coursed through his blood, rushed to his brain. His cock swelled harder, if such a thing was possible, and it was all he could do not to thrust upward with his hips and force himself deep into her throat.

Embracing his hard length in both hands now, Catherine drew him deep, sliding his taut, tender flesh over her teeth, down the caressing warmth of her tongue, almost to the back of her throat. And then, with tormenting languor, she drew away again. Sleek, wet warmth surrounded him, pulled at him, and left him quivering as though he were an untouched boy.

Slowly, perhaps in answer to his whimpering sigh, her rhythm shifted, deepening. Never in his life had he been touched so erotically. It was too much. Too much to be borne. Max no longer felt the pain of his broken bones, only the rush of desire which drove him. Again and again, she stroked him, sucked him, tormenting him with her mouth and hand, until, at last, he came off the mattress with a roar. He had to have her. Had to. Now.

Tumbling Catherine onto her back, dragging clothing and sheets as he went, Max pulled his weight on top of her. Her eyes flared wide with alarm. "Max, your ribs! Don't make things worse."

"Dio mio, cara!" he groaned. "What I feel for you couldn't get much worse." Ignoring the stab of pain in his chest, he pressed her down into the softness of his bed. The same bed in which he'd spent too many empty nights. Too many nights thinking of her, and long before he'd ever touched her.

His body ached, yes—but with raw, male need. It possessed him. Drove him. His groin was heavy with it, his chest bellowed with the strain of it. Catherine lay limply beneath him, her womanly flesh open and inviting, still damp with the pleasure of her orgasm. Max lifted his hips, and the sheet slithered down his legs. Still blushing beautifully, Catherine grasped his cock, taking the weight of it into her hand, and brushing her palm over the swollen head.

Max bit his lip, tasted blood. He reared high, threw back his head. *"Catherine—!"*

Max entered her hard on one thrust and lost what was left of his sanity. He drove deep on a groan which was ripped from his chest, from his very soul. And then he drew back and did it again. Fiercely, he pounded inside her, over and over, heedless of her fragility, of his shattered ribs. Beneath him, the bed began to squeak, the headboard banging relentlessly into the wall, until Catherine stiffened, her nails digging into his shoulders as she cried out. In lust? In pain? He did not know.

"No, Catherine," he begged. "Don't stop. Oh, no. Just *don't*—"

"Oh," she whispered. "I can't—I can't—I *can't* . . ."

He had to have her, had to take her. Hoped she would forgive him. He had never wanted anything like he wanted her beneath him. Just plain *wanted her*. The depth of it—of his need, his utter lack of control—was frightening. And still he thrust between her legs like a savage.

"Oh, oh, Max!" she cried.

He slid his hands beneath her buttocks, lifting her, filling her. And then she dug her nails deeper, came off the mattress against him, straining. "Aha, aha . . ." she chanted, her body convulsing, shattering to pieces beneath him, open and wet. She cried out his name, and Max was lost again, his cock and his heart and his soul dragged into her like a skiff torn loose by a riptide. Consciousness faded as his release came crashing over him. He arched hard against her and knew nothing but the sweet shimmering light of Catherine, the exquisite throbbing of her body around his as he exploded.

Max had never known a moment so pure, so sweet. For a long, timeless heartbeat, his life hung suspended from the stars. Everything was perfect. Anything was possible. His physical pain, his unspoken fears, the grinding hopelessness of his work—all of it was forgotten in one shining instant of peace. He gathered her to him, cradled her in his arms. Catherine still trembled, her lashes black against porcelain skin, and Max marveled that such an exquisite creature could want him. "Oh, *cara mia,*" he whispered hoarsely. "Did I hurt you?"

Catherine set her cheek against his chest, brushed her lips lightly over his nipple. "I don't think I care," she confessed in a small, soft voice. "Oh, Max. I never . . ."

He pressed his mouth to her forehead. It was warm, lightly sheened with perspiration. "Never what, Catherine?" he asked softly.

But Catherine did not answer. He rolled with her to one side and let himself drift with her in his arms. She smelled, as always, of springtime. Like home. In her embrace, he could dream of it, as it had been, verdant and fertile. He opened his eyes to the afternoon light, but his eyes still refused to focus. Slowly, inevitably, his physical pain returned, the shattered rib, the throbbing headache. And with it came the crushing pain of reality, the truth of what was happening to him. But it could not be. Simply could not. Max closed his eyes once more and tried not to think of it.

Good Lord, he had no business in a—what had she called it? *A relationship.* That sounded marginally less tawdry than an *affaire d'amour,* he supposed. But whatever one termed it, it wasn't meant for him, was it? He was neither charming nor handsome. He possessed nothing in the way of tenderness or tact. He was, just as she had once said, stubborn, dogmatic, and arrogant. But he really could not live without her. It was a simple, awful certainty. Max brushed the backs of his fingers along her cheek and felt a moment of fear. What if, when the novelty of bedding him began to fade, she saw the truth? At that very point when their passion should deepen to something sweeter, more enduring, what if she realized that he was nothing like the men of her world? Would it matter?

Rutledge had sneered that Max was "no true gentleman," the ultimate insult amongst the English upper class. But Max had not argued, for, in truth, Rutledge was right. Max looked at Catherine again and wondered why she'd even come back. Other than an enthusiastic bedmate, what could she possibly see in him? His eyes drifted over her, and Max suppressed a bitter laugh. Perhaps nothing. Perhaps it *was* just sex. That, at least, he was good at. When he could keep his wits about him. Gingerly, he shifted his weight to make her more comfortable, and Catherine stirred from sleep with a little sound of displeasure. "Max," she murmured, pressing her hand to his heart as if to stay him. "Don't leave. Don't."

The sweet plea broke his heart, and Max felt the hot press of tears behind his eyes. "Oh, *cara mia, non ti lascerò mia,*" he murmured, burying his face in her hair.

My dear, I will never leave you.

But that was a lie, was it not? The anger and distrust between them was gone, yes. But nothing else had really changed, no matter how far-flung his fantasies. Could he change? In some ways, yes, if he tried. But it would not, he feared, be enough. So he let Catherine drift in his arms, afraid to move. Afraid that if she woke now, and looked up at him with those innocent brown eyes, she might see him on the verge of sobbing like a child, aching with the loss of something he was afraid he'd never been meant to have.

Chapter Seventeen

A real man of fashion and pleasures observes decency.
It is by being well dressed that one should be distinguished.

—Lord Chesterfield, 1776,
The Fine Gentleman's Etiquette

Catherine awoke just as the afternoon light shafted through the crack in Max's curtains, catching her full in the face. Her eyes fluttered open, and she sat up, slightly disoriented. Max lay on his back beside her, breathing with the slow, shallow rhythm of a man whose ribs were splintered. The sheet lay tangled about his knees, as if he'd rolled onto his back to ease the pain. His body was beautiful, with layers of lean, hard muscle over his arms and abdomen, his chest lightly dusted with dark hair.

But in the bright light of day, it was all too apparent just what sort of life Max had lived. One shoulder looked to have been laid open almost to the bone, the gash roughly stitched to leave a nasty five-inch scar. Below his ribcage was the unmistakable pucker of a knife wound—a stiletto, if she had to guess. A broken finger, badly set. A deep slash, high above his right hipbone, the scar still red and angry. Catherine lost her nerve and quit counting. What made a man take such risks? Was he, as Sofia Castelli had suggested, simply driven by guilt?

With a sigh, she looked down to survey her own *dishabille* with a strange mix of mortification and delight. But it was too late for regret, not that she felt much. Gingerly, she slid from the bed and crossed the room to Max's washstand, the rough wooden floor gently catching at her stockinged feet as she went. A pitcher of tepid water was at hand, and above the walnut stand, a small mirror hung crookedly from a wooden peg. Bracing her hands on the cool porcelain basin, Catherine leaned forward to survey the contents of his shelf. A shaving brush, razor, and strop were laid out neatly, and beside them sat a chipped soap dish, along with a small comb missing three of its teeth. And that, as far as she could see, constituted the whole of Max's toilette kit. Inwardly, she smiled. It rather pleased her, his odd, perverse simplicity.

She picked up the soap and inhaled the subtle citrus scent she'd so often smelled on his skin. Then, swiftly, she tidied herself, borrowing his comb to re-dress her hair. She tiptoed back to the bed to see that Max still slept soundly. Her gaze drifted over him, and she was shaken yet again by his bruised ribs. She wondered just how he'd managed to make love to her, and swift on the heels of that thought came a moment of deep, shivering gratitude that he'd done it so delightfully well. And then, being a practical sort of woman, Catherine wondered how long it had been since he'd eaten. The body could not heal without nourishment. There was also the boy outside to be considered. Children needed to eat, and she did not doubt for one moment that Nate still stood guard on the front step—perhaps with good reason.

Catherine made her way through the parlor to the broad oak cupboard which sat in one corner and began rummaging through it with limited success. But she could make do, had certainly done so often enough. She went to the window which gave onto the front of the house, threw up the sash, and leaned out into the fading light. "Nate!" she whispered down at the boy, who still sat stoically upon the front step. "Can you peel potatoes?"

Max roused to the smell of something wonderful, and to the agony of his stomach clawing at his backbone. A reassuring sign, that. He knew from experience that hunger meant he would survive. Cautiously, he elbowed his way up through the pain and looked about the room. It felt oddly cold. Terribly empty. *Catherine*. Catherine was gone. A moment of loss gripped him. He had not dreamt it, had he? Max came fully awake to the sound of soft voices in his parlor. No, he had dreamt nothing. He could hear metal scraping against metal and something sizzling softly in the background. Onions? What on earth? Someone was cooking? Good God, he hoped so. And then he remembered.

Women like Catherine did not know how to cook. Did they? Curiosity got the better of him, and, still groggy, Max slid gingerly from the bed and pulled on his drawers. Stiffly lifting his arm so that he might rake the hair back off his face, he padded through the bedchamber, into the parlor, and froze. Catherine was moving to and fro with plates and bowls and teacups, murmuring softly to Lucifer, who was dogging her every step, whilst Nate—*Nate?*—stirred something in a skillet. Max's tiny table had been neatly laid, the teapot already out. The dog whuffed at Catherine's hems, whimpering pitifully. As she passed, Catherine leaned over Nate's shoulder and plucked a sliver of something from the skillet, blew on it for a moment, then dropped it neatly into Lucifer's mouth. The dog smacked it down, then gazed up at her in utter adoration.

Max must have made a sound—one of amazement, he did not doubt—and Catherine looked up with a smile that warmed him straight through the pain, right to the heart. "You are up!" she cried, setting aside the plates and swiftly closing the distance between them.

But Max's joy had quickly turned to embarrassment. He raked his fingers through his disheveled hair again. "I'm not decent," he mumbled, slowly backing toward his bedchamber. Good God, he was wearing nothing but a pair of linen drawers! Such familiarity would make plain to anyone—especially the boy—that he and Catherine had been intimate.

But Catherine already had him by the arm and was dragging him toward the table. "Nonsense," she insisted. "You are an invalid."

He glowered at her. "I am *not* an invalid."

Catherine merely smiled. "Yes, but you must think of your ribs, Max. A waistcoat and trousers are the last thing you need."

Max was pretty sure that dining in one's drawers violated all the rules on dress and decorum in Lord Chesterfield's blasted book. "I might at least put on a bloody shirt," he muttered as Catherine shoved him into a chair.

Nate looked blandly up from the skillet of potatoes he was stirring. "Yer looks awright ter me, gov," he said over his shoulder. " 'Ow about a cup o' tea?"

Impatiently, Catherine made a little circle with her hand. "Stir, stir," she ordered, lifting the kettle from the hob. "The tea isn't steeped."

Steadying one hand on his shoulder, Catherine leaned over Max to pour the hot water into the teapot. Briefly, she paused to draw in the smell of him: sleepy male mixed with warm citrus and a hint of liniment. The strange combination shouldn't have been pleasing, but it was. The sight of him strolling into the parlor had been pleasing, too. She liked the way the soft linen of his drawers had hung low across his lean hipbones, baring his navel, and the black hair which lightly sprinkled his stomach. On impulse, she glanced up. Nate had turned back to the potatoes. Swiftly, she slid one hand around Max, skimming her palm across his belly, and dipping her head to press her lips to the turn of his neck.

"Hmm," she murmured. "I'd best give you a shave after you've eaten."

"Hmph," Max grunted. "The day I can't shave myself will be the day the undertaker does it for me." But his eyes were smiling. Catherine smiled back and finished laying the table. They dined in companionable silence on a simple meal of fried potatoes, cheese toast, and tea. Max ate everything on his plate, albeit rather slowly. Nate, however, wolfed his food like a starving mongrel.

Catherine looked back and forth between them

quizzically. "Max, how long has Nate been sitting on your front stoop?"

Max's brows drew together. "Since he brought me home last night, I daresay."

Catherine turned her gaze on Nate. "You brought him home?" she archly began, then shook her head. "No, never mind. I can't bear it. Don't you have parents? Someone who will be missing you?"

Nate shrugged and shoveled in another forkful of potatoes. "Me muvver, I guess," he managed to answer. "But she'd be busy wiv the little ones."

Max frowned at the boy. "You should have slept on the settle, Nate."

Carefully watching the boy, Catherine laid her napkin upon the table. "Well, you must go home at once," she gently ordered him. "Your mother should know where you are."

Nate looked at her in mild scorn. "De Rohan 'ere might need me," he insisted. " 'E ain't in no shape ter be left alone, what wiv that murderer running loose."

Stubbornly, Catherine pursed her lips. "Then I shall stay," she persisted. "Nate, you are just a boy. You must go home."

Max shoved his chair roughly away from the table. "Good God!" he exclaimed. "Am I such a pathetic figure of a man? Must I now have a woman and a child arguing over who is to take care of me?"

The boy cast him a derisive glance. "Aye, well, yer needed a bit o' 'elp last night, I seem ter recollect."

Catherine, too, pushed back her chair. "Nate will go home for a few hours," she said quietly. "He may return later in the evening. I shall stay until then." When Max started to protest, she cut him off. "You promised me, Max, that I might read Lady Sands's correspondence," she insisted, hoping he would not remember she no longer had reason to do so. "Surely you do not mean to go back on your word?"

Max tried to scowl, but his eyes were still warm. Catherine could see he was tiring rapidly. Still, as Nate began to clear away the dishes, Max managed to circle one arm about her waist. "Thank you, *cara mia,* for dinner," he said, kissing her lightly atop the head. "It was a godsend. And yes, you may read the correspondence if that is still your wish."

And so it was that Nate and the leftover potatoes were soon on their way to St. Giles. Catherine shooed Max back to bed, tidied the little parlor, then carried Julia's lap desk into the bedroom. The light was beginning to fade, and Max was already asleep. Quietly, Catherine lit the lamp on his night table, then settled in for a long read. Every hour, she laid aside a calendar or a pile of letters, then woke Max to check his vision and offer a bit of the laudanum the surgeon had left by the bed. Max refused everything but water, and Catherine kept reading. Bentley might be off the hook, but her interminable curiosity still raged.

By the time Nate returned, the watchman was calling ten, and Catherine was not quite finished. With a whisper, she sent Nate in search of a hackney and made the boy a soft pallet by the hearth. Then she jotted out a note for Max and tiptoed back into the bedchamber. Quietly, she packed up Lady Sands's correspondence so that she might take it back to Mortimer Street. At the last moment, however, she made the mistake of turning back to the bed to look down at Max, and the warm surge of protectiveness which tugged at her was almost over-whelming. She felt as if something between them had shifted. Deepened, perhaps.

Strangely, not one word had passed between them about the horror of his life in Alsace. It was as if they had agreed not to speak of it. And why should they? The color of Max's blood, his mother's merchant roots, the string of near-unpronounceable names after his title— these things made no difference to Catherine. In truth, she wanted to laugh at the irony of it. Her late and not-too-lamented sire had taught her well that the circumstances of a man's birth said nothing of his character.

Impulsively, Catherine reached out to touch him, and, as if by instinct, Max turned his face into her hand, nuzzling his lips against her palm. His expression had gentled in sleep, leaving him with a countenance more handsome, far less fierce. Long inky-black lashes fanned softly over his cheeks, and with the hard lines of his face eased, he looked relaxed, finally at peace with himself and the world.

What, she wondered, had he been like as a boy of six-teen? How had he felt when he'd been forced to flee his country, his father taken from him so brutally, the ashes of his home still smoldering? And what must it feel like to know that some would always believe your father a traitor for having committed the egregious sin of trying to better the lives of those less fortunate? A caring and vulnerable young man would have been deeply scarred by it, Catherine decided. And he was, she knew, still far more caring and vulnerable than he wished anyone— even her—to see. Unable to resist the moment of tenderness, Catherine leaned down to press her lips to his forehead, then turned to blow out the lamp.

On Monday morning, Genevieve Durrett swept into Lord Sands's drawing room, her carriage the very picture of French grace. She was, Max had to admit, a fetching little thing, if a man liked his women small, voluptuous, and blond. He could see how easily she might entice a fellow like Harry into her bed.

But, despite her grace and beauty, Miss Durrett's poise nearly faltered when she saw the two men who awaited her. "Monsieur Sisk!" She dropped at once into a curtsey. *"Bonjour."* She rose and turned to face Max, her eyes flitting anxiously over his face. Only then did he recognize her as the servant he'd seen sobbing so pitifully on the morning Julia's body had been discovered. Max introduced himself and withdrew to one corner of the room to observe discreetly. Sisk settled into a chair and began thumbing through the pages of his notebook.

But, clearly, Genevieve Durrett had grown wary of the constable. She perched on the edge of her chair, her gaze focused squarely on the buttons of Sisk's uniform. Methodically, Sisk questioned her, going over and over the questions he and Max had agreed to. Genevieve admitted to having often accompanied her mistress shopping. And, yes, her mistress had had a fondness for visiting jewelers. But the servant vehemently denied knowing anything more.

When pressed, she said she knew nothing of counterfeit jewelry and even less about the names of her mistress's lovers. Relentlessly, Sisk continued to harangue her, and soon Genevieve's aplomb had vanished along with her color. Her posture grew increasingly rigid, her fingers went white as they grasped the arms of her chair. And still, she would admit to nothing. Sisk was getting nowhere, Max realized, for underneath all her hauteur, Genevieve Durrett was terrified.

Soon the sounds of her sobbing protests echoed through the town house, and, although the drawing-room doors had been pulled shut, Max could imagine the servants hovering in the corridor beyond. When Sisk nailed Genevieve with the question of her affair with Harry, the lady's maid completely collapsed. *"Mais non, mais non,"* she cried, violently wringing her hands. "Lies, et ez all lies! I have nothing to do weeth this miserable beezness. I know nothing of them, these English. I wish to leave. To go home. Please, *monsieur,* this you must believe!"

She looked so young, so vulnerable, and suddenly, something in her voice caught at Max's hardened heart. Perhaps it was the air of desperation. Genevieve Durrett was alone in a foreign land, confused and uncertain, at the mercy of strangers more powerful than she. That was a feeling he understood all too well. And Sisk had been haranguing her for a half-hour now.

At last, Max strode across the room to sit down beside Sisk, the blinding shaft of pain in his ribs a sharp reminder of why he'd been standing. Max gritted his teeth and smiled. "Miss Durrett," he said patiently. "Perhaps you do not understand that Lord Sands has already explained that the two of you were together that night. If necessary, he will swear to it in court—"

She cut him off with a sharp cry, her eyes flaring wide with terror. *"Non!"*

"—which is the last thing any of us wishes," Max finished, dropping his voice to a low, reassuring tone. "Now, perhaps I should tell you what I think? Would that be easier? I think you went to his lordship's bed under instructions from your mistress. Genevieve, is that so?"

He stared at her relentlessly, focusing all his persuasive energy on the woman who sat trembling before him. She held his gaze for a long, silent moment. *"Oui!"* she finally cried, bursting again into tears. "Sh-she paid me. She made a-a *prostituée*—a whore—of me, and for what? To be herself killed? I tell you, *monsieur,* I knew nothing of this. Nothing."

Gingerly, Max slid forward and touched the girl lightly on the shoulder. "Calm yourself, Miss Durrett," he said. "She was your employer. Perhaps you felt you had little choice?"

Genevieve had begun to snuffle pathetically. *"Mais oui, monsieur,"* she whispered, dabbing at her nose with a handkerchief. "It was just that way. Madame, she was— oh, how you say—*difficile, oui?"*

Gently, Max tried to steer her. "Think carefully, Miss Durrett, and tell us just what she said. What did she promise?"

Bravely, the lady's maid choked back another sob. "Madame told me I was to seduce milord as soon as he returned home," she answered, straightening in her chair and pushing back her shoulders. "Madame laughed and said there might be noise—*un peu*—in her *chambre.* But I must not let milord leave his bed. I must distract him, and for this thing, she promise me twenty pounds and passage back to Calais. Just this last thing I must do, she promised, and then I could go home."

Max leaned intently forward. "And why did she wish you to do this? Did she explain?"

Miserably, Genevieve nodded. *"Oui, monsieur,* she meant to entertain her lover."

"Which one?" Sisk gruffly interjected.

Genevieve's eyes widened innocently. "Her only one, *monsieur,"* she responded. "There were dalliances, *oui,* but this man she kept for the three years I have been weeth Madame. He came to her, this man, at the house in secret. Sometimes through the window."

Sisk gave a dubious grunt, but Max cut him off with a silencing look. "And do you know him? Do you know his name?"

"Monsieur Lumpkin," she swiftly answered. "Tony, Madame called him."

"Lumpkin?" Sisk lifted his pencil from the notebook and looked up. "Could you identify him?"

The lady's maid shook her head. "No, *monsieur,* I never see him. Long ago, she fixed the window, so that he might come to her in secret. But their *affaire,* it was not so secret. She often remarked that he was to meet her at this thing or that—balls, dinner parties."

Lumpkin. The name was vaguely familiar. Suddenly, a thought struck Max. "Lady Sands must have been quite devoted to this man, to risk permitting him into the house. But on this particular night, she did something even more unusual. She asked you to—er—to occupy his lordship. Do you know why?"

Genevieve looked uncomfortable. "I do not think

Madame was devoted to him," she said uncertainly. "When she was to see him, she was sometimes . . . *tourmenté*. Fretful. I do not think she encouraged him but pretended to like him."

Max lifted one brow. "Why do you think this?"

The lady's maid gave a Gallic shrug. "I am French, *monsieur,*" she said evenly. "She loved the men, *oui,* but this one, he troubled her. And this night, I think—I *think* she meant to end it. Perhaps she feared that they might quarrel loudly. She did say that after this night, he would no longer come to her bed. And that soon the stocking would be on the other foot. This I did not understand, but she was very pleased. Very satisfied. She even sent me to the butler for champagne."

Max watched her carefully. "How many goblets? And did Mr. Overturf open the bottle?"

She nodded with alacrity. "I watched him, *monsieur.* And I took but one goblet upstairs. But I broke it the next morning when I saw . . ."

Sisk exchanged a telling glance with Max. Clearly, they both sensed she was being truthful. "And was there any sort o' racket that night, Miss Durrett?" the police constable asked. "Anything which might have given 'is lordship concern?"

Again, she shook her head. "No, *monsieur,* nothing."

"*Hmph,*" said Sisk. "Did Lord Sands stir from his bed?"

Lips tightly pursed, the maid shook her head. *"Non."*

"Could he have done so without your knowledge?" interjected Max.

She paused as if to consider. *"Non, monsieur.* I sleep lightly."

Max relaxed against the back of his chair. It seemed Harry and Genevieve were almost in the clear. If the maid were guilty, she would have seized the opportunity to blame Harry. Moreover, her strange story of Lady Sands's mystery lover rang oddly true. "Lumpkin," he mused. "Perhaps Sands will recognize the name. I will ask him to join us."

"But this ez not possible, *monsieur,*" protested Genevieve softly. "Milord, he has left this very morning, at daybreak, weeth his sister the viscountess."

"Where did they go?" he demanded. But he feared he already knew.

Genevieve winced at his sharp tone. "To Milord Delacourt's estate, *monsieur,*" she answered. "I believe et ez in Derbyshire, *oui?*"

Max cursed softly, recalling his instructions to Harry. "Let's go, Sisk."

In the morning parlor at Mortimer Street, Catherine sat curled in Cam's huge leather armchair, her feet tucked up beneath her skirts. She wore her oldest, most comfortable muslin gown, and her hair was barely dressed, caught up haphazardly in a few pins. She was tired. Oh, so tired. This morning, she'd literally dragged herself from the warmth of the bed. Now, beyond the big bay window, the day was growing warm, but Catherine still felt oddly cold inside. She had toed off her slippers and pulled the mahogany tea table nearer, and now, Lady Sands's little rosewood desk lay folded open, carefully balanced across it.

Methodically, Catherine had been making a list of everyone Lady Sands had seen and every place she had gone in the last two years. It was a monumental task, and a fruitless one, too. Try as she might, Catherine could discover no pattern in the dead woman's life, and now, her penciled notes seemed to be swimming before her eyes. In truth, Catherine did not feel well at all. Her morning meal still sat on the small breakfast table in the corner. She'd been unable to eat it, and now she was heartily sick of smelling it, too. Impulsively, she rang the bell.

"I fear my appetite has failed me, Delilah," Catherine said when the housemaid entered. "You may clear now."

Delilah bobbed a quick curtsey. "Yes, ma'am. Will that be all?"

Catherine set down her pencil and pressed one hand to her abdomen. "Have we any soda water, Delilah?" she asked musingly. "I fancy I should like a glass."

"To be sure, ma'am. Just soda water?"

"With a pinch of ginger, please." Catherine turned back to her notes as Delilah quickly gathered up the breakfast dishes. But her stomach gave another faint flip-flop, and Catherine let her gaze drift from the page to the window which overlooked the tidy rear garden. With a vague sense of unease, she stared into the brilliant sunshine of a perfect May morning and watched as a house wren squatted beneath the fountain to pluck a fat worm from a freshly tilled flowerbed. Tossing back his head, he gobbled it down. At the sight, true nausea roiled in her stomach, almost into her throat. Catherine managed to choke it back, her hand flying to her mouth, her eyes squeezing shut. Good heavens! It was most disconcerting, this dreadful sensation. Catherine had never been sick a day in her life, but now she could feel the color draining from her face.

There was something else, too. Something a little more disconcerting. Her courses were two days late. A case of disordered nerves, no doubt. It had happened once before when her niece, Ariane, had disappeared. But Ariane had been safely returned to the bosom of her family, and Catherine's normal rhythms had soon resumed, dashing her hopes. Besides, it took weeks to realize such things, did it not? And that first time, Max had been so very careful . . .

But had he been careful enough? Catherine let her face fall forward into her hands. After eight barren years? It could not be! But good Lord, she should have taken one look at the man and realized the risk. Max was all male. *Virile* was probably his middle name. Oh, no. It was ridiculous. Impossible. No man was that potent. But suddenly, Catherine had a startlingly clear vision of Signora Castelli's frail hand lingering almost lovingly over that card—what had she called it? The Queen of Pentacles. "And above all, she brings great fertility," the old woman had gleefully cackled.

"Agggh!" Catherine cried aloud. "She has cursed me!"

Suddenly, Catherine was torn between hope and panic. She did not want Max forced into a marriage he was so clearly uncomfortable with. It was just bad milk. Spoilt fish. Frazzled nerves. Yes, one of those things. Slowly, the nausea lessened, and she turned her attention back to her work. Soon, Delilah returned bearing a small, silver tray. "I've brought a bit of bread and butter as well, my lady," she said, moving as if to scoot the tray onto the tea table beside the open lap desk.

But Catherine wanted the water rather desperately, and reached for it with an awkward gesture. Somehow, she jostled the tray, forcing Delilah to seize the glass. Catherine jerked back, and her elbow struck Lady Sands's desk, sending it sliding off the little table. With an awful crash, the wooden box landed on its hinges, almost snapping shut, and then rolled facedown, spilling out its contents. Delilah gave a little cry and dropped to her knees. "Oh, my lady!" she squawked, righting the little box and tucking the inkwells back into their compartments. "Beg your pardon!"

Catherine was on the floor beside her now, gathering up the scattered papers. "My fault, Delilah," she soothed. "I was awkward, and I fear I—"

They both noticed the damage simultaneously. A thin piece of wood, not much larger than a sheet of foolscap, lay beneath the scattered papers. Delilah met her gaze uneasily. "Oh, ma'am! I've broken it!"

Puzzled, Catherine picked up the slat. Beneath was a sheaf of papers, papers she'd not noticed before. Delilah rolled the desk onto its back in the open position, and Catherine laid the slat back inside, fitting it neatly into the deeper portion at the rear of the box.

Delilah gasped. "Lord, would you look at that!" she whispered. "A false bottom!"

Catherine tried to remove it again, but the slat would not budge. Delilah picked up a butter knife from the serving tray and slid it neatly along one edge until it slipped into a small groove, about a quarter-inch deep. Uncertainly, she lifted her gaze to meet Catherine's.

Catherine nodded with alacrity. "Try it."

With a deft snap of her wrist, Delilah popped the slat back out. "Ooh, what a clever little trick, ma'am!" she said breathlessly. "And just enough space beneath to hide those papers!"

But Catherine had already scooped them up and returned to her chair, her expression drawn into a tight, puzzled frown. The first item was a large, folded playbill, stiff with age, its corners yellowing. Gingerly, she opened it. The sketches inside were faded, but the words were as clear as they were insignificant:

Limited Engagement Only!
SHE STOOPS TO CONQUER
– or –
The Mistakes of a Night
A Work of Comedy
by Mr. Oliver Goldsmith
- at -
The Imperial Playhouse
Lower Washington Street, Boston

Catherine tossed it aside. Clearly, it was nothing but sentimental memorabilia of Lady Sands's girlhood in America. But the remaining papers looked to be letters. Impatiently, Catherine spread them out, and at once, an unusually short note caught her eye. She picked it up and held it carefully toward the light.

"My dear, dear, girl," it began, the penmanship a dark,

untidy scrawl. *"One can scarce imagine my amazement at finding you alive and well after so many years. Of course, I know that despite appearances, you could never forget your vows. And now it seems that you are richer, and I am poorer. Faith, my dear, for you will see me soon, perhaps when you least expect it . . ."*

Chapter Eighteen

If you cannot command your present humour and disposition, single out those who happen to be in the humour nearest your own.

—LORD CHESTERFIELD, 1776,
The Fine Gentleman's Etiquette

After leaving Harry's town house, Max and Lucifer accompanied Sisk on the short trip back to Queen Square. It hurt to walk, and yet it felt as necessary as air to Max's body. In Westminster, the day was a busy one, though neither man heeded the clattering traffic or the hawking vendors. Nor did they speak. Genevieve's story had left Max feeling confused, thwarted, and thoroughly ill tempered. Sisk, trudging along the street with his eyes narrowed and his brow furrowed, looked even less cheerful.

Suddenly, the constable slowed, and Max looked up to see they had reached the entrance which led to the Magistrate's Court. Max paused on the pavement, ignoring the passers-by who pushed impatiently around them. "I'd best come in," he said gruffly, leaning his weight on his walking stick.

Sisk eyed him up and down. "From the way yer carryin' yer ribs, wot yer'd best do is go home and crawl back in bed."

Max ignored him and started up the steps, Lucifer on his heels. "Tell Eversole to fetch all the statements," he demanded just as a huge coach and four clattered past, nearly drowning out his words. "Like it or not, we're going through this bloody case one more time."

Sisk gave his usual grunt, but just then, the coach turned round the corner, and a clear, sharp voice could be heard ringing through the air. Max swiveled about to see an immaculately dressed gentleman swishing through the crowd, making his way down the pavement. "Oh, I just couldn't wait!" sang Kemble, waving madly as he neared them. Then he jerked to a halt, the hand freezing in mid-waggle. "Christ, de Rohan! What happened to you?"

When Max just glared at him, Kemble let his assessing gaze drift boldly over Max's bruises. "Dear me!" he murmured as Lucifer began to whuff suspiciously at his footwear. "Has that pretty country miss a jealous husband somewhere?" Then his expression shifted mercurially. "Oh, but never mind that! Get a grip on that hell-hound before he pisses on my boots."

"What do you want, Kem?" grumbled Max, snapping his fingers to bring the mastiff to heel. With a parting snarl at Kemble, Lucifer obeyed.

"I'm dying to hear what your little French maid had to say."

Sisk tossed an inquiring glance at Max, who nodded tightly. "Aye, well, yer may as well come in," grumbled the police constable. "I don't need you pitching a hissy fit right 'ere in front o' the magistrates."

Kemble shot him an audacious wink, and together the four of them went up the short flight of steps and into the cool shadows of the corridor. The smell inside was both familiar and unpleasant; cold, acrid ashes and nervous perspiration had seemingly seeped into the planked floors. The fire in the grate had long since burnt out, and beside the ancient watch desk, a pair of uniformed constables stood, their heads bowed in quiet conversation.

"Eversole!" Sisk snapped as they passed. "Is the courtroom empty?"

The smaller of the two men jerked to attention, eyeing the mastiff with grave mistrust. "Yes, sir."

"We need a bit o' privacy," rasped Sisk. "Fetch me the file. Yer knows which."

They settled upon the narrow magistrates' bench at the far end of the room, Lucifer flopping down beneath. It took but a moment to bring Kemble up to date. When they were finished, Sisk snapped shut his notebook, and at once, Kemble burst into a peal of hilarity.

Sisk glowered at him. "Aye, and wot's so bloody funny?"

"Tony *Lumpkin*—?" managed Kemble between deep gulps of laughter.

Max scrubbed his hand down a morning's growth of beard. "I thought it was a dashed familiar name. Do you know him?"

"Know him?" Kemble spewed with laughter again. "In a manner of speaking. What a jolly joke! A killer with a sense of humor."

Max nailed him with an icy glare. "What the devil do you mean?"

Kemble's smile broadened. *"Tony Lumpkin!"* he repeated impatiently. "Act One, Scene Two of *She Stoops to Conquer!*"

Confused, Max shook his head.

Kemble tapped one finger impatiently. "He's the drunken young ne'er-do-well who sings the song at the Three Pigeons!" Abruptly, the willowy man stood before the rail and clapped an imaginary hat over his heart. Then, in a perfect baritone, he began to sway and sing:

> *Oh, when methodist preachers come down,*
> *A-preaching that drinking is sinful,*
> *I'll wager the rascals a crown,*
> *They always preach best with a skinful!*
> *But when you come down with your pence,*
> *For a slice of their scurvy religion,*
> *I'll leave it to all men of good sense,*
> *But you, my good friend, are their pigeon!*
> *Toroddle, toroddle, toroll!*

Gaining momentum, Kemble drew a deep breath for the second verse, but Lucifer roused to his feet, letting forth a blood-chilling howl. With an injured look, Kemble sat back down, as Sisk gave a low, soft whistle. "Well, I'll be blowed!" he said.

Suddenly, the door flew open to admit Eversole, who approached the bench with a sheaf of bound papers, keeping one eye on the dog. Sisk shuffled through the file. "These're just the case notes, you ejit," he growled impatiently. "We're wantin' the statements, too!"

His face flushing, Eversole left at once, leaving the door open as if he meant to return promptly.

Max returned at once to the topic at hand. "What are you saying, Kem?" he demanded. "That this name is some sort of prank?"

"Yes," admitted Kemble. "We have only to figure out why."

"Lumpkin," mused Max. "It certainly isn't a name we were searching for. We must go through Lady Sands's correspondence and calendars once again. There must be something we've overlooked."

With a heaving groan, Sisk stood. "Awright," he said wearily. "Back to yer place it is, de Rohan."

"I'm afraid I no longer have the lap desk," said Max, swiftly jerking to his feet. "Catherine—er—borrowed it. It is at her home in Mortimer Street."

Sisk rolled his eyes theatrically and began gathering up his things. "Christ Almighty, de Rohan!" he grumbled, stacking up the papers with quick, angry motions. "I can't think wot's got into you, givin' over evidence to some bit o' fluff wot's caught yer eye!"

Max shot him a dark look, but the barb had hit home. "Cecilia gave her the bloody desk in the first place, Sisk," he argued. "You were there when she brought it. Besides, Catherine has a remarkable understanding of human nature. She may well find something."

"Oh, just *Catherine* now?" teased Kemble. "Dispensed with that little formality of a title, have we?"

Sisk's head jerked up. "Title?" he archly interjected. "Thought she said her name was Mrs. Wodeway? Pr'haps, de Rohan, you ought to tell us just 'oo this woman is!"

Max felt his temper ratchet sharply upward. "It's none of your damned bus—"

Sisk cut him off. "If she's in possession of police evidence out o' this jurisdiction, it's plenty my business!"

Caught out, Max felt his face flame. "She is Lady

Catherine Wodeway, from Gloucestershire," he surrendered. "Her brother is Lord Treyhern."

"Treyhern?" mused Kemble. "From Gloucestershire? But that would be . . ."

Sisk's beady eyes began to glitter. "Why, that's Hell-Bent Rutledge's sister!" he exploded, tossing his notebook back down in disgust. "Gawd in heaven, de Rohan! Yer thinking with yer prick again! And this time, yer went and left key evidence with a suspect's sister!"

Just then, Eversole returned to place more papers on the desk. As if realizing their argument could be overheard, Sisk colored with embarrassment. "And shut the bloody door after yerself," he ordered his assistant, returning his piercing gaze to Max.

Max forced himself to be calm. Sisk should be reprimanded for upbraiding someone who so thoroughly outranked himself. Unfortunately, his argument was not unfair. "I didn't know who she was at first," Max confessed. "But it matters little, when Rutledge is obviously no longer a suspect."

Sisk still did not look pleased, but Kemble seized him by the elbow. "Leave it be, Sisk!" he warned, propelling the constable toward the door. "Looks like it's Mortimer Street for us."

By eleven o'clock, Catherine had managed to down her soda water and nibble a bit of bread crust. She was finishing the last of the newly discovered letters when someone dropped the front knocker with a determined thud. Morosely, she sighed. It was market day for Mrs. Trinkle, and, with the new butler not yet in residence, it fell to whoever was at hand to open the door. It was Isabel, no doubt, for they had planned to pick out new hats and gloves for the Flemington ball.

But to her shock, it was Max who stood on her threshold, looking startlingly masculine for a man who was bearing half his weight onto a walking stick. Catherine's heart leapt with happiness, and the rest of her very nearly leapt into his arms, but she was compelled to restrain herself. On the pavement below stood his friends, Mr. Kemble and Mr. Sisk, who was gingerly holding the dog's leash. She stepped back and threw open the door. This was not, it would seem, a social call.

"Come in," she called brightly to the men below. And then, in an arch sotto-voce to Max, "And what, pray, are you doing out of bed?"

Max smiled grimly as he passed. "My job," he said bluntly. "A moment of your time, if I may? It's about that lap desk."

Catherine lifted her eyebrows. "Good," she said very gravely. "Won't your friends come in, too?"

She caught a flash of rueful uncertainty in his eyes. "Shopkeepers and policemen loitering about his lordship's house?" he softly inquired. "Whatever would Treyhern say?"

Catherine shot him a dark look. "Probably 'Would you prefer coffee or tea?'" she snapped. "My brother doesn't put on airs."

Max cut an odd glance toward her, then gently inclined his head. "Might I hope for an introduction to this paragon of egalitarianism?" he murmured.

Catherine forced a smile. "If I don't strangle you first." Then, impatiently, she turned toward the men outside and lifted her chin. "Bring the dog and come in at once," she demanded. "I want your help."

Ten minutes later, Delilah was pouring the coffee and laughing unabashedly with Mr. Sisk about how they had discovered the hidden compartment. Catherine had pulled the tea table between the four of them, and they now sat shuffling through the various letters. Lucifer, to her pleasure, had settled at her feet and was now minutely examining her slippers.

"But this is what most perplexes me," she murmured, spreading the theater playbill across the table. "At first, I'd dismissed it. After all, it's just a Goldsmith play, but then I saw the sketch of this woman in the lower corner, and—"

"Goldsmith?" cried Mr. Kemble, snatching the play-bill from beneath her fingers. Protectively, Lucifer half rose from his haunches with a low, malevolent rumble, but Mr. Kemble was transfixed by the paper. "Well, hang me if it isn't our favorite, boys!" he exclaimed. *"She Stoops to Conquer!"*

Max let his eyes drift down the cast. *"Maledizione!"* he swore, stabbing a finger down at the second line. "Star-ring the renowned Julia Astwell as Mrs. Hardcastle! *Ast-well!* By God, that was Lady Sands's name before she wed!"

Kemble leaned over the table. "And who had the role of Tony Lumpkin?" he asked. "Oh—here it is. Richard Ventnor. Never heard of him. Oh, hello—! What's this . . . ?"

Absently, Catherine slicked a soothing hand over the dog's head. "What do you see, Mr. Kemble?" she asked. But she thought she already knew.

Kemble was glancing back and forth between Julia Astwell's headline and, on the opposite page, a penciled sketch of a pretty girl striking a theatrical pose. "This!" He tapped an impatient finger upon the sketch. "Isn't this the woman we knew as Lady Sands? The caption says her name is Nancy Coates, 'a rising star cast in the role of Miss Neville.' Not Julia at all!"

Catherine slid forward, almost off her chair. "Just so!" she said. "I saw Lady Sands but once. Still, I would swear this Nancy Coates is the woman I knew."

Sisk and Max exchanged confused glances. "I saw her briefly at Delacourt's wedding," admitted Max. "But I could not swear this young lady is she."

Sisk shrugged. "Never laid eyes on the woman until she was stiff as a board," he muttered. "And folk do take on a queer color when they've been throttled."

"Charmingly put," interjected Max dryly. "But still, look at those eyebrows. Is there not a vague resemblance to the dead woman?"

"Hmm." Sisk leaned nearer. "P'rhaps."

Kemble struck a more decisive tone. "Well, I'd seen Lady Sands a dozen times, and this Nancy Coates"—he tapped the sketch again—"is the woman I knew. Less ten years and two stone, of course. But it's Harry's wife."

"I fear it gets worse," said Catherine softly, drawing a folded piece of foolscap from her pocket. Suddenly, three sets of eyes lifted from the table to her face. "This letter was addressed to Julia not too long after she married Harry. It is unsigned, but the handwriting looks masculine. Someone who knew her in Boston, I collect. It sounds . . . well, rather ominous."

"From the mysterious Tony Lumpkin, perhaps?" remarked Kemble, snatching the letter and spreading it out. Together, the three men skimmed it.

"Unsigned," remarked Max softly, dragging his hair back off his face. It was a gesture, Catherine had learned, which meant he was thinking. "It would appear this Miss Coates came to England and assumed Julia Astwell's identity as Lord Hoage's estranged grand-daughter. But was it done with or without Miss Astwell's knowledge?"

Kemble shrugged. "We'll never know, but this play-bill implies that Miss Astwell was quite famous. Perhaps she was none too eager to give up her career to go dance attendance on a condescending old man? After all, there was initially no promise of an inheritance."

Max nodded grimly. "Although her grandfather did finally acknowledge her, he did so out of desperation, when his health failed. And only after he'd cast her mother into a life of poverty. Miss Astwell may have been bitter."

Sisk gave another nasty laugh. "P'raps it was even her idea of a joke? Send some low-born American actress ter pose as that pompous old windbag's lost grand-daughter?"

"Revenge, more like," muttered Max. "But the joke was on Julia Astwell, was it not? Nancy—if that's who Lady Sands really was—ended up inheriting the old man's money."

Catherine picked up the letter again, reading it for the tenth time. "There's something else here, Max, that I just cannot like," she mused. "This horrid, dark hand-writing. It looks so angry. The whole thing has an almost apocalyptic tone to it. And these phrases—*your vows, richer and poorer*—do you think . . ."

"Do I think what?" He stared at her fixedly.

Catherine lifted her gaze to catch and hold his. "Well," she said softly, "isn't it just possible that these two were married?"

Abruptly, Max snatched the letter, his eyes running frantically over it again. "Yes. It is quite possible."

Kemble peered over his shoulder. "Well, well," he murmured. "It seems our mysterious Nancy Coates was a bit of a bigamist. Find this actor Ventnor, and I daresay you'll have found your murderous Mr. Lumpkin, Max."

Abruptly, Max stood, his rangy length looming over the little morning parlor. "Sisk, take the playbill and that letter," he ordered, jerking out his silver watch and flicking it open with his thumb. "We've a long journey ahead."

Catherine jerked from her chair, alarmed. "Max, where—?"

"Derbyshire," he said grimly, restoring the watch to his waistcoat. "A mail coach leaves the Cross Keys Inn within the hour. I want to know if Harry ever heard of either Lumpkin or Ventnor."

Catherine frowned. While it would be fast, she did not think an arduous journey in a badly sprung mail coach would be good for Max's ribs. If she begged him to stay, would he? Probably. In fact, she was beginning to harbor the faintest suspicion that, given time, she might be able to wrap Max round her little finger. But how dreadfully wrong that would be! She had sought this *affaire* with her eyes wide open. And she had come to love him for what he was. And what he was—just as he had always insisted—was a policeman.

So Catherine escorted her guests to the door and, with much restraint, smiled brightly when handing Mr. Kemble his exquisite top hat and stick. "How I wish I could offer you a carriage," she said, turning to Mr. Sisk. "But I came in my brother's and sent it back again."

"Thank you, ma'am." Sisk's ears turned faintly pink, then he and Mr. Kemble disappeared down the steps.

But Max held back, his gaze drifting over Catherine's face. "I must thank you, too," he said quietly.

Catherine looked at him uncertainly. "For . . . ?"

Max shrugged his big shoulders uncomfortably, as if his coat were too tight. "For going through all those letters. For being kind to my—*my friends*. And for not mollycoddling me." He gave her a lame smile. "I daresay you've bitten your tongue hard enough to draw blood over that one."

He looked so solemn, so unexpectedly defenseless. Impulsively, Catherine shoved shut the door, ignoring the men who stood below. "Perhaps," she said, twining her arms behind his neck, "you'd best see for yourself?"

Fleetingly, Max hesitated. And then, as if unable to resist, he swept Catherine into his arms. His eyes were guarded and intense, and as he closed them, he lowered his mouth to hers in a kiss that was exquisite in its tenderness. His big hands were warm and gentle as they splayed over her back, enfolding her against him, seemingly *into* him. For long, sweet moments, he kissed her, parting her lips, delving into her mouth, sliding his tongue sinuously along hers, his heartbeat slow and strong against her breasts. And then, on a sigh, he feathered his lips over hers, across her jaw, down her throat.

She expected him to pull away, take his leave, but instead, a bone-deep shudder wracked his body. "Ah, God, Catherine!" he whispered, bending over her to bury his face against her neck. "I do not like this. I do not like to leave you."

Setting her hands on his shoulders, she pushed him a little away and gazed up into his eyes. "Good," she answered. "I should never wish it to be easy."

"It is not easy," he answered, his voice more raspy than usual. "Nothing about this is easy."

"Oh, I disagree." Catherine managed a weak, crooked smile. "I fell in love with you easily. And very quickly, too. Perhaps the rest of it will become easy in time? I shall wait, Max. I am a very patient woman."

For a moment, he looked stunned. His mouth opened, as if he meant to say something, but words apparently failed him. And then he shook his head, turned abruptly to open the door, and went down the steps into the sunshine. On the pavement below, it seemed Mr. Sisk and Mr. Kemble had broken into a quarrel. "No, no, no!" fumed the latter. "I'd sooner have a tooth drawn. I shall sneeze! And there will be mud! There is always mud in the country. I just won't go, do you hear me?"

"Good," grumbled Max, slapping Lucifer's leather leash across Kemble's palm as he passed. "You can watch the dog. And don't worry, he'll eat anything."

"Oh my God!" wailed Kemble, staring desperately after the disappearing men. "That's what I'm afraid of!"

Chapter Nineteen

*Vice is so deformed that it shocks us at first sight,
and would hardly attract us if it did not first wear
the mask of some virtue.*

—LORD CHESTERFIELD, 1776,
The Fine Gentleman's Etiquette

Not too many hours after Kemble went trudging up the
Strand with his burden, mentally preparing himself for
a miserable night, little Lord Branthwaite was already
suffering one. He was stuck in a pokey little village hos-
tel somewhere south of Leicester, after having been
carted halfway across Essex like a sack of meal in a coach
which pitched and swayed like a dinghy. The day had
grown hot, and his nurse had swaddled him in garments
which were too snug. And now, the dust of the Five
Feathers' courtyard was drifting through the window of
his private parlor, tickling his nose.

So when the evening mail coach came clattering in at
dusk, its horn blaring, its passengers bolting, and the
grooms buzzing about like bees, his young lordship lost
his barely tethered temper and screamed with all his
might, right into his mother's left ear. "Oooh, what a
fit," complained Cecilia, peeling him away from her
shoulder, only to find Lord Branthwaite was taking a

fistful of her hair and an onyx ear bob with him. "You're your father's son, aren't you?"

The babe began to kick and flail his displeasure, but just then, the parlor door flew open to admit his blame-worthy sire. "What's that, my love?" Lord Delacourt murmured, shoving a lock of sweaty hair off his fore-head. "Oh, is Simon cranky? Poor boy! Come to Papa, my precious."

Gladly, Cecilia surrendered her burden. "Yes, do take him," she said irritably, collapsing into a nearby chair to restore the ear bob. "He is half yours, after all, and it's the cranky part, I'm sure. Now, what news of that wheel? Are we to spend the rest of May in this wretched place, or only the night?"

"Just the night," Delacourt cheerfully answered as he settled the babe onto his knee for a bounce. "Your brother is standing over the wheelwright even as we speak. We'll start anew tomorrow."

But, again, the door flew open. This time, it was the harried innkeeper. "The queerest thing, my lord," he began, clearly intimidated by something. "A, er, gentle-man has just come in on the mail coach. A big, dark-looking fellow, he is. Asking after you and my lady. And for the other gent, too. Him most particular."

"My brother—?" asked Cecilia, rising from her chair. "Who on earth would ask for Harry?" But over the innkeeper's shoulder, she caught sight of the lean, black-clad figure who towered in the shadows of the taproom.

Delacourt, too, saw him. "What on earth?" he mut-tered. "De Rohan? And Sisk? Good God, come in at once." And then, to the relieved innkeeper, "Two tankards of ale, please, and another platter of food."

Max removed his hat and bent his head to step beneath the lintel. "My lord," he began solicitously. "I'm given to understand you've lost a wheel?"

"Max!" cried Cecilia, rushing to clasp his hands in hers. "What has happened? Why are you looking for Harry?"

Max looked back and forth between them and gave up all pretense of politesse. "Would you call Lord Sands at once?" he asked. "I have something I urgently need you to see. A sketch of someone you and your brother might recognize."

Delacourt went to the door, bellowing for the innkeeper to fetch Harry. A little nervously, Cecilia motioned them to the table by the window. Sisk smoothed the wrinkles from the playbill and pushed it into a shaft of sunlight. "Right 'ere, my lady, if yer please," he said in a crisp, businesslike tone. " 'Ave a look at this, and tell us if you recognize anyone?"

Quizzically, Cecilia's gaze flew from Sisk to Max and finally to the playbill. At once, her finely arched brows snapped together. "Look, David!" she exclaimed to Delacourt, who was now attempting to jiggle the babe back to sleep. "This pencil sketch! It is—why, it looks about like Julia when she was young. And oh, dear, an *actress*—? And why have they got the wrong name underneath?"

Max met her eyes with a level gaze. "Cecilia," he said quietly. "I don't think they do."

Placing his free hand affectionately on his wife's shoulder, Delacourt gazed over her head. "But it is Julia," he insisted, lifting his eyes to meet Max's. "Those eyebrows are unique. Who the devil is this Coates woman?"

Max exchanged an uneasy glance with Sisk. "Cecilia," he said quietly. "Precisely what did you and your brother know of this woman he married?"

Cecilia shrugged. "Just what I told you. Her grandfather was our neighbor. He sent for his granddaughter in America, and we met her at a ball which he gave shortly after her arrival. Soon she'd quite set her cap at Harry, and she seemed . . . well, nice enough." Her eyes caught Max's pleadingly. "Why, Max? What is it?"

Max pursed his lips for a moment and considered Harry. Like most good sharpers, it seemed Nancy Coates had picked her pigeons well. She had tricked a lonely old man into believing her his granddaughter, then married Harry—an act of bigamy, no doubt—all in order to inherit a fortune. And poor Harry hadn't suspected a thing. "How did she represent herself to you?" Max asked. "And to her grandfather? I mean, what credentials did she have?"

"Credentials?" she whispered, suspicion dawning in her eyes. "H-her grandfather had written her letters. Several pleading, pathetic letters. I remember, for she tried to show them to me once. I thought it in quite bad taste."

Suddenly, Harry burst into the room, puffing hard, his face more florid than usual. "What, ho, de Rohan!" he cried a little anxiously. "Thought you told me to leave town."

Max held up a staying hand. "My mistake, my lord," he apologized. "I fear I must now ask you to return again."

Harry shrugged good-naturedly. "To be sure," he agreed. "But did you come all the way from London to tell me that?"

"No, Harry," said his sister, motioning him toward the other chair. "Come, sit down. Max is asking questions about Julia."

Harry's fuzzy red brows knotted. "Think I told you all I know."

Sisk shoved the sketch across the table. "Oh, that's old Julia," Harry readily agreed. "A mere sprite of a thing when I married her."

Max paused, holding Harry's gaze. "Lord Sands," he began awkwardly. "Did your wife—when you wed, was she—or perhaps I should more simply ask, did she ever mention having been married before?"

Harry's face deepened to the color of an overripe cherry. "Why, good God!" he blustered. "What sort of question is that to ask? Of course not! A fellow would know that sort of thing, w-wouldn't he?"

Cecilia planted her hands palms-down on the scarred wooden table. "Harry, don't be thick," she said sharply. "Max is asking, *was she a virgin—?*"

Max tried to intercede. "Cecilia, that is not nec—"

"Yes, it is!" Cecilia cut in. *"Harry?"*

Harry's blush deepened to something akin to eggplant, and Max began to ponder the possibility of an apoplexy. "Well, er—I, ah—she said . . . she said she was."

At that, mayhem erupted. "And you believed that?" shrieked Cecilia, pressing her fingertips to her temples. "A bit of alum water and chicken blood, and you fell for it?"

"Cecilia!" roared her husband, looming large over the

table. "You are *not* being helpful!" At once, Lord Branth-waite lifted his head from his papa's shoulder and erupted into another wail. Fortunately, a harried-looking nurse burst in and, with a nod from Delacourt, swept the lad away in her arms. Then, with one hand, Delacourt hefted a solid oak chair and fairly hurled it against the table.

Sitting down with a stern expression, he studied them as if they were unruly children. "Very well!" he said commandingly. "Now, explain, Max, just what the devil is going on."

Because he could see no better way, Max was swift and blunt. At the end of his story, Harry looked almost relieved, and Delacourt looked deeply thoughtful. "And so Julia wasn't Julia at all," he grumbled. "I can't say I'm surprised. She acted the fine lady, yes, but there was always a coarse edge to her."

"And she was *married!*" said Cecilia more softly. "I daresay it's that American banker—the one who claimed to have been in Scotland."

"Perhaps." But Max was deeply doubtful.

"That's why Julia was selling her jewelry, wasn't it?" Cecilia continued. "She abandoned her husband and came to England as an imposter. And when her husband found her, he began blackmailing her slowly."

Max hesitated. "It would fit the facts, yes."

But Harry still looked mystified. "So, I wasn't married to anyone atall?" he mumbled as a serving maid entered bearing a tray heaped with food. "Be a bit of a relief, that would."

Max turned to Sisk. "What was your impression of the banker?"

Sisk looked chagrined. "Well, Eversole took 'is statement," he admitted. "Said the fellow 'ad a receipt from 'is hotel in Edinburgh."

Max pondered that for a moment. "And Eversole is competent? You trust him?"

Sisk hesitated. "Well . . . as much as I trust any of 'em, I daresay."

A long, anxious silence held sway over the tiny parlor. Max leaned forward in his chair, the wooden bottom creaking beneath his weight. "Sisk," he said very quietly. "I hear a disturbing hint of doubt in your tone."

The constable shifted uneasily. "Awright, de Rohan," he admitted. "That bribery scandal last month shook us, and no mistake. But no reason ter think Eversole's been lining 'is pockets, eh?"

"Perhaps, Sisk, you'd best tell me." The words were grim, almost threatening.

Sisk blanched. "Well, 'e did drink right reg'lar down at the Fiddling Dog wiv those two wot got caught on the take," he quietly confessed. "But I'd tipped a few wiv 'em meself, I daresay."

With a muttered curse, Max pounded his fist on the table, rattling the dishes. "Eversole has been intimately involved in this case!" he roared, sending the serving girl darting back out the door. "My God, just today he brought us this file! And left the bloody door open whilst we talked about it! And he knows—" Max jerked to a halt, then almost shouted. "Good God, Sisk—now he *knows* where Lady Sands's letters are!"

Sisk leapt angrily from his chair. "Oh? And just 'oo would you trust, de Rohan? The whole bloody lot of 'em are rife wiv filth. And it sure as 'ell ain't my job ter clean it up, is it? No, it's *yours!* 'Cause I gots ter work wiv 'em!"

Swiftly, Delacourt reached out to lay his hand over Max's fist. "Calm yourselves," he said quietly. "You are on the same side. Now, Max, where is that damned lap desk?"

Max pressed the heels of his hands into his eyes, which were raw with a day's worth of road grit. "At Catherine's," he answered hollowly. "Damn me for a fool! I left it at Catherine's."

Cecilia gasped, but her husband shot her a dark look. "This constable—Eversole—does he know you've come here?" demanded Delacourt. "That you've found this letter and playbill?"

Max shook his head and let his hands drop dejectedly onto the table. "Catherine found it just this morning," he admitted. "We went straight from her house to the Cross Keys and caught the mail coach."

Delacourt rose from his chair, looking very grave. "Cecilia," he said sharply, striding toward the door. "See that these men eat now."

"Y-yes, to be sure," she agreed. "Where are you going?"

Delacourt threw open the door. "To check the wheel and have fresh horses put to," he said grimly. "And to make sure my carriage pistols are loaded. We shall hire a conveyance and follow them in the morning."

The evening following Max's departure for Derbyshire, Catherine begged off her engagement with Isabel. She'd felt unable to suffer through another ball, even for the Flemingtons, whom she actually liked. Isabel surrendered with good grace, and Catherine dined instead with Bentley—then quarreled with him again over Max. This time, he'd gone so far as to threaten to reveal her secret to Cam. It seemed Sofia Castelli's eerie prognostications just wouldn't stop coming true. Then, after tossing and turning with worry over Max all night, she arose with a headache to match her queasy stomach.

What on earth was wrong with her? In the country, she always felt fine. Perhaps it was the foul London air? Determined to best her weakness, Catherine sent round for her horse and a groom. She would have a long, hard ride, she had decided. And why not go to Hampstead? Whilst there, she could roust Bentley from his bed and have it out with him once and for all.

Yes, Bentley be damned, and Cam, too, if it came to it. She was going to do what felt right in her heart, she decided, stepping into the skirt of her favorite red habit. She was going to marry Max; beg him if necessary. Of course, it was remotely possible, she considered as she struggled to fasten her skirt buttons, that neither of them was going to have much choice in the matter. She'd gained a half a stone, it seemed.

But at last, the buttons were coaxed into place. It was fine. Surely it fit as perfectly as ever? She had let Signora Castelli spook her, that was all. In this prediction, at least, Max's grandmother had erred. Catherine was almost sorry for it. The only thing she wanted more than a child was to be with Max. But on his terms, not because they'd had no honorable alternative.

She went to the window and stared down into the street as she shrugged into her jacket. She had the oddest hope that if she simply stared out long enough, Max would return to her sooner. A foolish fantasy, that. Just then, the groom came round leading two horses. Orion craned his glossy neck to whuff suspiciously at one of the small holly bushes which flanked the front door. Curious, Catherine threw up the sash and leaned out. Good God, surely the silly beast did not mean to eat it?

And then, she saw it, the faint outline of someone—a very *small* someone—crouched in the shadowy crevice behind the holly. She leaned a little farther and looked straight down. *Nate!* That little rascal! What on earth? Suddenly, she laughed aloud. Had Max sent him to keep watch on her? Perhaps he was afraid she'd go careening into trouble without him. Well, fine! A spot of worry would do Max good. Catherine would keep Nate's secret, at least for now. With a song in her heart, she went tripping down the steps and threw open the door to greet her groom.

But, to her shock, a fine high-perch phaeton drew up before her doorstep, and a tall figure in a black cloak leapt effortlessly down. He noticed her habit at once. "Ah, Lady Catherine!" said Rupert Vost, his voice rich with disappointment. "You are on your way out? I had hoped most desperately to take you for a drive!"

Catherine looked at him in some surprise. "Good afternoon, Mr. Vost."

Vost smiled at her pleadingly. "I'd hoped to speak with you further about that little matter of a wedding gift," he reminded her, unfurling his cloak and tossing it over his arm. "I thought we might take a spin through the park."

"Through the park?"

He shrugged boyishly. "Yes, so you can give me your

advice. After we've settled on the right thing, perhaps we might window shop a bit? I don't mind admitting that I feel like an idiot to be at sixes and sevens over what ought to be a simple thing. But I'm so keen to impress Amelia, and the happy day is but a fortnight hence."

Inwardly, Catherine sighed. Good heavens! Was the man never going to give up? Perhaps it would be best just to get it over with. Vost would find her dull, and interested in neither flirtation nor flattery. Then he would go away. "Well, I was on my way to Hampstead," she began.

"Oh, excellent!" he interjected, bounding up the steps. "We shall have lots of time to chat."

Catherine forced a smile and motioned her groom away. "I meant to call upon my brother," she clarified, reopening the front door. "A heated discussion between siblings. I shouldn't want witnesses—in case I do him some injury, you see. I'd best go another time."

Rupert Vost laughed as she showed him into the morning parlor. "Ah!" he said jovially. "And I daresay I can guess what that might be about! Brothers are very protective of their sisters, are they not?"

Catherine's smile faded. "Whatever do you mean?"

Vost looked suddenly embarrassed. "Oh, my apologies," he murmured. "I'd been given to understand— but perhaps I mistook the matter . . ."

"What *matter?*"

He gave a chagrined smile and draped his cloak over his arm. "Well, that you and the charming Mr. de Rohan had, er, formed an attachment."

Catherine felt herself tense. "Whoever would say such a thing?"

Vost coughed into his fist. "Well, ah, actually, it was

Lady Kirton," he confessed. "At the Flemingtons' ball last night."

"Isabel!" Catherine felt her eyes narrow.

"Oh, dear me!" he said, leaning forward to touch her arm lightly. "You mustn't blame your aunt! I was just inquiring after you—expressing my regard and all that—and perhaps she mistook me? I'm ashamed to admit I was once thought an awful rake, so I daresay she wished to discourage me. Silly of her, really, when I am so devoted to my Amelia. Now, about those pearls of yours—where did you say you bought them?"

"I didn't," she responded. "They were my mother's." Suddenly, Catherine wished to escape the room. "Will you pardon me whilst I change?"

"Oh, absolutely," oozed Rupert Vost.

It took Catherine but a moment to change from her habit into a carriage dress and pelisse. For reasons she did not perfectly understand, she wanted this little jaunt over with. It was foolish, really. Why stay at home on such a lovely day? Max had gone all the way to Derbyshire, a journey of some two or three days. And although she saw Vost for the unabashed flirt he was, he was charming. It was no great inconvenience to help him surprise his bride-to-be. It would get her mind off other things.

With one last tug on the sleeves of her pelisse, Catherine rushed back down the stairs. Vost, too, was impatient, for he had drawn shut the door of the morning parlor and was awaiting her at the foot of the twisting staircase. "You look charming, Lady Catherine," he said, offering her his arm. "Shall we?"

They stepped out the door, and suddenly, Catherine remembered. "Mr. Vost! Your cloak!"

Vost lifted his hands, palms toward the sunshine, and smiled. "I'll fetch it later. Now, careful, my dear, whilst I help you up. A high-slung rig, is it not?"

Quickly, Vost whipped up his horses and headed south toward Oxford Street at a fast clip. They chatted amiably, and soon they were whirling through the gates at Hyde Park Corner. It was a most unfashionable hour for a drive, and Catherine saw no other carriages. Around the Serpentine, nannies in starched white smocks pushed their perambulators along the path which rimmed the glistening water. Halfway up the slope, a young boy struggled with his kite strings, but otherwise, the park was empty.

"Why do we not go farther up the hill?" Vost asked with another blinding smile. "I always find children so tedious."

By ten o'clock, the little village of Luton Hoo was vanishing into the dust of Lord Delacourt's traveling coach. His ribs still aching miserably, Max sat stoically upon the box, as either he or Sisk had been required to do since the beginning of their journey, because someone had to keep the poor coachman awake. To his credit, the hearty fellow had made decent time. The moon had been nearly full, and they had paused often to rest and change out the horses.

From his lofty perch, Max watched as the hedgerows and hills of England flowed past in a rich, green panorama. As midday approached, they lumbered through the fringes of north London, almost to Marylebone. He would not rest until he had seen Catherine. Until he had that bloody lap desk back. He was furious with himself for not having realized the risk in permitting her to keep it. Furious he'd not considered the possibility of police corruption in this case. And, as usual, Sisk had been annoyingly right. It was Max's sworn duty to think of such things—not to mention his deep moral obligation to see to Catherine's safety. He had been *bedding* her, for God's sake, an act which could have grave consequences. And it made her his responsibility, regardless of how she might see it.

Yes, somehow, he'd become careless, and in more ways than one. He'd let himself begin to *feel* instead of *think*. And he did not know just what to do about it. Sometimes he wondered if he oughtn't just beg her to marry him. The thought no longer alarmed him so much. Indeed, it sometimes seemed the only way to keep her truly safe—*if* she would have him. If he could bear to give up his job and settle into a less dangerous, more mundane life.

Catherine. *Catherine*. He squeezed shut his eyes and felt his anxiety ratchet up another notch. Confidentiality bedamned, he should have shown her his list of suspects. Should have warned her about Eversole. Still, there was no reason to believe the constable a turncoat. All would be well once he reached Catherine and saw that she was fine. Then he would be able to get his heart out of his throat and draw a decent breath again. It wouldn't be long. The rumble and clatter of midday traffic along the Edgeware Road surrounded them now. Delacourt's coachman yawned for the hundredth time, then turned to Max for directions. Soon they were rolling up Mortimer Street.

But, strangely, the scene unfolding before Catherine's house was almost as he'd left it. Kemble still stood on the pavement at the foot of the steps, his heels dug in, nervously clutching Lucifer's leash. And the dog was still straining hard against it, radiating canine irritation. And then Max caught sight of the small head poking from the tangle of shrubbery near the front door. What the devil? *Nate?*

In his bewilderment, he signaled the coachman too late, and the carriage halted well past the house. Max leapt down, apparently unnoticed, and started down the pavement. With a pained expression, Kemble had thrust the dog's leash almost into the shrubbery. "But he likes you," the dapper fellow was whining. "Now, come out, Nate, do! If Lady Catherine can't take him, you really must! I insist!"

"No, I can't!" Nate whimpered, pale-faced as he picked his way out of the bush. "Look 'ere, Mr. Kemble, bad trouble's afoot, and—oh, praise Jesus, Mary, 'n' Joseph! There's de Rohan!"

Kemble whipped around. "Well, thank God!"

Lucifer began to wiggle with excitement as Max drew up beside Kemble, who summarily stuffed the leash into his hand. "Why on earth are you hiding in Lady Catherine's shrubbery, Nate?" Max demanded, oblivious to the dog's happy sniffing.

Kemble must have caught the arch tone of Max's voice. "I had nothing to do with it!" he insisted, backing away, palms out. But Max had nailed Nate with an angry gaze.

"I've been cramped up in there orf 'n on for a sen'night," the lad admitted weakly, ripping his shirt as he leapt free of the holly. "But never mind me! It's Lady Catherine yer ort ter worry about!"

"What?" demanded Max, alarm surging. "What about her?"

Normally unflappable, Nate began wringing his hands. "She's gorn orf wiv that gentry cove," he blurted, eyes big as sovereigns. "Not five minutes past. I smelt 'im, de Rohan, I swear ter God Almighty. It was 'im—that fellow 'oo followed yer out o' St. James! Same fancy cloak, too."

Just then, Sisk lumbered up beside Max. "What's the whelp yammering about?" he asked on a yawn.

All seriousness now, Kemble clamped a solid hand on Sisk's shoulder. "He thinks Catherine has been kidnapped. Is that it, Nate?"

Nate looked sicker still. " 'E tricked her, is wot I thinks. She let 'im in the 'ouse. And but a minute after, I 'ears the side window scrape open. So I creep under the ledges"—here, the lad pointed along the front foundation—"an' I peeped round the corner. And 'e's shoving that fancy cloak out o' the window, pretty as you please! Wrapped up in a ball and clanking something awful, it was, an' big as a spring sow. A silver candlestick fell out, an' the fellow below stuffed it—"

"What fellow?" Max demanded.

Nate's eyes narrowed to little slits. "That weaselly-looking blue-coat 'oo works out 'er Queen Square. Eversole's 'is name."

Terror seized Max's heart. But Nate was still explaining. "I followed 'im a fair piece, then thought better of it. But by the time I run back to the house, the carriage was turnin' the corner inter Regent Street."

Max squatted down on the pavement and stared Nate straight in the eyes. "And the man with the cloak,

Nate?" he asked, unable to keep the surging panic from his voice. "Did you catch his name? Or where they were going? Anything?"

Eyes pooling with tears now, Nate nodded. "Vost," he whispered. "She called him Mr. Vost. Drivin' a high black phaeton, 'e was. Said they were orf ter Hyde Park. But 'e's a wrong un, de Rohan. And I just *knows* it."

As Rupert Vost's phaeton spun along the park's upper carriage drive, Catherine studied her companion's profile. Amelia might be plain and shy, but Catherine could certainly see how Lord Welbridge's daughter had fallen in love with Vost. The dappled sunlight flowed over them, emphasizing his angelic good looks and glinting off his golden hair.

As he slowed the carriage, Vost turned to her and smiled. And suddenly, inexplicably, Catherine remembered Max's long-ago admonition about being alone in the park. But how foolish she was! It was broad daylight. She was with a gentleman. Vost turned left and made his way into the depths of the park, then drew up his horses near a deep thatch of rhododendron. Catherine recognized it at once. It was the very one in which Max had first kissed her.

"Let's stroll, shall we?" he invited, leaping gracefully down. "There is a lovely bench in the shade just past that thicket."

He caught her easily about the waist and spun her around and down. It seemed Vost had begun to perspire, for it was then that Catherine noticed his cologne—opulent sandalwood, and far too much of it. She regained her footing and brushed quickly past him, the hems of her carriage dress sweeping along the gravel. As they reached the point along the path where the bushes began to grow higher and thicker, Vost grew oddly quiet.

The silence set Catherine's nerves on edge. Perhaps she should say something. "Now, about this jewelry, Mr. Vost," she began, pushing away a low branch and ducking around it. "Are you quite set on pearls? Some people think them, you know, a young girl's jewelry. Mightn't your Amelia be better pleased with colored stones?"

"Sapphires, perhaps," he lazily agreed. "I've always had a fondness for sapphires."

They reached the bench along the path, and Vost turned suddenly to look at her. To her surprise, every ounce of his facile charm seemed to have drained from his face. Instead, he looked suddenly harder, quite ruthless, really. Catherine must have betrayed her shock and half turned back toward the path.

Vost reacted with lightning speed, grabbing her and dragging her back against him. She drew breath to scream. One hand slapped over her mouth, sending her heart into her throat. Roughly, he shook her, knocking her hat into the grass. "Be still, damn you!" he hissed. Panic surged, and she struggled against his iron grip, tossing her head, trying to jab him in the ribs with an elbow. But he was quick. Strong. His scent was heavy and choking. She bit into his hand, thrashed her head, tried to cry out.

The soft, unmistakable sound of steel sliding against leather stopped her. A cold, hard edge pressed against her throat. *A knife.* Oh, God. Beneath Vost's fingers, Catherine whimpered. "Not another bloody sound," he hissed. "I will use it."

She tried to think. Tried to reason. No clear thought came. Someone would come. Oh, pray God someone would come. Vost jerked her head hard against his chest, bent his lips to her ear. "I'm removing my hand now," he whispered darkly. "Make a sound, and I'll slit your throat, then swear we were set upon by footpads."

She tried to crane her neck, tried to see his face. Again, he slammed her head back against his chest. "Nod if you understand," he rasped.

He was perspiring heavily now, the stench of sandalwood revolting. Catherine tried to nod, felt the back of her head scrub against his lapel. "Good," he said softly. The fingers fell away. She dragged in her breath, gasping for air. For sanity.

"What do you want?" she softly cried. Still holding the knife to her throat, Vost let the other hand slide down, cupping her breast, weighing it in his hand. "No," she whispered, shuddering at his touch. "Not that. Please, not that."

Vost pressed the blade harder against her flesh, his hand tightening roughly over her breast. He squeezed until it hurt, but Catherine refused to cry out. "By God, I'd like a taste of you," he hissed, lightly touching his tongue to the turn of her throat. Catherine felt her whole body tremble with revulsion. He laughed softly. "Oh, yes," he whispered. "I should enjoy fucking a real woman instead of that frail stick I'm about to marry. Someone who'd put up a bit of a fight. Julia did, you know. And you're the very same. So very fine in your ways. But you'll give in before I'm done with you. God knows she did."

Catherine shook her head, shut her eyes. "No," she

whispered, her voice small and plaintive. "Please, no."
Rape. It would be rape. Why her? Dear God, horrible
things like this didn't happen to ordinary people like
her. Did they? She should be at home on the farm. Gar-
dening. Riding. *Knitting*, for pity's sake! Tears welled up
into her throat, hot and choking.

Vost moved his hand higher, fondled her nipple
through the fabric of her gown, pinched it hard. "I want
you," he whispered. "I won't hurt you if you'll promise
not to scream."

She felt the knife tremble against her throat as his
other hand slid lower, eased between her thighs, touched
her obscenely. Catherine squeezed shut her eyes. If she
screamed, how fast could he cut her? *How fast?* Oh,
God. Catherine began to fight for breath. "A-are you de-
ranged?" she managed to whisper. "I could not live with
myself."

Ever so gently, he pricked at the flesh of her throat
with the tip of his blade. Involuntarily, she jerked. Vost
laughed, low and wicked. "My dear, I'm afraid you
shan't live to regret much of anything," he whispered,
his voice mockingly seductive. "I fear you might know
too much. I've no notion, you see, just what my dear
Julia might have kept in that little desk of hers."

She was trembling now with every fiber of her being,
afraid to move, afraid to scream. But knowledge rushed
through her, and somehow she found the strength to
speak. "Y-you are Julia's husband," she said in a horrified whisper. "I found her letters. Let me go. You are too
late."

"I think not," he said softly. "You see, a terrible robbery occurred in Mortimer Street whilst you were up-

stairs changing. That little lap desk is gone, along with three sets of silver candlesticks. Really, my dear, London can be such a dangerous place. You should keep more servants about."

Wild with panic, Catherine could barely speak. "Wh-what are you t-talking about?"

He jerked her body closer, and, to her shame, Catherine could feel his rigid erection pressing against her hips. "You don't think I'm fool enough to work alone, do you?" he asked, his breath hot on her neck. "The policeman I bribed was hidden in your garden. By dusk, he'll be down at the Fiddling Dog, drunk as the fool he is."

Catherine's whole body shook. He was going to rape her. Kill her. Kill his henchman, too, she didn't doubt. But from somewhere deep in the reaches of her soul, Catherine found a shred of composure and dragged it up out of sheer desperation. *Stall. Stall*, she thought. Keep him talking. Someone *would* come.

"I hope your accomplice enjoys his riches, for I'm sure his days are numbered," she managed. "As you mean mine to be."

Vost's hand returned to squeeze hard at her breast, pushing the swell of her flesh almost from her stays. "After I've tasted these," he grunted, brushing the cold blade down her throat, over her nipple.

"So, a thief, a rapist, *and* a murderer?" she bit out, wrenching his hand from her breast.

Vost laughed against her ear, his lips moist. "Beg me, Catherine," he whispered. "Beg me not to hurt you. I always made Julia beg first. I think she came to like it. But she didn't like paying for my silence." He tightened his arm about her waist, dragging her hips against his.

"Go to hell!" she managed weakly, trying to wrench free. "I've already given your letters to the authorities!"

Vost laughed again. "I don't believe you, my dear," he whispered. "You are too desperate. I like that. If you are good, I'll hide you away for a few days. Until I tire of you. And then I'll send you on your way to—oh, say, the Barbary Coast?"

"No—!"

He slipped the cold blade of the knife beneath the ruching of her neckline and flicked his wrist, as if he might slit it open. "Yes, creamy flesh like this would be worth a small fortune to those dark-skinned devils. You've developed a taste for the swarthy type, I believe? It would be better than death."

"No, damn you, kill me," she swore. "And then you'll be hanged. My groom saw you arrive. He'll bear witness to this." *And Nate,* she remembered at the last moment. Nate had seen him, could probably identify the carriage . . .

"You mean to be tiresome, I see." Vost heaved a weary sigh. "Then I'm afraid there will be a dreadful phaeton accident, my dear."

"You'll never get away with it!"

Vost kept talking, his voice almost melancholy. "You demanded the ribbons, of course," he mused. "So headstrong! Unwisely, I indulged you. Of course, you overturned us." The blade brushed almost lovingly over her throat. "Your lovely neck! It will snap almost instantly! Stunned and grief-stricken, I shall rush for help. But it will be too late."

"My servant saw you, you fool! No one will believe you innocent!"

Vost threw back his head and laughed. "Amelia will," he answered. "Plain women will forgive a handsome rake anything. Already she has lied to the police, and of her own volition. To save us from the taint of scandal, she said. Amusing, is it not? As to the others, especially that hulking bastard de Rohan, yes, they will suspect. But they will prove nothing."

Catherine tried to squirm from his grip. "You will be ruined!"

"I think not, my dear. Amelia's father has too much money."

"That is why you killed your wife, is it not?" Catherine demanded. She fought down her impulse to struggle, to run. It was too soon. Not yet. Stall. Keep him talking. Splinter his focus. *Watch the knife.* "Your wife— the actress, Nancy—she was about to turn the tables on you, wasn't she?" she whispered. "You were just a petty blackmailer until Amelia Lane fell for you. You stole the sapphire and killed your wife, for you knew that as soon as you married Amelia, Nancy would have her revenge."

Vost's fist tightened involuntarily, his fingers digging into her flesh. "Yes, God damn her!" he gritted. "She was very sly. Smiled and wished me well, even. But I knew that the minute Harry divorced her—and he meant to—she'd be blackmailing *me*. The bitch probably has our marriage lines in that bloody damned desk. I won't risk it. Not now, not when I've got my little sapphire nest egg safely hidden away in my rooms. I'd bled everything else out of her. She was of no further use to anyone."

"But she was a human being!" Catherine cried. "You must have loved her once!"

Vost jerked her angrily against him again. "She was a selfish whore!" he growled. "She left me without a word in Boston! She tricked that idiot Sands into marrying her. And she rid herself of my child—me, her own husband!—as if she thought herself too good to carry it."

Catherine had touched a nerve. "She—she kept a memento, you know," she somehow stuttered. "The p-playbill. *She Stoops to Conquer.* You are Richard. Richard Ventnor. That was your last work together, wasn't it? Nancy couldn't bring herself to throw it away. She must have cared."

"Shut up, you blue-blooded bitch," he spat.

And then, his hand was about her mouth again. His fingers shoved between her lips. She tasted dry, bitter linen. *A handkerchief!* Oh, God. She lashed her head wildly, to no avail, and screamed. Too late. Too late.

Chapter Twenty

❧❦❧

*Let your enemies feel the steadiness of your resentment;
for there is a difference between bearing malice,
which is ungenerous, and a resolute self-defense,
which is always justifiable.*

—Lord Chesterfield, 1776,
The Fine Gentleman's Etiquette

Vost dragged Catherine bodily into the shadows, deeper into the bushes. He pushed her facedown into the cool grass, came down on top of her, forcing her breasts and belly hard against the ground. Catherine curled her fists into the turf, tried to claw and squirm away. He dragged her back, struck her hard in the temple with his elbow. "Scream, my fine lady!" he hissed as her tears began to flow. "No one will hear now. You won't make me feel guilty. You *won't*."

He lay spread on top of her now, the tip of the knife touching her just below the ear. His hand fisted in her skirts, dragged them up. Cold air. Ice-cold. Catherine shuddered again. Nausea roiled in her stomach. She felt his weight lift slightly away to fumble at his trousers. She wanted to vomit. Wouldn't give in to the urge. Had to fight. *Fight.* Better dead than this. Beneath him, she squirmed, tried to cry out, dug her fingers deeper into the ground, tried to push up. And then the cold tip of the knife pricked at her flesh. He grunted. Started to lift himself, to look back. He made a half-noise. A curse? A moan? She was not sure.

But he did not finish it.

A roar filled Catherine's ears. Her body jerked, convulsed. Pain, hot and fierce, burned through her. *Not her throat. Not the knife.* Something else. Daylight faded. Catherine tried to think. Tried to breathe. Couldn't. A horrid sound surrounded her, a cacophony of snarling and snapping, as if the pits of hell had cracked open all around her. Dimly, she sensed someone—or something—dragging Vost's weight off her body. Then total oblivion roiled up, blotting out the flood of pain. Sucking her down, and down and down. Until Catherine knew no more.

It is, perhaps, a blessing that the most horrific moments of a person's life are often lived in a sort of murky reality, never to be clearly remembered again. Max de Rohan was one of those rare, confident men who had dealt daily with the ugliest, most depraved cesspits of human nature, wading through them mentally unscathed, never pausing to question the wisdom of each action, never doubting the righteousness of his path. But in one blinding instant, all of that changed. Max jerked the trigger, felt the recoil of the pistol in his hand, and suddenly shattered his own moral certainty. His own infallibility. And perhaps his dreams.

Vost's chest was bleeding copiously as the dog dragged him away. Max spared his wound no thought. Instead, he flung Delacourt's carriage pistol into the grass and fell to his knees beside Catherine. Oblivious to the gnashing of Lucifer's teeth a few feet away, he gingerly turned her over. Rage receded. Terror seized him as he tore at her clothing. "Oh, God!" he prayed as Kem knelt beside him. "Christ, Kem, I—I meant to shoot him through the shoulder."

Kemble was kneeling beside him now. "Oh, you got him," he said swiftly. "How badly is she hurt?" Swiftly, Max shoved away the hem of Catherine's pelisse to study the wound, a wide, angry gash near her waist, oozing blood and bits of fabric. Catherine moaned softly at his touch.

Max gave a cry of agony and began ripping off his neck cloth. "Kem, *Dio mio,* what have I done?"

"You'd no choice, Max." Kemble cut a swift glance over his shoulder at Lucifer. The dog was making quick work of what was left of Rupert Vost, leaving a swath of blood across the grass. Now he had hefted him up by the coat collar and was snapping his head from side to side as if he were a rag doll.

"Catherine—" Max choked, gingerly examining her with his shaking hands. "Catherine, you must—oh, God! Please. Don't die."

But her dress was darkening with blood. Her blood. "Seems the ball went through Vost, then into her," murmured Kemble, helping to rip free her clothing. "But where, damn it?" Hastily, he seized the bone-handled rondel which lay glittering in the grass by her neck and began to hack through the sodden fabric, ripping it away to reveal the full extent of the damage. "Thank God, not the heart," he whispered. But blood was seemingly everywhere.

As they frantically worked, Sisk's portly figure

popped over the hill. He reached them and collapsed to his knees, seizing his chest, gasping for breath. "Gawd in heaven, that dog's broke the bastard's neck," he wheezed. Then his gaze softened on Catherine. "Poor lovey! Any hope?"

Kemble was swiftly padding the wound with his makeshift bandage. "Give me your neck cloth, Sisk. Max, can you stanch a gunshot wound?"

"Yes."

"Then do it," warned Kem, his hands flying now. "Press here and here," he commanded, dragging Max's fingers to the critical points. "Do not let up. Sisk, have the coach brought up. And be damned quick about it. I'm off to fetch Greaves. Meet me in Mortimer Street."

Somehow, Max and the coachman managed to move Catherine's limp body into the carriage. And some-how—later, he couldn't even recall the journey—he managed to hold her steady in his arms until they reached her house. The housemaid, Delilah, met them at the door and promptly fell to pieces at the sight. Greaves, who lived just yards away in Harley Street, had already gone up to Catherine's bedchamber, thank God. With his throat so tight he could barely breathe, Max carried Catherine up the stairs and into the house. In-side, he bolted up the steps two at a time, pushing past the housekeeper, who stood gaping after him on the landing. He heard the rustle of her stiff bombazine skirts as she spun about to follow him, and still he did not hesitate.

He knew Catherine's door lay at the top of the stairs and carried her in without preamble. Already, a strong medicinal smell hung in the air, and Greaves's leather bag was open on the washstand. Kemble helped him position her on the bed.

At once, the surgeon seized command. "Her pulse is weak but stable," Greaves pronounced, his fingers pressed to Catherine's limp wrist. "Kemble, you've some medical training, I recollect? I've laid out bandages in the dressing room. Prepare them whilst I mix a tincture of opiates." And then he pulled a brown vial from his bag, keeping one eye on Max. "Go downstairs, Max, and pour yourself a brandy. I must examine the lady now. Do you understand me?"

Already, the housekeeper had begun to draw off Catherine's stockings with quick, desperate motions. Max bent to touch her lightly on the forehead, and Catherine's eyelids fluttered ever so slightly. He wanted to stay. Wanted to demand his rights. But he had none. "I will go only so far as the drawing room," he finally answered. "And I shan't take my eyes from this door, Greaves. Damn it, you must fix her! Call me at once if— if there is anything . . ."

Greaves laid a steadying hand on Max's arm. "You may trust that I will do so, my friend."

For the next half-hour, Max watched through the open doors of the drawing room as servants scurried up and down the curving staircase bearing basins, towels, and lamps. He felt guilty. Unwanted. Horribly out of place. In the corridor, he could hear a footman being dispatched to Hampstead, tasked with the mission of finding Bentley Rutledge. Slowly, the hush of illness fell over the house, and Max found himself alone, clutching yet another snifter of brandy he didn't want and staring at the portrait of a man he'd never known.

Randolph Rutledge. Bentley had his face, but Catherine had his eyes. Eyes she might never give to her children. Max caught back a sob, dropped his head, felt it shudder through his body. She was so real, so honorable. Catherine was a good person, a rare thing in this world. And beautiful beyond words. Had he ever told her so? Perhaps in the throes of passion, when a man might say anything and scarce remember it. But that did not count. He loved her, and he had not told her. Why had he shut away the truth? She deserved better. And still, despite his failings, she had fleetingly been his. *Almost* his. And because of it, because he'd gotten her into this mess, she might very well die.

Oh, he was used to blood. Even death. Saw it often— too often—in all its infinite, appalling forms. He should have been inured to it. But he could not escape the vision of the deep, ragged wound slicing through Catherine's ivory flesh. Better it should have been him. Surely, the pain would have been easier to bear than this? He had promised to keep her *safe*. And he had failed. He felt something damp on his cheek, vaguely bewildered that he even possessed the ability to cry. He had not done so since his father's death.

Not so long ago, Max had believed that his life had ended then. That he was incapable of feeling, of holding anything or anyone dear again. He now wished desperately that that were true. Instead, his life was seeping slowly away as surely as Catherine's did. He had not mistaken the gravity in Kemble's eyes when he'd torn away the fabric of her dress. There was too much blood.

A grave risk of infection. Not the heart, Kemble had said, and he knew about such things. But there were other vital organs.

Max squeezed shut his eyes and relived the wild rage that had surged forth at the sight of Vost on top of her. And *Dio,* that knife! Glinting against her carotid artery. Moving. Lifting. As if he'd meant to slice her cleanly through the neck. And, like the hellcat she was, Catherine had been fighting him. Risking her life. Max had taken aim, swiftly but so very carefully. Or *thought* he had. Had he let his rage shake him? Or had Vost truly moved? He did not know. Would never know. Yes, he had killed the bastard, and for that he had no regret. But the ball had sliced through Catherine. And for that, he wanted to die.

The late-afternoon breeze puffed at the underdrapes, billowing them into the room like small, ivory clouds. In the street beyond, a raspy-voiced lad was shouting the evening headlines, hawking his newspapers with undaunted vigor. Somewhere deep inside the house, a clock kept ticking. *Ticking. Ticking. Ticking.* Until Max wanted to find it, rip out its mechanical workings, and hurl them to the floor. Every moment was precious. Critical. How could time roll on as if nothing had happened? Where was Greaves? Where was Kem? Why did they not come down to—to tell him something? His grief became edged with anger. Was he truly such an insignificant part of Catherine's life? So insignificant he could be left alone in a murky drawing room, ignored and uninformed?

The answer was, appallingly, *yes.* He was not her husband. Not even her fiancé. So far as her friends and servants knew, they were the merest acquaintances. In short, he had no rights at all. And that, too, was his own doing, was it not? This despite the fact that she had tried at every turn to forge something between them. And always—at least, until yesterday—he had held her at a distance. Held some part of himself in reserve. He had been afraid to confront the depths and the complexities of what he felt for her. Afraid he wasn't good enough. Afraid she wouldn't understand his dreams. Or his fears. Or the choices he'd had to make. Afraid that loving her would change everything.

Well, everything had changed now, had it not? Too late. His duty to Peel meant nothing. His position in Wapping was but a memory. His father's murder, his mother's grief, even his own attempts to prove himself worthy of—of something he no longer even *understood*—good God, all of it seemed so insignificant now. *A bloody zealot for justice,* Peel had called him. Well, fuck that. Max's noble ideals had suddenly given way to a simple wish for one small, very ordinary thing. A thing most men came by so easily and so often failed to cherish. He wanted a normal life. A home. A wife. Children. Not very much, not by most men's standards.

For what felt like hours, he sat alone, desperate to go to her, reliving the moment he'd squeezed the trigger. As if he might take it back. Somehow make it right. Darkness fell, unheralded by anything save the watch calling the hour. And still he waited. For Greaves. For Rutledge. For the end of his life. Upstairs, a door softly closed, and someone came lightly down the steps. Max leapt at once to his feet.

Kemble appeared in the shadows of the corridor, his shirt open at the throat, his fine coat still stained with blood. In the fading light, he looked drawn, almost fragile. "She is resting," he whispered as Max closed the distance between them.

Max laid a hand on the smaller man's shoulder. "Resting?"

Kemble nodded, looking at him with unutterable sadness. "Greaves cleaned and stitched the wound," he said quietly. "He says it was deep but not fatal. It nicked her high on the pelvic bone but cleared her organs. There's still a risk, of course, of infection."

Dumbly, Max nodded. *Infection.* Infection was bad.

Kemble smiled wearily. "She was asking for you," he said. "Greaves says you are to come up now, stay with her, and never mind that catty bitch of a housekeeper. I'm afraid I must run along, old fellow. The shop, you know. It's quite late."

Oddly, Max did not want him to leave. "Yes, of course you must go," he reluctantly agreed. "Thank you."

Again, Kemble smiled. "Sisk took the boy and the dog to Wellclose Square. I'll go round to his station tomorrow and clean up the paperwork. You'll be all right?"

Max tried to smile and failed. "I suppose, Kem, that I shall have to be."

They walked together through the shadows of the corridor. At the foot of the staircase, Kemble turned to go, then whirled back again, seizing Max firmly by the arm. "Look here, old boy," he said gruffly. "I know what you're thinking, and you must stop it at once. He'd quite lost his mind, you know. He meant to kill her, and you had no choice but to shoot."

Max shook his head. "I lost my head. I aimed poorly."

Kemble squeezed harder on his arm. "That's balderdash, Max, and you know it. It was a hard shot. Through the trees, with them writhing in the grass like that. It's a damned good thing you hit him when you did. And Catherine—she will be fine, Max. She *will*."

But Max had pulled away and started up the stairs.

Catherine lay upon the bed in the empty room, her hands flat upon the neatly turned-down bedcovers, dressed in something white and frilly. At once, Max slowed his pace, crossing the room quietly. He bent over the bed, stared down at her pale, porcelain face, and swallowed hard. Catherine was as still as death, barely breathing, it seemed. He squeezed shut his eyes, knelt, and began to pray. For some inexplicable reason, he thought of his grandmother's rosary and wished desperately that he owned one.

Behind him, he heard the housekeeper enter, listened as she drew in her breath haughtily. One hand tightly gripping the bedcovers, Max lifted his head and turned, nailing her with his darkest glower. She stopped dead in her tracks, her expression indignant, her mouth opening and closing soundlessly.

By God, he would not be refused! If she thought his presence in this room improper, then she'd best bring a regiment of light infantry along when she came to throw him out. It was time to seize the rights he meant to have. Slowly, he rose from his knees to stand beside the bed.

"Grow accustomed to the sight of me, madam," he warned in a voice as dark as death. "I shan't be leaving this room until she is well again."

Just then, the dressing-room door swung open, and Greaves came into the room, carefully wiping his hands on a thick white towel. He cut a swift, knowing glance at the housekeeper. "Ah, Maximilian!" he said softly. "I am glad you are here."

Max turned from the bed. "She is—?" Words failed him.

"—as well as can be expected," finished Greaves, tossing the towel over his bag. From a corner of his eye, Max saw the housekeeper swirl about, then, softly, the door clicked shut.

Max struggled for composure. "Tell me," he quietly demanded. "Tell me the truth."

Greaves smiled across the bed. "She is fine, Max. Full of opiates, and like to sleep through the night, but it will deaden the pain."

"Is there infection?" Max demanded.

The doctor made a little *tch-tch* sound in his throat. "Max, it could be days before we know," he murmured consolingly.

"When will she awaken? When may I speak with her?"

Greaves leaned his substantial weight onto a wing chair, the very one which he and Rutledge had overturned during their graceless fisticuffs eons ago. "Tomorrow morning at the latest, I should say," he answered. "Now, come join me by the hearth. I wish to speak with you."

Reluctantly, Max left the bed and crossed the room.

He wanted to feel relief, wanted to breathe normally again, but he was still too frightened. And something in Greaves's demeanor worried him. The surgeon took a chair, motioned for Max to do likewise, and cleared his throat rather formally. "Lady Catherine must have complete bed rest, Maximilian," the doctor began. "Under no circumstances can she be overset or disturbed. Her—ah—her condition is quite delicate. Do you fully comprehend me, Max?"

Max managed to nod. "A gunshot wound is a serious thing," he agreed. "I've seen enough to know."

Greaves twisted uncomfortably in his chair. "Yes, to be sure," he murmured. "But . . ."

The terror returned anew. "But *what,* damn it?"

The doctor studied his knuckles for a moment. "She was asking for you rather determinedly, Max," he said quietly. "She's had a terrible shock to the system, but she's an incredibly strong woman. You . . . you have a long-standing relationship with her, I take it?"

Max almost rose from his chair in anger. "We are—" He swallowed hard, considered his words, then threw caution to the wind. "We are to be married," he said quite certainly, relaxing into his seat. "As soon as she is well enough." *And as soon as she says yes,* he silently added.

And she would, he vowed to himself. He would do whatever it took. He would read every page in Kemble's bloody etiquette book, polish up his signet ring, and rig himself out like a damned Regent Street dandy if that's what it took to prove he deserved her. He would even dust off that god-awful mouthful of a noble title fate had saddled him with and make her a viscountess, if only she would say yes.

Yes. Yes, Max, I will marry you.

If only she lived to say the words, his life would be right again. Or perhaps right for the first time ever.

Greaves exhaled with obvious relief and dropped his hand into his lap. "Then the sooner the better," he said softly. "Under the circumstances."

"Circumstances?" Max wanted to explode. "Good God, man! Will you speak plainly?"

Amusement flickered across the doctor's face. "Plainly, then, had the wound been two inches lower, I fear we might have suffered a terrible tragedy. You see, I very much suspect Lady Catherine is with child."

In the ensuing silence, Max could hear his own heart beat. The medicinal smell grew stronger, the room hazier. A carriage rumbled through the street below, the noise echoing softly through the chamber, drawing him back from the edge of unconsciousness. "W-with child?" he finally managed. "How do you—I mean, how can you . . . ?"

Greaves shook his head. "I can't be absolutely sure yet," he answered. "But she murmured something suspicious and demanded to see you. And women often know these things, Max, long before a doctor can make a definitive diagnosis."

Max shook his head. "Well, I don't see how . . . that is to say . . ."

Suddenly, Greaves lost his color. "Good God, the child is yours, I hope?"

Max didn't bother to count the weeks and days. He knew Catherine. He knew the truth, as clearly as he knew his own name. "Yes," he answered certainly. "Yes, of course it is my child. I will speak to her brother, Lord Treyhern, as soon as I may. We will be married at once."

The doctor smiled and relaxed into his chair.

After Greaves gathered up his things and made his way out, Max drew a chair to the edge of the bed. Some time later, Delilah came shyly into the room bearing a pot of scalding coffee and a cold supper laid out on a silver tray, compliments of the housekeeper, she said. Max shot her a grim smile. His presence was to be tolerated, then, it would seem. Or, at the very least, they did not mean to starve him out. He took the tray and thanked her profusely. But, try as he might, he could not eat.

The coffee, however, was a godsend. He sipped it slowly as night deepened over Marylebone. Like the old riverman he was, Max could feel the wind rolling up from the water, cooling the city and making the house creak. Inside, the doors and footsteps slowly fell silent, and the traffic in the street below rumbled to a halt. No one disturbed his vigil. Quite likely, they did not dare. Eventually, Max drew his chair up to the edge of the mattress, splayed his elbows across the counterpane, and rested his forehead on his hands as he listened to the sound of Catherine's shallow breathing.

She was alive. And as long as he sat here, as long as he listened to her every breath, she would remain so. He was convinced of it. And yet he still could not block out the memory of her bloodless face as he crouched by her side atop that awful hill. There, Max had suffered an epiphany. In one of those blinding flashes of self-knowledge that hits a man like a lightning bolt, perhaps

once or twice in his lifetime, his brain had finally acknowledged what his heart had known at first sight. He
loved Catherine. Desperately. With every fiber of his
being. No matter how hard he'd tried to hold a part of
himself away from her, it was too late. She was already a
part of him, his heart, his soul. And he had the most
dreadful suspicion that Catherine had known it. Had
embraced it. And now it was up to him to put things
right.

Around two the morning, Catherine stirred, and Max
leapt to his feet. Her hand lifted unsteadily from the
counterpane, and her head turned ever so slightly
toward him. "Max," she whispered hoarsely, never
opening her eyes.

Max seized her hand, carried it to his mouth, and
brushed his lips across it. She felt warm and very much
alive. "Catherine," he choked. "I am here, *cara mia,* I am
here."

Perhaps it was his imagination, but he thought he saw
the faintest hint of a smile crook one corner of her
mouth. But Catherine did not stir again. Gingerly, Max
settled himself onto the bed, still clutching her hand.
And it was there that Bentley Rutledge found him, some
time near dawn.

Catherine's brother came into the room on silent feet,
his presence betrayed only by the soft creak of the door
hinge. Max rose and turned but did not release Catherine's hand. Rutledge looked like hell, sporting what appeared to be a two-day growth of beard and a coat which
had undoubtedly been slept in. He reeked of stale to-
bacco and brandy as he drew up along the edge of his sister's sickbed.

With a strange, sidelong glance at Max, he dragged one hand roughly through his hair and set the other on his hip. "How is she?" he asked in a voice which was surprisingly tender.

"Alive," said Max, his voice catching on the last syllable.

Rutledge came nearer and bent to brush the back of his hand across her cheek. Catherine did not stir. After a long moment had passed, he jerked his head toward the tray atop the night table. "Coffee?"

Max nodded. "Cold."

"I'll take it," said Rutledge, thumping Max almost companionably across the back and settling into his chair. Uneasily, he splayed his elbows on his knees and leaned forward to study his sister's face. "Go home and get some sleep, de Rohan," he said, without looking at him. "My man downstairs will run you home in my rig."

"No."

Rutledge looked up with a faintly amused expression. "I really think you ought, old boy," he said gently. "Unless I miss my guess, you've a couple of broken ribs, and you're running short of sleep."

"Your point?"

Rutledge let his gaze slide over Max's bruised and battered face, then down his dusty clothing. "My point is that you look worse than I, which is rather an accomplishment," he answered. "You want a nap, a bath, and a clean shirt, in that order. I shan't stir from this chair until you return. I swear it."

The young man's kindness was almost Max's undoing. "I just can't leave her yet," he choked.

Rutledge heaved a put-upon sigh. "Oh, dear," he said. "You mean to hang about and do the honorable thing, do you not? But in truth, de Rohan, you look a damned ugly sight. She might well refuse you, eh? After all, you did shoot her. So go home, old chap. Just for a bit, eh?"

Chapter Twenty-one

Do not be in haste to marry,
but look about you first, for the affair is important.

—LORD CHESTERFIELD, 1776,
The Fine Gentleman's Etiquette

There are some visions in life which come upon a man so unexpectedly and so illogically that his eyes can never be quite prepared to take them in, and his mind cannot quickly grasp them. And so it was that when Max returned to Mortimer Street, he found that the world had been turned upside-down. Convinced that Catherine still languished on the verge of death, he had rushed past Delilah and up the stairs to her bedchamber, only to have his tentative knock drowned out by a burst of raucous laughter from within.

Curious, he pushed open the door to find that Catherine sat up in bed, propped lamely on a stack of pillows far larger than herself. He breathed a sigh of relief. Her face was still pale and drawn, but her eyes were alert, and she was smiling. Smiling not at him—for, amidst the commotion, she'd not even noticed his arrival—but at the three ladies who sat around a folding Pembroke table which had been rolled to the side of her bed. Bentley Rutledge, too, was smiling—his an ear-to-ear grin. One hip hitched high on the edge of his sister's bed, he cradled an empty soup bowl in his lap, but his bemused gaze was fixed on the old woman shrouded in black and seated at the head of the table.

Softly, Max cursed.

The old woman did not notice. Instead, she bent her head over her work, a spread of cards, face-up on the table. "Ah, *Dio mio,* Signor Rutledge," announced Nonna Sofia gravely. "Such scandals! Such vice! And what is this, eh? I see something else here, too! The path of love, it does not run smoothly for you. No, not at all."

"My dear *signora,*" murmured Rutledge in a dry, languid tone. "I'm known to like it a little rough."

The other ladies exchanged horrified looks, then burst again into titters. But Catherine drew back an elbow and jabbed him hard in the ribs. With a squawk of pain, Rutledge slid gracefully off the bed and onto his feet, then set the soup bowl on the table. He swept into a deep, mocking bow.

"Dear ladies!" he said smoothly. "I see the invalid no longer requires my delicate ministrations. So, I must take my leave, for today the rough path of love leads me to Tattersall's. I've my eye on a long-legged filly there, and it most assuredly feels like *amore.*"

Nonna Sofia looked up with a bemused expression. *"Va bene,* my boy," she said softly. "Go! Go! And hide behind your laughter if it pleases you. But when you tire of it, you must call upon me. We shall share a bottle of burgundy and sort out this mess you have made with your life. Maximilian will give you my direction."

"Will I?" intoned Max dryly.

Five sets of eyes turned at once to the door. Cousin Maria jerked from her chair with a gasp. Lady Kirton blushed deeply, like a schoolgirl caught out in some trifling mischief. Only his grandmother remained impassive. *"Buongiorno*, my grandson," she said, cutting him a sly, knowing glance. "You were abed quite late this important day, *no?"*

Max stood, hands clasped tightly behind his back, his heart pounding wildly. It was a condition he was growing frighteningly accustomed to. "Out," he barked, struggling to hide his agitation. "Out! The lot of you! She is ill. She must rest."

The ladies leapt to their feet like flustered hens, gathering up cards, gloves, and reticules as they clucked and scattered. With a rumbling laugh, Rutledge pushed past Max, pounding him on the back as he went. Catherine's eyes grew round with amazement, until at last the room was empty.

Max went at once to her side, but he did not touch her. "You are awake," he managed to say.

Feebly, she smiled. "Only just," she answered. "Weak as a kitten, and hurting like the very devil. But oh, Max, I am ever so glad to see you!"

Max clasped his fingers behind his back until they ached. "My grandmother has no business disturbing you," he said stiffly.

Catherine blushed. "It was just that Nate told her of my accident," she explained. "How he came to be hiding in that holly bush, I'll never know, but Sofia seemed genuinely concerned. Maria brought a delicious broth, and Isabel and Bentley had their fortunes told. It was quite diverting, really."

"So I'd wager," he murmured.

Uneasily, Max settled himself on the edge of the bed, and stared down at her hand where it lay upon the bed covers. Her skin was so pale, he could see the tracery of soft blue veins against her flesh. Almost absently, he began to draw one finger over them. "Catherine—" he began, then lost his nerve.

"Yes?"

He let his hand fall away. "Thank God you are feeling better," he whispered. "I am so sorry. Words cannot express . . . I was a fool to . . . it is—all of this is . . . my fault," he lamely finished.

Catherine gathered his strong, warm fingers into her own and looked up at Max. "It certainly is not," she insisted. But she could see the myriad emotions which flitted over his face, could sense the turmoil within him. She, too, felt it. Yesterday, she had come within a breath of dying—and perhaps something almost worse than dying. It was not a thing even a Rutledge could take lightly. And she had Max to thank for saving her.

Oh, she knew what he thought. Saw the guilt which tore at him. The surgeon, Dr. Greaves—he, too, had understood. He had returned shortly after daybreak to examine her wound and to mumble soft, soothing words. In pain and still disoriented, Catherine had nonetheless found herself oddly comfortable in speaking with him. How pleased she was to know yet another of Max's friends. He chose them well, and they were loyal. What better measure of a man's character was there?

Impulsively, she tightened her grip on Max's hands

and drew him closer. "Max," she said softly. "You needn't worry. I'm safe."

"And I mean to keep you so," he interjected gruffly. "Catherine, there's nothing else for it. We must marry. I . . . good God, I *shot* you. I'm responsible for you. I—I can't think how else to explain it. You are mine."

"Goodness." Catherine laughed a little unsteadily. "It sounds rather as if you've been hunting big game. You shot me, so I am yours? Am I to be mounted on your chimney piece?"

Max shook his head, pressed his lips tightly together. *"Dio mio,"* he muttered. "I must sound like a lunatic." He drew in a deep, ragged breath. "Catherine, Greaves told me. About . . . about the baby. I feel, oh—so incredibly . . ."

"Responsible?" she finished, feeling a little shaft of pain through the heart. "Is that it? Because, if so, we should wait. It may yet come to naught. Perhaps—why, perhaps you would be relieved."

Again, he shook his head and drew her hands to his mouth. "No, no, *cara,"* he rasped, pressing his lips to her knuckles, each in turn. "I am so happy. And so bloody frightened. Oh, God, Catherine, just don't fight me on this. I can't bear it. I don't know if you're carrying our child or not. It does not matter. You must marry me. Tomorrow, if at all possible."

Catherine sat up a little straighter. "Why, Max? Tell me. Let me inside that heart of yours. Please."

Max closed his eyes and bent his head until it rested on their joined hands. "Because I love you, Catherine," he whispered. "I love you so much. Just marry me, and, with God as my witness, I swear I will do whatever it takes to deserve you."

Incredulous, Catherine stared down at the back of his head. "To *deserve* me—?"

But Max was still speaking into her counterpane. "I will pay more attention to my clothes and my temperament, I swear it. I shall learn to make idle conversation. I will buy a new house. You may choose the grandest thing in Mayfair—I daresay I can afford it—and style yourself Lady de Vendenheim-Sélestat if you wish it. I will be a true gentleman, I promise."

Catherine forced his head up. "Max, what on earth are you talking about?"

He looked at her, unblinkingly. "I sent my resignation to Whitehall this morning," he said quietly. "An English gentleman cannot have my sort of career. I know that. Besides, I must think of your welfare. Of our children. And I wish your brothers to have no cause to look down on me."

Catherine reached up to caress his lean, hard cheek. "Oh, Max! My brothers don't have any cause to look down on you!" she said softly. "Especially that rakehell Bentley. Really, my dear, what are you talking about? Why did you give up the work—*important* work—that you love?"

"That sort of work is dangerous," he said solemnly. "It is best left to men without families."

Catherine stroked him again and shook her head. "Oh, life is never certain, Max," she whispered, gazing into his anguished eyes. "I've already buried one husband, one who lived a dull, quiet life in the country, doing nothing more dangerous than shooting pheasants.

I won't have my second husband die of boredom, and that is precisely what would happen to you. Besides, my love, I am so very proud of the work you do. Did you not know that?"

Max held her hands in a death grip. "But will you marry me, Catherine?" he demanded. "Just tell me that. The rest can wait."

"Yes, yes, I will marry you this afternoon, you exasperating man!" she cried. "And a house—something small, a little closer to Sofia—yes, that would be lovely. Do as you will with your title. But what's all this nonsense about clothes and conversation?"

But Max simply leaned forward to kiss her lightly on the lips. "Oh, Catherine, I will make you so proud."

Catherine shook her head. "Faith, I must be still witless with laudanum," she moaned. "Did I not just tell you how proud I am? Proud of you, and proud of your work, Max. Surely you knew?"

"And you will do it?" He held her gaze with an agonizing desperation. "You will marry me?"

"Did I not just say so?" Catherine felt as if she was about to burst into tears of both joy and vexation—a portent of what her future with Max would be like, she did not doubt. "Just send someone to Whitehall to retrieve that letter of resignation, Max," she sighed. "Get it back, do you hear me? Then fetch the parson and a special license. I'd best marry you straightaway—this very afternoon."

Max started to shake his head. Just then, a light knock sounded upon the door, and Greaves hastened in, snapping the lock behind him. "Ah, good morning, Maximilian!" he said, cheerfully plopping his bag down and leaning intently over the footboard. "And Lady Catherine! You've a little of your color back, I fancy."

Max had leapt to attention. "You must congratulate me, Greaves," he said very gravely. "Your patient has just made me the happiest of men."

The surgeon smiled broadly and scrubbed his hands together. "Capital! Oh, capital!" he said, circling around the bed and folding back the covers so modestly that only the bandage about her waist was revealed. "Then I can use your help here, Max."

"My . . . help?"

Greaves shot a swift wink at Catherine and unfurled a length of clean cotton bandaging from his bag. "Indeed! I've only a moment to redress this wound, and then I'm off to another patient. Another duel! Such a messy habit!" Gingerly, he began to peel away the dressing below Catherine's waist. "Anyway, you're well accustomed to the sight of blood. And since you're to wed, there's no impropriety in your helping me a moment."

Max cleared his throat. "Well, I . . . I'm not perfectly sure—"

But inch by inch, Catherine's bruised skin was already being exposed. "In any case," Greaves interjected, "I'd as soon not have that sour-faced housekeeper—your pardon, ma'am." The next layer came away, slightly damp and brown, and the old army surgeon tossed it expertly over his shoulder. "Ah, there it is! No pus, no drainage, and the sutures are holding nicely! Now, look just here, Max, and you'll be much relieved. I noted that the ball took just the merest chip from the arc of the pelvic bone—I saved it for you, by the way—and then exited neatly through the—"

An awful clatter stopped him short.

Catherine screamed, and Greaves whirled about, too late. Max had pitched backward into a heap, taking the folding table and two chairs down with him as he went and sending the soup bowl careening across the floor. His impressive length lay spread-eagled over the broken table, its little wheels still spinning merrily. Max's intense black eyes had rolled back into his head, making his nose look even more prominent.

"Oh, dear me!" murmured the surgeon as he squatted to peer at Max's bloodless face.

Catherine's hand had flown to her mouth. "Oh, my God!" she whispered through her fingers. "Is he hurt?"

Greaves shook his head morosely. "Nothing a couple more sutures won't fix," he muttered, lumbering down onto one knee beside Max. "But I've some sound medical advice for him, my lady."

"Yes! Yes, by all means!"

Gingerly, Greaves rolled one eyelid back with the ball of his thumb. "When your labor pains commence, have young Mr. Rutledge take the father-to-be down to Piccadilly and keep him utterly, mindlessly drunk for a few days."

Epilogue

It is time to put an end to this long rambling, in which if any one thing can be of use to you, it will more than pay for the trouble I have taken to write it.

—LORD CHESTERFIELD, 1776,
The Fine Gentleman's Etiquette

Max awoke to find that the early October sun had settled low in the sky, cutting at an angle through shutters which had been left open to the heat of an afternoon breeze. Lifting his hand to shield his eyes, he sat up, watching as Catherine wandered through the gardens toward him. So captivating was the sight of her, lithe and lovely against a backdrop of green, that Max let his sheet slither unheeded onto the cool marble floor. Lazily, he yawned and stretched, but his gaze never wavered. This custom of taking an afternoon siesta had become a luxurious habit. Almost as addictive and enduring as watching his wife.

Catherine. Catherine, who moved as if time held no meaning. Here in the lush, rolling vineyards of Spain, it scarcely did. The grapes, not the calendar, shaped the rhythms of one's life. He watched his wife stroll through the verge of thick grass along the terrace, her bare feet peeping from beneath the skirts of her bleached-linen sack dress, one hand on her rounding stomach, the other holding open some sort of letter. Her hair was down, the mahogany tendrils catching the sun and air as she approached, still reading.

Gaea. His earth goddess. He had known it from the first. Though to his grandmother, she had been the Queen of Pentacles, the symbol of generosity and wisdom. All that was good and productive. And above all, great fertility. Max laughed out loud at that. Catherine must have heard him, for she looked up with a bemused smile. It was a look of pure happiness, which pleased him. No, thrilled him. Max searched his mind for a better word—in any language—and found none.

She crossed beneath the shadows of the flowering vine which draped the door, lifting a low swag with one arm. "You are laughing," she said, her feet silent on the marble as she approached his chaise. "A drowsy, naked, laughing man. What is in your mind, I wonder?"

Max curled one arm about her burgeoning waist and dragged her down beside him. With the other hand, he pushed a rope of hair over her shoulder, then smoothed the tendrils back from her face. "What I am always thinking," he murmured. "That I love you. That I want you—"

Catherine cut a swift glance down. "Oh, I can see that."

"Saucy wench!" He dragged her face to his for a kiss. "And I'm thinking that you drive me to distraction. That I wish we may never leave this place."

Casually—too casually—she shrugged. "If you really wish that, then we need never leave," she said simply, brushing the back of her hand across the stubble of his beard. "This villa is yours, after all, is it not? And now that the roof no longer leaks and the spiders have been vanquished—"

"Really, Catherine, it was never that bad!"

She let one hand drift down her belly. "We need only refurbish the nursery, and *voilà,* we may stay forever. Bentley can tend Aldhampton for us. God knows he needs something to keep him out of trouble."

Max lay back on the chaise and pulled her close against him. "Your brother is no farmer," he said quietly. "And I cannot stay here. I've promised Peel. But we will come back every year. It was wonderful to see the harvest, was it not? Like a miracle to me, really. I can't think why I stayed away so long."

But he did know why. Catalonia was too close to France. To Alsace. There were too many memories, too much pain. At first, even the scent of the ripening grapes had choked him. Still, as a child, he had come here nearly every year. This was but one of his father's estates, yes, one his grandmother had brought to her Alsatian husband as a dowry. But he had loved it. Had loved the richness of the earth, the incredible sunshine, the lyrical language. How many harvests had he missed? Or perhaps *ignored* was a better word. The villa, the outbuildings, the acres of once-prime vineyards—they had all suffered a bit from their absentee landlord's inattention. Catherine was only half joking about the roof.

He had brought her here for a romantic honeymoon, or so he had told both her and himself. But he now realized he'd done it so that she might banish a few more of his ghosts. And so she had. Max stroked his hand down the swell of her stomach and felt a moment of deep gratitude.

She made a murmur of pleasure and rolled into him, crushing something in her pocket. "Oh," she said softly. "The letter!"

He crooked his head to look down at her. "I saw you reading something. Who is it from?"

"From my brother," she answered. "From Cam. He wishes to know when we mean to return and what chores I wish done at Aldhampton when all the crops are in. And he sends you a message."

"A message for me?"

Max was surprised. He had met Lord Treyhern just prior to the wedding, when they'd gone to Catherine's childhood home to be wed in her old parish church. His lordship had carefully scrutinized his potential brother-in-law. Max had assumed it was a given that he and Catherine must marry, but apparently a child born out of wedlock would have been less distasteful to Treyhern than a marriage in which his sister might be unhappy. Catherine, of course, had wrapped her elder brother about her finger, and the ceremony had been held within a fortnight. But during their short visit, Treyhern had never quite warmed toward Max. He was sending, Max knew, a subtle warning. Max was expected to keep Treyhern's little sister very, very happy—or suffer the consequences.

Abruptly, Catherine sat up. "Let me read you what Cam says," she said, extracting the letter. "Your friends have been conspiring, I fear."

Max crooked one eyebrow. "Who? Kemble?"

Lightly, she laughed. "Yes, he and the word *conspire* quite go together, do they not?" she agreed, shaking her head. "But this time, it's Walrafen and Peel. It seems they have found a higher and better use for—let me see, yes, here it is—your *social zealotry*. My, what important words your friends use—"

Max grabbed her by the wrist and kissed her hard. "Get on with it, *cara mia*," he growled. "I might have a higher and better use for you. Work is not what I wish to think about on my honeymoon."

With an impish grin, she tossed the letter aside, stood, and gathered up her skirts. As she had been for much of the summer, the lusty wench was bare from the waist down. Drawers made her wound itch, she had complained, though it was now little more than a fierce red pucker—which he found perversely erotic. Max laughed and reached out to touch it. Touch *her.* "*Bella,*" he growled. "What do you mean to do to me?"

"Torture you for your insolence," she said, slowly straddling him across the chaise and lowering herself onto him. "I, too, have many talents."

Max sucked in his breath when she touched him, gently guiding him between her legs. "Ah! God, Catherine!" Many talents indeed.

Atop him, she slid down just an inch and sighed with contentment. "It is good?"

"Ah, *paradiso!*" he groaned. "This does not feel like torture."

Her spine arched elegantly back, and she impaled herself fully on his length. "There," she sighed when he was up to the hilt in her luscious feminine heat. "Now, as I was saying—" She rose up, pausing to lick her lips. "Peel wishes you to give up your position in the Home Office after all."

"Who?" Fleetingly, Max couldn't breathe. "Give what?"

Slowly, she sank down again, tightening her muscles around him, cutting off the blood to his brain. "They expect the government to call for an election soon."

First the lungs, then the mind. "An—an election?"

With a shudder of delight, she rose up again. "It seems my lordly brother has a pocket borough languishing somewhere in Devonshire."

"Pocket *what?*"

"A political jurisdiction," she panted, perspiration lightly sheening her lip. "Whose voting he more or less controls."

Max watched her incredible breasts rise and fall. "I know—good God, Catherine—I know what it is." He tried again to breathe, without much success. "Oh, *per amor del cielo!* What are you doing?"

"Explaining the letter."

"Bother the bloody letter!" He looked at her with a mix of incendiary lust and utter confusion. "Catherine, can you really talk politics whilst we do this?"

She gave him a wicked grin, looking frighteningly like her younger brother. "I may as well learn," she said with an amiable shrug. "If I don't, I mayn't get any when we return home."

"Oh, Catherine, don't be a fool!"

"Then don't be cross, darling." She slid up his length again, tightening her every muscle as she moved in sheer, sweet torment. "You promised you'd mind your temper if I'd marry you."

"Yes. I did—*will*—oh, God, Catherine, just don't stop."

But Catherine was still working her body against his, panting now rather desperately. "They want—you to—stand for Parliament," she managed, picking up her rhythm. "For the Commons—because Walrafen's Tories—are frustrated—and hard—"

"The Tories!" Max interjected. "They can't comprehend *frustrated* and *hard.*"

"Hard *pressed,*" she finished. "And Peel needs—support. For—the police reform bill. And after that—oh—oh, God! Max!"

Deliberately, Max held himself back a little. "The police bill—?" he asked.

"Oh! Max!" Catherine's lashes began to drop shut. "Just—never mind. Just—oh, no—harder—!"

Max shifted position ever so slightly, just enough to torment, then reached up and drew down the bodice of her loose linen gown. "Frustrated yet, Catherine?" he asked, running his tongue around her left nipple, then sucking it into his mouth.

Her head went back. Her eyes squeezed shut. "Ah—ah, Max, just—just—just—"

Her breast was warm in his mouth, her skin fragrant and feminine in the autumn heat, and Max could not hold out; he had never been able to hold up against Catherine's onslaught. For long, sweet moments, she rode him as the sun slid into the westerly sky. And then, subtly, he rocked forward, lifted his hips, and urged himself perfectly against her. It worked. It always worked.

"Oh! Oh, God! Max!"

And then Catherine's eyes rolled back in her head.

* * *

"And so you will do it?" she asked him some half an hour later. They had moved to the big featherbed in the corner, and Catherine was now slowly stroking one hand down his spine.

Flat on his belly, Max roused from his stupor, weakly lifting his head to peer at her through a shock of black hair. "Do what, *cara mia?*"

Lazily, she uncurled her body from his. "Stand for Cam's borough in Devonshire."

Max gave one of his disgusted grunts. "No, Catherine," he said firmly. "My respect for Peel aside, I can't see myself as a part of his party. Moreover, the whole concept of pocket boroughs is corrupt."

Vehemently, she nodded. "Indeed it is," she agreed. "Which is why Cam pays it so little heed."

"The bloody system of English politics should be changed," he groused, rolling onto his back and drawing her into his embrace.

"Indeed it should." Her voice was cheerful.

A strange feeling crept over him. "Catherine, why are you agreeing with me?"

She was silent for a long moment. "Only Parliament can change the government," she said quietly, stilling her hand and pressing it over his heart. "If the system we have is so bad—and if your ideas are so just and so noble—then why do you not help fix it?"

It was Max's turn to fall silent. So silent, in fact, that he felt Catherine nearly drift to sleep in his arms. They had slept thus for months now in this idyllic, isolated villa, with servants who came only sporadically and neighbors too distant to see. It had been perfect. Blissful. But it was not real. He knew it, and she knew it.

"Ah, Catherine, perhaps you are right," he said at last. "It is easy to complain. Easy to fight small battles. We will go back to London in another month, and I will at least discuss it with Walrafen and your brother, of course. In any case, I suppose we ought to buy that house in town—"

"Near Sofia," she interjected.

Max looked at her warily. "Perhaps Bloomsbury," he countered. "That's as far east as my wife and child are going." He turned his head to kiss her hair.

Catherine crooked her head to look up at him. "And Nate? Nate will live with us, will he not?"

Max's black eyes narrowed. "You may well believe it," he grumbled. "I'll have that boy where I can keep an eye on him, and far from my grandmother. Together, they are far too dangerous to be unleashed on an unsuspecting populace."

Catherine laughed. "I fear you're right."

Max frowned and kissed her again. "And as to my grandmother, *cara,* I'm afraid that when the babe arrives, you can expect to see far too much of her. Still, since she'll soon have a grandchild to occupy her time, I shall try to persuade her to let Trumbull manage the business. He is really quite capable, and it is time she began to rest more."

Catherine felt her heart surge with love. "You will convince her, Max. You can be most persuasive when you wish it."

His eyes held hers, his gaze warm, like a smoldering fire. With joy surging in her heart, Catherine stroked one palm down the rocklike surface of his thigh. Max was beauty and strength, his legs stretching forever across their bed. "Do you know, Max, I could touch you forever," she whispered. "You are so very hard and sleek and beautiful. So every inch a man. I am proud of you. So proud."

"I am ordinary," he answered, his voice suddenly hesitant. "You are perfection. I've wanted you, Catherine, since the moment I first saw you thundering through the park on that big chestnut gelding. It tore at me, I wanted you so. And I knew—I just *knew*—that if I touched you even once, my life would be forever changed."

But, as she always did, Catherine blushed and turned away. "Look, Max!" she said breathlessly. "The sun—it is almost gone."

She rose from the bed like a round, perfect Venus, wrapping the sheet about her as she went toward the still-open doors. "Come, my love," she said, stepping onto the veranda and stretching one hand back in invitation. "Come outside and feel the sunshine."

But he already did. He had no need to step outside. For Max de Rohan had been blessed by a sun which never set, an earth which was ever green.

Historical Note

Philip Dormer Stanhope, fourth Earl of Chesterfield, was a Georgian statesman and courtier who began his ascent as a Gentleman of the Bedchamber to the future George II, during whose reign he accepted the embassy at The Hague. There, his mistress gave birth to his illegitimate son, also Philip, whom he barely acknowledged. In later life, the earl married the King's illegitimate sister for political gain. But his obsession in life was to be, always and above all things, "a true gentleman," and he held a narrow and intolerant view of just what a gentleman should be.

Despite his hesitance to claim his son, Chesterfield maintained a prolific stream of correspondence with the young man, primarily letters of advice, instruction, and, often, admonishment. After his death in 1773, his lordship's letters were collected and published under a variety of catchy titles, including *The Fine Gentleman's Etiquette* and *The Principles of Politeness*. The letters were wildly popular with some, but his bold and often self-serving opinions laid open the earl's memory to scorn with others.

His lordship reached the pinnacle of his posthumous infamy when Dr. Samuel Johnson uttered his now-famous set-down which declared that Chesterfield's letters "teach the morals of a whore and the manners of a dancing master." And, indeed, his lordship did value style over substance, self-interest over morality, and pride over principle. Much of his advice sounds shockingly Machiavellian to our modern ears. None, however, can deny his literary genius and scathing wit. Or, as Lady Catherine might say, "at least he wasn't boring."